COLLIER SPYMASTERS SERIES

Consulting Editor: Saul A. Katz,
Founder, 999 Bookshop, New York City

Also by Richard Llewellyn

THE
END
of the
RUG

Richard Llewellyn

COLLIER BOOKS
Macmillan Publishing Company
New York

Collier Books
Macmillan Publishing Company
866 Third Avenue, New York, NY 10022
Collier Macmillan Canada, Inc.

Library of Congress Cataloging-in-Publication Data
Llewellyn, Richard.
    The end of the rug/Richard Llewellyn.—1st Collier Books ed.
    p.   cm.
  ISBN 0-02-022551-2
  I. Title.
PR6023.L47E5   1989
823'.912—dc19   88-13771   CIP

First Collier Books Edition 1989

10 9 8 7 6 5 4 3 2 1

Printed in the United States of America

THE
END
of the
RUG

1

I suppose it all began when that beautiful Pan American hostess put a breakfast tray in front of me and I sat up to reach for the orange juice. My hand never touched the glass because sitting up brought my back against the cushion. Instantly I missed the bump of my automatic in the right-hand hip pocket.

I'd left it under the pillow. I could see it grinning at me.

In the white sear of that blinding moment I felt the wreck of a career, loss of pension, hardship for Mel, both children having to leave the university, disgrace and utter ruin for everybody. I wasn't in a department or in a position where people normally carry a gun. It hadn't been declared to Swiss Customs and I hadn't a permit except from Scotland Yard, which of course didn't reach Switzerland, and diplomatic passports don't confer the privilege of leaving firearms in hotel bedrooms. The gun would be found and sent to the police. Their inquiries would end in a report to London. As a result, obviously, the entire department would come under close examination, not only by the Swiss but by other interested agencies. If I were asked why, in my position, did I carry a gun, I could only say that a month or so before, Hawtrey had warned us that we must expect trouble from a certain quarter and to keep our eyes open. My people would accept the fact, but not the carelessness, especially since it involved the department. But if the question were put to me by the Swiss police, I couldn't think offhand of an answer. There wasn't one.

I sat there, eyes shut, mentally ill. I knew my face had gone white. I could feel it. But the brain worked. We were about twenty minutes outside Geneva. Next stop Paris. If I found the right excuse, I could catch a return flight, go to the hotel, pray the gun was still under the pillow, call Dr. Parnell, complain of an old appendix pain, fly back to London, and simply say I was sorry, blah-blah-blah.

It might wash.

"Are you feeling well, sir?" the hostess—bless her—bent to murmur in my ear.

"No," I whispered, with great truth. "I've got a bad appendix. Sorry. Have to get off at Paris."

"Would you care for a little cognac, sir?"

Would I! I nodded. She took the tray and I looked around at Paul Chamby, glasses up on his forehead, dozing with a newspaper in his lap. Paul—we called him the Little Cham—was Australian, one of the best, top drawer, excellent mind, the very devil of a fellow to work for, my immediate superior and nobody above except the Minister. He had the job I'd been waiting for, and I didn't have much longer to wait. He, too, had been in the Service, though we'd met only at the end of the war, when we were trying to find out what the Russians were up to in Saudi Arabia. Then I'd gone into the Colonial secretariat for a few instructive years, and we'd met again in Cairo when I was on my way home from handing over another piece of the Empire, and he was going to London to start the smallest, though certainly not the least important, department in the civil list. Over a couple of drinks he decided that I was right for the second spot, and within the week, there I was, happily at work and using the last scrap of energy to bring us up to date with every move, anywhere, by the six nations already in the European Common Market, so that when we were admitted, we'd be on top of the job, little to learn and few growing pains. We all knew that when it happened there'd be at least a barony for Paul, and a few knighthoods, certainly one for me, and I knew how Mel wanted to hear herself called y'ladyship.

Then why must I jeopardise a career, my family's lives, hopes, ambitions and God knows what, by leaving a gun under a pillow? Criminally careless. *No* excuse.

I felt like crying.

A hostess took Paul's breakfast down, and I followed, holding on to chairbacks. I stood aside for her, and Paul saw me with the cup almost at his chin, paused, frowned, put the cup down and let the glasses fall to make pinpoint grey eyes suddenly enormous.

"Well," he said quietly. "Feel as crook as you look, Edmund?"

"Appendix. I'd like to go back to Geneva. See Dr. Parnell. Operation or not, I can get the next plane to London. He wanted to operate a couple of months ago. I suppose this is it."

He nodded at the chair across the aisle.

"Rest your hard luck. By all means get off at Paris. I'll book your flight from the cockpit."

He pulled the letter pad out of the chairback, touched the bell, and took out a pen.

"Your breakfast is going to get cold."

"Long as you don't," he said, writing. "Can't afford to lose you, boy. Specially now. Be tragedy."

He gave the note to the hostess, and nodded at his breakfast.

"Make you feel worse if I eat this?" he asked, smiling sympathy. "I was on a flight with Mr. Molotov—remember The Hammer?—I got sick over Berlin. Crook? I felt terrible. He stopped eating his lunch, ordered the plane down and put me off with his personal physician. Hardest man I ever met, The Hammer. Never been a kinder heart. The doctor gave me a couple of pills and a shot of cognac, and we were off inside the hour. I see you're getting at least half the same treatment, eh?"

The hostess pulled down the table and put a glass of cognac on a paper mat.

"Swissair's making the reservation, sir," she told Paul. "Take-off's ten minutes after we get in. The car'll meet us."

"VIP stuff," Paul said, sliding a fork under fried egg on a corner of toast. "Any idea why we're going to London?"

"Bit of a surprise, wasn't it?"

"While I think of it, you'd better sign this," he said through a chew, and took a folded sheet out of his breast pocket. "The messenger couldn't find you. At three in the morning? Sure it's your appendix?"

"Why couldn't the dolt use a telephone? I was at the club. Playing a little bridge. Got back to the hotel about four. After all, today's free. Or should have been!"

"Too true. Well, I tell you, Edmund. I've got an idea we're in. We're going up. Notice the Ambassador and all the other top jocks taking the R.A.F. jet? Cholly-Mi-Golly must have waved 'em on, thank God, at last!"

General Charles de Gaulle had never been other than a perfect bugbear from the start.

"You think we'll be opening in Brussels? Or based on London?"

"Brussels'd be the likeliest move. At least, for one of us. You, probably. We've hidden our light under the old Swiss bushel a lot too long. I've enjoyed it. I'll be sorry to leave Geneva. Lot of good friends there. No pain going to Brussels though. City's overcrowded, but it's a lovely place to live. Moira'll be overjoyed. She's had a go everywhere, but she can't like it. Prefers London. At least she understands what's going on. Languages aren't her strong point. Funny. Anything else she's bright."

But dear Moira was the last I wanted to think about at that moment. Mel's face seemed to float, tragic, appealing, and I could hear the quiver in her voice—"Oh, darling, how could you? Ah, darling!"—I hadn't any idea how I was to tell her, that is, if I had to. If. Staring at Paul's disappearing toast-and-marmalade I felt really sick. Perhaps it was the cognac, but I heaved myself up and lurched down the aisle to the lads' room, locked myself in, and sat down, alone with myself, staring.

Curious, but only then, with the twin bones of my backside

4

biting through thin skin at a hard seat, looking at greenish light in the mirror, I realised what a swine I'd been. Had? Still was. And if I got out of this frightening mess, still intended to be. That's what surprised me.

I'd suddenly been made aware of a new side of myself, one that *wanted* to do, that refused to do anything else but what *it* wanted. The other—official, apparently disciplined—side, that blanched at thought of disgrace, ruin, sat there looking on, pitifully weak, crying inwardly, but offering no word. It liked enjoying itself with the other. The third side could look at both, criticising the one, despising the other, without volition, *aut*. The true I—who on earth exactly was I?—seemed to be somewhere in the middle, professional diplomatist of sorts, accountant by and large, banker here and there, economist now and then, planner, yes, of impressive parts, a couple of good degrees, a few honors, always certain of a good Press—"*Darling*, do you see your *photo*graph's in the paper *again*? You look simply *ghastly*!"—ah, poor Mel, what I am to say to you?—because if the Tale of the Gun is told, then you're bound to hear about Roiki, and Ghislaine, and of course, Peggy, but God Almighty, not Tanis, never Tanis, please God, not.

Even through the cloy of aircraft deodorant I sniffed the elixir of her passion, felt the strength of her arms that only a couple of hours before I'd had to take by the wrists, but gently, to break a clasp that could have kept me with her into daylight, and I had to be careful. That last kiss, when she bit the side of my jaw—leopardess!—still burned when I got out to blueing dawn, and thank God I'd had the sense. The slip of paper at the hotel desk warning of a flight to London at 7 and a car coming for me at 6:10 almost put me in a dither, but the official side took cold grasp, and I asked the porter to telephone the club to post a notice, that Mr. Edmund Trothe presented his compliments, and regretted his inability to finish the bridge tournament of the previous night, or keep engagements in the foreseeable future because of a sudden journey, and would acquaint

5

his friends on return. Considering what had happened, it seemed a remarkably defensive glimpse into the future. It could help to save me, but I still had to find somebody to say I was at the club.

It was probably because of Tanis that I overlooked the gun. I undressed and lay down for fifteen minutes to dream of her, and when the coffee came I had a bath, shave, packed a bag and briefcase, and I was ready when the porter rang to announce the car.

Except that I forgot to look under the pillow.

FASTEN SEAT BELTS flashed. I got up, washed my face, and went down the aisle slowly, a sort of dignified wabble befitting the Spartan ignoring pain. Paul gave me a smile suggesting approval and sympathy, or it could have been an urp of indigestion.

We landed, and the hostess came to tell me the car was waiting.

"If it's got to be an operation, ask Dr. Parnell to ring me," Paul said, shaking hands. "I'll have things readied."

Into the airline runabout, and over to the waiting Swissair jet, and in minutes I was on the way back to Geneva. Then I had breakfast, though I first made sure nobody aboard knew me, and I'd hardly wiped the egg off my chin, and we were there. I got a cab to the hotel, and went in as though to an Auschwitz gas oven. The night porter had gone. I asked the receptionist, an old friend of mine, for the key to 408 and up I went. The corridor was quiet, no maids, brooms or carpetsweepers. With almost a prayer I went in.

The room hadn't been touched!

Two leaps, and I tore the pillow away.

The gun seemed to exude a bluish smirk.

I felt limp in every bone and nerve. I sat on the bed and put the steel to my face almost as a caress of assurance that I was awake. Carefully I buttoned it into my hip pocket, blew Mel a kiss, breathed a long, shaking sigh of thanks to God, and picked up the telephone, dialled Dr. Parnell and spoke to his secretary.

"Oh, yes, sir," she said. "Dr. Parnell was telephoned from Paris. Should I send the car?"

I was there, clothes off, in ten minutes, and Dr. Parnell went over me with fingertips he must have been keeping on ice.

"Don't like my patients taken ill on planes, y'know," he said. "Doesn't do the old firm's reputation any good, does it? Well, it's a grumbler. Probably exacerbated by an early start. No need for an operation, yet. I'll let you know later. I thought you looked a little under the weather at the club last night."

"Wasn't feeling a bit well. But I didn't think of this!"

I couldn't tell him it was excitement—that always makes me pale—at thought of meeting Tanis. But he was my witness, ready-made.

Clothes on again—happy?—my God, nobody's ever been happier—and out to that perfect Swiss morning of warmish air from the lake, blue sky, pale yellow sun making tramlines flash electric silver, bells striking ten, my lucky number, and the entire world my lobster.

Back at the office I went in to a stare of surprise from Miss Furnival, doing the day-before's filing. I told her what had happened, but she appeared oddly uninterested. She was, in fact, unemotionally, superlatively efficient, never said much about anything, had an elephantine memory, and to top it off, she was quite the nicest woman in the building.

"There is something rather strange going on, sir," she said, breaking into a memory about having seen her once with her dark glasses off, surprise of small surprise, a real beauty. "Did you know they're dismantling the computer room?"

"Dismantling? Who?"

"A team of men came from London this morning, sir!"

"Aha. Well, that bears out what a little bird's been saying."

"Did the little bird mention they were taking it to Bomber Command at Ravensmere, and our computer staff's gone back

7

to London? Mr. Raile just left. He wasn't a bit pleased. He's been sent to the London University economics section. Most of the others are going to Manchester or Bradford, and a few to Edinburgh. Seems rather like a tear-out, doesn't it?"

She looked up from an open file. A phantom seemed to float from a face like a smudged mask in green glasses. I've remembered it ever since. She looked like a sybil pronouncing oracular doom. But I wasn't having any, even if I was extremely sympathetic. She doubtless hadn't quite got over her brother's death.

"Don't know what you mean," I said, brusque as that. "Is the day report in?"

"That's something else the little bird might have sung about," she said, and took the pile of files, gentling her hips over to the cabinet. "There'll be no more day reports or correspondence. It's being redirected to Whitehall. Postmaster confirmed it!"

But I wasn't to be drawn.

"Isn't that why we've been called to London?" I said. "We'll know soon enough. It might be useful if you started thinking about packing."

"That's what I'm doing, sir. We were warned when we came in this morning. The packers will be here this afternoon."

"How long have we been here, Miss Furnival?"

"Almost eight years, sir."

"If you'll remember, we came at twelve hours notice, didn't we?"

"Yes, sir"—back to me, head down at the files, question mark figure in that dress, black as always, rounded calves, small bottom and clearly no girdle—"though there wasn't this atmosphere, was there? I mean, sort of—mmm—dismal?"

"I don't find anything dismal about it," I said, and took my hat, umbrella and briefcase. "I'll expect to see you in London one day this week. Did you telephone Mrs. Trothe?"

"Yes, sir"—still with her back to me—"there was no reply at eight-thirty!"

8

"No reply?"

"No, sir. I repeated the call half an hour ago. I've got a call in for eleven o'clock."

Mrs. Cloney, the daily maid, first to drop tools and gallop for the telephone—prime source of fresh gossip—not in at 8:30? Five telephones in the house, one beside Mel's bed, and where was she?—"*Can't* face the world before *tenn*ish, darling. Im*poss!*" —out shopping? Comedy grunted in the thought. She might have gone to see the children. Might anything.

"When you reach her, would you please say she can get me at Whitehall after midday?" I said, a little surprised at the thinness of my voice. "The moment I know anything official I'll call you. Goodbye?"

"Goodbye, sir"—wistful as a child, turning slowly away—"and I hope you have a pleasant journey. I know exactly how the last of the Mohicans felt. Distinctly *en seul!*"

I looked back, surprised.

"I have no doubt we'll be unpacking in a couple of days or so," I said. "Is there something wrong? Anything I can do?"

"Everybody's waiting for the midday papers," she said, a little tiredly. "Another speech. De G again. I don't think we'll ever get in. On any terms. He's afraid of us, and that's that. I think it absolutely shameful that these politicians can make it so hard for ordinary people. That fossil doesn't care what happens. Politics, that's all. Women and children don't matter. We haven't got a single champion anywhere. Our lot are just as bad. Nothing except their ugly little politics. I detest the word. I loathe the people. I took this job because I believe in a united Europe. I believe we have a wonderful part to play. I've seen enough here to know I'm right. I've loved working for you because I'm certain in my very soul you believe in what we've been doing. I can't bear the thought it's all come to nothing. I'll turn my back and walk out!"

"Good heavens!" I said, quite startled. "I don't think you can mean that, surely? Walk out? But we're just beginning!"

9

She shook her head, tightened her mouth, looking away. "I've always had a curious, well, a sort of proprietorial feeling about being here. I mean, doing this job. The morning I got your telegram to come to London for an interview, the mother of the man I was more-or-less engaged to phoned to say he'd been killed in Korea. I was quite mad. He was the nicest. Best. They always are, aren't they? Well, that morning, I saw you, and I thought it was some sort of miracle. He'd always believed in a united Europe. I thought I'd in some way be helping him. Projecting his way of thinking. His ideals. The things he really died for. That's why I came here. That morning I was certain I'd been sent. I mean, to see you. You were so sure, in a shining sort of way. I didn't hesitate. I haven't since. Till now!"

"But why now? We always knew that the nearer we got, the rougher the fight, at least, over the table. All that has still to be gone through. Why this faltering?"

She picked up an armful of files and turned to put them on the OUT shelf.

"I've never faltered," she said, and I believed her. "This is that nonsense-thing called 'feeling.' I've got a 'feeling' it's all over. It's a tear-out. I'll resign. I'll be brain-drain. I'll sit for a degree and go to the United States. I think it's the only place where natural gifts are appreciated. Here, they're merely kicked aside. I shall only be sorry to leave you. I've learned such a lot. Enjoyed every moment!"

Her voice had filled the room, but then I had to listen to catch the whisper.

"That's not the way to look at things," I said, for want of something better. "It's destructively unlike you, to begin with. As to speeches, we've survived any number. And our Charles won't always be there, you know. Pull yourself together. Stop listening to gossip. Nothing quite gets my goat like pessimism. I'll telephone at four-thirty. Till then!"

That little talk, not perhaps the longest we'd ever had, but certainly the most personal, brought worry's small vinegar dripping at the back of my mind. I'd wondered sometimes why such a lovely girl hadn't married, but I didn't know about the Korean business. However, it had nothing to do with me, and a passing glance at the computer's entrails spread over the floor of Sanctum One, that holy of holies, did nothing for comfort. I didn't know any of the men in there. It's an extraordinary mental experience to be quite sure of oneself and one's intentions, and to be unsure to the point of sharp distrust of everybody and everything else.

But the automatic made a reassuring bump on my hip, and once I was in the street, doubts and fears seemed silly. I raised my umbrella to call the car, and off we went to the airport. I was quite happy. After all, worry must have a reason. The more I thought, the less reason there seemed to be. The fears of the morning were gone. That wound in the gut, which seemed to spill the very blood of presage to disgrace, was healed.

I could almost have sung because a choking memory of Tanis was near and dearly beautiful, and beyond her, I was quite sure I hadn't a care in the world.

2

Euphoria doesn't endure. It's a tender plant that shrivels in the first whiff of reality, and mine got hit by a couple of polar blasts at London Airport. Two messages waited for me, one from Paul to say that the Lord Blercgrove would see me at 3 not 4, and the other was a puzzler from Mel, relayed by Miss Furnival, telling me to go straight home instead of meeting her at Pamela's, and not to worry because she wasn't, and she was sure the children would be all right.

I remember standing there like two pennorth of soft-soap, wondering what I wasn't to worry about. How did she know I was coming to London? Had Paul telephoned her?

Then, like a punch in the nose, I saw a newsbill scrawled in crayon THAT BIG CHARLIE SHAKES HIS NUT AGAIN. I can see the sixpence I put down, and the headline DE GAULLE: ENCORE NON!

An inch of print got sucked into my mind, and while the words disintegrated wherever words go, I knew Miss Furnival's "feeling" was a bright light.

We were finished. A second refusal left no room for hope. London had issued the fiat, obviously to save money. A small section could deal with the daily paper.

Our poor understaffed department, with all its enthusiasm, sweat, everything we, from messengers to Paul and up, had given in time by a clock we never looked at, and the days of our lives, Saturdays and Sundays too, all of it, and every shining, dedicated idiot, was dead.

I've never been nearer going berserk. I could have wrecked the entire place with an umbrella and bare hands. But ridiculous feelings serve their purpose. They bring a sequent swing to sanity, the calms of decent thought. There was I, black homburg, grey overcoat, grey suiting, white shirt, school tie, umbrella, black briefcase, I suppose a perfect specimen of all I was supposed to be, turning in contempt from the murder in my mind, holding up my luggage tabs, nodding to a porter, and knowing, by the quick shadow of respect in his eyes and the salute, that he recognised me.

I didn't ask why, though if I'd been in better humor I might have had a word with him. One can always learn.

There were perhaps three hundred million like that man and his wife in Europe. They all lived much the same sort of life, all had about the same basic domestic wants—which made our Common Market job so much easier—and were quite often content if they were met, plus a few "luxuries" like television, football pools, and a couple of weeks off a year with pay. They were product of people who'd been guided in baronial law through almost two thousand years of Christian history, which in terms of barbarism could have given Medes, Tartars or Bolsheviks more than a run for their money. Fear of cruelty so ingrained had imposed an almost serflike compliance with authority, and that mark was still on the generations that had come through the industrial revolution and two world wars, for the most part quiet in conduct, orderly of habit, restive only by threat of unemployment, or any hint of further war.

Our design was to bring them all into one purchasing unit with one currency and thus to become the world's largest single market. Exchange of goods and services, adoption of common political ideas, and a sharing of the business of government were steps toward a federation of all the countries in Europe, each state self-governing on the lines of the United States of America, which some of us saw as the only way to avoid being squeezed between the Eagle and the Bear, and, by allying with them on better than equal terms—because we'd be more powerful than either—to face and defeat a miscreant China.

"Miserable fellow!" the Lord Blercgrove—whom some of us called the Blur—grumbled, on the morning we'd first heard of Cholly's liverish unhelpfulness. "He's been cuddling La Belle Marianne for years in what must be a classic case for all time of political incest. He's chosen to forget our hospitality of 1940. We're not the sort to remind him. Of course, he's a soldier. Principles of the military academy, and competent. But no ideas. That's his weakness. He could have been the father of the United States of Europe. Instead, he'll go down as Europe's most ungrateful tele-actor. A moody Jack Pudding. A farceur. Ridiculous creature!"

But underneath all that, I was worried about Mel's message. She wasn't the type to say anything of the sort to a secretary unless something was out of line. Perhaps she'd heard we were shot down from one of our many Common Market friends. There's always a "friend" ready to get on the phone to relay a choice morsel of Gorgonzola.

Sergeant Quatrell saluted when I went in, but he was too much the old soldier to say anything. That straight face was enough. Bad news lay on the air.

Everybody was out to lunch, which gave me an hour or so to clear my desk. Three times I called Mel at home. No reply. But Mel had never been anything but a home-bird. In the years I'd been abroad, I couldn't remember ringing the house and not getting an immediate reply. Where the devil was she or Mrs. Cloney? Miss Furnival called while I was halfway through a sandwich, and some of the salmon and cucumber fell out.

"Sir, do you know a Mr. Hofferman, Hobelman, or Heffelman?" her voice came in loud and muted whorls. "I believe we've got a sunspot or something. The line's terrible both ways. Well, he rang about ten minutes ago. He said something about 128, Glenver, or Glenville or Grenville Gardens. I couldn't get it. Anyway, that's where he said Mrs. Trothe is, and for you to get

14

in touch with her. From the directory here, I think it's in Kensington somewhere. He spoke from London."

I felt an extraordinary run of ice through every vein. It wasn't any of those names I knew, but they brought back the stare in the eyes of Gerhardt von Hollefendorm just before I'd shot him. Was this a first warning that I was a target? It was, as Hawtrey had said, how they worked. They gave the victim a tantalizing little crumb of memory, twisted in some way, to make him jumpy. Then they stretched out the time. I wondered who, near me, could inform of my movements. Somebody had to know. They weren't mind-readers.

On sudden thought I called Joel Cawle at M.I.6 and told him.

"D'you know anybody at that address?" he asked.

"No."

"Ever heard of any of those names or the other since that time?"

"No."

"I'll check and report."

I gave the address to Quatrell and told him to run through the directories. In the hour or so it took him, I finished everything, and about ten minutes to three a secretary rang to say his lordship was waiting.

"Information got that address, sir," Quatrell said, and gave me a slip. "Rare job finding it. Only thing right's the number. Name's Ebbleton. It's off the Brompton Road."

Looking at the slip in the dark corridor I had the most horrible feeling of something awful hanging over me. I've never been the emotional type, the sort that shows every feeling from a pinprick up, as it were, on the sleeve. I don't have visions, or hear brumal voices, or odd signals from the underworld. But I must say I felt something curdle, though I could never have told why.

Ebbleton was my brother-in-law, Terence, married to Pamela, Mel's sister, though how Mel could have appeared in that family had always been a mystery to some of us. Pamela and her mother were a couple of fashion plates from the mid-marts of the women's magazines, colorless as plastic, as devoid of character, except that both followed the dogs and horses, spoke of little else, and kept that type of company. Their tabletalk came direct from the men's bar. Mel didn't like it, and on a famous occasion had told them so, and walked out, though nobody was less prim than Mel. That, I'd always supposed was why they'd rarely visited us when I was at home. Ebbleton roared them on. Good for his business friends, possibly. But I hadn't known they'd moved to that address. I'd thought they were still in Finchley, just outside London, in what Mel had called that Oldye Tudorye Mishyemashye of a place, with peacocks moulting all over the lawn, and a fatty assurance of steak and kidney pudding everywhere, in the drawing room as well, walled solidly in gold frames with colored prints of all the Derby winners since Koh-I-Nor. I'd met Ebbleton there, and at a couple of other places. We'd never had much to say to each other. I don't like the sort of ingratiating manner that conceals a snigger. In the City over a few years he'd made a fortune, though now and again he'd got himself in a tight corner and had to borrow from Mel's mother, but it was always paid back with a "little" present, generally from Van Cleef and Arpels, since his other base was Paris. With those forgivable exceptions he'd never, so far as I knew, put a foot out of place. He did it all with aplomb, a personable man, dark, greying, with a fine blue eye which actually twinkled, always well-dressed, nearly always a new car, never without a new joke, and a cigar he waved as a baton while talking. He always reminded me of somebody, but I could never think who. He and Pamela were simply not the sort of people Mel and I wanted at home. For that very reason I wondered what on earth she could be doing at that address. And if she was, then why not tell me so, instead of leaving me such a curious message. Mel, however, was anything but a soft-center, and something unusual might have happened. I relied absolutely on her cold common sense, and while

16

I went into the waiting room I was putting an affectionate arm round her, dear girl, and I took her face in my hands.

But suddenly, in that moment, my kiss was for Tanis, and I felt her cling. It came rather more than coldly that things had got quite out of hand.

"I'll save you a nasty shock," Paul said, looking over the trees, no greeting. "We're finished. We're being transferred. Christ!"

I just heard the whisper. I might have said it.

"They've got something for you in this new education business. Sounds all right. All our people are getting pushed in somewhere. Minister thinks the department's got to be reorganised. Couple of ambassadors taking our places. We're getting plastered in the cracks. Dear old Chollie. You can see his game, can't you? He couldn't hold Germany, and us. We'd tip him up. We've been wasting our time!"

"I have that feeling. But why are they reorganising?"

"They've come up with the idea the department's got to have a lot more weight. More names. Publicity. One thing, they look as if they've made up their minds. That's a change!"

"Did you read the speech?"

"Just now. Same old nonsense. None of it holds water. No, if we got in, he'd be just another *clochard*. As it is, he's the boss, he knows it, and he'll hang on."

"A tear-out," I said, even then not believing it. "If my two weren't in their final year, I think I'd resign!"

He looked at me, about to speak, but Miss Tulliver opened the door.

"His lordship will see you, gentlemen. Miss Furnival will call from Geneva in fifteen minutes, Mr. Trothe. I'll put you through here."

"Make it my office, please."

"Sir, I'm sorry, but your office has been taken by Administration. Since three o'clock!"

"So's mine," Paul said, and walked in.

Lord Blercgrove's pink skull poked through small bushes of white hair over his ears. His manner was always distant, as if he'd no intention of demeaning himself by dealing with lesser souls, but if he had to, then he'd lower a barge-pole for propriety's sake.

I believe we both felt the point. It was quite clear his lordship had little use for displaced persons. His image of himself as the Power behind Power—as Paul called him—didn't permit acceptance of failure anywhere, in anybody, for any reason.

We were Out.

"You've heard the news," he said, in that far-off tenor-y drawl, as if everything was too damn' much trouble. "There's nothing I may usefully add. I'm sorry, of course. A great deal of hard work apparently for nothing. Our day will come, I'm sure. Mr. Chamby, you'll be going ov—"

"I'm going nowhere," Paul interrupted, but so quietly. "I've had enough. You'll get my resignation with my report by about next Thursday or Friday. That's the lot!"

"Sorry to hear that," his lordship said, and leaned back, looking at a pencil. "This *is* promotion, you know?"

"I'd have liked it in our department. Can't have it? Right. I'll go home!"

"And Mr. Trothe?" his lordship asked, almost slyly, still looking at the pencil.

"I shall serve," I said. "I have a family, and there's a pension to consider."

"Ah, yes. Yes, indeed. One's compelled to think practically these days, what? Well, I've spoken to Mrs. Lesley Shafford. She's the new Junior Minister. Across the road. Miss Tulliver has your letter of introduction. As I've said, it's also promotion in your case. You'll find plenty to do, I'm sure."

I nodded, and Paul and I got up together.

His lordship came round the desk, and offered a hand.

"Goodbye to you, Mr. Chamby. I've always enjoyed working with you. Trothe, I'd like a word more, if you please."

18

"I'll see you before you go, Paul?"

He nodded and walked on. Looking at that bowed head I felt desperately sorry. I had a feeling that neither of us would ever advance quite so far again. A barony, a knighthood, such pleasant dreams!

"Do sit down, Trothe," his lordship said amiably, which surprised me. "There's something I want to air. Merely that, for the moment. As we both know, I have ample reason to trust you. We've never mentioned that matter, have we?"

I knew what he meant but I had no intention of discussing it. Shooting his paramour had preyed on me for a long time. I could never remember her name. Her bottom lip bled when I put the barrel against her teeth. But she kept her smile. She was brave.

"As well not," I said. "There are cemeteries even in the mind. Those days and times are gone. I often wish they hadn't happened!"

The Blur sat back, elbows on the chair, pencil held across his chest, looking at me. His eyes seemed to change in tones of grey. I felt myself approaching head-on collision.

"A sense of gratitude is often selfish. I'm selfish enough to be grateful. But I must say you did put her away without much fuss!"

That a brutal idiocy, committed by order, in wartime, when anything was duty, could be regarded years later as done "without much fuss" became not so much a studied—because unthought—perhaps unmeant—insult—as a horror that had to be relived. I don't think we become less sensitive in later years. We may remember less, perhaps, but what stays is infinitely more poignant.

A short nod seemed the best answer.

"You asked Security to make a check of a man called Hoffenden, Hoffernan or something of the sort. Why?"

"He telephoned me."

"Do you know anyone of that name? Or have you ever?"

19

"Some years ago. Von Hollefendorm. I had to kill him."

"Ah. Yes. It was after my—er—"

"Yes."

"You think he mightn't have died?"

"Impossible. I think of somebody using his name."

"Revenge?"

"Sounds a little too fourpenny-thriller. But one never knows."

"One really doesn't. Let me show you a precis of a report."

He gave me a sheet of green paper. The block of type wasn't signed. It was headed from a town in West Germany, and listed, first, the names of Nazi ex-officers' guilds, alliances, clubs and sporting fraternities, and others for NCOs and men, most in the cities and towns, quite a number in rural areas, and a few in European capitals, two in London hidden, one as a card club and the other a bowling alley. Each had a board of directors, all members paid subscriptions, and all swore the same oath, of fealty and obedience to their officers, and all were devoted to the purpose of joining the two German states and of bringing up their sons to believe in a united German nation. All swore to defend the country's frontiers, but never to take up arms against any except the attacker. All sports were practised including horsemanship, aviation, and yachting, and local, state and federal athletic associations were regularly supported with funds.

The sting was very much in the tail.

It had been found that most units had a small body of men, mostly youngsters under the surveillance of veterans, sworn under oath to kill or in other ways bring to ruin, those whose evidence had sent ex-Nazis to prison. At notice of the death of any marked man, special meetings were called to "drink the swine under the table and drown him in the beerwash of honest men."

I gave it back.

"More serious than I'd thought," I said. "We must be fairly high on the roster."

"Somewhere among the top seeds, I imagine. Considering what

type of chaps they are, all modern appliances, as well as complete liberty of movement, I think it time to take a closer look at them."

"Might be wiser."

"The position you're going to's only a stop-gap. There are better things in wait. But I feel that since you're—as it were—in center-stage, you might think about taking charge of this. If only as a form of self-protection!"

"But I thought Hawtrey was in charge?"

"He's been supervising reports, that's all, and generally keeping everybody informed. He's excellent in his way, of course. But not for command."

"I'm a little rusty—"

He laughed at the pencil.

"An hour's instruction will be enough. Newer methods don't take long to learn. Think it over. Meantime, everything's being done to find this Hollefendorm fellow."

"I'd like to know how he got my telephone number, and right to my desk!"

The Blur sat back, and positively simpered.

"I should have thought that facile in the extreme!" he almost whinnied. "Weren't you friendly with a Frenchwoman called Ghislaine Ivry? You supplied her with your telephone number, and she called you from Oran, didn't she? Why should it surprise you that others know? I can't think how such a grizzled old fox could be so limitlessly naïve!"

I could only stare at pale grey eyes above fingers twiddling a red pencil.

"I'm a little surprised," I said, not untruthfully. "Are the names of these 'others' known?"

"But of course. We know that Communists have infiltrated these ex-Nazi organizations."

"I can't imagine her mixed up in anything of the sort!"

"I could show you a list of at least twenty girls, all extremely able, most of them quite lovely, working in this country at the moment. Secretaries, models, so forth. All doing a little job of one kind or another. You know our system. Just enough rope to let us hang them!"

Three buzzes sounded from the box beside his elbow. He pressed the switch as if the caller must be God.

"M'lord, Mrs. Lesley Shafford's secretary's on the line to say that the Junior Minister's free for the next half hour if Mr. Trothe's available," the loudspeaker grated. "She has a Chequers appointment tomorrow, that's why."

His lordship got up.

"Take advantage of the opportunity," he said, and looked at his watch. "Could you be back here at five? There are confidential matters about this appointment I'd like to stress. It's hardly what it appears on the surface!"

I went out feeling I had both feet stuck in a nasty morass. Mention of Ghislaine's name after such a long time was a shock made worse by her status as an agent, which I'd never guessed. Clearly, I'd been under close observation. Tanis must also appear on that file. That was highly uncomfortable for both of us. Instantly she threaded herself through my mind until literally I couldn't think of anyone or anything else, refused to be bothered by thought of The Eye.

At my stage of the game, falling in love was no joke.

I remembered the contempt I'd felt for others stupid enough— as I'd thought then—to fall over themselves for somebody or other. My somebody-or-other was twenty-seven, slim, thick chestnut hair below her waist, greeny-grey eyes, Swiss-French with a Hungarian mother, and all that temperament. She'd come for an interview with me, an unbelievable reporter for a local paper, though the article and others that followed proved she knew her job. As I know now, because I'm rather less of a benighted idiot, they were written for her, and she was never on the staff. Then she was given the women's page, or so she told me. That night we had a little party to celebrate her success, and then was when the unbelievable happened.

22

Until that time I was a sort of Daddy-Come-up, somebody to go to dinner with, or a picnic-lunch on Sundays, or a concert or cinema, well, anyway a pretty drift from here to there, with latterly a kiss on the cheek when we met and when I left her at her apartment door. There's no fool like an apparently mature one, specifically he who never thought of himself as more than twenty-one. I never had. I wasn't playing any game, and I certainly had no idea of anything more serious than a charming—charming is the one word to describe her manner—companionship since I was old enough to be her father, even if I've never been able to see what that's got to do with it. As Robbie Burns said, "a man's a man for a' that."

If I'd any idea in mind that she'd be wonderful in bed, I must have stifled it, but of course that thought was alive at any time I cared to dwell on beautiful legs, hands, the faraway dream of her eyes, sometimes the wrinkling of a mouth that seemed never to have been kissed. Those were thoughts that senior civil servants, heads of departments, fathers of families, ought never to have. They came at times to me, and I put them aside, though on many a drive home I was caressed by silken wraiths all in her perfume, whispering with her mouth, tickling my face with her hair. And that, at any age, can be maddening. In my case, it was worse. I found myself daydreaming, and I won't say it's not enjoyable.

It is.

But it's dangerous. The mind goes from the wish to the want, from dreaming to desiring, and on to passion, I thought I was simply infatuated. That's a funny word I've never taken much notice of. I've been made to. I could have been infatuated in the beginning with such items as a way of walking in an almost distrait lift of the chin, a sidelong smile of narrowed greeny-grey that opens in a sudden flamey stare, of lips that pressed in a pink cone look like the apple itself, of hands used gracefully, not largely, in conversation, and a discrete perfume that only sometimes stuck a sweet knife in the senses. They were

23

part of memory that made me hungry, shut my eyes almost against my will, brought her name bursting from my mouth in a groan.

I found it all funny, that is, at the start.

You immoderate ass, I said to myself. Here you are, at your age, behaving like a schoolboy. Your own son probably feels like this for somebody he's met, and you'll pull his leg. Puppy-love. Is that it?

By God, it hurts.

Hurts.

Christ, somewhere in the gut, near the heart, in the throat at the back of the head, it hurts.

But *what* an idiot!

All right, an idiot, but in all enlightened Creation, no idiot happier, or more grateful, or more determined to be my kind of idiot, than myself.

3

Mrs. Lesley Shafford looked a youngish forty, cropped coppery hair, grey eyes behind glasses, thin mouth, very little make-up, and a grey tailleur. She appeared to be all her career as a headmistress had made her, quietly smart, pleasant in a scholastic way, and very full of her new job. The Minister—oh, a charming man!—had the most wonderful ideas and she was thrilled, but thrilled, to be even a small part of what could only become a wonderful chapter in our history, and on, until she must have seen what I thought.

"I'm very grateful to Lord Blercgrove for suggesting you, Mr. Trothe," she said, in a different tone, and I noticed she had the Blur's habit of fiddling with a pencil. "We're new, and I know I haven't got the right people. But I think your coming here'll be a really auspicious start. What we're doing is looking into the matter of scholarships to and from all the countries of the Commonwealth and the rest of the world. Then new universities, technical colleges, endowments, grants, investments, and so forth, coalescing everything, as it were, and bringing it all under one head. It'll take a long time, of course. That's why I was so glad you were suggested. Your record makes you an ideal choice for personnel, first, and then on the committees, finance, economic and so on. If you'd care to begin on Monday I'd be most grateful. I shall have time to get the Minister's views on paper, and we'll work from that. Shall we say here, at eleven?"

Any sympathy I'd ever had with women's suffrage disappeared

then and there. Male politicos had to take notice of women, had to flatter, coerce, and then, an election won, throw them a sop among the Ministries, though not, of course, where they'd do any damage. The misfortune was that the male staff had to put up with them, and at times bow and scrape to keep their jobs.

I suppose most of what I felt showed unhappily in my face.

"You know, Mr. Trothe," she said unexpectedly as I got up to go. "I've had a great deal of experience in working with men. I'm not the maternal sort. Neither do I plead. My method of working is to take the Minister's directives, and see they're carried out. That is my intention. I do hope we shall be able to work together. Good morning!"

I went out deflated, fuming. I hated the idea of working for a woman, and especially a bluestocking, and having to take orders. Sounds silly, it *is* certainly silly, but silly or not, that's how I felt.

While I digested gall and aloes, walking down the corridor, I ran into Errol Hinter, whom we called Yorick, perhaps because of the empty skull.

"Why, hullo, Edmund, good lord, what're you doing here?" he falsettoed, agreeably enough, even if I'd had to give him the boot from my department a couple of years before. I'd thought at the time he must have been about the most ineffectual nonentity ever. For all that, he had his uses, he certainly had human appeal, besides being on Christian name terms—because of his family's ramifications—with the top o' the land. Whether it was the Court, the Embassies, the City, Lords or Commons, or Society as it's properly understood, there was nobody he couldn't get to in two minutes flat. I saw immediately why he'd been sent to a new department. He'd be useful. Then he'd do something so absurd as to defy speech, and he'd be pushed elsewhere. He was tall, frail, pale, with black-rimmed spectacles that minimized sloppy blue eyes to concentric points, a completely open manner—I don't suppose I've met a man more absolutely honest—and an air about him of complete good humor, almost as if he were laughing at the entire world for every reason, and summing up the person he was talking to as one of the prime comedians of all time. That—naturally—did nothing to endear him to heads of departments wanting to keep him on for sweet charity's sake, yet having to get rid of him before he drove everyone potty.

"Oh, De Gaulle," he said, when I'd told him. "I heard the most awfully funny story about him the other day. Can't remember what it was. Goes in one ear, gets stuck in the sinus. I think I've got TB. Hope so. Camellias and whatnot at the grave, what? Voluptuous damsels throwing themselves in. Don't know any. Still, an early death's about all I can look forward to. They speak so kindly of one, don't they? Awful bloody fool, but frightfully good-natured, what? You must have guessed I've just been the glowing heart of the most unutterable debacle? I gave the wrong ambassador the wrong despatch. Dear me. I've never *heard* such a caterwaul about a paragraph or two, really!"

I let him ramble on. Knowing him, I knew he had a peculiar method of communication. If he had news, a message, a warning, of any worth, he'd never say so outright, but entwine it in the conversation, though only with those he liked. Others, of course, might just as well have tried opening oysters with a broom.

"I suppose you know the Management's a great friend of Lady Blercgrove?" he said, in a flash of lenses toward Mrs. Shafford's office. "And of my lady mother's. There's more than a possibility the Management's going elsewhere. Education, or some such. Don't know why people bother. Only gives the lower classes ideas. Of course, it'll leave that desk vacant, won't it?"

He looked down the long corridor. A green runner stretched the length to a window reddening in winter's setting sun.

"I'm thinking of hiring a mechanized bath-chair or a mini-scooter for this job," he said, in his weary way. "D'you see where they've put me? I mean, look at it. A mile to go for a cup of tea. Or a sacred pee. I've got a little dungeon down there. Table and chair. No telephone. Stone floor. No carpet. Frightful come-down. Don't you think? Girls here look at me as if I'd just got out of a dribble-coop. I suppose they've all read the case history. People write the most frightful nonsense about one, don't they? All Christian souls, I suppose. But the effect, great heaven!"

"Come and see me on Monday," I told him. "I'll shift you a little nearer the earth's center. You mentioned a desk becoming vacant?"

"Personally, from what I hear, I think that's what you're here for. After all, Junior Minister isn't far from other things, is it? The higher we go, the merrier. I do hope I can keep on here. It's so near the Tube, and there's an awfully good pub round the corner. A rather more comfortable chair, one less ruthless to the old rump'd be a step in the right direction, don't you think?"

"I'll get you one with a cushion," I said. "Even if it's against Standing Orders, Inventory, Grades, etcetera!"

He mimped unbelievingly, and brushed something off his cuff.

"Thank you, Edmund. Enjoyable, I must say, meeting you again. Well, here we go for the mile dash. That length of green's really a scabrously defeating job, don't you think? One rather fears chlorophyll poisoning!"

I looked at the doors opening off the corridor all the way down to the window.

"Which one's yours?" I asked him.

"On the right, at the end," he said, hands in pockets, bent-shouldered, gloomy. "I mean the end. That nasty little stable-door crack down there. Can you see it? It's nothing but death's anteroom. If I get scuffed here, I've had it. Awful thought. Imagine. There isn't any further except the window and those most inhospitable flagstones down in the courtyard. Death, I love thee, but not that!"

28

There was even a waft of old winding-sheets in the way he said it.

"Oh, I remember!" he called, and turned back. "The De Gaulle story? He was breezing off somewhere, and he called his Minister-fixer and said, 'Look here, I might roll up while I'm away, so we'd better decide where I'll be buried.' 'Ah,' says the Minister, 'I'll get in touch with Les Invalides immediately!' 'Les Invalides?' says De Gaulle, almost out of his socks. 'Me, buried with a nasty little Corsican NCO? Rubbish!' 'Then let's try the Arc de Triomphe,' says the Minister. 'Me, buried with an *UNKNOWN* soldier?' says De Gaulle. 'Ridiculous! Get on the blower to Rome and see about the Holy Sepulchre!' The Minister rockets away. Back he comes, all smiles. 'Everything's fixed for a slap-up do,' he says. 'Only snag is, they want ten million new francs, gold.' 'Ten million?' says De Gaulle, absolutely purple. 'But the old fool knows perfectly well I shan't be in there more than three days.'"

We laughed at nonsense, and a messenger came up the stairs with a slip of paper for me.

MRS. TROTHE TELEPHONED TO SAY SHE MIGHT BE AWAY NEXT WEEK AND WOULD YOU PLEASE SEE THAT MRS. CLONEY ASKS MRS. TRESS TO CLEAN THE BOOKS IN THE LIBRARY AND SHAKE OUT THE BLANKETS IN THE UPSTAIRS CLOSET. THERE MIGHT BE MOTH.

I folded the paper, and looked at Yorick's admiring stare.

"Of international importance, doubtless?" he said, and turned. "Ah, me. An inconsequential spot of cosmic urine. Half a tiny fece of obscurity's own droppings. Shall I ever be anything else? I envy you, Edmund. Marked for greatness. What more wonderful destiny can there be?"

"At the moment I'm to see about moth on the second-floor landing," I said. "Stop worrying. You'll get your chair this afternoon if I have to carry it up myself!"

He looked at me without the smile, took a hand out of his

pocket to push his spectacles up between his brows, looking over my shoulder at something quite new, or so it seemed.

"Thank you, Edmund," he said, as if I'd offered him a cigaret. "Back to the hutch, what?"

He turned and went away in long heel-and-toe strides.

I felt awfully sorry for him.

Some people seem to have everything except that all-important little something up top. That's what I thought.

But for God's sake, how *can* one be so wrong?

4

Big Ben struck the hour as I went into the Blur's office. One sheet of paper lay on the blotter. I saw it held a paragraph.

"I can imagine your interview," he said, arch as a vixen. "You look as though you'd been rehearsing a rebel battle cry!"

"Can't stand the thought of working for a woman," I said. "Must be a worse fate, but I can't think of it. Is there really nothing else?"

"Of that importance, no. Because now you get the other half of the story. You're going there for one specific purpose. Of all the students, mostly African, already in the country, and the others coming here, we know there are some who aren't students at all. They're manoeuvred into scholarships however carefully we try to sift them. Most have been to a Russian university, or to Pekin. They're sent here to keep an eye on their colleagues, and in other ways make themselves useful. We want to root them out. We'd like to know where their money comes from, what they spend it on and where. We want to know the source. The dossiers have been sent over to your office. I'm quite sure it won't take you long to spot most of them. Send their names to M.I.6. You'll be free sooner than you think, I promise you!"

"A happy day," I said. "Depending, of course, on what the next appointment's going to be!"

He smiled down at the paragraph.

"Put your mind on our friends, here," he said, tapping the paper. "They're going to be troublesome. We've put out a short net, but it's not going to be enough. The people we're after won't be guileless enough to frequent a bowling alley or a card club. Their friends will. The people who help them. But that's like trying to pot rabbits in the dark. It's got to be Germany, and you're the only real runner. First, you know the form. Second, you've seen blood. The others haven't. Apart from that, you're one they'd very much like to put in the bag. As they've already done with Andrew Furnival and Tom Law!"

"What's the evidence, there?"

He turned the chair to look through the window.

"We'd managed to get a Misadventure verdict in both cases. We put on more than a little pressure. They'd been very much a part of us, and the evidence was uneven, to say the least. But we had to dig. Without going into detail, Andrew was found dead in his own car with a pipe from the exhaust through the window and the cracks stuffed with newspaper. But there was a large bruise above the neck. Tom Law was found with his head in a gas oven. But it was proved there wasn't enough gas in the meter, and it'd run out while his girl was there. He'd walked her down to the corner. Andrew was a staff member at Nuremberg. Tom, at Gelsen Kirchen. He had a very large practice in Manchester. Why would a first-class physician with every comfortable means at hand choose a stupid little gas oven? That, in any case, wouldn't work? The murderer overlooked the meter."

He swivelled the chair to face me.

"But within a week of both deaths—and there was an interval of almost four months between them—a party was held in the bierkeller in Regsmund. All the flags, etcetera. Fortunately we had somebody there. We know the names of the men who got the welcome, and others since. But of course there've perhaps been French, Belgian, Dutch and American victims, and others we may never know. We don't know which way the roster works. They may take the easier marks first. The more difficult, us, for example—"

He got up and walked to the window. He was hunched as a

vulture, shoulders back, hands in jacket pockets pulling at the coat.

"They don't have to shoot us, you know, Trothe," he said quietly. "All we need is a putrescent whiff of any sort of scandal. That's all. We'd never survive it. We'd be finished. Publicity would murder us. That, I confess, is my fear. We're out in the light. Naked, vulnerable. These people know it. My instinct is, they'll play on it!"

"Any plan in mind?"

He shook his head.

"No use without some idea of the terrain," he said. "You'll have to go to Regsmund. That's a primary requisite. What they need is a lesson. The loss of a few 'heroes' would do it. Meantime, our people are reporting. That's why I'd like you to go across the road for a little time. The work I've asked you to do there will not—repeat not—come under the scrutiny of the Junior Minister. You'll attend meetings and committees, of course, and give what advice you think fit. That's all!"

A perfect end to an interview with the Blur, I thought, walking down the stairs. I don't know whether I felt resentment at being used as a sort of catspaw, or if I basked in the unspoken compliment of having been handpicked, as it were, for what must be a dangerous business. I'd been in too many to think much about it, though I felt the old, sweet sap of excitement in rise, and tried to stifle it in thought of Tanis. My present position wouldn't permit the weekend flight I'd promised myself. Starting on Monday meant I'd have to go in on Saturday, perhaps Sunday, for a few hours to bring myself up to date with the paper. But I wanted Tanis with me. I could then and there have caught a plane and gone to her. That's how I felt. I couldn't tolerate any thought of days, perhaps weeks away from her. It simply maddened. But I couldn't telephone. Letters could be opened, cables read. In the light of the Ghislaine report, any direct communication would be stupid, because it would encourage the Eye. I had to find a way of bringing her over quietly for a day or so now and again. Even a thought that I could was a pacifier of sorts, and I rolled my umbrella a little tighter, and walked toward Trafalgar Square.

I took a bus to Kensington, thinking of Eric Coates' music and marvelling how it seemed to fit the shops, houses, side-streets and even the people, especially when a squadron of H. M. Life Guards rode beyond the trees in a flash of scarlet and burnished steel.

Ebbleton's house, I found, was one in a wide square, with three bow windows one above the other, and a portico with two pillars and six worn steps up to a black front door. I knew exactly how it would look inside because an aunt of mine had lived in the same type of house not half a mile away.

I rang the bell and waited for a minute, and rang again. I'd decided to write a card, and the door opened. Instanter, a sense of warning bristled. The mood of door-openers can be told by the way the doors open. Why does a man fear to open his own front door?

Terry looked at me. He was at least two days unshaven, in a dressing gown that reminded me of what our dog slept on.

"Edmund!" he whispered, hollow-eyed, blue-patched, as if I were earthy from the grave. "Good God! How did you get here?"

"Bus," I said. "What's wrong with you?"

"Oh," he sighed, and dropped his shoulders, frowned, looked about, opened the door perhaps two inches wider. "Had a rotten flu. And the damnedest mess with telephones. I've been trying to reach Montreal since this morning. Can't connect!"

"I was told there was a sunspot or something."

He looked round as if pleased.

"Really? That might account for it, then. But it won't account for losses. I—well—I hope I've got something left!"

He stood in shadow of half-drawn velvet curtains, dusty windows, a living example of the frowse in a room which hadn't been looked at for at least a week. Something about his attitude made me look at him a little closer. It suddenly struck me that his accent wasn't quite English. I'd never seen him alone before. We'd always been in a party. His dirty nails trembled in lighting a cigaret. He stared out at the laurel hedge.

Suddenly enough to make me start he turned, nodding at some telephones humping among an assortment of sheets scribbled with red pencil, a calculator, ashtrays piled with butts, and lifted his shoulders, leaving them at level of his ears. Which I thought excessively foreign.

"What's the matter?" I asked, on the brisk side.

"Telephones," he said, quickly, as if pleased by any excuse. "What is the use if they don't work?"

I wondered if he were drunk.

"Couldn't you cable?" I asked, still brisk.

"I've spent pounds. Not a single reply. I simply don't know what to make of it!"

"Seems curious. Cabling your brokers?"

He nodded, smoke wisping up his nose to his eyes, hands in the pockets of that horrible dressing gown. I wondered why a man always faultlessly dressed in public should take so little care of himself in private. Our char, dear Mrs. Cloney, wouldn't have worn those slippers.

I didn't believe a word of his story about telephones or cables because I'd spoken to Ottawa only an hour or so before. Both ways were clear. I had to ask myself why he would dare lie to me. But then I thought of M.I.6. They might have been up to something.

"Look here," I said, rather louder than required. "I came to find out what Mel's doing here. Where is she?"

"Mel?" he said, through cigaret smoke. "What d'you mean? How did you find this place?"

"Somebody called Hoffenden or Heffernan took the trouble to ring my office in Geneva this morning. Any idea who it could have been?"

His frown changed to a clear stare, almost, I could have sworn, of fear.

"Only my secretary knows this address," he said shakily. "Not even Pam knows. Geneva? It can't be!"

"That's why I'm here!"

He reached for a chair and rested on the back. I never saw anyone so utterly unlike his usual self. I even felt sorry for him.

"Go and sleep for a couple of hours," I said, and put down my umbrella and overcoat. "I'll take care of the phones. If a cable comes, I'll call you."

He shook his head at the floor.

"Can't. Going to be smashed if I don't!"

"You'll need a clearer brain than the one you've got now. I'll wake you when it's necessary. Go to bed!"

It was a command, and he obeyed like a small boy. He shambled in those slippers to the door, stood for a moment, sighed, and creaked up the stairs. I heard a door slam, and open again. I felt the weight of a listener.

Was somebody pulling my leg? Who could have telephoned Geneva? Why?

I didn't want to touch the desk or look at the papers, though I saw that most were European and Russian. I didn't even empty the ashtrays. I opened the window to freshen the air, cleared an armchair of reviews, and sat down to think. It took two moments to resolve a picture of Pamela, and I reached for the nearest telephone. I had to try four of them until I found a live line in the fifth, on the other side of the desk.

I asked the operator why I couldn't get a number on the other four, and she put me on to somebody who said that any query should be referred to the Chief Engineer. I dialled Pamela's and spoke to Mrs. Tewkes, the cookwhatall. Mrs. Ebbleton was out shopping but she'd be back by teatime. I left my name and rang his Pall Mall office, and rang again. No reply. I rang the operator. She had no better luck, and neither did the supervisor. I thought of taking a cab to Pall Mall to find out what was happening but a key snickered in the front door.

I sat still, expecting a secretary to come in. But somebody went in high heels to the front room.

"Terry? Terry?"

Mel's voice.

Terry seemed to waken, if he was asleep, and his shout covered her second call.

"Up here. Come on up. Don't touch anything down there!"

"Darling, as if I would. I've got it. You're safe, darling. I knew there was nothing to worry about. And I've got a new sort of coldpill. They're said to be awfully good. Did you miss me?"

"Come on up here. Get those letters off?"

"Of course"—going up the stairs—"you've got a fever, poor sweet. Tacky temper. Never mind!"

The door closed.

Mel?

I swear the entire world swung, and swung, and hit me full in the face.

I couldn't think, I couldn't see. Yet something prevented me from going upstairs. I didn't want to find her there. Everything, every sense, recoiled, froze, died.

I couldn't, I wouldn't see her there.

With barely a pause I took my hat and overcoat and went quietly into the passage. There wasn't a sound. The house was even without echo. But what was he going to tell her about me?

She'd left her coat and handbag on the hall table.

Impulse—what else?—made me open it. I took her wallet, snapped the bag shut, opened the front door, closed it without a sound, and walked, almost ran away.

I suppose, thinking back, the worst, incomparably the worst, because the most dishonest act of my life, and the one I most bitterly regret.

5

I deliberately read the evening paper in the train going home. It was rather more than an hour's journey, for the most part through fields and gardens of that English green which always shocks those who've been away and may have forgotten its delicacy. I saw flashes of it from the corner of my eye, felt warmed by it, loved it, and I also saw Bladen looking at me from his reflection in the window. He and his wife Dora were neighbours, or at least, we lived in the same village, went to the same church, ran stalls at charity fairs, though without any intimacy so far as I was concerned. I couldn't remember having had a drink with him, though we always nodded with that silly set of the mouth which tells of mutual approval. He was something in metals, I'd heard, and he'd read all about me in the press, so that we knew where we stood. I didn't want to talk, I didn't want to think, and I sat there pretending to read, though of course not a word went in.

All I could hear was Mel's voice.

Had I obeyed that first instinct I'd have gone up there and killed the pair of them.

I hadn't, because I'd thought of Tanis.

I could hardly play the heavy with Mel when I'd had at least four other affairs without her knowledge, and now had another, far more serious, with a girl not much older than our daughter. Perhaps it offended a sense of propriety or justice, or whatever it was, but I felt I couldn't go up there and do the thing properly. That sort of scene needs sincerity and lots of steam. I hadn't either, or a leg to stand on.

I was going home because I suddenly felt quite sick and I wanted to sit in my library and see if I couldn't find a little mental peace.

Mel, unfaithful? Melisande, mistress of dear Terence? I wondered if Pamela knew. It was unbelievable.

I had the evidence of my ears.

That was the voice of Mel's love. I'd known it for almost thirty years. Was I heartbroken? Was that what I felt? Mel, the magnificent and most beautiful pillar of my existence, girl-bride and mother, that dearest, sobbing bundle in my arms, unfaithful? Another man's toy, her brother-in-law's pet, traitor to her sister and everybody else? I felt the anger, but it was damped by knowledge that I was equally guilty.

In all that welter of thought and counter-thought, I tried to imagine who could have called Geneva with that address. Again I thought of Ebbleton, wondering how Mel could have had anything to do with him in that state, though she must have been used to it. For how long? Has she been, at times, mistress to both of us? How dear Terence must have sniggered!

The thought stung and I lay back, putting the paper down, closing my eyes.

I could feel Bladen looking at me.

I opened my eyes, and he was.

"Erhm—Mr. Trothe," he began. "Erhm—it's been some time since we met. I'm sorry to disturb you like this. But—erhm—I erhm—I felt I had to ask if there's any truth in these rumors?"

"What rumors?"

"Erhm—well, that the banks have foreclosed on erhm—your brother-in-law. I detest repeating gossip, but I thought it my duty to ask?"

"I returned from Europe today. I know nothing about it."

"Quite. It's erhm—it's a little worrying, that's all."

"Why should it worry you?"

"Well, erhm—uh—Dora and I put a little money in. In the pool, I mean. We thought the twelve-and-a-half percents'd take care of Christmas presents and insurance, don't you know? Always useful. Since Melisande and yourself were in, and all the others, we thought it worth a crack, as it were?"

I hated that he should use my wife's Christian name, damn it. I detest familiarity on that basis.

"I know nothing about any pool. I certainly have no money or anything else in any sector of Ebbleton's business. Who gave you to understand I did? Or that my wife had contributed a ha'penny?"

His frown cleared.

"I prefer to say nothing more, Mr. Trothe," he said, immediately withdrawn. "I don't want to purvey gossip. Forgive me for the interruption!"

"Not at all. I shall get the facts and telephone you later tonight, if I may?"

"By all means. Thank you!"

A flux of rage seemed to tear a hole in my throat. Mel, mixed up in share-pushing? Mistress of the tout? By his suasion? Mel, selling shares for her lover? It was ludicrous. Incredible. I knew it was true. I shrivelled. In my position, married to the doxy of a common trickster?

The train slowed, we said goodnight, and I got out almost into the arms of Dr. Tomsett, our vicar, a big man of fairish-grey hair, heartwhole blue eyes and the face of a football player.

"Ah, Mr. Trothe!" he greeted me, with a grin of broken teeth. "Welcome home. We hadn't expected you, but I'm awfully glad you're here. There've been the most disquieting stories flying about. Is it true you're leaving us?"

Good God, I thought, how do these things begin? Where?

"First I've heard of it," I said. "We've been here for nine generations and I don't doubt the tenth intends to carry on!"

"Oh," he said, and stared, very bluely, seriously, and looked at the train going away, drawing a deep breath. "I think I should tell you that many of my parishioners put some money in your brother-in-law's companies. They've paid very well for the past couple of years, so the Parish council thought we might invest a little for the organ fund and so forth. I don't like to think it's gone?"

"What makes you think it has?"

"Bladen's a stock broker, as perhaps you know? He said Ebbleton's being looked for. I don't know who by, but this afternoon, a friend of mine went to his offices in Pall Mall. It's shut. Mrs. Trothe told me he's in Scotland!"

"When did she tell you that?"

"On the telephone last evening. You know, if you're just back, this is a very poor welcome—"

"I shall find out the facts and let you know. So far as I'm concerned there's not a penny of mine invested with my brother-in-law. I've never liked that type of market. I like it less now!"

He was staring at me, a blue challenge, even unbelieving, head slightly sideways. He opened his mouth to say something, thought better, shut it, pulled his overcoat to the top button.

In that time my mind raced. Could Mel have been the swine's mistress for a couple of years? Had she been share-pushing for that time?

I pulled in the sort of breath that makes no noise. Perhaps he saw the fury I felt.

He suddenly smiled in the kindliest way.

"Let me drop you at the Manor," he said, almost his old self. "These things are worrying, but there's always room for doubt, isn't there? People really don't mind what they say—"

"Thank you, but I'd promised myself a walk. I've been sitting in planes, offices and trains all day."

"Oh, I quite understand. Then I'll wait for your call!"

He went to the man he'd met off the train, and I turned down the other way.

I was absolutely in a seethe. A couple of villagers touched their caps, and some waved to me, but I merely lifted my umbrella in answer. At other times I'd have stopped, happy to hear rustic speech again, and learn the latest about crops, bulbs, seeds. I could always depend on something good for the following season and I had many a friend since I always paid on the dot. It was therefore really infuriating when old Tim Garfield crossed the street to say "Good Even', zur. When could ui carl f'r the 'count? Bin a long toime ewtstandin'. Ev' since las' Ap'ul, ah."

I owed him three pounds eight, I remembered, and I'd given the cash to Mel. I took the money out, apologised, said I was just back, and gave him goodnight.

I wasn't just seething. I was crawling. It occurred to me that other local bills might be outstanding. I was passing the village grocer, and went in to ask for a packet of tea.

"I haven't seen the account for a couple of months or so," I told old Freeman. "How do we stand?"

"It's more'n that, sir," he said. "Fair amount. I didn't like bothering!"

"Send it to me and you'll have a cheque in the morning. Didn't you send it to the house?"

"Every week, sir. Mrs. Cloney gen'ly took it herself!"

He looked as if he might say more, but I suppose my glance stopped him. It must have been a freezer.

"That's all," I said. "Goodnight to you!"

Seethe, blaze, creep, crawl, burst with shame and rage. These people had been friends of my parents and grandparents. The house was known for monthly clearance of all accounts. Were any others months behind? What was Mel doing with the money? The monthly cheque I sent her was always comfortably over expenditure. The rest was her pin-money and I never stinted or asked questions.

What had the stupid woman been doing? Supplying her lover? Savage rage, that I suppose I had never before experienced almost pushed me into the pub for a half of bitter to moisten my aching throat. But I felt I couldn't talk to anyone. I had to get home, put my slippers on, pour myself a really good drink, and sit down to consider what was happening.

I crossed the Common, passed the post office, the constabulary house, both shut, and turned down our lane with a feeling of relief. The trees spread black veins against a darkening sky.

A star shone, almost as sign of hope for me. Those trees, that star I had known since boyhood, coming back from fishing, or playing cricket for the village. They'd always given me, as it were, an assurance that I was "of" them, and they "of" me, a steady feeling, of being wholly part of order, part of time itself, of carrying my name correctly into the future for the decent use of others I'd never know, who'd never think of me. How I'd have loved to talk to my great-great-grandfather, that Vice-Admiral at Trafalgar! Could he have known then, that I, Edmund, named for him, would feel cold pride that he was of my tree? But what silliness! How does a man, abroad in sweaty gusto of glorious living, think ahead into the fourth generation —granted the fecund womb of the beloved—and what is he to imagine?

Suddenly I thought that the world turned, that the horrors of one generation were the prideful equanimity of those following, that the shocks of the moment were matters of living nerve, and things were not so bad as I'd assumed, that Mel might have a perfectly reasonable excuse, that my guilty mind and conscience might have distorted things, that the rumors could have been started by the envious, that anything and nothing, and for God's sake stop worrying.

My property began where the trees ended. There was the grey stone wall. The main gate was on the right of the lane, and I saw with approval that the new shrubs had topped the stone by almost a foot.

But above the gatepost a white board glowed in the dusk. For a moment I looked at it, trying to think what it might be, and then broke the stroll and half ran.

I couldn't believe what I saw. But I knew why Dr. Tomsett's heartwhole blue eyes had suddenly flashed hard in disbelief.

I simply gawked at a sign of red letters:

BY CONSENT OF THE OWNER
THIS DESIRABLE PROPERTY
FOR SALE
BILLIN & HODGE
AGENTS

I don't suppose I shall die again. When I do, it'll be child's play.

6

It was the same scotch and the same water I'd always had, but I never lifted a drink that tasted worse or did less. Of course I'd smashed the board, which made me feel better, if any thought of it, or what it meant simply petrified me. Mel's message recurred. Was this what I wasn't to worry about? What was I expected to do? The place was freehold, left to me by my father. It had never had lien or mortgage. I couldn't see how Gilman could have dared furnish deeds without my consent. Or how anything could have been done without my permission. Wasn't I owner, absolute? It all seemed a black comedy. It wasn't a bit funny to me.

I got Gilman on the third try.

"Oh, Mr. Trothe, yes, indeed. Would you mind if I dropped in? It's not a matter I care to discuss over the telephone!"

"I'll expect you."

He came after I'd cut myself a sandwich, about an hour later. I'd known Gilman since my father's time. He refused a drink, and without preamble, took a legal folio out of a cardboard case, turned it right-side-up to me, and pointed to the signatures on the last page.

"Did you sign that?" he asked, looking at me over the top of his horn rims in a way I can only describe as peculiar.

It wasn't my signature.

I simply shook my head.

"It isn't? Is that the signature of your wife?"

"Yes. At least, I think so. What on earth *is* this?"

Without replying he took a file of letters out of his case.

"Have you ever received, or have you ever read, or has anyone read any of these letters to you? You'll please note that the first is dated more than six weeks ago!"

I looked through them without reading more than a line or two.

"Never. They should have been forwarded. They weren't."

"I was assured on more than one occasion that they were!"

"By whom?"

"Mrs. Trothe."

"She was mistaken."

"I hope the Judge is as charitable!"

"What the devil *are* you talking about?"

He held out the file of letters across the table.

"I'd like you to read these tonight. Let me have your comment as soon as possible, by telephone if necessary. I shall be in my office at 8:30. I shall apply for a warrant against Mr. Terence Ebbleton!"

"But what *for?*"

"He sold this property. With—though I hope not—the connivance of your wife. Has she visited you in the past four or five months?"

"Yes. At Easter."

"The conspiracy must have been sealed then. With the most impressive stamp of the Geneva Municipal Court. It attests the validity of your signature, yourself at the time being abroad in the interests of your Country. I sniffed a hulk of rats the moment I saw it. All I shall say is, don't let it worry you unduly. The property's safe enough. Now, yes!"

I sat back when he'd gone and had another tasteless drink without, I swear, being able to tell which end of me was up. I've never been so astounded, and I wasn't the least bit angry. I hadn't the energy. I looked through the letters, all from Gilman, warning me that Mel had applied for copies of the deeds, and so on, until not ten days before, he'd warned that a sale was announced and wanted to know urgently by cable whether I knew anything about it, and if so, why, without previous notice to him as my solicitor.

I shook it all out of my tired brain and dragged myself to bed. I set the alarm at 4, woke fresh, made a cup of tea, and jogged down to the station. In London I taxied to the Turkish bath, shaved, breakfasted, read all the papers, and at two minutes to nine, I walked into my new office and stood in the doorway, laughing at a bed of files two feet high covering my desk.

The Blur was good as his word. I took off my jacket and turned back my cuffs.

Work and I were old friends.

7

My long, and apparently lazy days in Africa gave handsome
return. Wherever I'd been, I'd made a study of tribal names,
because governing families are always somewhere near the top,
in or out of office. At that time, our Registries covered many a
generation in every country, so there was ample material, and
I had the friendly help of the old hands in the various Civil
Services. Jeremy Cavendish had long ago told me to run the
sound of the name over a few times, and then look for a similar
sound, perhaps the same run of letters. If you find anything
approaching it in a "root" name, you can bet he's of the same
clan, probably of the same family. The system didn't fail except
when a student had taken a "western" name or two, but then
I didn't bother. He went on the list. By noon I had a page to
send to M.I.6, and a pile of dossiers beside my chair. I felt the
loss of a secretary. I hadn't heard from Miss Furnival. I had a
feeling she'd kept her word. She was of that timber. But there
was less fun in working. She hadn't said much, but a hint of
perfume, a whisper of satin in all she did took a lot of the drag
from the day. I was sorry as I'd been when my right hand had
once gone in plaster. I had all feeling of it, but not the use.

I spent a couple of hours after lunch with Gilman and his
partners, looking over the damage Mr. Ebbleton had tried to do,
had been prevented from doing. There were links to Canada,
the police were in, banks were helping, and I signed the papers
they put in front of me. I'd always thought the Law to be an ass.
I was surer when I left for the office. I couldn't get hold of Patti,

and only Frederick had a telephone at his digs. Patti had to be got through the university. Both had lectures, and I left messages to meet me for luncheon next day at noon, and a five-line whip, code in our family for immediately, and no nonsense.

Kensington was a little out of my way, but I took a cab there in just the right mood to give Mr. Bloody Ebbleton the hiding of his existence. No luck. I rang for minutes. I'd hoped to find Mel, and yet I didn't want to. If I'd found her there with him, I was quite sure what I'd have done. My little friend on the hip made a most compelling bump. And if I did, what would I say to the children? I didn't know. In truest fact I didn't care.

A personal call to Jeremy Cavendish came through from his home in Northumberland. It was like old days again. He'd retired more than ten years but his mind flashed as crystal.

"Yes, well now, look here," he began, when I'd told him. "You can substitute any one vowel for any other, for a start. The musculature of the Negro's mouth and lips doesn't always tend to clear English enunciation. Consonants and glottal stops are most difficult to render. In the early days it wasn't always done with care. Now that some of them have been to school and learned to write, they're spelling their names differently—a prime cause of confusion—or else, to show independence apart from a change of flag, they're using some other form of the tribal or clan or family name. You've got quite a job on, at this distance. All I'd have had to do was call in my chief clerk. You can't. Anyway, I've got a packet of stuff here I'll look through tonight. Call you in the morning!"

I was looking for the source or sources of funds, but since the students came from thirty or more countries, it was difficult to find any link. School costs, books, rent and pocket money were supplied by the department, not lavishly, but I was surprised what the taxpayer had to fork out. It simply made me the more determined to find out who deserved a free ride, and which should be tabbed. Nobody got benefit of doubt, though in the light of Jeremy's advice I went through those I'd "done," and saw nothing to change my mind. But perhaps because I'd whispered so many names so many times in different ways, a pattern was forming, a rhythm of syllables which I came across in odd dossiers, without being able to say them out loud, or even write them. It was like having a fair idea of a tune without a notion how to whistle it. One of the smaller frustrations, and a perfect example of the mind's own computer having the answer and failing to spit it out. I wondered if it ever happened with its electronic brother.

Paul called me just before I left.

" 'lo, there, Edmund! How's Parkinson's Law operating?"

"Hasn't caught up, yet. No secretary. Where've you been? How's Moira?"

"She's fine. Just back from Geneva after packing my bits. D'you know anybody called Desarbier?"

I felt a burn widen between the eyes.

"Yes?"

"She called Moira to ask if she knew where you were. Moira said London. That's all. She didn't give any details, except to say you probably wouldn't be going back. Didn't say what she wanted. Hasn't called since. All right?"

"Perfectly!"

"Good. I'll be in London tomorrow. Drop in and see you. About four?"

I turned from any thought of Tanis for the moment. But, of course, she was always just below the surface of my mind. I didn't feel like going home. A room at the club, a slow dinner and bed seemed right. I wanted to be at the office before eight. I read the *Economist* before it sent me to sleep, still thinking of that flow of syllables. I woke with it, and shaved to its rhythm. Once in the office I lost the drift and it didn't seem to recur.

Jeremy called a little before eleven, and said he'd just posted a list of the more important names and origins, and had also been in touch with Sir Ryder Chapman at Scrymgour, Tyle's, the Canal banking agents.

"If you happen to find a link anywhere, or if you want information to do with accounts, hidden or open, get on to him. He'll be waiting. You could get it, of course, through our people, but it'll take longer and it won't be as exact. Got anything yet?"

"Merely a ripple of syllables—"

"Common experience, Edmund. Keep at it. You're absolutely on the right track!"

I went back to my Mbatabe Sdubokuvas with considerably more heart, almost charmed by a Konopsaka Churchill Bganigki, except that I couldn't find where he'd been for three years, and since he was taking advanced Economic Administration, I suspected Moscow, and he went on the list.

Twenty minutes before Big Ben struck I walked in a drizzle down Whitehall to meet the children, and I was halfway up the Strand in time to see Patti in front of me go through the courtyard to the Grill.

She'd grown since I'd last seen her. I suppose there's nothing more touching than remembering a mite in a pink shawl, and then seeing a girl with Mel's early beauty and my eyes, but hugely so, almost as tall as myself and a wonderful air of complete self-possession.

We kissed and Frederick came hurrying in, and we sat at a window table. I had the time of my life listening to them and trying to realize they were my children. I didn't tell them anything about Mel, but I chose a moment to mention that Gilman was going over the family's business and the year's accounts, and wanted to know where the document was that they'd signed.

Patti made her There-What-Did-I-Tell-You face, and looked at Frederick.

"Mummy!" she sighed. "If only she'd keep her darling head shut!"

"We may as well tell you," Frederick said. "But I must say, I agree with Patti. It was going to be our birthday present to you. You remember the money Uncle Geoffrey left us? Uncle

Terry told Mummy it wasn't doing much in three-and-a-half per-cents, and why not buy that piece of land behind the house? It goes out to the main road and crosses it. Sell the piece on the other side for development, and incorporate the main part with the property. That'd give us each a nice-sized plot one of these days, besides more than doubling existing value. Well, Mummy said she'd have everything done through Mr. Gilman. We signed the document about a couple of months ago. Wasn't wrong, was it?"

"Have you had any money?"

They looked at each other, a brother-and-sister flick that didn't require words. Frederick shook his head.

"Promised some, that's all," he said vaguely.

I was becoming quite used to fury. I knew it made my face thinner. I could feel it.

Patti stared at me, dear girl, and put a hand on my arm.

"Daddy!" she whispered. "What on earth's the matter?"

"The piece for development's been sold for much more than we gave for the entire lot," Frederick said quickly, anxiously. "Please don't think we lost anything. Or that we were under-handed—"

"Underhanded? Don't you realize that I'm responsible—"

"But it was our money, wasn't it? Mummy told us—"

"You've been the victims of a confidence trick," I said, and put down my napkin. "Go on with your lunch. I'm going to telephone!"

I left them absolutely stricken, poor kids, for the first time in their lives face to face with the poison of the thieving mind.

"So that's how it was done," Gilman said, when I told him. "Pelion upon Ossa. He was paid ninety thousand as first money for the property. Remainder with the deeds. Cheque was cleared yesterday. Who was guardian of the children's money?"

"Mel and a cousin, now dead."

"Ebbleton has petitioners wanting to put him in bankruptcy. There's a warrant out for him. I fear there'll be one for Mrs.

Trothe. Accomplice. It's fraud, you know. She was privy. And may I make it quite clear that I was not consulted at any time?"

I went back to a silent couple.

"Dads, I can't tell you how sorry we both are," Frederick said, looking as he once had when he broke a window. "We thought it was a good idea, that's all!"

"We won't lose anything. But I'm afraid your mother's in very serious trouble. The three of us'll meet it head-on—"

Patti broke down, poor sweet, and I passed her my handkerchief.

"I've felt something's been wrong," she said. "There's been a sort of—well, she—she isn't always at home. She never comes to see us."

"How long's that been?"

"Oh. A year, perhaps? Or more. And, well, you sort of—sort of stopped writing—"

"I wrote every week to both of you. They went in your mother's letter!"

Two pairs of eyes looked at each other and turned to me. Patti's glistened.

"Never got them," Frederick said.

"Why don't you come home at the weekend?" I said. "Let's have one of our lazy parties. I'll grill the steaks. You make a marvellous dessert. Frederick scours Fortnum's for goodies. Howzat?"

"Sa-moo-flee!" Patti said, in spirits again, laughing.

"New word?"

"Probably. There's two or three every day. It's esque. Meet you there, or go down together?"

"Meet you there. I don't know what time I can get away. I've got a new appointment. Tell you all about it later."

I suppose we looked an ordinary trio going out, but I knew they were frantic to ask questions, and I was torn in bloody

53

sweat to think how I was to answer them. I knew it was my fault.

Neglect.

Taking Mel too much for granted. I'd loved, honored and cherished until we'd agreed she'd stay at home to keep mildew out of the house and have a place ready for the children and their friends at weekends, and also to go on with her work in the Parish. Our village was all the better for Mel and a few like her. Besides, staying at home saved money. The expense of an apartment for two anywhere in Europe, with travel, and the upkeep of the house wasn't covered by my expense allowance. I wasn't getting any younger and there were the pensioned years to consider. Saving seemed to be the wisest course, and so I moved into a bachelor's hotel. During the first few months I flew home when I could for the weekend. Then I met Roiki, a simply delightful Finnish girl studying languages, and she simply and delightfully studied English with me until she graduated and went home to Helsinki. After that, months of lonely walks and a great deal of work until I met Ghislaine at a party and found that I'd worked with her father in Algeria. That led to other meetings, all perfectly innocent, until one evening I'd called to take her to the cinema. She'd got home late from the office, and opened the door in a bath towel and one around her head Arab-style, and all the wonder of the harem in her powdered feet and the cologne on her body. She took my face in cool hands to apologise, and kissed the dimple in my chin, and I put my arms about the towel and felt a sand-glass waist, and that was that. But only a little while later, she went home to Oran, and then her letters stopped. After her, well after, perhaps a year, Peggy and I met at Paul's house. She was Australian, buyer for a women's fashion group in Paris, but from that first night—we lost no time—she flew in almost every weekend until that idyll, too, came to an end in her leaving for Melbourne and a directorship. And, I later discovered, marriage. Then lonely days, nights, months until I met Tanis.

In those days I often thought of Mel. Unfortunately we don't use our brains, much less our hearts at such times. Lovely gifts come easily. It seems silly to refuse. Women, after all, can be just as lonely, and in want, as men. A release for the nerves, as Ghislaine once said. That attitude accepted, everything follows without question. But ridiculous as it may seem, I never forgot my duty to Mel. I flew home when I could to take her out to dine and go to a theatre, and flew back on Sunday night. She often came to stay with me. But she was having trouble with what she called Girl's Business. I didn't ask any questions. I suppose I should have done. But after all, we knew each other well enough to speak out and she never had. She only wished to sleep in another room.

But she also had a duty to me. She should have said something. What *could* she say? I've found a lover? He's Pam's husband. For the love of God!

I went back to the office in a frail mood, thinking of all the things I ought to have done that I hadn't, and all the things I'd done that I oughtn't. At the end I felt an abysmal misery that Mel could have deceived the children for any reason. If she'd been cheating me out of property, I might have accepted it and said nothing. I was the guilty party. But when had she put her arms about me? When was the last time? In later marriage one doesn't think of those things, but they're important. They become important when misery strikes. A woman's arms about a man's neck may not be much, but they're a constant reminder that someone loves, has need, wants to be sure that life isn't just a matter of going it alone. I should have been more thoughtful. Mel had always been avid, but then I'd look at her, and she'd widen her mouth and shake her head just slightly. After a little of that, I simply didn't bother her, and she never made the slightest move. I saw, then, that she hadn't been meno at all.

Ebbleton had my place. It wasn't the prettiest thought.

I suppose they'd met when she stayed the night with Pamela

as she often did, going to London for shopping. But how could Pamela have been so blind? For two years? It didn't seem possible. Yet I'd had my affairs over the years and I was certain Mel never suspected. I could have been wrong, of course. But if she'd known, I was positive she'd have raised the very devil. She wasn't the sort to keep things hidden. My mind went on endlessly thiswaying and thatwaying and my head felt like a shredded onion. I couldn't make a stand on moral grounds. I wasn't in a position to preach. I was quite unable to point a finger anywhere. I couldn't be myself.

I tried not to think of it, or of her. I tried not to, but I did. Because I loved Mel, or my dignity? I don't know. But why hadn't she thought of the children?

Why hadn't I?

It cuts both ways.

8

Mel was at home when I got there. It was something of a shock. I went in rather spindly at the knees, though I shall never know why. I'd never felt like that before. As though she were not my lawful wedded but some chanced-on griffon.

The wife of my bosom sat in the with-drawing room in front of a tea-tray. She smiled a glint of frost when I went in, but the frost became ice as I looked at her.

"Didn't you think it necessary to let me know you'd gone to see your mother?" I asked her, in quite the wrong tone of voice, though I knew it too late even to kick myself. "Isn't Mrs. Cloney ever here? There's nobody to answer a telephone!"

"I closed most of the rooms except ours and the spare," she said, perfectly at ease. "This, the library and your study don't require Cloney all day. A woman comes in to help her once a week. A great barn of a place, yawning with emptiness. I couldn't stand it!"

She bit into a sardine-paste toast.

No kiss, no effort, no invitation to have a cup of tea, drink, or anything else. We might have been passengers on the same bus.

"Do you know an address in Kensington kept by somebody called Ebbleton?" I asked, pouring my cup.

"Of course I know somebody called Ebbleton. Address in Kensington? No. There isn't another Ebbleton, surely? Terry. Terence. Is this some sort of elaborate word game?"

"Lost anything recently?"

"Not that I know."

"No money? Fifteen pounds and some change?"

"Not aware of it."

I took the wallet from my pocket, and put it on the tea-tray. She stared down at it. I saw the sudden quickness of breath.

"How long have you been telling fibs?" I asked her.

"Not as long as you!"

"Would you please explain that?"

"Would you please explain your running about with a lot of shopgirls?"

Stopped cold.

I couldn't say they weren't shopgirls. They weren't, but that was neither here nor there. I couldn't deny I'd been, as it were, running about. It hurt.

"I don't want to bandy words," I said. "Have you been interfering with this property lately? Signing documents or getting the children to sign what you knew to be wrong? Not merely wrong, but criminal?"

"I think you're talking the most abject nonsense!"

She was perfectly herself again, beautiful, graceful, half-smiling out at the garden.

I lifted the telephone and dialled Gilman. He'd just got in.

"Trothe here. I wondered if you'd care to speak to Mrs. Trothe. She doesn't seem to know what I'm talking about!"

"By all means, please."

I handed the telephone over and she took it as if it were the most natural thing in this world to do, leaning back, playing with the pearl necklace.

"Mr. Gilman? Oh, yes. Very well, thank you. Yes? Yes. Document? I know nothing of any document. Of course. My brother-in-law. Selling the what? I really don't understand a word you say, Mr. Gilman!"

A car came around the drive. Only one motor in this world sported that sort of asthma, the village cab, with Harry Baylis driving. He stopped, and the bell rang.

"I understand, of course, but you must please realise that I deny it first to last," Mel said, ineffably tranquil, stroking her curly back-hair. "And I haven't been a victim of anything, except the deceit of my husband-that-was. What? Yes. I'm leaving him. I want a divorce. I have all the evidence I require. A detective agency here and in Switzerland. Yes, well. Being sorry's rather late. 10:30 tomorrow? Thank you. Goodbye!"

I felt as though I wasn't in the room. She put the receiver down, stood, gave her hair a couple of pats, and went out, no look, word or gesture.

I sat there, cold, not a word within a mile, but marvelling at a performance. Clever girl. Cleverer than I'd thought. It was no use my asking questions. I knew her too well. No use trying to plead. In that frame of mind she was monolithic. Not a bit of use trying to hold her. That would have been stupid. I'd never used physical force, and I wasn't going to start. Especially with a villager on the step as a witness.

She came back, hat and coat on, and looked at me.

"You'll find everything on your study table," she said. "I'll be at Pamela's for the moment."

"Aren't I entitled," I began.

"You're entitled to nothing," she said, graciously glacial. "I want nothing more to do with you. You thought I'd reached the age, is that it? Well I did, and I suffered, and you didn't care one jot. Now, you can go to hell!"

She turned, no tears, no feeling, and called out to Baylis along the hall, walking down to open the door.

"Only these two, madam?" Baylis said, and grunted. "I'll close the door, 'm. Getting proper cold, ain't it? Going to be a 'ard winter, so the old 'uns do say. Ah!"

The front door closed, the car door shut, the motor fired and gravel crunched.

I still sat there.

The damnedest thing that ever happened to me.

I simply couldn't find the energy to move. I knew she'd been lying, but superbly, and I knew that if I'd felt more honest, or if I'd been innocent, then things would have gone quite another way. But I was chained by the thought of Roiki and Ghislaine and who else, and Tanis.

Thinking of her, almost feeling her presence beside me, I began to like the idea of divorce. I was indifferent to any threat it might have to my career. I knew divorced colleagues, and nothing terrible had happened to them. Divorce was an accepted fact of life. At my age it was ludicrous, but then, it was Mel's idea not mine.

I got a drink and went in my study, a small room off the hall. The blotter was neatly piled with three thin heaps of paper. In one, unpaid bills. In another, correspondence addressed to me, opened, of up to five months before, a note from Ghislaine that brought me in a scarlet flush, and I couldn't look at the rest. In the third pile, a series of letters from an African agency, arranging an inspection of the house, and contents, with a view to rental or purchase.

In sudden nausea I took the drink out into the garden and strolled among the roses trying not to think. I couldn't feel anything for Mel. Not anger, not disgust, not anything. She seemed a stranger, met and passed. I couldn't understand her lack of feeling, her indifference.

I couldn't understand myself. That's what really hurt. I'd been disgracefully furtive. I didn't think it was in me. That hurt too. Because of it, I'd simply sat there and let her have the stage. I couldn't for the life of me have understood it in anyone else. Reason for it, yes. I suppose I could have given one or two. But the real reason was that I'd been a traitor, to her, to the children, to myself.

Worse than that, I knew, looking down at the greenhouses, that I didn't care.

I wanted Tanis.

Nothing else seemed to matter.

I suppose we all go slightly mad at times. It seemed to be

my turn, though I must say I felt sane enough. Just standing there, holding the drink, taking a sip, looking at flowers and shrubs folding themselves in early winter's browns, I could have laughed. That's when I felt mad, though I was certain I wasn't.

A blue Rolls-Royce followed by another came in the gate and stopped.

Five really black men, in that garden an alarming apparition, very well-dressed, all toothily cordial, came toward me, and one, the youngest, bowed and held out a card I didn't take.

"My name's Trothe," I said, before he could speak. "I'm the owner of this property. I assume you're here to inspect? Then I must tell you that you've been deceived. This is my card, and here's the name and telephone of my solicitor. He'll tell you everything else!"

All the smiles had gone when I'd finished writing. There were moments of most unhappy silence.

"But, sir, we came to meet Mrs. Eb-laton at six o'clock, now, because we have bought this place!" an older man said, hesitantly. "We have paid. It is ours. We have everything in order. We arranged that the house should be delivered at six o'clock this evening. The staff comes tomorrow. Where is Mrs. Eb-laton?"

"I'm extremely sorry. This house has not been sold, and it is not on the market, and while I live, won't be. Have you been here before?"

"Oh, yes!" the young man said, and held out the bag. "I have the list of furnitures and crockeries, everything. But what shall we do, sir? If we have paid, and it isn't ours?"

"You have legal redress," I said. "Who let you in, here?"

"It was the Mr. Eb-laton. He showed everything, with the Mrs. Eb-laton, also. She promised to be here!"

"She's gone. That's all. I'm sorry I can't be of any further help!"

The oldest man opened his hands, pink in the palms, a gesture of almost unbearable pathos.

"Oh, my God, my God!" he whispered, and turned to the car. "A scandal, my God!"

They followed, got in one or other car, and in a moment I stood alone in the drive listening to whispers in the lane, a rippling when they passed through the brook, fowls enjoying their evening cluck, and the sough of our elms.

I felt like a warrior dead-tired after victorious battle. Almost without energy I went in for another drink, and the telephone rang.

Pamela wailed, an extraordinary noise.

"Oh, Edmund, Terry's left me! What am I to do? What can I do? Oh, what do I do?"

"Talk it over with Mel. I believe she's on her way to you."

She gulped.

"First I've heard of it," she said, quieter. "Why's she coming here?"

"To stay, I suppose. She's going to divorce me."

"She's wha—she's *what?*"

"Divorce. That's what she just told me. Where did T—your husband—write from?"

"I think it must be Ireland. From the stamp. There's no address."

She began that hopeless sobbing.

"Pull yourself together. For the sake of the children. Go to your mother's for a few days. That's the best thing."

I'd hardly put the phone down when Gilman called.

"Ebbleton's in Ireland. They don't know where. He crossed by air the day before yesterday. They can't extradite for the moment. The cheque for the house was cashed by a woman. She took it in a large handbag. Mrs. Trothe, d'you think?"

"Probably. There were some Africans here this evening. They wanted to occupy the house. I told them to go to the police."

"Best thing. When are your children coming to see me?"

"Tomorrow at 10:30. I suppose this property's safe enough?"

"If we can prove your signature's a forgery, yes. If they can

62

prove it *is* your signature, then it's fairly hopeless, I'm afraid. Remember, there are two separate deals involved. The house and garden, and the piece at the back. The money's been paid, so of course they'll fight. It won't be easy!"

I went to bed slightly drunk.

9

That Friday morning, I was almost down to the last layer of dossiers and pretty well up-to-date with the department's paper, or just about five fairly hard days without a secretary, when the messenger came in with a cup of tea, and announced Miss Furnival, lo, without the glasses.

She was, in fact, a beauty. I wondered why I'd never quite appreciated it before. Perhaps because she seemed part of the office equipment, or because I'd made it a rule never to be familiar with those I had to work with. However it was, she surprised me, and she noticed it. With a blush.

"I thought I'd call and deliver these letters instead of posting them," she said, rather more expansively than usual, and put the package on the desk. "I've resigned. I've started at a crammer's. I don't think I'll have much trouble."

"I'm sure you won't. If you need any help, let me know. But I'm really very sorry indeed you're not coming here. I'm working without a right hand. Just when I need one. Yourself, for preference?"

She shook her head, smoothly combed, long, deep-gold, and looked me in the eye perhaps for the first time without the glasses. They were clear, deep blue, in that light almost violet. I was startled, not so much by the color. They held a smile I couldn't quite place. Mischievous, perhaps.

"The work wouldn't interest me," she said. "I stayed with you because I liked working for you. And I learned, as well. That phase is over. I'm going after gowns and mortarboards!"

"I haven't the remotest doubt they'll be yours. Do you know anyone fit to take your place?"

"Gillian Roule," she said instantly. "Best brain in the Service. She's young, but a little time with you, and she'll knock spots off everybody."

Again that smile, brighter, and I thought I knew why. Miss Roule could hardly be called prepossessing. A pekinese face, gold-rimmed ovals, tri-focal, that magnified the blackest eyes I think I ever saw, black hair combed in a way that always reminded me of cushion-spill, and a voice like a very old record played too fast, she was—as I once heard her described by a messenger—"a right lump o' stuff, but mark you, nice to talk to!"—and she also made the best cup of tea in the Commonwealth.

"Take some settling in," I said. "But I'll accept your advice. Not for the first time!"

Sheer flattery. She knew it, and she blushed again. I'd never known she blushed before. This was a new Miss Furnival. For the life of me I couldn't think of her Christian name. I'd never heard Andrew use it. She'd never mentioned him. I respect that kind of reserve.

She got up, looking at the package.

"Don't want to waste your time," she said. "There's a note and some telephone calls from a Mademoiselle Desarbier. Tanis Desarbier. She was extremely insistent. And—may I say—distressed?"

My face turned away to burn. It wasn't just a blush. A sudden hilarious wave of enjoyment picked me up, held me, and I couldn't speak or think. I couldn't see through a mist, not of tears, but of a sudden, and absolutely vicious, passion.

I didn't care what else happened in this world.

I wanted Tanis.

"Thank you," I said, and cleared my throat, and used blessed time to walk around the desk to take her to the door. She walked in front, in a blue dress that fitted a remarkably small waist, slim hips. My goodness, she was a beauty, and I damned myself for thinking nonsense and yet it wasn't. One can't always pretend to be blind.

She turned so quickly that I almost ran into her.

"Would you mind if I called in one night?" she asked. "There're some things I'm not awfully strong on. I mean, that we didn't deal with. Especially accountancy. I know you meant what you said."

"Anytime after seven-thirty. Come whenever you please. Take pot-luck, if you like."

She smiled quite beautifully. I wondered again why I'd never noticed it. She turned away and called "Thank you so much, goodbye," over her shoulder, and I watched her walk in the shadowy corridor, shutting the door quietly, trying to make up my mind whether she really needed help, or if she was baiting me. In which case, I'd swallow the bait.

Tanis' note was a joy to read. She'd been desolated to learn I'd gone and wasn't coming back, and when could she come to London? And why didn't I telephone the office or her apartment or send a telegram or at least say that I loved her, because she loved me, but gloriously, and missed me, but terribly, and she held my heart preciously as she hoped I held hers, and when, helas, would they beat together again?

That was enough.

I knew I had to finish the African business in quick time, make it known I didn't want to stay in the department, and get off to Germany. It was the only way to meet her.

I'd just torn up the note and burned the scraps, and Paul put his head round the door.

"Handed in my last report," he said, cheerfully enough, though I was surprised at the always soft-collared Little Cham in starched linen, black and stripes, unusually Order of the Day. "Look as though you'd grounded down, Edmund?"

He picked up a memo-pad, and began writing.

"I'm cleaning up African education for the next couple of

years," I said, and turned the light on. "You look as though you were due at St. James's!"

"Not far off," he said, and put the slip in front of me. "Carlton Club. And afterwards a reception. I *do* wear shoes sometimes!"

What he'd written gave me a jolt. *This office might be bugged*—it had never occurred to me—*so on the off-chance, would you like a drink tonight? Have a matter to talk over. I'm on your way. Come home with me. A nod is yes.*

I nodded, and he grinned.

"Glad to see you're looking so well," he said. "Got to be at the In and Out at seven. So long, Edmund. Be good!"

He crushed the note in his pocket and strolled out. I thought for a moment about the mystery, decided he might be right—depending on what he had to say—and got on with the job. At seven I was at the In and Out, and the porter said Mr. Chamby was waiting at the garage.

"Sorry for the rigmarole," he said, when I got in. "I don't like that building. Never have. Don't suppose they demiked the place since M.I. moved over. Just as well to remember it. Mrs. Shafford's no fool. She likes to know what's going on. She was in M.I., do you know?"

"I didn't. Not very comfortable sailing!"

"Bony article, what I've heard. That's why I thought of you when this came up. But we'll wait till we get home. What's Osterley doing?"

I gave him an account of our old staff, or of those whose whereabouts I knew. He was able to fill in most of the others, so obviously he'd made it his business, and since there were dozens, all of them first-class in their way, I began to wonder.

We arrived at his house, bumped gently over the bricked surround, and saw the Chrysler parked up on the garage ramp.

Paul went up the ramp to the big four-door, tugged at the handle. It was locked. He turned and walked down, waiting for me to catch up.

"That Williams!" he said, half laughing, half annoyed. "Good bloke, but he's deaf in three ears. How many times I told him to put that bloody car in the garage? He *will* leave it there. Too idle to get the keys. I'll boot him right in the powder-keg!"

We went into the bar in the billiard room, and after he'd poured the drinks, he tapped out a roll of maps from a cardboard tube and spread them on the table.

"I'll make it short," he said, in his terse way. "If you don't like this first tick, that's it. Tell me straight off. This is a new market. It's world wide. It's Middle East, no politics, and the capital's private. It's not oil. Mineral gas. Pipelines. Interested?"

"Very!"

"We're in at the top, I'm number one, you're my assistant. I'll be in the chair for two years. Then you go up. Your contract's for five years with option of renewal, starting at £17,500 sterling. Plus expenses and a pension that'll make yours at the moment look like a lunch check. Still interested?"

"Even more!"

"Good. Here's the makeup of the company. These are the bankers. Stock brokers. Lawyers. Names of the shareholders. They're the people I met today. Objections?"

The company directors were Arabian princes and European bankers. Names alone inspired confidence. I felt that at last I'd fallen on my feet.

"None!"

"Good. When d'you want to start?"

"If I go to the end of next June, I earn just a little more pension," I said, but I was thinking of Tanis, and Regsmund, and that's about all I thought about. "Always useful, a little extra!"

"I'll more than make up whatever you might lose. I want you in by latest, the end of March. If it goes as I think, it'll be January. We've got to do some picking-over of that Soviet deal. Your area's Saudi Arabia, Iraq and Syria. Anyway, be ready to move when I drop the flag. You'll need a secretary. Anybody in mind?"

"No."

Paul shrugged, pushing a tube of maps in the cylinder.

"Well, that's the lot, Edmund. Here's a selection of notes you can go over. Any questions, I'm nearly always here, or you can get Angela at the office. Number's on the cover. Williams'll run you home. Let me know as soon as you can, won't you?"

"Of course. In principle, I accept. And gratefully. Let me settle details, that's all. Does Williams know the way?"

I'd seen how to get in touch with Tanis.

10

London was grey in fog, but I found a cabman who must have had a built-in radar and he put me in front of the office at 8:30 on the chime of Big Ben.

A note from Gilman had been on my desk since the night before. *Please telephone me as soon as possible. It is most urgent.* I had to wait until almost ten to get him.

"Sorry," he said. "Fog. Just got in. Edmund, I'm terribly sorry to add to your worries. It's your son. On the strength of that sale, he borrowed some money and bought a car—"

"I didn't know that—"

"I was sure you didn't. There's a complication in that boy who lent him the money's a son of the minister who 'bought' the property. They're sitting for the same degree. I believe the boy went home with your son and that's how he met Ebbleton. Then the father was introduced, and so we go on. Well, the father's absolutely raving about the loan—especially after the property business—and Frederick can't pay. The car firm won't take the car back except at a ridiculous price. The boy's a minor and so is Frederick. The father's threatening to sue you. I couldn't find Frederick. Could you possibly see him and ask what happened generally? With the other business so closely involved, it could be made to look like false pretences—"

"Depend on it I'll speak to him today. I'll let you know immediately!"

I hadn't the heart to say any more. I'd always regarded Frederick as a sensible, thoroughly decent fellow. I was proud of him, not only for winning a scholarship, but for being both sportsman and scholar. Except in the matter of religion—or lack of it—he'd never given me a moment's worry. Then this. Owning a car and not telling me? That was deceitful where it wasn't sly. I detest sly people.

Miss Roule tried all day to find him, but no luck.

I was in and out of committees during the morning, worked through lunch, and then Yorick saved the day, and perhaps my head and a few others.

"Oh, Edmund," he called along the corridor. "There's this enormous load coming in this evening from Sudan and Tanzania, and other holes. Any idea where they're going?"

"See Miss Avery," I said, a little annoyed at an idiot question. "Surely you've managed to find that out by now? Transport, accommodation, Miss Avery!"

He was looking at me fondly as any collector examining a remarkable specimen.

"Then I'm the runner from Thermopylae!" he cooed, in gentle triumph. "Point is, nobody knows which end's what about a dam' thing. They simply don't!"

"Don't?"

"Don't. Was there ever a more nugatory conversation, d'you suppose?"

There's a mental state called nonplussed, and I know exactly how it feels. There were seventy-seven students, law, classics, chemistry, veterinary, etc., coming in that night. No accommodation? Transport to the various hotels? It wasn't my business to worry about such things. Thank God I did. I found that nothing had been done because the Junior Minister had said she'd settle the timetable and let everybody know. But in the interim her chief secretary had been taken to hospital, memories were unjogged, and nobody thought of asking a question until time had become dangerously short.

We still didn't know if, in fact, transport and accommodation

71

had been laid on. I told Miss Roule to telephone the High Commissioner's offices. She got the same reply from all of them. They thought, because of the new plan, that we were doing it. I let poor old Brantley give her highness the news. He got his ears singed.

"Never mind," I told him. "Supposing they were all stranded. What a story for the Press!"

"Quite. I was at some pains to point out we couldn't afford many errors of that magnitude."

"What did she have to say to that?"

"She catted into a spitting tantrum. Told me when she needed my observations she'd ask for them. I don't think I'll last. I'll shift coal rather than grovel here!"

"Let's see what happens at five!"

At five o'clock we all waited almost twenty minutes until Madame appeared. She took the chair without apology, we ran through the agenda, and then she looked at me.

"I've spoken to the Minister," she said, slightly flushed. "Apparently, he thought of meeting this party this evening. His office was arranging everything. Somebody told them we were doing it. That's why nothing was done. I have to be at the House at six. Anything outstanding?"

My turn.

"Transport," I began.

"Nothing much there," she interrupted. "We'll deal with it on Wednesday. Here, the same time!"

"We've got another term of students coming next month," I said. "Air passage has to be arranged. That's not such a simple matter. We haven't the *modus operandi*. No permit from the Treasury—"

"We seem determined to make the Treasury into a bogeyman," she said, smiling, head on one side, gathering papers. "I'll talk to the Minister. This time, he'd like to meet them. Press party, so forth. Leave it to me."

Poor old Brantley got something like a wigging for daring to suggest that the Treasury wouldn't look at many of the school items up for budget.

"Please don't waste time in trying to assess the Treasury's opinion," she said remotely sweet. "They'll come to heel, you'll see!"

The prospect of Sir Gerald Ambridge and his colleagues coming to heel for any soul on earth was wryly funny, and some of us laughed, which didn't improve her temper. Yorick, sitting at the end of the table, iced the cake by sneezing his everlasting head off.

"Dear me," he sighed, lily-like. "Openers for a wasting bronchial condition, mh?"

"Perhaps a day at home might improve your health?" Mrs. Shafford said, with tempered asperity, because she wanted very much to know the sort of people he knew. "It might save a few absentees by contamination with all those germs. Do you think?"

Yorick seemed to get the point.

"I sometimes do," he said, through a stuffed nose. "It isn't always obvious, I fear. If anyone catches any of those germs, I hope they'll give them back. In my state I can't afford to lose anything so healthy as a germ. I'm sort of caving-in as you look at me. What?"

"I didn't say a word," Mrs. Shafford said, and lifted the sheets of agenda, forgot herself, and worse, quite mistook her man. "I've always thought people who insist on sneezing in public are perhaps the worst type of bore!"

Yorick put the handkerchief back, and in that hush, pushed aside his chair and stood, half-bowed by inclination, no more, of the head.

"Mrs. Shafford," he said, without looking at her. "Lifelong, I've always been taught that the only bores are those who're bored. They, truly, are the deadweight. If I'm required, which inspires me with hideous doubt, I shall probably be in the vomitorium, or in G-One-O-Six. I'd much rather be in space, or a nice marble urn. Everybody please forgive me!"

His departure was shattered by enormous sneezes, which perhaps stopped some of us from cheering. Mrs. Shafford got up, we got up, she sailed out, we jammed the far door.

"I'll call Fosden," Brantley said, mouth behind a paper. "That drivel about the Minister was a crashing lie if ever I heard one!"

"Leave it alone," I said. "Face saving isn't lying. It's protecting. All's forgiven. Sense of humor, sense of honor, in some quarters, both the same. After all, the Minister's god. He can put his pen through you!"

"Healthy feeling. You know, I can't stand her!"

"She does her best. Would you verify all's in order and let me know?"

I didn't want him to think I'd discuss a superior. Once that sort of gossip takes hold, then there's no longer a department, but top to bottom a hotbed of malice. I'd seen it happen. But the Junior Minister had to be taught a severe lesson. How, was another matter. She was a smart woman.

Smart, that is, of her day, and the day is cheap.

Miss Roule held up a slip from behind a life-saving tea-tray.

"Long distance, sir, Ireland," she squeaked. "A Mr. Ebbleton's calling. He'll come through at six o'clock."

He came through almost on the dot.

"Edmund? Terry here. Listen, please. I'm in Dublin. The parties of the second part who bought the house—Scipio Africanus, if you follow—won't take further action. They want to avoid publicity. I've arranged payments, and they'll have had the first this afternoon. I'm staying here to avoid any nonsense. I've got a deal going which'll satisfy everybody. Won't take more than ten days. Edmund, please think of Mel. If you jump to conclusions, you're mistaken."

"You're talking to a Government department—"

"I don't give a curse! I've been trying to get you for three days. This is what I wanted to tell you. The children's money's safe. The bankruptcy application was cancelled, you may as well know. How can they make me a bankrupt?"

"I shall have you arrested for selling my property under false pretences!"

"Mel did the selling, not me. She did me a big favor. I've told you the money she lent me's going back. Be careful what you do. I don't want to say any more. I've told her to call you. She's in Paris."

"Paris?"

"She didn't know where else to go. She's on the moon!"

"What do you mean?"

"What I'm telling you is that next year, with the development of the piece at the back, your property's worth ten times more, at least. You've lost nothing. You've got Mel to thank. I've given your secretary her telephone number. Call her. Find her. Go over and get her. I told you. She's not well. Goodbye!"

Miss Roule called the Paris number, an hotel at Saint-Germain-des-Prés, but Mel wasn't in. I rang Gilman.

"That's correct," he said, surprisingly. "I'm still trying to gather ends. The others, the Africans, sent their representative to see me this afternoon. It seems we're in the blue. And by the way, a Mr. Nganojokwe settled Frederick's loan. The terms are well within his means. I'll let you know the details."

I had a porridgy feeling in my stomach. Something was going on I knew nothing about. Terence's defence of Mel upset me. That he didn't like me didn't surprise me. We'd never met comfortably. So far as I was concerned, he was merely a be-monocled used-car dealer, and comported himself on about that level. But why a used-car dealer, wearing a monocle to help vision—an otherwise honest man—should be used as a comparative for contempt defied analysis, except that it was snobbism at its heinous worst. I hadn't known I was that sort of snob. Obviously I was, because I thought like one. Which surprised me.

Miss Roule came almost to the desk, but instead of looking at me, turned to the window instead. In her attitude I sensed pity or sympathy.

"I got through to Paris, sir," she barely said. "Mrs. Trothe refused the call!"

Some silences are unbearable, but there's nothing to say.

"Is there something more I may do, sir?"

"You might telephone Dr. Norris and ask for an appointment tomorrow night, please."

I should have put that Paris call in myself. It never occurred to me that Mel wouldn't answer a telephone. Ebbleton had said she wasn't herself, but I was surely entitled to be treated with courtesy. Kindness, or any of the other virtues apart, we'd had almost thirty good years of marriage and two children, and I'd always made ample provision. I'd had a few affairs, though not until she'd told me she wasn't ready for bed. After that, she hadn't mentioned it, and neither had I. If she'd suffered, she'd never told me or given any sign of wanting more of my company. She had pride, certainly, no woman more, but she was a wife, and she could have written it if she'd found herself unable to say it. She'd kept silent. She'd acted a part in her own drama. Well, that sort of mulish rebellion had to be paid for. I wondered if I should send Frederick and decided I would. If she refused to read a letter, he could tell her what I wanted to say.

I felt a dead sort of anger mixed with pity, and a disgust for what I thought was an unhealthy situation that could have been avoided by a heart-to-heart talk. Whether it would have prevented the affair with Tanis was quite another matter. I doubted it.

I smiled, thinking of her, and her name whispered out of me. Her presence was never far, her perfume was only a half-sniff away, and her smile was just behind the back of my eyes.

I'd never felt that for Mel, and that was her crass misfortune. Ours had been what many call a "healthy" marriage, of two young people wanting each other in bed, and having got there, finding they liked it enough to keep on, and never worrying about anyone else. What energy each had went to the other, and never left much for the wayside lay.

I still had about two hours paper work to do. I didn't feel like telephoning anybody, but I knew I had to do something about Frederick. I couldn't do any more than Gilman, either for him or for myself. That helplessness, that dependency on somebody else, took the stuffing out of me. Anyway, I'd finished by a little after eight o'clock, and went to the club for a plate and a tankard. A little after nine I walked up St. James's, along Piccadilly and through Shaftesbury Avenue to the room Frederick had in a building I'd leased to an insurance company. The watchman said he hadn't been in for a couple of days. He pointed to a number of messages stuck in the rack.

I walked down High Holborn and turned toward Patti's place, not far from Ludgate Circus. The streets hadn't yet filled with newspaper trucks, but a stream of vegetable wagons went up toward Covent Garden, and I thought of buying her some flowers, but it was rather too early for the market. The house hunched between skyscrapers, on the site of the Fleet Prison, and I walked up to the third floor, almost smelling the mental detritus of how-many generations, and the fetor of their lives, left behind as certainly as the cracked paint on the walls. Patti had found the place. I'd been there twice, for the house-warming when she moved in, and last year when she won an essay competition and invited an unending company of student friends in to have a drink. They were all over everywhere, up and down the stairs, all colors, all conditions, and of course I paid the drink bill. I didn't mind a bit. It was wonderful to see a princess in a white shantung sheath among a court of cavaliers, seeing her mother in her, and not less touchingly, a little of me.

There was a light under the door, and I rang.

It was one room with a window looking over the Thames,

bathroom, closet and kitchen, all about the size of a stamp, but perfect for her.

A shadow crossed the light.

"Freddie?" Patti's whisper almost didn't pass the walnut. "Is that you? Wait a minute, will you?"

"It's me," I said, and heard the *ough!* of recognition. "May I come in?"

"Just—just a moment," she said, in her normal voice, with something of Mel in it, Mel, that is, at her newest. "Let me pull things together. Shan't be a chord!"

I heard the bed creak.

She was still at the door.

From the silence I understood the odd, obscene language of gestures.

I knew there was a man in there.

My virgin daughter?

I could have walked downstairs so easily.

If I was jealous, or possessive or God knows what, but I felt a sudden, thick hate for anyone who'd taken her. Anyone she'd allowed to take her.

"Take" her?

Yes, take. Use her body. That mite in the pink shawl I'd so often nursed. My virgin daughter. Why do we dream such nonsense? Mites grow into women. Women have bodies. Bodies make demands. In sudden, garish light I saw Tanis, and her father, whoever he was, both looking at me.

What was there to say?

The door opened. Patti smiled a little baggily under the eyes, holding an old wrap of Mel's about herself. The divan bed was more or less straight except for crinkles here and there. All else was in the usual state of disorder. Patti wasn't a picker-up. She was a flinger-anywhere, and anywhere was where everything was.

"I don't want to stay more than a moment," I said, still in the doorway. "I want to talk to Frederick. Where is he?"

"I wish I knew," she said, no attempt at a kiss or embrace. She was honest. "I've been trying to find him. He's such an idiot. All sorts of people have been looking for him. What's he done?"

Still no kiss or attempt, no Daddy, nothing. Was I no more to her than a passer-by? A nuisance? Somebody who merely paid quarterly rental, fees, food, and all that nonsense?

Suddenly I was looking at any baggy-eyed girl disturbed in midfling, and impatiently anxious to get back to bed.

"When you see him, tell him I want to talk to him," I said. "It's an extremely serious matter. That's why I'm here. I didn't mean to disturb you!"

She smiled, the old Patti, and quickly, on impulse put her arms about my neck and kissed my cheek.

"Daddy, please forgive me for being so disgustingly rude!" she said, but she didn't move or ask me in. "It's my night for beauty, nails and toes 'n things. May I come to lunch tomorrow? I'll scurry about in the morning, I promise. I'll find him!"

"Neither of you mentioned he had a car?"

She stood away, looking at my tie.

"He asked me not to," she whispered pleadingly. "It was a surprise!"

"Indeed. It may go, surprisingly, as far as the police!"

She put a hand to her mouth and her eyes frowned terror.

"Now you know why I came here. Not to interrupt your affair!"

She turned her back. Her face was crimson.

"Please go, Daddy!" she whispered. "It's—it's my life. Not yours!"

"So long as I pay the expenses for the life which I helped to give you, all's well. Is that it?"

I was acting like a fool, I knew it, and I didn't know how to stop. Anger hit me in the throat, sudden, stupid anger made worse by tiredness.

"Haven't I a right to ask that you comport yourself as the

daughter your mother and I were so proud of? Is there any pride in knowing you're a slut?"

She turned in fury, but the wrap fell open. She wore nothing underneath. She made a hopeless gesture, tied the belt, and held the door handle.

"You may as well know, now," she said. "I'm going to be married. Quite soon. I'm not a slut—"

"If there's a man in that bathroom, you're a slut!"

The bathroom door opened.

A man stood in the light with a towel round his waist. Short, bony but muscular, about my age, greying.

African.

Black.

"Sir, this isn't the time for social niceties," he said softly, easily. "I'm a barrister-at-law. I'm not poor in this world's money. I can claim and supply enough. I can provide all proof at any time. I shall take your daughter back with me. She will never want. I wish I could have met you in a more appropriate manner. However, we meet like this. I am not sorry. I love Patti—"

That finished it for me.

Again I saw myself and Tanis. The only difference was his negroid skin. If I could take another man's daughter with all delight and not a qualm of conscience, then why couldn't somebody take my daughter with the same delight, the same disregard?

Despite myself, I saw a mite in a pink shawl, saw her toddle, picked up a warm bundle, and tears blinded, flashed in light and thorns prickled in my throat.

There was nothing to say. Fight wasn't in me. It was her life. I couldn't argue, there, in a doorway.

I turned and walked down the stairs. When I reached the landing she shut the door.

I looked up Ludgate Circus toward St. Paul's. It wasn't much good praying, but I was wondering if there was anything I could do for a little thing in a pink shawl. Of course there wasn't.

That little bundle had become a woman.

I hadn't thought of it before.

11

Just after midday Frederick met me for a sandwich and a glass
of ale. I couldn't be angry with him. He was contrite and dis-
couraged. He looked so tired. I didn't like to see that. He said
the loan had been a spontaneous thing. The friend was wealthy,
a son of the Minister for Foreign Affairs, and since he thought
he had a considerable sum coming as his share of the sale, he
accepted the offer of enough to buy the car and a couple of
other things. I didn't ask what they were, but I scented a girl
somewhere.

"Do you know any of Patti's friends?" I asked, more or less
casually.

He looked away.

"A few," he said. "Harmless enough!"

"Harmless enough to marry her?"

Still he didn't look at me.

"Do you know of any African 'friend'?"

He turned direct to me and looked me in the eye.

"Dads, you'll have to prepare for a bit of a blow," he said.
"I tried to talk her out of it. I nagged and chinned. It's no
good. He's quite a decent sort. Got a Rolls. Lives in Park Lane.
She's always been interested in African stuff. He lectured us a
couple of times on African tribal law. That's how they met.
Nothing to stop her. She's of age."

"Is she out of her senses?"

"Patti's the coolest. She wants a rich husband. She doesn't care a hoot about color. Africa's adventure. Money's money. So far as she's concerned, that's all there is to it!"

"I think it a great pity your mother and I had to deny ourselves so much to send her to a good school!"

"If you hadn't, she wouldn't have had the chance of meeting a millionaire!"

"How do you know he's a millionaire?"

"Ask Lloyd's about him. Dads, you're worried about color, aren't you?"

"Partly, I suppose."

"It's got to come. The sooner we're all properly mixed up and one tint, the sooner we get rid of the color bar. It'll take time. But somebody's got to start!"

He spoke moodily, still not his own bright self. I put it down to the business in hand, which was still a worry, and told him to go along to Gilman. I went back to the office, thinking about Patti, and not, I must confess, getting very far. I had a color prejudice—which I hadn't been aware of before, perhaps because she was my daughter and not someone else's—and I had a prejudice about his age—which was about my own—though I'd never thought twice about it, and never questioned my right to do as I pleased—and I also had a prejudice, if not a hate, for her conduct of the night before, and how many other nights. But I'd been in the same boat for more years than she'd been adult, and I'd never doubted that I had every right to do whatever I wanted with any girl, and without once considering her parents and never a single thought for any father.

Was I miserable because Patti had treated me with such absolute disregard? Disrespect? Heartlessness? Perhaps. Perhaps anything, but it was too much of a problem, and the appointment book was filled and I had to see Dr. Norris that night. Despite all, I took the car early, an anonymous crawler in evening traffic.

The vicar waved his umbrella and I pulled up going past the Common.

"I'm so glad to see you!" he called. "We've had excellent news about our shares. Apparently those awful rumors were only that. I'm really terribly sorry to have worried you in such a manner. If you're in church on Sunday, do come and have a drink after. We'd be delighted!"

"Why don't you bring Mrs. Tomsett for a drink on Saturday? I believe I'll be in London on Sunday. And Blennerhassett might let me see the accounts."

"Excellent. Of course!"

I was a little dumbfounded. At one moment the entire world appeared to be falling apart, and the next it was almost mended. But there was still Mel. And Patti. And I wasn't altogether happy about Frederick. I knew that Gilman was still not satisfied about the property deal. But they all had to be dealt with reasonably, and they could all be brought to a sensible conclusion, and that, in itself, was a comforting thought.

Mrs. Cloney had just finished cooking my dinner and I told her I'd serve myself, paid for the day's shopping, ordered the next night's dinner, and off she went.

Dr. Norris had left a large practice in London to come to our village in semi-retirement, though he still had the patients he'd been attending for forty years or more. He wasn't young, but he certainly didn't look old, and under the lamp, showing white hair thinned over an amateur gardener's bronzed scalp, sharp black eyes, a small grey moustache, I gave him fifty-odd, but I'd been told he was nearer eighty. Unbelievable, but there he was, sharp as a tack, and active enough to give any of us eighteen holes of Sunday golf and often a beating.

He leaned back, an inveterate spectacle-chewer, and looked across a bowl of greenhouse carnations at me.

"I feel it my professional duty to tell you, since you ask," he said, no smile, quickly. "I warned her more than a year ago that she ought to go into a clinic I recommended. She refused. That's all. If a patient refuses, there's very little I can do!"

He put his spectacles in the case, closed a book, and locked a drawer.

"What am I to infer?" I asked, after too long a pause.

"If you could get her to consent to see me, you'd be doing your plainest duty."

"If I'm not told anything, what *can* I do?"

He nodded, looked at his book, obviously waiting for me to go.

"Could I offer you a scotch?" he asked, surprisingly.

I needed a drink, but I wanted far more to breathe cold air.

"No, thank you. I'll go tonight."

"Oh. Where?"

"Paris. May I please use your telephone?"

"By all means. I'll get you a little pick-me-up."

I called the airline and got a seat on the eleven o'clock flight, and sent a telegram to the office explaining my possible absence in the morning.

Dr. Norris came in with a glass of water and a couple of capsules.

"One now, one before you go to bed. I hope you're successful. As I said, there may still be time!"

I swallowed, thanked him and got in the car, drove round and asked Constable Parnes to keep an eye on the house, and to lock up for me.

In that drive to London I thought of little else than finding Mel, and shaking—if I had to—some sense into her, and bringing her back for an examination. At the air terminus I telephoned Frederick and told him I might be away a day or so, and to tell Patti to be ready with him to fly to Paris on Saturday, so that we could meet as a family and fly back together. I didn't think Mel could refuse that.

"Not Saturday, Dads. We're both right up to here on Saturday!"

Rage burst at last.

"You'll both kindly do exactly as I tell you. Be ready to fly to Paris at midday on Saturday. We'll try to become a family again. For the sake of your mother. She needs our help!"

"Look, Dads. It's no use before four o'clock. It's—it's—you'll have to know, anyhow. Pat's getting married. Special license. I'm best man. You see? Four o'clock at BEA, London Terminus. Right?"

I couldn't answer him. I put the receiver down. My flight was called. I walked down that hundred miles of concrete, but I shall never know how.

I needed the scotch the stewardess gave me, and I was surprised to find the aircraft bumping over the tarmac at Le Bourget when I awoke. I telephoned the Paris number and got the address of the hotel. Paris wasn't asleep, and somewhere or other in all those lit streets, I got the feeling that all wasn't lost.

Until I saw Mel.

The concierge went up to her room and beckoned me from the stairhead. I went in the open door, and stood there, poleaxed.

I'd never seen Mel drunk before. A little tiddly after a party or a birthday, but never tight, certainly not drunk.

That glazed, sloppy stare, which barely focussed where I stood, yes, to see it brought more pain than I'd thought possible. Of pity, of hate, tenderness, horror, pain that's nowhere, can't be described, almost isn't of the body, that takes the heart and crushes, holds the lungs without breath, pulls at the gut, weakens legs and knees, dries the throat, bleeds from the eyes.

"Mel, darling," I said. "I've come to take you home."

"Not going," she said, clearly enough.

"Well, it's late. We'll wait till the morning. You go back to sleep. But everything's all right. You haven't a worry in the world!"

"'detest you!"

"Yes, well, you've probably had cause. But there's time for forgiveness, isn't there?"

"Forgive—hm. Talk rot!"

"Go to sleep, Mel. Shall I tuck you in?"

"'n't come near me. Misbred hound. Not fit to sleep'n a kennel. Go 'wayl"

There seemed little use in extending the dialogue, so I went out and shut the door. The concierge was sorry, but there wasn't a room available. He went a few doors down the street, and came back all smiles. I was given a room under the stairs with a bathroom I seemed to be sharing with half Paris from the cheer of flush, which went on waking me all night and was still going when I woke in the morning. Mel wasn't up but she'd had coffee, so I knocked on the door and went in.

Her look petrified me. This wasn't a Mel I'd ever known.

"Get out," she said, in a toss of an uncombed head, and that, in itself, was most unusual. "Outside, immediately. How dare you come in here!"

"Mel, darling. Please. I've come to take you home."

"Don't talk nonsense to me. Get out!"

"Mel. I'm going to wait here till you're ready to go home!"

I sat down on the only chair.

She looked at me for a moment, a frightening look, and I knew she either wasn't sane, or she was drunk, or drugged.

Without hurry she picked up the telephone.

"There's a man in my room without my permission," she said, calmly, in her excellent French. "Would you please have him removed? I'd call the police. He might be violent!"

"Mel, for God Almighty's sake! How could you say such a thing?"

She put the receiver down and sighed, head turned, at the wall, a miracle of ennui. I must have waited a good five sound-less minutes before I sat on the bed, but she jerked her hand away.

"Mel, please. Darling. I had a talk with Dr. Norris—"

"Would you please go away? I don't wish to talk to you, or see you, or listen to you, or be anywhere near you ever again. Please don't make yourself a nuisance. Go away!"

At that moment the door swung open.

Two policemen stood there, large, blue-caped, impassive. Somebody in an alpaca jacket I supposed was the manager walked in, bowed to Mel.

"Take that man away," she said, still sitting up, arms folded, tray on her knees, looking at the coffee pot. "He insists on being a nuisance!"

"I am the husband of—"

"I am in process of divorce. He's being a pest. I fear bodily harm. I ask your protection. He has no right here!"

"Absolutely," the manager said. "He isn't staying here!"

One of the policemen hooked a finger.

"Come," he said, in a voice so absolutely French—small, a boy's and yet not—that I could have laughed. "Make no more trouble. Go downstairs, go out, and don't come back. You understand?"

"Perfectly. Mel, I'm terribly sorry about this—"

"I don't wish to talk to this man. Please take him away—"

"Mel, for God's sake, what *is* the matter with you? Why won't you do as Dr. Norris says?"

"Would you please remove this offensive thing? He's insulting me!"

The nearest policeman took me by the arm in what felt like the paw of a bear.

"Outside," he said. "Before you go IN-side!"

He wouldn't let me say another word, and he very nearly tore my arm off leading me out.

"Frederick'll be here on Saturday," I called from the stairhead. "You'll see him, won't you?"

"You and your brood!" she shrieked, and the manager shut the door.

Funny that Patti and her mother should give me the same feeling, down a flight of stairs, and into a cold street.

12

In London, it took me a little time on the telephone to find that Patti had been married about thirty minutes and the party, mostly of Africans, had left for nobody knew where. I didn't know how I felt. The business with Mel had been too much of a shock. To have tried to stop the marriage might have been worse than silly. Patti was strong-minded. She wouldn't have listened, anyway. She simply had to learn, and get on with it. I'd heard of other Afro-Euro marriages that turned out excellently well. But I was far from happy.

Frederick looked more than a little guilty, even sordidly under-brow, when we met at the air terminus. I gave him some money and his return ticket and a single for Mel, without comment on his conduct or his sister's. I spoke only of his mother.

"Do all you can," I told him. "You could save her life. Remember that!"

"But what's the matter between you? Is there anything wrong?"

I hadn't told him about the scene. I didn't think I should. He'd learn soon enough from Mel. But he had to be told something.

"Your mother wants a divorce. She believes she'd be happier with someone else."

"Terry? I'd have sworn there was more than brotherly affection there. He was always at the house. I wish I'd known for sure!"

"You could at least have let me know you had doubts?"

89

"When did we ever have a chance for a real talk? I tried to write—oh—a dozen times. Looked so ridiculous, I tore them up. Mums said there was nothing in it. I asked her. So did Patti. More than once. But she got the same answer. Nothing to do with us. We just let it go."

"I wish to God I'd even suspected anything. Might have saved a lot of this. Who'd imagine such misery?"

He linked his arm in mine and we strolled toward the airbus. We weren't a demonstrative family, and his gesture touched me.

"Cheer up, Dads," he said gently. "I'll climb a cloud, you can bet your boots. I mean, what's she going to do in Paris? She ought to be at home. We couldn't understand why she wasn't. I mean, she never was. Whenever we've wanted to go down for a weekend, there's never been anybody there. Place was absolutely haunted. Everything locked. That's one reason Patti's gone. She said the only two things missing from us babes in our little wood were the robins and leaves. Her room wasn't even cleaned. She was really stabbed about it. Well, now she's happy enough. About the time I get to Paris, they'll be in Rome. Then Marrakesh."

We hadn't mentioned her, I'd asked no questions, and any thought of her having gone without wanting or even trying to see me brought that feeling of nausea. I didn't want to think of it. But it chewed, kept chewing. My Patti. Not a kiss, not a word. I couldn't believe it.

I didn't reply, and he saw I didn't want to hear any more. His flight was called, he gave me a filial peck, and I turned to go back, lonelier than I had ever been in my life.

Saturday afternoon in London, all the shutters down, a Sunday air over everything, nowhere to go except a picture gallery or a cinema. Any notion of going home and having to be reminded of Mel gave me the shivers. I couldn't feel anything for her. That's what surprised me. I felt I should have been thinking lovingly, or yearningly. I couldn't. I never had.

That was a truth I had to face.

90

Then how on earth had we lived together all that time? Simple enough. We were a couple of well-schooled people, we'd got married, we'd had two children, we'd liked each other in bed, we had a house and garden that belonged to us, we had all the worldly goods we needed and a lot left over, I was in a good position and Mel could do as she pleased. That's how it was. We'd made the best of a very good thing. I didn't regret a moment. For that sort of pleasant, ordered life I'd have done exactly the same all over again. Selfish, perhaps. But that was the cold truth.

But I'd never loved her, truly, urgently, as I loved Tanis. It wasn't the happiest thing to have to admit. But I'd gone a long way past telling myself pretty stories.

Possibly, Mel'd never loved me. Perhaps she resented my taking her for granted. She might even have hidden a dislike, or perhaps a hatred for me over many a year. I didn't know. But the active hatred in her eyes and voice that morning couldn't have grown in a couple of minutes. I could think of nothing I'd done, except, of course, giving a few women what was properly hers.

That was hard luck.

But had I neglected the children?

We'd lost the first, a silent little bundle which endured only for a few days. The nurse hadn't wanted to show it to me, and when I insisted I knew why. I also knew why Mel couldn't kiss me as she had. There was always a sort of arm's-length distance I couldn't see but that I felt, and I know she felt it in me. Why should love produce horror? Was this a reason why two healthy people should go to bed? But why should the silent little thing induce horror? Because it marked us as being indifferent breeders? Wasn't like the general run of the children of our friends? Nincompoops later on, possibly, but healthy as infants? We made love—but what ridiculous terms we use!—we, the hopelessly genteel, who tolerate the four-letter words in open publication and laud the authors, but obstinately refuse a correct use of

language in our more intimate relations—relations, Great God!—
with each other—we, Mel and I went to bed because we were
all we had, and we didn't at that time want anybody else, and
we were infinitely sorry for each other. That was about all the
feeling between us. When Frederick came we were happier.
He was a fine little fellow and grew to be rather taller than me.
When Patti came along, Mel said that's enough and had something done to her ovaries. I don't think we had much of a discussion about it. The two of them grew up without incident
except the usual mumps and scarlet fever, and when they were
ready, off they went, Frederick to my old school, Patti to Mel's,
and we went to visit them when we could, and took them to
France or Italy for holidays. I never had any "deep" conversation
with either of them. Mel said there was no earthly use in telling
them anything since they got all the information they'd need
from books that we, at their age wouldn't have dreamed of, and
in any event it was no use putting ideas in their heads. After
all, neither of us had ever had any "instruction" and we'd done
well enough.

But how had they grown up to be strangers to us? What had
caused the split?

Because that's what it was. Neither of them had telephoned
me to ask how things were going. The weekend had come to
nothing. We'd grown apart, and I couldn't for the life of me
think why. The only time I'd had an argument with them—
and it really wasn't that at all, but simply a query about what
I'd learned were called "beat groups"—the entire house rocked
with twangy-bangy, and the mewlings of callow importunates—
they looked at each other, not with pity or derision or any other
expression that I could see, and Frederick took off the record.

"Granddad didn't like jazz, and you did," he said, rather
tiredly. "We don't like jazz, either. We prefer this. I suppose my
kids'll like something else. Perfectly all right with me. After all,
the entire world grows up, too. And there must be something in

it because the entire world's buying it. That's why these lads are millionaires. Don't I wish I were one of them!"

"Fool if you didn't," Patti said, and got up, stretching. "I'm going back. Got a little drinky-winky tonight."

"I thought you'd come to church," I said, and I was really disappointed. "We haven't been as a family for far too long!"

Patti shook her head, drawing back the hair behind her ears. "No church for me, Daddy, thank you," she said, formally as she might refuse sugar in tea. "But absolutely *never!* Not even to get married. That stuff went out with the waltz!"

"I'm surprised to hear you say that," I said, and she saw that I was, and her face pinked and her eyes warned. "You were brought up rather differently, surely?"

"I feel exactly the same, Dads," Frederick said, putting the records in a pile. "None of that business has the smallest pull for me. It's locked!"

"Locked?"

"Doesn't go in. We've escaped. Might have impressed once upon a time. Obviously it did. There were martyrs. They didn't do much good, though. Then Hitler comes along and does away with six million of the most inoffensive people on earth. You did your part to let him, and you still go to church? What for? The question I'd like to have answered, is why people who think themselves intelligent can be deceived by an outworn form of social activity? That's all it is. You call it spiritual discipline. But you're only doing what your grandfather and his granddad did. I'm not following form. That's all."

"I deeply regret it. I believe it does one good to submit oneself to judgement at least once now and again. To ask for, and give thanks, for example, for health. Life. All the pleasure it brings. One's got to give thanks somewhere, surely?"

"I don't in the least see why," Patti said, staring out at the roses waving against the pane. "We're not here because we wanted to be. We weren't given the slightest choice. We're here, that's all. Parental or family love's a question of usage. We're

93

supposed to love fathers and mothers because it's thought natural. It's not natural at all. It's because everybody's been brainwashed into thinking so. So it must be the thing to do? Doesn't follow. And as for religion in general, darling Freds can say all that again. But you should hear him when he's had a couple of stuttering martinis!"

"I didn't know he'd started drinking? That's hardly the way to a four-minute mile!"

They both laughed, and Frederick put the last of the records in his suitcase, I remember, with a gesture of almost impatient finality.

"It's out, Dads," he said. "I left the team months ago. Exams are going to take every moment. That's all I'm waiting for. Then Kierkegaard, Berdyaev and ol' man Mose' can all go and chase themselves!"

"I don't like your attitude. It doesn't become you. Either of you. You're being deliberately provocative. Why?"

Frederick stood, feet apart, and looked at me, knuckles on hips.

"I didn't mean provocation, sir. We were discussing whether or not we were going to church, surely? Now then, if you'll be the Dads we know you are, you'll lend us the car so that I can drop Pats and go about my own encumbrances. I'll leave the car at the garage tomorrow. Washed!"

"Do let's, Daddy!"

No use acting the galloping blimp. They went away with a touch on the cheek each, stopping en route to say goodbye to Mel, tea-ing in the village with the Blennerhassetts.

That was the first time, almost a couple of years ago that I'd realised there was such a gulf between us. Mel had said naturally there must be. The same gulf existed between her mother and herself.

"Leave everything alone, then they'll settle down. Don't criticise. They've got to find their own feet!"

94

But leaving them to find their own feet had taken them a thousand light miles further away, until now I couldn't talk to either of them. We weren't a family. Had we ever been?

In a sudden fit of irritation I put everything out of my head and went up to Gunter's for tea, and bought a paper on the way.

Who should be sitting there but the Misses Furnival and Roule. We smiled and I sat down at another table. It wasn't even on the surface of my mind to consider inviting them over. I simply put my nose in the *Standard* and read what there was of the news while I drank a couple of cups of tea. When I looked up, a waitress smiled and came closer.

"I beg your pardon, sir," she began, and looked across the room. "That young lady over there presents her compliments and wonders whether she could speak to you?"

Miss Roule had gone. Miss Furnival sat alone. She wasn't looking at me. I put the paper aside and walked over. She turned her head, widened her eyes.

"I told Rouley I'd pay," she said, in that little-girl manner of hers. "But I haven't enough money—!"

Well, of course, I took the bill and sat down, and she told me she'd been swotting all afternoon at her crammer's and she was going home to do some scribbling. Without knowing what I was saying—and I'd take that with a grain or two of salt—I asked her how she was going, she said by rail, and I offered her a lift in the car, and she said lovely.

Away we went, and we prattled, heaven knows about what, all the way to her place in Gover's Grange. Its size surprised me, but the Furnivals were an old family.

"I'm going to be quite daring," she said, getting out. "In the places where you ought to be using my name, there's a blank because 'Miss Furnival' doesn't fit!"

"I've been racking my brain," I said, and I had. "I don't think I ever heard it. What is it?"

"Consuelo. But *please* don't call me Connie!"

"Would I, do you suppose, be likely to? It's a very beautiful name."

"Thank you. I think Edmund is, too!"

"Good. Then it's Edmund. Goodnight, Consuelo!"

The telephone was ringing when I reached the house, and I had to scramble down the hall in the dark.

Frederick, from Heathrow.

"She's with me, Dads. But she isn't well enough to go home tonight. I'm taking her to Aunt Pam's. She just said I could. Dads, she doesn't look at all well. Think I ought to call a doctor?"

"I'll ring Pamela and ask her. She's bound to know who's the best. Leave it to me. You did splendidly. I'll drive over!"

I didn't look forward to it, though when I got there, late, it wasn't as disagreeable as I might have thought. But it certainly wasn't happy. She seemed only partly her old self. She half-smiled all the time, moved slowly, even painfully, and not only didn't mention Paris, but didn't say a single word. Not one. Not even thank you. That wasn't like Mel.

"Dangerous for her to travel tonight," Dr. Smythe said, when he came downstairs. "She's going to sleep now, and I'll come in the morning. What's the name of your physician? I'll phone him."

"Have you any opinion, Doctor?"

He settled the contents of his bag and locked it.

"I regret I'm not in a position to say. Until I've spoken to Dr. Norris. If there should be any change, I mean restlessness, have no hesitation. Call me immediately. I shall be here at eight-fifteen tomorrow morning."

He put on a bowler, looked at Pamela, fair hair, gold-rims, gentle grey eyes, birdseye blue tie, holding up the bag to go out, and Mel upstairs asleep.

"I suppose you've got to go," Pamela said inconsequentially. "Everything's very quiet."

"If I get the Tube, I'll catch the last train very comfortably. It's got a buffet car."

"It's a long way. You're going to need your energy. I know you have a high position. That was Mel's fear. I think it might have been cause of this."

"What? Mel's fear? Fear of what?"

Pamela shrugged, rattled the ice in the glass.

"Well, that she mightn't measure. Mightn't be able to do all she should. She was awfully afraid of your going up. She felt she wasn't able to cope. Other women were so much cleverer. She used to cry."

"I wish to God she'd told me."

"You were always so—well, sort of, far away. You never seemed to have any difficulty. Every time she saw your picture in the paper, she shivered. She was terrified!"

"Of what?"

"I suppose of making a mess of things. She went through agonies when she had to give a dinner. The one you gave for the French Ambassador, remember? She was a wreck!"

"It was marvellous. But, silly girl, everybody said so. What did she have to be afraid of?"

"Failure. That's all. Letting you down. And you never even put out your hand. Did you?"

"Well, I don't know. I took it as a matter of course. She'd lived in that circle for long enough, surely? When did she ever fail?"

"I think it got worse as time went on. I think she was sickening for—for this. She went through her worst time, you know. I thought she sailed through."

"One has to treat people as grown-up."

"You can put your arms round them, sometimes!"

"And be pushed away?"

"Try, try, try again. It pays."

"Did it, with your husband?"

"That's hitting under the belt!"

97

"You were probably as unknowing as I. Why didn't you try and try again?"

"Why don't you call him Terry?"

"I'd be delighted to call him anything else!"

She picked up her drink, and raised it.

"Don't blame you a bit. D'you know, now that he's gone, I'm even rather glad?"

"More freedom?"

"Much, my dear. I'm going to be cosily-me for a change. Freddie's the gloryboy. He brought a positive *scal*lop here. *Sloozy*. Half-Chinese. The other half wouldn't care. She was brewed when she got here, and Freddie gave her a hypo in the max"—she pointed a forefinger into her half-turned buttock—"right at the pool out there, and rolled her in. What went on, I daren't tell you!"

"Are you talking about drugs?"

"Of course!—"

"But are you sure? Not some joke or—"

She laughed, the sudden, chin-up vwaah-huh!

"Joke? Edmund, they were all on the weed—"

"Who were?"

"The party he brought. From the U. A dozen or so. Perfectly lovely kids, all of them. Often been here. Nearly every Sund—"

"What's this 'weed'?"

The laugh went, and she looked at me sideways, plainly sorry she'd spoken.

"Oh, Edmun', please, can't we forget all about it?" she said sharply. "I shouldn't have—well, it's all fun, anyway. They enjoy themselves here, and I enjoy *them*. I look forward to my Sundays, I can tell you!"

There was no sound outside Mel's door before I put on my overcoat, and downstairs I murmured goodnight—and Pamela said nothing—and I left that house of kitchen-and-bar smells, and all those horses, quite sure I'd never go there again, and coldly certain I'd take Master Frederick by the ear. I might have suspected drink. His appearance suggested a thick head. But "weed," which I took to be marijuana, and hypo's in the buttocks of scallops, however sloozy, were a quite different matter. A cruel thought forced its way against my will. Patti. Could she have been one of the party sometimes?

It was a little late to ask.

13

There wasn't a vacant room at the club, and I didn't feel like walking back through a drizzle to the Turkish bath. I slept in the armchair, and went over in a smoky morning, changed, and got to the office a little before eight.

I'd been at work for an hour or so, and suddenly, for no reason I could have given, that run of syllables started again, a definite rhythm at the back of my mind. I looked through Jeremy's list of names without being able to pick out anything that matched, and then asked Miss Roule to find Frederick. She caught him in the canteen. I could hear the cutlery and yelp of orders.

"How does your brother-in-law spell his name?" I asked, without preamble. "I want to write to Patti. Any idea where they live?"

"I understood they were going as far as the Ivory Coast and back here. About three weeks. I don't believe I could spell his name if you paid me. We always called him Wepo!"

"I couldn't find him in any of the directories. Not, at any rate, under the name he gave at the Registry Office."

"I saw that. But he said the other was a business name, and he was married in his real name. It's the name of his mother's family. Lot of G's and K's in it, I remember. Pats said she'd stick to our name!"

"Good of her. When are you coming home?"

"Not this week, Dads. Too much of a drag!"

"Poltroon!"

100

"I'm not turned on for bucolic revelry. Minus-minis and no bra's. That's Frederico!"

I copied the name of my son-in-law from the Park Lane rental agency's report—misspelled, with a middle name I hadn't seen before—though the syllables, with every change of vowel didn't fit the run in my mind.

"Pass that to Security," I told Miss Roule.

I got a large sheet of paper and a thick pencil and began to give letters to the pattern running in my head. It took a solid ten minutes to bring Brebabaki Okojiko Kajogoni to fit in some way the stresses my mind insisted on.

Joseph Colethorne came in after a triple knock. I knew him slightly, though anyone less like an agent would be hard to imagine, a tiny, stooped, baldish, self-barbered-moustachish sort of fellow, with a Yorkshire accent. Behind him, Miss Roule raised her eyebrows.

"That second call to Geneva," he said, and I nodded, and she shut the door. "Went from Victoria Station Hotel. Fake name, of course. Operator doesn't remember the caller. You've some idea you know the man?"

"None at all."

"Any idea how he'd get this number? And the extension?"

"None."

He nodded as if it were no matter.

"That house in Kensington. I suppose y'know it was rented by your brother-in-law, do y'?"

"I'm told so."

"What'd be the idea of putting you on to him?"

"Not the faintest."

"Know anything about that office in Pall Mall?"

"Some sort of engineering business, isn't it?"

Toothsuck came of superior knowledge.

"Export to Eastern Europe, Russia and China. Ebbleton's in Dublin, I suppose you know? Yes. We're hoping he'll fly to Canada. We'll get him there."

"What sort of charge?"

He cleared his nose without opening his mouth.

"That office was a proper nest. Economic intelligence, mostly. They've all gone back. Bunked overnight. We let 'em go. Be easier when they come in again. Ebbleton's blotted his copy-book, though. I don't doubt there's a couple of his own mob looking for him."

"His own—?"

"Lads he was working with. He was doing a nice lot of business on the side. It was not allowed. So they'll likely give him a number."

"Where?"

"In the mortuary."

That hadn't occurred to me. Or, far more seriously, that Ebbleton could have been any sort of agent. I felt my position a little slippery underfoot.

"Sorry to hear that," I said. "Anything you want from me?"

"Brigadier Hawtrey warned y'bout that Nazi lot, didn't he? Right, well, I'll underline it. That's really why I come over. We don't want any accidents!"

"What makes you think there might be?"

He sucked his front teeth in a chirrup and turned to the door.

"They're a rough lot, and we don't know-yet-who they are, or who we're looking for. But *they* know *you*. And a few others. I don't want to hear y're a suicide one of these lovely mornings. Spoil me breakfast. All right?"

He opened the door to go. I never saw anyone look more like a newspaper-seller.

I sat there a little cold. Who, in London, could possibly know my telephone number and extension here? Mel, of course. But if she'd given it to Ebbleton—and obviously she had—why would he give it to somebody to put me on to a hiding-place? Some-body wanted me to find out about Mel, perhaps?

Miss Roule came in to call me to a three o'clock Shadow, which turned out a little darker than usual. The Junior Minister was bothered about an item in the morning papers, playing up an African student, thrown out of his lodging for cooking food on a gas ring he wasn't supposed to have.

"The Minister was very upset about it," she said. "We might have intervened, I feel, Mr. Trothe?"

"If we'd been told. But I hardly think it anything to do with us if a man breaks a rule against cooking in his room?"

"Anything that disturbs racial feeling is something very much to do with us. Anything to do with students, of course, is exactly what we're here for!"

"We seem to be narrowing the terms of reference—"

"Nothing of the sort. I was able to assure the Minister that the man's in other lodgings where he's able to cook. I checked personally. Nobody else seemed to think it worth the trouble!"

I caught the half-smile in Brantley's eye, and let it go.

If there's one thing I've learned in my time, it's never to try to "fit" appointments in. It's a pernicious habit that almost always ends in disaster. It must. Official appointments are exactly that. Tardy arrival is not only discourtesy, but smells of inefficient staff-work and the staff, of course, resent the slur.

I had to leave when they were discussing whether the Junior Minister could "fit in" a meeting with a delegation of Scottish school teachers before attending the House, and a conference with the Minister. I would have said no. As it must happen, there were supplementary questions, and Brantley warned her she might be kept longer than she wished. She was kept more than an hour longer in a roaring battle, had to see the Minister immediately afterwards, and the delegation, breathing Gaelic fire, went off just after 8:30 that night without seeing her.

Next morning it was in the papers, and while the department got a black eye, we were all perfectly happy.

"That'll learn her," Yorick said, over the ten o'clock cup. "Cocky is as cocky does. That desk's going to be vacant sooner than we think. The Minister's absolutely apocalyptic. Riding four foamers at once!"

Miss Roule came to say that I was required to speak to Delhi in twenty minutes, and filled the plate with biscuits.

"Pity we couldn't have done something," I said, having read about it and feeling guiltily innocent because I don't like crowing over a corpse. "We could have made an appointment for another time, surely?"

"Too late for the North," Yorick said. "It fell on me to tea-and-bun them. They're going to cancel the Highland Games, stop the flow of butterscotch, and declare the frontier closed to the Sassenach. Scotland's agin her. Devil of a handicap. And I'm agin her, and by George, that's no small business!"

"I believe you deliberately kept them there!" I said, seeing light.

He chose an oatmeal biscuit, looking across me at Miss Roule, and his eyes smiled.

"But Edmund," he said. "I have so little opportunity of listening to the Doric. How could I possibly let them go?"

14

Mrs. Cloney woke me with a lovely cup of tea.

"Market day, sir," she whispered, in the dark. "Thought I'd give y' call 'stead o' the exchange. They said you wanted a sixer. Ain't quite that, but 'time you bath 'n shave, your omelet'll be ready. Paper'll be here in a minute!"

A woman like that can't be thanked.

While I broke a hot roll the doorbell burred.

"Call for you down the Post Office, sir!" Mrs. Cloney bellowed along the passage. "Want 'em put it through here, sir?"

"Please, Mrs. Cloney."

I was halfway through *The Times* editorial and the phone rang.

"Hullo? Mr. Edmund Trothe?"

"Speaking!"

"Ah, Mr. Trothe. This is John Oram. You may remember me? Mr. Lane's office? I'm speaking from London. Couldn't get you direct. Something wrong with Trunks."

"Yes, Mr. Oram?"

"Brigadier Hawtrey's office asked me to present compliments, and to say they'd prefer you stayed at home today, sir. There's distinctly bad news from the east. If you follow?"

"Unfortunately I'm seeing the Lord Blercgrove. I shall go direct from the station to the office. How's the weather?"

"Haven't been out all night, sir, but they say there's an inky fog and it's supposed to be getting worse!"

"That'll help cloud things over, won't it? I'll call when I arrive."

If somebody was after my blood I intended to give him a pretty fast gallop. I had no doubt about my little talisman. For closer entertainment I decided on an umbrella which had been useful on occasion. I looked through the collection in the brolly-pot and the malacca came to hand as an old friend. The ferrule catch snapped back easily enough, and even after so many years the knife of razor steel was still bright.

I walked through thin mist to the station, caught the train and read the newspapers in the pullman. London was ugly with piled brown snow in gutter-drifts, slush over the ankles, and a thick fog that stank of old chimneys. I didn't want to go by Tube. Instead I walked out of the station looking for a cab, kept on past an empty rank, and out to the street.

Not a sound.

Fog came down thicker. All I could see in front was a lamp post, a tall shadow. I walked on, sure of the way I'd been going since schooldays, hearing traffic whine here and there as coursing dogs, and gone.

It hadn't occurred to me that I could lose my way anywhere in London. I'd always walked to Whitehall in fog and enjoyed it. I so often remembered walking hand-in-hand with my father in the days of hansom cabs, he pretending he was lost, and I sure he wasn't, and laughing at him.

But this was no ordinary fog. It was neither grey nor green, and it wasn't brown or blue, but something that seemed part of each as the minutes went by and then turned stinkingly black. A smell of soot became a stench of burning rubbish and altered to traffic odor, oil, petrol, rubber, asphalt, and as suddenly changed to the stale reek of garden sweepings in old glow doused with water, and in a moment, back again to soot.

I rambled on, sure of my way, feeling for kerbs with a questing foot, tapping voids with the umbrella, absolutely in no doubt until I touched a knee-high wall with the ferrule. I put out a hand and felt railings. Railings left, railings right.

But there shouldn't have been railings where I was going.

I tried to think where I was.

I'd turned left from the station, counted the turnings, crossed over, and turned right—as I'd thought—and I should have been in Edgware Road going toward Marble Arch.

I wasn't.

Then where the devil was I?

I couldn't hear a soul.

There was nothing to see except the fog. Even the paving was hidden. I swung the umbrella in a wide arc. It touched nothing. I took two paces toward the railings, three. Four. I had to go back the other way to reach them.

I'd lost all sense of direction.

When I heard those footsteps behind me, I suddenly realised what a complete fool I was to have tried that walk by myself, more especially in view of Oram's warning. I took the automatic out and let it drop in my left-hand overcoat pocket. In the right hand I carried the umbrella. Shooting, unless absolutely necessary, is not the best idea in London. I couldn't see a yard. The stealth of those footsteps, slidden, slow, made me think of a cat crouch-pacing after a bird.

A nightmare of years, that always wakened me in cold sweat, was being broken. I dreamed of being stalked in fog, no chance of defence, no glimpse of the murderer. I knew I was going to be slaughtered by sudden whip-slashings of a sabre. It seemed furthest siege of idiocy to suppose that somebody would try to kill me in the middle of London in the open street.

But it was murderer's weather.

Black.

I got to the shadow of a pillar-box and edged all round it, keeping that bulk of metal between me and the approaching steps. They were near, a few yards away, and they passed.

I saw no movement. I couldn't see the ferrule of my umbrella, or my shoes, and all traffic seemed to have stopped. Somebody shouted from far off. No cars had passed. I tried not to breathe to be able to hear any smallest sound.

I sensed without actually seeing a movement to my left and half-paced to the right, but the umbrella handle—I was holding it upside down—struck the metal the lightest touch though it sounded like a bell-ringer's toll.

I stood where I was, not a move. I put an eye around the metal to look for shadow, one side, and the other.

Nothing.

I believe I would have given everything, heart, soul and property only for a glimpse, to know who he was, to store the memory, to break that dream, to have just one bash at him.

Cold got into my feet. I shivered. I unscrewed the umbrella's ferrule to open the blade. In trained hands—and mine were well-trained—the innocent umbrella can become a lethal weapon. All I asked was a fair target. I prayed for it, standing there, cursing to control shivers of cold, trying with movements of my nose to stop the drips from itching, blinking to free my eyes of water, staring one side and the other for any move.

The sound of a car's tires became a certain whisper. I saw the shadow of its bulk. It was passing, almost touching the skirts of my overcoat.

"Stay where y'are, Trothe!" somebody said urgently. "My God, what a run—"

I turned from behind the pillar-box.

"Don't move!" the voice shouted behind me. "He's on top of y'!"

Instantly I felt rather than saw a motion, to my right.

I threw the umbrella as a spear with all the force in my body.

I heard it hit. I could have howled triumph.

I went forward a pace at a time. The groan came from a

few yards on. He might have been foxing. He could have been to my right, or somewhere near the railings. I danced sideways to the left and crouched.

Two bullets clinked a ragged ricochet off metal, two mauve-pink balloons exploded almost in my face.

A .45 *BANGED!* an ear-splitter just behind me and nearly gave me a nose-bleed. I felt that ginger-ale sting.

"Stand still, Trothe," the voice said, quietly. "I hit him!"

A reddish anti-fog beam showed bricks and railings, and green ends of shrubs poking out, and a man in a blue overcoat lying in a heap. My umbrella lay under him, and a fattish aluminium cone had rolled toward the gutter. The left hand still held an automatic.

"Something new here!" a voice said, and a shadow picked up the cone. "This is how he was going, sir, see this? This is that funny light!"

"What we thought was X-rays?"

"'s right, sup!"

"Doing very well so far!" Joseph Colethorne said, near me, and put the .45 back in the holster under his jacket. "You gave us a right headache, didn't you?"

"Wasn't thinking. Who is this?"

"Don't know. He's been behind you since you left this morning. He took a party down to your place on Friday. Tourists. Bus trip. He stayed at the pub, down there. *Clark!*"

"Sup!"

"Give us a hand, here!"

"Sup!"

I picked up my umbrella. The man was fair, flabby-jowls, mid-thirties perhaps, well dressed and shod. I'd never seen him before.

Colethorne turned out the pockets. He had a thick wad of notes doubled in an elastic band, some change, but no cheque book or papers.

Clark, somebody anonymous, reached visible hands and took

his feet. I helped, and we lifted him in to the back of a Rolls-Royce that must have been half a century old from the height of roof and width of body, and still in fragrance of leather and a faintest hint of perfume.

"We'll get him down to the doctor's," Colethorne said. "You can walk where you like now. No use asking me where you are. Take a bit of time. Talk to a policeman. He'll remember you. If this fella comes around, doesn't matter what he says, you're safe as the bank. All right?"

"Why can't I come with you?"

I could barely see Colethorne's face, but I felt the resigned impatience.

"Gunshot wound," he said. "Time we get there he might be dead. I've got a pass. And the story. Have you?"

"No."

"Just go on walking. If there's any follow-up, Mr. Cawle'll phone. All right, Clark!"

"Sup!"

The door shut, and though I hadn't heard the motor, the car was gone even to the sound of tires.

I walked into the roadway, tapping the ferrule against the edge of the kerbstone, following the gutter. Where the stone curved in a corner, I crossed, taking the straightest way over the crown to the other side.

Fog was lighter and drifts of breeze moved smoky clouds, but I couldn't see the houses. I walked along the gutter, so far as I knew, going west. Several times I saw the lights of buses, engines running but stationary, and veered away. I didn't want identification or any lively chatter too near the scene.

An hour and twenty-five minutes by my watch of tapping and walking took me into a signal light. I still couldn't see anything much more than a yard in front. I wiped the fog murk from my face. My handkerchief was black. I blew my nose a couple of times, a trumpeter's effort, and cursed aloud.

Somebody laughed heh-heh-heh! close by, and nearly lifted

me out of my skin. I almost ran that way and pulled up sharp to see a policeman's helmet and oilskin cape in a doorway. I walked into the beam of his torchlight and took off my hat to wipe the band. I intended he should remember me.

"Filthy weather, Constable," I said.

"Ah, lovely morning, sir!" he said, gay as a bird. "Want to know where you are? Three doors down from Camden Town Tube. Want a nice cup of tea, there's a place just the other side. Where y' come from, sir?"

"Paddington," I said. "I'm disappointed. I thought I was somewhere near Whitehall. My office—"

"You ain't half!" he said. "Just had a bloke passed here, thought he was up at Highgate Arches. Started off from Stoke Newington. I send 'em all down the Tube. Best way, lovely mornin' like this!"

"I don't see anything 'lovely' about it," I grumped. "Late for the office, fog-soiled—"

"That's right, sir," the constable said, in a large dandle. "It's only Londoners 'joy the fog. My ol' dad, he used to tell us tales, there. Once he was down the Elephant 'n Castle, took him two days to get to the Kennington Horns. Driving a wagon 'n two pair, he was. They don't do too much better today, do they? Them buses ain't moved since last night. Look o' things, they'll be here tonight. Fog, sir, that's our mother's milk. Love it!"

Sure enough, in thick, sooty-smelling darkness, the lights of the Tube entrance glowed suddenly as by magic. I walked farther on, hugging the wall, and found the door to the café. It amazed me to find it crammed with people in blue mist of tobacco, frying bacon, coffee, pepper, and fainter, the soupy smell of cooked greens. My tea in an enormous cup tasted like the nectar of the gods. While I read the newspaper, I never ate anything better than the rounds of toast, one with beef-blood dripping, and the other one, half with butter and two poached eggs, and the other half thick with strawberry jam. I went out absolutely a brand-new man, and turned right for the Tube, wondering why Italians always seem to run a café so much better than anybody else, and why a meal eaten in the discomfort of an overcoat, with people crowded all about, has more taste than in one's own breakfast room at home.

I turned into the Tube and booked to Green Park. There were very few passengers in my car. I hid behind the newspaper for most of the way, but then I was by myself. I got out and felt my way down to the Ritz, tapping the umbrella as a blind man's stick and thanking God for my eyes.

A phone call to the office got Mansell, the messenger.

"Been on duty all night, sir," he said, disgustingly cheerful. "Day man ain't in, yet. Nobody's got here. Don't think they will, in this. Worst fog for eighty years, the B.B.C. says it is. I don't believe it. I seen worser 'n this. This un's blackish. I seen red—"

"Listen, Mansell, just leave a message for Miss Roule, will you? Say I may be a little late, but I'll be there within the hour."

"Well, uh. Sir, there's a message here, just come in, sir. Mrs. Pamela Ebbleton. Been trying to get you, sir."

Pamela's number was engaged for more than ten minutes, and then I was listening to an amazing jumble of sounds and somebody sobbed into the receiver.

"Hullo?" I shouted. "What *is* the matter—!"

"Oh, *Edmund!*"—Mel's mother—"oh, thank *heaven!* Please come here quickly, my dear. The most awful—"

"What is it?"

"The house. It's full of police. And Mel's been taken to the hospital. Just gone. Oh, Edmund—!"

"I'll be there within thirty minutes. Which hospital was she taken to?"

"I don't know. I—Pamela's in raving hysterics—"

I put the telephone down. I tried to call Dr. Norris. Hopeless. I went out in the black, feeling a way to the Green Park Tube. The train was express, passing two or three stations at a time. I couldn't think what the police might be doing in the house. I

112

couldn't bear to think about Mel. I tried to do the crossword puzzle. I usually do it while shaving, propping it against the mirror. The sway of the train, low light, the moan of the motor, impatience, a hurt in the throat thinking of Mel, but I had to put it away, blank.

Morning was clearer when I got out, and a cab put me outside the gate. Mel's mother was at the door before I could ring. She looked desperately tired, wept dry.

Pamela sat on the sofa in a dressing gown. She was drunk, barely able to keep her eyes open. The bottle on the floor was almost empty.

"The great Edmun', himself!" she said, flinging out her arms. "I'm not married. Hoor—eee! My children are bastards. Nice? I'm still Pamela Scoones!"

"Now, Pamela, I insist you stop drinking and talk sensibly!" her mother began, and turned to me. "The police have been here for the past couple of hours. Why they *must* come at such an ungodly time only they know. That creature Ebbleton—I never liked the man—has a wife in Europe somewhere. Three children. He's a bigamist, of course. Question is, what can Pamela do?"

"There isn't much anyone can do until we've got a few more facts," I said. "Why did they come here? Did they have a warrant?"

"'course," Pamela said, drunkenly superior. "Wouldn't lerrem in without, wourra? Frighten the children, I said. Go on, frighten 'children. 'n my sister, very ill. Then he told me'p. So I had a drink!"

"Then Mel woke up screaming," Mrs. Scoones said. "I called the doctor—Dr. Smythe?—yes. He came and the police called an ambulance. One good thing they did!"

The telephone rang. Pamela reached out and threw the receiver off.

"Ringing all night!" she grated. "Hell with—"

"Pamela!" Mrs. Scoones scolded, and bent to pick it up. "Hullo? Yes?"

Her face smoothed of any line or wrinkle. She turned staring eyes to me that suddenly glazed and I had to jump to catch her.

"—really am terribly sorry," a man's voice was saying. "There was nothing we could do. I'm trying to get—"

"My name is Trothe. Would you please repeat that?"

"Oh. Mr. Trothe? This is Dr. Smythe. I'm speaking from the Winchmore Hill Hospital. I brought Mrs. Trothe here a little over an hour ago. A heart condition. I regret very deeply there was nothing we could do. She died at twenty-two minutes past the hour. If you'd care to come here, we could discuss the transfer of the—"

Pamela fell against her mother weeping quietly, deeply. I poured the rest of the whiskey, drank it in a short gulp, and left them.

15

I didn't know how many friends Mel had until she lay in St. Matthew's. Dr. Tomsett wrote to say he permitted the lying-in-state because Mrs. Trothe had always been such a dedicated parishioner, most attentive to her duties, and, moreover, of up-right and most wholesome character, a woman everybody loved and respected for her human, to say nothing of her moral qualities, and I couldn't see the rest.

Mel, lying there surrounded by lilies-of-the-valley and damask roses, from her own greenhouses, seemed as she had been on the day I first met her, not a moment older, perfectly, youthfully beautiful.

I had a few days off until the funeral was over. I'd no idea what to do with myself. Even the garden no longer held interest. It reminded me too much of Mel. I saw her in every corner. The house whispered of her. I couldn't stay there. There wasn't a room where I felt comfortable.

Paul and Moira called just after tea. He came in but she waved from the car. They'd just come from the church. He said the obvious things, tried to appear feelingless.

"I told Moira I wanted a quiet word with you," he said. "Got to get back. There's one little matter, first. Did the Blur say anything more to you about this Nazi business?"

"He mentioned it, yes."

"I'm out of it. I refuse to accept any official warning, and I don't want cover. Told him so. How about you?"

"We're both on the short list. Forgotten that?"

"I can't be worried, Edmund. I can take care of myself. Anybody starts anything, he'll get it. You won't believe what happened, though. He tried to get me to rewrite my report!"

"How d'you mean?"

"Rewrite. Cut the factors against the Common Market, or anyway, water it well down. The figures came from your summary. He'll probably talk to you about it. I don't believe he ever looked at it before. At least, not him, but whoever-it-is interested. Anyway, he said we weren't there to sabotage. Imagine that!"

"The figures are plain enough!"

He gave me the old-time Little Cham stare, the Long Swords, we'd always called it, that asked a question and answered it in one.

"Ever go back over those days, Edmund?" he asked, one eye shut. "I had plenty of time to make a real autopsy. Going in the Market's a gift for socialists. They join up with all the other parties. Makes the trades unions the only lasting power. But when you look at the cost to the nation, you've got to start blinking. The Blur's supposed to be protecting Government policy. I'm glad I went when I did. I wouldn't have lasted!"

"Is this an early warning?"

He shrugged.

"You know the game, Edmund. I'm just saying you can resign *now*. You can sign your contract when you like. When y'going to be your own man?"

"I'm more than tempted, I may say!"

"Good. I know this isn't much of a time to ask you to cock an eye at anything. But I brought a few papers along. I'd like you to size things up. What I'd really appreciate is a comparison between the Russian scheme, and ours. We're their only competitors. Then call me. Any time!"

"I'm getting very worried about you, sir," Mrs. Cloney said, when I refused more than a cup of tea. "You're not eating anything. Ruin your constitution you will, sir!"

"Don't feel like it, Mrs. Cloney."

"I felt the same when my mother went, sir. I'll frummle me brains, see if I can't think of something tasty for your dinner. I dare's you'll eat something 'fore I leave this house tonight, an' that's *it!*"

I had to smile because she meant it, and upon my soul, that crack in mood, just that sudden unthought smile seemed to make everything rather better. I took the package of papers and spread them on the table. Instantly, I knew that Paul was considerably more advanced than I'd thought. A couple of hours' study and some pencilling convinced me.

I looked through what I'd written, emphasising the geographical and logistic weakness of the Russian scheme, however imaginative, and heard a car arrive. I—rather impatiently—went out and opened the door.

Joel Cawle and Bernard Lane looked at me. A large car held a mattress of frozen snow on its roof.

"We'd like a couple of moments, please," Bernard said, and I opened the door wider. "Sorry to appear like this. We're wordless. But it couldn't wait!"

I led the way into the library.

When they took their coats off I had that porridgy feeling again. Both were pudding-faced and neither smiled or made any attempt at breaking an ice-cap. I'd been at school with both of them, so there were no formalities. Joel put a little grey box on a corner of the desk.

"We'd like you to answer a list of questions," Bernard said, largely. "On the morning of the eighth of this month you turned back at Paris from a flight to London. Why?"

There was no sense in garbling, or denial.

"I'd left an automatic in my hotel," I said. "The second, I was in pain from what I thought was a recurrence of an appendix—er—trouble. I got the automatic, and then I saw Dr. Parnell. I then caught the next flight to London."

Joel tapped his ballpen on the desk and half-smiled.

"I'm glad we got so far," he said, and opened the little box, pressed a button, the lid flew up, and a small projector shone a light on a screen about the size of a sheet of typing paper. First, the manager of the hotel spoke of me, and gave a fair picture of my stay there, including women I'd invited to lunch and dinner and to my room.

Joel switched off.

"How many, altogether?" he asked. "Names, please!"

"I refuse," I said. "My friends are entirely my affair."

Bernard sat back, nodding.

"Let's go on with the film," he said, and Joel pressed the button.

I went absolutely cold to the soles of my feet to see a door open.

I knew that door.

To see ourselves as others see us?

Merely as sweating spectator I saw myself for the first time as others saw me. I didn't like what I saw. I detested that air of god-ism that I've seen so often in others but never thought I'd managed to acquire. I wasn't aware of it. But I could see it. It could be missed in a still photograph. In film it was plain as a pikestaff. When I leapt for the bed, a gigolo in airy twiddle, and tore away the pillow and sat, holding the gun to my face and whispering like a lunatic, I really did wish the floor would open. I've never felt so naked, spiritually or mentally. Never was any being on this earth so consumed with shame.

Light changed, and a woman sat with her back to us, sobbing, speaking in a voice of utmost weariness. I knew she'd been interrogated—a bout of questioning by a team of brutes—for hours until she broke.

I knew the hair, and that suit could only have been Ghislaine's. I'd given her the tweed.

She told of our meeting, what we talked about, what we did, where and when, with dates and times and places. I was simply appalled at the amount of restricted information I'd apparently given her. I knew I hadn't, because some of it was new to me, and it could only have come from the French side. But I hadn't a leg to stand on. The information was correct, so far as I knew. If I hadn't given it to her, where could she have got it? I didn't see her face, but the only time she put a shaking hand to the back of her head in that familiar gesture of hers, I saw that her beautiful nails were short and there were strips of sticking plaster round four of them. I thought of her tenderness, and our quite lovely hours together. Thinking of her being "persuaded" to tell that tale—most of it absolutely untrue—brought on the same berserk fit that had made me want to wreck the airport. I'd have gambled my life that she was truthful to her fingertips, of joyful heart and dear, womanly moods. I was sure she'd been reading her statement, and that was why she had her back to the camera.

Joel turned on the light.

"Well?" he said.

"No need to say anything about the gun episode," I said. "Somebody was extremely clever. But the last part, yes. What she said I told her is quite untrue. I didn't. Those words were put in her mouth. For some reason or other. Who's she working for?"

"Does it matter? What we've just seen is part of her confession. I ask the next question in general fashion because we have a list. Do you know any other women? Most of them aren't worth talking about. Which of them might be?"

I would much rather have cut my throat than mention Tanis.

"I'm very deeply concerned with that statement," I said. "It's not true. I didn't give that information. It's not part of normal conversation. She never asked questions. I'd have been the first to be on guard. She was my friend, let's say, because I could relax in her company."

"All very interesting," Bernard said distantly. "We want to

119

get at specifics. You don't know any woman who might be on this list whose company, let us say, you'd prefer to any other's?"

I knew then that the trap was baited, ready.

"None more than any other," I said.

"Allow me to orient your mind. Joel, switch that second roll on, will you?"

Lights went out, and again the little screen filled with a long shot of the lake, and in the forefront, two mites sitting at a tablecloth, picnicking. The lens zoomed, the figures became larger, larger, until one face filled the screen, hair blown, laughing like an idiot.

Me.

The camera moved, and another head laughed, spitting crumbs.

Tanis.

Then she was walking up the ramp at Zurich Airport, and a man met her.

Me.

Then we were in the car, passing at speed. We went in a hotel. We came out and walked hand in hand. We went back to the hotel. We went into the airport, we talked, and I kissed her hand. I hadn't known the extent of her feeling for me—unless she was the most accomplished actress—but it was so obvious in her manner, in the way she closed her eyes before she turned away.

In that, I shut my eyes in sudden, blinding love of her. Ridiculous, at such a time, to feel so vapidly, some might say. There was nothing vapid about my feeling. I could have killed both those men I'd always thought to be friends of mine, then and there, with my bare hands. And enjoyed it.

"Nothing to tell us?" Joel asked, and switched off. "We've got a dossier here, if you'd like me to read it?"

"Unnecessary. I don't want that girl hurt. That's all."

"She won't be. We don't use force. As you know. Prison's another matter."

"What could you charge her with? Adultery?"

"That's her business, not ours. No. She could be sent to prison as a convicted agent—"

"You're insane!"

Bernard looked at the end of that infernal pencil.

"You'll have to believe us," he said quietly, firmly and I knew too well they had all the evidence they'd require. "We don't play for matches, as you should know. You had long enough to learn. Why not save yourself a great deal of trouble?"

"How?"

They looked at each other, blinked like a couple of hens, and looked point-blank at me.

"Miss Desarbier—that's not her real name—should be here shortly to represent a newspaper at the Birmingham Fair," Joel said—and astonished me—"and you have my word that if you'll work with us, she can leave the country when she wishes. She can move as freely as yourself. If you refuse, we shall have to take other steps."

"Such as?"

"On the testimony you've seen, we could put you in arrest as, let's say, a suspected person. It would take some time for you to clear yourself. Undoubtedly you could. But what would be the inevitable effect?"

"Unpleasant, I should say."

"That's what you have to think about. We require your decision now. Without further discussion. Are you prepared to help us in this matter of an agent known to you as Tanis Desarbier?"

I thought of the children, my name, reputation, career.

I saw Mel among damask roses and lilies-of-the-valley.

In those few seconds, when the air in the room seemed to expand until I thought my head would burst, I thought of everything I was or had been. I had served my country to point of murder in cold blood. I'd parachuted, laid explosive charges, killed and maimed God knows how many. That, and more, most details forgotten. And to be asked by a couple of clerks—I regarded them as nothing more—to betray?

"I've taken my decision," I said. "The answer is no."

Both of them got up. Neither looked at me.

"Very well," Bernard said, and only then I understood that he was in charge. "You may expect to be called during the next day or so. If you reconsider, this is the number."

"There'll be no reconsideration. I refuse to decoy, or to inform. That's all."

I saw them to the door, a couple of prime examples of the type of social order they pretended to defend, impoverished in every sense, anti-individual, pro-herd so long as the animals were of their type, flocked in school-and-college paddocks, kept well away from the hoi polloi whose mites, taken in tax, helped to pay them a wage, called—since the Saxon tongue is laborer's jargon and rude, and Latin more flowery—a salary. A salary for both to indulge a natural bent for dishonesty, not as forthright policemen but as the slyest type of human rat, palliating conscience and relieving self-doubt by describing themselves as of the Secret Service, numbered as clinical exhibits, among other sordid activity, to keep an eye on others wily as themselves, including Tanis.

I couldn't believe she was an agent.

I tried to recall every moment I'd spent with her. I couldn't remember any warning breath, any word or gesture, never a question, and certainly, away from the office I wasn't the one to discuss anything to do with what I did. It was a nasty shock, but unless I was being led up the garden for some reason, I knew they had firm ground for more than suspicion.

But why should I be led up the garden? It was years since I'd had a number in the Service, and only then because of the war. The moment it was over, I was out, sick of it, sick of subterfuge, sick of the worst—because the most subnorm-people I'd ever met.

Glory, laud and honor shone out from two silly words, Secret

Service, which every ass in creation seemed to think was a paradise of demigods, whereas there never existed a more humdrum or cheaper lot of neo-gangsters, putting up with themselves by breathing the same criminal air as any other thief or murderer, the while faking visions of duty, patriotism, a people served, a country protected.

Most was nonsense, some was accident, and the rest was play on the rottenest part of human nature, by blackmail, or subornment by gift of money.

I watched the car go through the gate, and walked through the rhododendrons, looking at leaves dripping the little tears of half-thaw, wondering whether to resign then and there, or go on a little longer. Resignation might well bring instant arrest. For the moment, at least, my official position was defence of a kind. But I was far from safe, and I knew I must warn Tanis.

Frederick turned into the lane and I pulled myself together.

"Hullo, Dads. Couldn't get down before. Just been to the church. Beautiful!"

The boy couldn't finish.

"Come on," I said. "Let's have a good walk. Get some of this out of our systems. Not a bit of use acting like a couple of dishrags!"

He nodded, sniffed, used his handkerchief, turning with me.

"You were always the tough one, Dads," he said. "One reason I admire you. You're never rushed. Never moved. Or knocked over. I think I've got more of Mums. She'd cry over a hurt dog. Or trampled plants. Remember that time Mills' pigs got in the garden and made a mess of her spring flowers? She cried all day. Poor Mums. I didn't know how I'd miss her. Took her as part of the furniture. What I'd give to put my arms round her!"

One has to listen, and the knife goes deeper with every word. In that cold wind, in the whisper of brown briars, we talked of her, only of her, and sometimes I didn't hear him, and he didn't hear me, but we never repeated what we'd said that the winds had taken, never turned to look at each other.

123

It was almost dark when we got back. But that short walk had done us both a lot of good. We could talk in a normal voice.

Outside the house he looked at his watch.

"I'm going to catch that six-ten slow. I can work tonight. By the way, Patti flew back last night. She's seen Mr. Gilman. Dads, I asked her to come down with me. She wasn't up to it. Poor old Pats. She's completely smashed. I wish you'd go and see her?"

"I can't go tonight. Where is she?"

"The Savonia. She's got a suite."

"I wish you'd ask her to come home. She's got to come for the funeral, anyway."

"No. She won't. She says she can't. She'll wait till after, and go back to Wepo."

"Wepo?"

"Her husband, Dad, I don't want to hurt you. But I shan't be there either. Churchyards and cemeteries are beyond me. I'd rather remember her as she was!"

I don't think I've ever disbelieved my ears before.

I looked at him, palish in the dusk, even beginning to wonder if he were really my son, the Frederick I'd rolled on the lawn, taught to use bat and ball, ridden with, followed beagles, taken to Paris for dinners, watched grow up, been proud of, this tall good-looking young man, tenth generation Trothe, within a few years of taking my place in the house behind us.

He seemed to sense that if he came near me I'd knock him down.

He stood away, putting his hands deep in his overcoat pockets.

"Goodnight, Dads," he said, backing off, sounding relieved, almost cheerful. "I'll tell Patti. Sorry if we're a disappointment. But that's how it is!"

He walked off, a long stride. I couldn't see him in tree shadow and the night.

I tried to see Mel. I wanted to hear what she might say. I heard no more than the sough of the elms she'd loved.

124

Suddenly I didn't give a damn about the children, those selfish little brutes I'd helped to pamper. On the way back to the house I was quite sure I'd never again give either of them a second thought. Curiously, I'd often wondered how Victorian fathers could have sent their errant children into the street without a qualm.

It was almost a satisfaction, now, to know exactly how, and to agree there was no other way.

But I wasn't altogether certain that my righteous mood would last.

Mrs. Cloney almost ran out of the front door.

"Miss Roule, sir, very important for Mr. Lane, sir!"

I went through the hall to the shadowy niche, lifted the receiver.

"Miss Roule? I'm sorry but Mr. Lane's just gone—"

"Oh, Mr. Trothe—"

"If it's very important I can have the car stopped somewhere—"

"Well, sir—I'm awfully afraid it is—there's a message from Scotland Yard—"

"—yes?"

"Sir, the coded message is that Mr. Terence Ebbleton has committed suicide. The Glasgow Police sent in to say Mr. Lane should be warned there's an inquest tomorrow at eleven o'clock. Could you please let me know if you managed to reach him?"

16

Mel's funeral had to be walked white in a whirling snowstorm that made all of us anonymous, and blew the vicar's voice into a turgid echo. The earth I picked up was frozen. It wouldn't crumble and I didn't hear it fall. It seemed impossible to say a final goodbye in such a heartless rite, but that's the way we treat ourselves.

What a lugubrious lot!

I was sure, walking back, that my two were right to have stayed away. I wished I had, but I hadn't the moral courage. Mel would have hated it just as I hated it for both of us. Left to myself I'd have ordered cremation. Before Pamela had been called to Glasgow to hear about her estate, we'd had something of a discussion about it. But what *is* the use of arguing with a Grandmother Scoones in drear drone about the place, and a Pamela, never less than slightly drunk, wearing weeds even in the house, both in open-mouthed horror at the bare notion? I didn't waste time in trying to convince a couple of dyed-in-the-wool nihils, who fear any mention of death, hate the idea of the grave, and can't bear the thought of being burned before their time. I let it go when Pamela accused me of wanting to "get rid of" poor darlin' Mel. I told the pair of them for God's sake to keep out of my way, and went up to my room.

Anyway, we got back frozen, Grandmother Scoones and I, and I must say the old lady at seventy-something trod the snow-banks without a whimper and thanked me for my arm when we reached the blessed warmth of the house. Mrs. Cloney brought in coffee and brandy, which picked things up for the moment. Several people came back, which was kind of them, but I didn't talk. Anything said to me I ignored. Not rudely, I hope, but I hadn't the heart or mind. The telephone never stopped ringing. Mrs. Cloney or somebody answered. People who hadn't been able to attend gave excuses, roads blocked, ice, snow, whatever. I wasn't listening. I went up to my room, took one of Dr. Norris' blackout pills, and woke next morning. I tried to eat breakfast, felt wretched, took half a pill, and slept again.

At a little after midday the bedside telephone rang.

"Edmund, sorry," Mrs. Scoones said. "I think you might want to speak to a Miss Roule? It's on the study line."

"I'll come down. Thank you."

"Sir, the Lord Blercgrove presents his compliments, and if at all possible would like to see you at eleven o'clock"—the squeak came over distance—"that is, tomorrow morning."

It was exactly like coming to life.

"I believe I can manage it. Thank you, Miss Roule. Goodbye!"

Mrs. Scoones was looking at me.

"I suppose you intend to marry again, do you?" she asked me, moving hooked thumbs in her lap almost as if she were shuffling cards. "Poor Mel, y'know. I was always sure she'd go before me. Never very strong. Like her father. Turned rather funny and went off. Edmund, why weren't the children here?"

A little shaky at the end.

"Preferred not, perhaps?"

"Why wasn't—why wasn't anybody invited to Patti's wedding?"

"Rather a sudden business."

"You didn't know about it?"

"Until Frederick told me, no."

"I can't look any of my friends in the face. How could she go off like that?"

"She's of age."

"While her Mummy was dying?"

127

"She didn't know. I didn't. Nobody did."

"I've cut her off. She won't get a penny!"

"She'll have enough."

"I'm terribly glad Mel didn't know."

"So am I."

"Even Frederick. Her favorite!"

"I wasn't aware of that?"

"Of course. He'll get nothing, either. I'm leaving everything to Pamela!"

"Good!"

"I think you always gave them too much of an idea of themselves."

"Rather better than too little."

"They never knew where they were. Went off on their own."

"Their privilege. I've no doubt they'll do very well."

"Patricia, married to a black?"

"He married a white."

I amazed myself. I was defending the children. It was then that I began to think, or tried to, about them both and of my responsibility. I couldn't see that I'd been a bad parent. They'd had what I thought was a normal childhood. They'd always seemed healthy, at times a boisterous pair, went off quite happily to school, did well enough to make their report cards an agreeable surprise each term, and an excellent excuse for a family party and special presents.

It wasn't any use blaming the "modern" generation. Frederick and Patti were "modern" in that sense, wore what I thought were curious clothes and Frederick let his back hair run over his collar and generally seemed ungroomed. I'd never been like that. I wouldn't at his age have been allowed to. But we gave them a lot of personal freedom to prepare themselves for the very different world in front of them. As Mel said—having been to a couple of lectures, one of them, I remember, called Whither, Youth?—give them a chance to know and contend with their own time and the people they'd have to grow up with, and, as it were, in the hurly-burly of their youthful day, round off the disciplines, moral or social we both thought we'd been successful in teaching.

Well, Patti had married a Negro, wealthy or not, and Frederick had borrowed a large sum of money without telling me, and bought a car I knew nothing about. Both were minus a personal sense of honor—what, exactly, was a sense of honor? I knew, of course, but I'm hanged if I could explain it—(and had our conduct been any less dishonorable at times? There was more than excuse for Mel. I had none)—or had they, in the past few years of sharpening senses against the wit of their own age, seen what was going on and taken a leaf out of our book? I was damned if I knew, and even if I had the answer it was too late.

Late.

Horrible word.

17

I got in purposely early and put Miss Roule to work. She had sisters, not of blood but of bond, in most departments, and in an hour I had a pad of notes covering all that was known of Tanis and the paper she was working for. It turned out to be capitalized from East Germany and gave a distinctly Communist twist to the news, something I hadn't realised since I'd never read it. There were sparse details of her family, a mother, and three brothers, the eldest a professor of law, the second a currency exchange operator, and the youngest a travel agent, all without a dossier, harmless. A paragraph each described her acquaintanceship with Lord Imbrett when he was knightly Sir Ronald Hinter and Lord Blercgrove when he was unctuous Sir Tristram Kells. Those two reports should have warned me, but didn't. Obviously she'd been quite a girl when most of her age were still in school. One report was signed by Paul, which startled me. M.I. files, of course, were not available, and that was a pity, because I was hoodwinked by a report that the name Desarbier was that of her mother's second husband, and before that marriage she'd called herself by her maiden name of Svertlov. I should have dug a little deeper. Tanis had told me her father was French. Certainly she spoke French as a Frenchwoman. For that matter she also spoke German, English and Italian fluently, beautifully, though I wasn't surprised since all foreigners are supposed to. I don't know why we're not.

But there was still one of those Little Men whispering at the back of my mind.

Who—if anybody—was she working for? What did they expect to get from me? Well, of course, there are times when we're all, I suppose, elementarily dull. At that time, I was. Because I was in love, and blind. Pity I couldn't have got somebody to boot me into sanity. Even Mel's death had done nothing.

Yorick helped. His lanky stroll bowlegged down that green length of carpet in the late afternoon, giving me a tuneless *hollo!* when he saw me, and quickening his step.

"Rather like calling yoo-hoo across the prairie somewhere," he said, and turned to nod down the corridor. "I wet the end up there and dropped in a few seeds. Dashed if they didn't sprout. I'm thinking of trying a few packets. Brighten the joint, what?"

"Enough daisies about the place now. Listen to me, Errol. Were you with the department when the Blur was rather sweet on that little Hungarian thing? She left a book of hers in the debris. I'd like to return it."

"But most of us knew her," he said, in an entirely different voice. "I took some of the Blur's notes to her. As office-boy-in-chief. He might have got shopped over her. Except that somebody dropped a hint to Lady Blercgrove. She almost steamed him open. That's when he came back to London. La Goulasch went back to Budapest, I heard. Most dangerous harpy in the business!"

"Which business?"

He looked sideways at me with that expression of faintly surprised amusement.

"Now, Edmund!" he chided, from behind the hand pretending to scratch the tip of his nose. "I was questioned by our people, I remember. I didn't know anything. I make it a point not to. But I've since heard she's really poisonous. I think I'd burn that book if I were you. Forgive my saying so?"

I knew I was being warned, but again, it wasn't the time to ask questions. He called most of us by our Christian names because of his social position, perhaps, but mostly because he hadn't a particle of respect for the Machine or those who tried to

make it work. His information came, I supposed, from the din-
ner-table chatter of his father, the Lord Imbrett, a large cog in
the depths of the Central Office of the Party, and none better
informed about the events of the day. I'd met him both at his
desk—a real tiger—years ago, and latterly at dinner parties,
though all we'd talked about was Yorick.

"Of course, there isn't a more exasperating oaf in human ken,"
he'd told me, the last time. "And since he's my son, I get the
blame. Really, sometimes his mother looks at me as if it were
my fault. But after all, his grandfather—ah—on *her* side, of
course!—was a raving blob. Fellow simply gibbered. Why look
at me?"

There was rather more to it than that. Some I'd known made
it their business to appear half-wits in order to delude or lull.
They were always the most dangerous people to get on the
wrong side of, and it was so easily done, a word, a look, a tone
of voice not to their liking. They were part of the Management,
a small caucus ruling over the Establishment, that nexus of
families in solid walling of the Crown, at once their demiurge
and protector, and only reason for their existence. I was a little
different. I knew my place as Small Gentry. I had property
that had been part of my family for more than three hundred
years, same place, same name. Some of us died with this or that
royal bully, others died with Cromwell, or lived with him and
managed to hang on to the property when he died, that warty
puritan, or earned a right by the sword when the second
Charles came back. But however deep those roots, I was no
match for the Establishment, still less for the Management. I
could be ruined by a word in the right place, especially in view
of my official position. I could be relegated without hope of
appeal. I had to be careful. The Blur was part of the Caucus,
the Power behind Power—as Paul always called him—and he
was merciless.

It had always interested me that such a personality, at risk
of name and reputation, could go heels-over-head for a pretty

face. But I had only to look at myself. It had never entered my mind that Tanis could be anything but what she'd told me she was.

In those moments of walking beside Yorick I knew I was hanging by my fingertips from a cliff edge. One wrong move, and that would be that. I knew it better than anyone could tell me.

Yet I couldn't seem to give a damn.

That heat, of a simply vicious passion broke through everything, swept down any other thought, made all other considerations into so many static shadows. I was prepared to suffer loss of any description for one more glorious meeting with her. Without hesitation I'd have sold myself to the Devil only for that. Absurd, yes, but fact. I had to face it. For the first time in my life I was in love, late, but the years only seemed to have gathered brighter coals, and I burned, burned inwardly, burned in the head, in my soul I seemed to burn, and her name burned my throat in the sigh that tore from me without volition, despite all attempt at control.

I was in gravest danger of making more than a fool of myself.

And I didn't care.

"Well, here we are," Yorick said, outside my office. "I've sometimes nuzzled the thought of occupying the throne in there. Often wondered how it'd be if I were you. In command. Beastliest mess that ever was, I suppose. I'm not cut out for it. Not cut out for anything. Just cut out, that's all. Miserable thought, what?"

"Cheer up. I'll see what I can do!"

He nodded, turning away.

"Do get rid of that book, Edmund," he said.

I went into the office, and Miss Roule held up a slip.

"Call from a Mr. Von Hoffenden, or something, sir. I couldn't quite get it. I could barely understand him. It was a local call, sir. And your appointment's in six minutes!"

My hackles jagged above my collar in peaks that seemed to have the height and weight of icy mountains.

Von Hollefendorm came into mind clear as in the moment I'd shot him. I did it in cold blood, my fifth, I think. A very handsome, fair-to-gingery fellow, about thirty, and I'd caught him in his library outside Oran. He'd been interfering with our submarine net across the Straits of Gibraltar, or something of the sort, and I'd wrecked an enormous radio station at the top of the house. Anyway, I never forgot his eyes. He knew me, of course. We'd been at school together, though he'd been slightly my senior.

"Please, Trothe, God help me. My wife's got a child coming. There're three in the—"

That was all. In cold blood, on duty, by direct order. In this day, unbelievable. But true. And would I do it again? But of course. And as a matter of course, were it given as a duty.

Discipline can only be sacrosanct. Without it, chaos.

But it also applies to others, to the enemy. Then what? Kill, or be killed? But it's not a Christian concept. There's nothing Christian about killing. For any reason. I'd never thought much about it before. But in those moments, I had to wonder if killing in the service of one's country as part of duty can be ignored in the face of the Second Commandment. It was an old theme, argued over the generations, but a time comes when each man has to find an answer for himself. I didn't have one. Was I merely a lip-service Christian? Was churchgoing only an outworn form of social activity? Were the children correct?

I gave Miss Roule the paper.

"Pass that to Security. Urgent!"

18

I could see about two yards in front of me over to the Blur's office, and groaned to think of the journey home. He looked not tired so much as harassed, red-eyed, and in shirtsleeves—which was unusual, I thought—and from the pile of files spread over that at-any-other-time desert of polish, his desk, he seemed to have been doing a little work.

"Hullo, Trothe. Please do sit down. I hope you got our note?"

"Thank you—"

"Not a bit. We tried, but the roads were hopeless. Best we could do was Thursday evening. You weren't available. I was surprised to see so many Russians there!"

"All the eastern Embassies. She had any number of friends. One of the few they could all talk to."

"It's a profound loss of most helpful influence. I don't think many of us realise what extraordinary power good women have. However."

He looked at a report sheet.

"Bernard sent me the inquest summary," he said, half-smiling. "So they had a good try, did they?"

"If Colethorne hadn't come along, it might have been on target!"

"Unfortunately, it's somebody we don't know. They're trying to trace him. I believe some of us'll have to be very careful for a long time. It's a nuisance!"

"I think I'll close the house. Stay in London."

"Might be a good move. But you'll have to be armed. I told Bernard to see to it."

I didn't think it worthwhile mentioning my little friend.

He waved at the desk.

"I've been collating available information," he said, almost reluctantly. "Things have happened. When we last talked, I wasn't quite sure what we were up against. Since then we've had this fellow Ebbleton to talk to. He was most useful. Up to a point. Unfortunately he used his shirt to strangle himself. It's pretty well certain he was working for the East Germans, though his agency here worked for Soviet and Chinese export. Why that sort of man does *what* he does really defies analysis. He could have made a fortune—did, in fact—privately, by sticking to common or garden business. He chose to mix it up with espionage. But then we have a further complication."

He chose a green file and untied the tape, put on half-moon spectacles, and began to read.

"About nine years ago, on a visit to my mother in Regsmund, we—my younger brother, my sister, and myself—were asked to join the Brotherhood of Veteran Fighters Number 43, in memory of our father. We agreed, and we were installed with great ceremony. My older brother and my mother refused. We found it was considered a great honor. Membership was a social cachet. When we went back for Christmas, it was six or seven years ago, I think, we attended a New Year meeting. We were told of plans to make all the brotherhoods into a political party to fight the next election, first in the state and then in the nation. We would represent the new Germany, new ideas, new everything. I was asked to stand. Sigmund, my younger brother, has political flair. He went on the planning council to attract the younger generation. We were not to make the mistakes of the old Nazi party. We wanted a united Germany within the old boundaries. Our nuclear scientists would make us the first power in Europe. After all, we helped the French to achieve nuclear parity. We wanted all foreign troops out of our country. They had been useful in spending their money. We didn't need it any more. We wanted to be ourselves. It sounded good. But I had a better job. My sister, Bernice, was also tempted. But then she was too young. There is nothing I wish to say about her. I cannot answer your question. About myself, yes. Let me see, now. We would, of course, in a few years, command the Common Market. We are more people, we work harder, we produce more than the French. The Italians offer more competition. They have brains. But we would command. At that meeting we were told of this plan to punish those responsible for the death or imprisonment of our brothers for the extermination of the Jews. I say what I say. I make no explanation. I don't know any names. I was a member of a table. Each of us had a number. We accepted the responsibility for punishing the accusers and witnesses. My table was given Mr. Edmund Trothe. At that time I didn't know him. Yes, we had many Communists. Supposed. East Germany has many Communists. Supposed. When we have one country, we have no Communists, supposed or not. Trothe, yes. We knew about him. All details. The exact way to deal with these people had to be agreed. Each one at the table had to do something. We paid our own expenses. If the kill came off, the money would be paid back to us by the committee. Many have been successful. Trothe was difficult. He lived in the country, not in London. He worked in Switzerland, and that's more difficult. The Swiss Police are ultra-efficient. We could not afford suspicion. We found that the sister of Mr. Trothe's wife worked in the library of the United Nations in New York. I often went there on business. It was simple to get a letter of introduction. We met and I found her an excellent partner. At this time I was transferred to the London agency. No, I was in charge of the legal and financial side. A little later she moved to Paris. We were married that Easter at Le Touquet. I was already married, yes. But a domestic life is always more comfortable. In any case my children are provided for. I met Mr. Trothe. It was always impossible for me to talk to him. It was not easy to earn the

confidence of Mrs. Trothe. I gave her reports of his friendship
with women in Geneva. At that time, Mr. Trothe was living
there. I worked closer with Mrs. Trothe. She had not the simple
character of my wife. I met his son and daughter and often
entertained them. Well, to lunch. At special times to dinner and
the theatre. Well, as I say, we move carefully. There could never
be suspicion. In this period I thought I could make a better life
for myself in Canada. I began to make a large account there.
Then Mrs. Trothe became unwell. I gave her drugs. I also gave
drugs to her son. At first benzedrine. After, others stronger. Mrs.
Trothe told me she must go into a hospital. I said the illness
could be cured without that. At the end I knew she would die.
She knew it also. She was not afraid. She was English. It is
enough to say. I promised I would help her children. It was my
part to ruin Mr. Trothe. I could have done it, but I had to use
his money to bring myself out of a commercial disaster. His
lawyers worked too quickly. I had to pay back to be free again.
But what I did is known to my superiors. It will not be forgiven.
I have failed. I sometimes wonder if we do not live for nothing.
I do not wish to say more. Signed."

He threw the file on the desk and walked to the window.

"I wouldn't pay the slightest attention to that nonsense about
Melisande and your children," he said, and took off his glasses.
"That type of creature always thrashes about to make all the
trouble it can. As to the rest, it's not much, but I think startlingly
enough. How are we—any of us—to defend ourselves? These
people can come in the country at any time as tourists. They
can work here. They can scout, make plans, take all the time
they want. Quite unknown to us. There's no hurry. The patient
massing of detail appeals to that type of mind. Suddenly, when
it's least expected, the *coup*. A new form of sport. Man-killing.
In perfect accord with our time. Can't get our sights on any of
them. Except, of course, we have a clear lead in Regsmund."

"But why did he confess so much? Surely, his best line was to
say nothing. Make us prove the charge!"

138

"And if we did, he'd get thirty years. In this statement he lays himself open to five or six. With remissions, possibly three or four. And if he gave us the other information we wanted, a few weeks or months. We use our advantages, too, you know!"

"I'm very worried about that drug business!"

He made the slightest grimace of distaste and stuck a fore-finger down his collar to set his tie.

"Take no notice, Trothe!" he said, up at the ceiling. "You've had enough experience, heaven knows. They'll do all the harm they can. They rely upon the credulity of the hopelessly medi-ocre. It's the mediocrities, you know, who govern the world in these days. They have the votes!"

"Again, whether I'm solid concrete north of the septum, or not, but what's this ex-Nazi business got to do with espionage?"

The Blur put his jacket on, arranged his tie, and turned to me.

"It's something I'm trying to decide," he said, and nodded at the piled desk. "That's what I've been going over today. As I see it, and it's based on what's known, these three were Communists at their university. When they got their degrees, they went directly into East German intelligence. After all, for youngsters it was a very good life. They went at odd times to China, Russia, Cuba, the United States, here, all over the show. They each spoke at least six languages. Their only religion was implicit in the Communist manifesto. Their only apostles Hegel, Marx, Lenin, Stalin, Mao Tse-tung and others equally drab. I don't think it can ever have occurred to them that their father was anything *but* a prole. He was by genealogy an aristocrat, a captain in the German Navy, which was never by tradition less strict than our own in choice of personnel. I find it quite dispiriting that so many young people like this are poisoned through and through by long outdated, and in these days in-senate theory!"

At any other time I suppose I'd have been amused by the arch-Tory permitting himself the luxury of a few moments' soap-boxism. But I didn't feel like it. I couldn't bear to think of Mel, or of my crass—where it wasn't criminal—stupidity.

I was getting more of what I deserved.

Suddenly, and for no particular reason I could readily have given, I hoisted myself out of a steaming marsh of self-pity or self-denigration—it didn't matter any more—and nodded at the files spread over the desk.

"I don't give a damn who they're after," I said. "But a recrudescence of Nazism? I don't want my son throwing six years of his life away as I had to. Why hasn't there been any warning about this?"

"Oh, but there's been plenty. Most people are rather tired of it. Same old Germans doing the same old thing? In many ways I'm reminded of 1938, and on. We didn't do anything then. We can do far less now. You can't stop people from joining a beer club, or forming a political party. It's a free country."

"Because of us and equally forgotten Uncle Sam!"

"All long buried. Our task now is to single out these people and put them out of business. Regsmund could be a start. One or two out the way could be a warning to the rest!"

"What's the form?"

He walked round the desk and sat with great deliberation in the chair, spread his hands, looking up from them to me. I'd never before realised that he had possibly the palest and most disagreeably granitic eyes I'd ever seen, until he smiled.

"You see, Trothe, we're not on solid ground," he said. "As I see it, the matter falls into two distinct compartments. Is this idea of killing off those of us named in court proceedings a purely local ex-Nazi affair? Or has the idea been borrowed to be exploited by one or other, or a combination of iron-curtain intelligence agencies? If it's the first, then we're dealing with amateurs, gifted, perhaps, and we can erase with minimum fuss. If it's the other, then we're up against a far more serious enemy. We have to find out which. I suggest we'd have to begin in Regsmund. We already have an agent there. What we need is somebody of wide experience at the top. Bernard Lane's been handling it. He's done very well, but he's too young to have tasted blood. The only man I know, in whom I'd repose the slightest confidence, would be yourself. You also have a personal interest!"

"I don't like to think of myself as *revanchiste*," I said. "But I suppose that's inherent in a thought of my wife."

"You might also take into consideration your children. They're not immune, as you've just heard!"

"Does any particular plan suggest itself?"

The Blur took a black leather notebook out of the middle drawer of his desk.

"At the moment, no," he said. "We must appreciate that we don't know who exactly the enemy is. But 'they' know us. We can't disguise ourselves. I can't become somebody else or go anywhere else. We don't want to alert them in any way. What we've got to do is to pretend to plod on. Good old British muddle, and so on. You're in a different position—I hasten to add—not in spheres of substance or dignity. You could take a month's leave of absence. In view of recent tragedy, not unexpected. But is it enough? I mean, if you're going to accept this assignment?"

But I'd been thinking of Patti and Frederick. A thought of anything happening to them, unlikely though it might seem, brought that cringe of the spirit.

"I've got a better idea," I said. "My physician will prescribe a stay in a nursing home. Incommunicado. From time to time he'll visit me. Carry back discreetly dire tales. They'll be repeated."

He was looking impish.

"I'll have you transferred in the most abject circumstances. Then what?"

"Then I shall go to Regsmund. Start life as a slightly deranged odd-job repairman with expert knowledge of radio and TV. Well up my street. Have you any suggestions beyond Bernard and Joel as assistants? I could name a right-hand?"

"Errol Hinter, of course," his lordship said, without hesitation. "Certainly. He has the requisite command of German. You'll need somebody to collate reports, so forth. Very well. When do you begin?"

I stared at the calendar's figures, that hid so much in their nakedness.

"The end of the month'll give me time to put things in order, solicitors and that sort of thing," I said.

"Don't overdo it," the Blur said, at his blandest. "I think the nursing home idea quite sound. You'll write notes to your housekeeper at intervals. Arrange for her keep. Local birthdays, charities, etcetera. Gillian will supervise. She's rather good at that sort of detail. You'll reply by hand to those who signed the book?"

"It's being done."

"You'll acquaint everybody you've, well, more or less, retired to recuperate?"

"Not my idea at all. No. You might have a bulletin sent to Fleet Street. 'Mr. Edmund Trothe, recently so forth and so on, was yesterday taken ill and removed to St. George's Hospital where he passed a comfortable night.' Watch where the enquiries come from. That night I could fly to Hamburg, and on to Regsmund."

"I'll have the papers in order," the Blur said, writing. "Passport?"

"I have some documents I've used before. I shall be Simeon Rotbart Eck. I can prove my ancestry. I can meet, if necessary, any or all the members of the family and bamboozle them that I was a prisoner in Russia. I speak fair Russian with a German accent. I'll shave my head, clip my eyebrows, wear steel spectacles, and grow a moustache, with a small beard, not an imperial, but something of that kind. You will please arrange a tattooist to put a number in the right place, together with the symbol against a use of penicillin. I'm allergic. You will please have bought for me the sort of leather bag the superior type of German workman uses. He's always extremely particular, if you've noticed? And a box—not bag—of tools, a wide range of the latest and best, please, not forgetting the meters, oscillographs and whatnot. I repair anything from pocket radios to electric washers, and I'll wire anything from a building to a bomb. What infuriates me is that it's necessary. Jew-baiting and all, they're almost back again!"

The Blur looked up at the window, and I was instantly reminded of a seagull, beak in the breeze, scenting.

"Depressing, I agree," he said, incisive with distaste. "We're not what we were. Not what our fathers were. Simply the catsmeat of what's left!"

The box buzzed and Miss Tulliver's clear voice announced Sir Herbert Tate.

"All right, Trothe," the Blur said, with a slight wrinkle of the eyes to suggest a smile. "Miss Tulliver will arrange a further meeting, d'you see?"

"A Mr. Gilman called across the road and they put him on downstairs, Mr. Trothe," Miss Tulliver said in the anteroom. "Could you please call his office. It's urgent!"

She gestured to the telephone but I had a better idea.

"Thank you. I'll take it outside!"

"And a call from Miss Roule, sir—"

I used the inter-office line.

"Oh, Mr. Trothe! Miss Furnival wondered if she might speak to you—"

"Certainly. Is she in London?"

"She's here, sir!"

"Then could she meet me in the Ladies' Annex of my club at seven o'clock?"

A moment's pause.

"Perfect, sir. Thank you!"

19

A taxi with oil lamps came by and I pointed the way to the club. It was still foggy and I asked him to wait. Oil lamps pierced better than electrics.

The waiter looked a little strange when I ordered tea, and I sat in the comfortable phone booth and called Gilman.

"Trothe? Thank heaven you managed it! The police have been on to me. They'd called Mrs. Cloney. She put them on to Dr. Norris—"

"Yes?—"

"Frederick. He's in serious trouble. He and a party of friends were down at Ribbett's Lock, on the Thames. About three this morning, one of the girls in the party telephoned her father, and he got on to the police. The girl was in a nervous collapse. The rest of the party, half a dozen or so girls and four or five chaps, including Frederick, had taken a drug—"

"Taken a what?"

"A drug, called LSD. The police surgeon sent them all to Kingslake Hospital and they're there now. One of the girls is daughter of a Cabinet Minister. The fathers are all something important. Extremely grave matter!"

"What do you advise?"

"My partner's just come back. He fears we shan't be able to evade prosecution. I'm profoundly sorry. Could you possibly go there tonight? If the police are there, you might be able to do at least something to help him?"

"Thank you. I'll be there as soon as this fog'll let me."

144

One of the nicest things about living, I've always thought, is the accident of surprise.

It pulls one out of the rut if only for a moment, though there's nothing wrong with the rut. It's necessary for the sake of order, discipline, duty. I've had my own rut marked for me I suppose since I was born. I was trained in what to do and how it must be done, encouraged to do better, found that I liked it, went on doing it and still am. Or trying to. I'd always thought I'd done exactly the same with Frederick. He was born in the same room, in the same house, went to the same schools, the same university, and had—I'd hoped—everything I'd had, plus the extraordinary technical benefits of the past twenty years.

Then how the devil could a sensible fellow with two good scholarships, and an excellent sportsman—he had a tableful of cups in the dining room—how could he become mixed up in this drug business? Intelligence must have told him it was criminal. That alone should have been enough. As for the others of "good" family, I didn't know what to think. I told Consuelo in the lounge. She was there on the dot. She didn't look at all shocked.

"I smoked opium," she said. "Thought it was terribly wicked and 'advanced,' poor little me. I was sicker than a cat. It cured me. I did it for bravado. I was challenged, and that's all this is. Probably!"

The waiter came to bend over me.

"A Mr. Colethorne presents his compliments, sir. From the office!"

I excused myself, and went out to the hall. Mr. Colethorne really startled me. No longer the newspaper seller. Smart, barbered, and a straight, unsmiling eye. He gave me a package.

"Mr. Oram sent this, Mr. Trothe. Would you please sign this receipt?"

I signed, and watched the bowler jaunt down the steps into darkening mist. The package was heavyish. I took it into the cloakroom, making sure I was alone. Wrappings of oilpaper and

145

thick tape took minutes to strip. Out came a blue flannel bag stitched at the edges, shaped for the deadliest handful I've ever hefted, a superb example of the gunsmith's art, of a type I'd never seen before. The small boy who'd always loved guns came alive. I itched to use it. The firing range was just downstairs. I went down the flight, switched the lights on, wound a target down, slipped in a clip of twelve small, nubby bullets that looked harmless, childish, in fact, and fired. The first shot took the entire bull out of the card. What it would do to a human being I could only guess. I fired again at the remaining left corner. It flew in bits. I became aware that it had almost no sound at all. I fired again to make sure. A kitten's sneeze had much in common.

I don't know why, but I went back to Consuelo feeling far happier. We took the waiting taxi, and I was thankful because those oil lamps with magnifiers got us along much faster than the white moil of electrics crawling beside us. I must have sounded like a real old fogey bugling off on the way down, and when, at last, we got to the hospital.

"Depressing business," the physician told me. "We're not very well up in LSD. Causes mental disturbance, we know. Often with very serious aftereffects. We've done a lot of cabling to hospitals in the United States. They've had more experience. This is the first time most of us have seen a case. One of them's a medical student. Sorry about that. Should have known better!"

"Are they really ill?"

"Physically, no. They'll have the most horrendous dreams. Bad go. Especially for the girls!"

"Where could they get this stuff?"

"The medical student's under suspicion. It's not easily come by, I can tell you that. Enough of a dose for all of them'd cost the earth. One of the Africans had a lot of money on him. Would you care to take charge of your son's personal possessions? Might be as well. The police haven't impounded, yet!"

"Will they?"

"Waiting till they get word from us that they're awake. Then they'll be charged. Drug Squad. Scotland Yard job. We're expecting a sergeant and a matron any moment!"

"May I see him?"

"Just going up. He won't wake till some time later tonight or tomorrow. That's when he'll feel it most."

We got out of the lift and walked down a quiet corridor to a long room. A nurse sat under a green lampshade reading a paper, and got up, but the doctor shook his head. Frederick was second of a row of five, all with their mouths open, all of them double-belted to the bed.

"They've been extremely violent," the doctor said, in a normal tone that sounded like a bellow in a vault. "It's all right. Fifty car horns wouldn't wake them. Their temperatures are dropping, I'm very glad to see. No change?"

"No, Doctor. This patient had a nosebleed a few minutes ago. I think he punched himself. They were all struggling about for a time. But they don't make a sound. It's giving me goose pimples!"

In fact, that's what they gave me. They looked dead. Waxen. Frederick reminded me horribly of Mel. I hadn't realised he was so like her. Suddenly I wanted to put my arms around him, that warm little chap of those few years ago, dragging himself up on my knee for a bedtime story, often a little nuisance though he generally got what he wanted. An infant voice singing Puff, The Magic Dragon came back to me in heartrending memory. I thought of Patti.

In sudden surge of a curious type of sickness that made my legs weak, I turned away from those shapes, away from a green lamp, the dry complaint of a newspaper, the chiaroscuro which shadowed my son whom I couldn't help.

But what can a father do? There's no control over a young man who insists on ganging his ain gait into a midden.

"Doing fairly well, so far," the doctor said, out in the corridor. "Now I've got to look at the girls. Far more pathetic!"

"Why?"

"More delicate. Less chance of picking up. We've got into the habit of treating girls as hobbledehoys, comrades, all that sort of rot. They're not, y'know. They have a limit."

"Difficult to see sometimes."

"Poor little things try to do everything the lads do. They rarely try to do what they're best at. Insisting on it. They don't. It's not I-yi. Poor little bitches!"

"Don't what?"

We were waiting for the lift. I saw him for the first time, black tufty hair, recondite—no other word for brown eyes so probing, knowing—a true physician's eyes—and the pale complexion of an athlete, not pallid but minus the apples of false health.

"Don't insist on being women," he said. "They carry the cradle of birth. They're not taught so. We've become such effete pricks, they haven't any difficulty in keeping up with us. It's our fault. We nip into bed now and again, we squirt our brains out? That's only using what we're given. The girls nip in, too. They're using what they have. Apart from that, what are we? Lumpfish!"

In the ward office he unlocked a steel cupboard and took an envelope from the shelf.

"He's got a suit, an overcoat, hat, underwear in Matron's store," he read, from a list. "Everything was checked by the night sister, pending a decision where to move them. The only reason you're taking this, he's a minor. You're his father. Just look at that packet. With the pink band. That's amphetamine. The one with the blue's a type of benzedrine. Not the sort of thing to be carrying about. And amphetamine's dangerous. Any idea where he got them?"

"None!"

"I'd destroy both, if I were you. Just tap it down the sink, over there. Tear up the paper!"

148

I rattled the pellets down the brass O and turned the water in a splash. I lit a match to burn the wrappings.

"Some swine make a good living out of peddling, you know," he said. "I feel sorry for kids hung on it."

"Was he?"

He shrugged, nodding at where we'd come from.

"He's not there by accident. Doesn't take long to make an addict. You had no idea?"

"Of course not!"

But I had a very distinct idea. In the wallet, among club vouchers, a season ticket, notes from Adela, Inky and yur U, a card, Terence Ebbleton and a telephone number. On the back in a scrawl *The Dorchester, 9, Friday.*

"If he's an addict, what treatment would he require?"

"See any doctor!"

"Any?"

"Advice isn't my business!"

"Are you very popular here?" I asked him.

He looked at me with a sideways half-smile.

"Extremely so," he said. "That's why I'm on night duty. Mind if I leave you? The girls are upstairs."

I went back to Consuelo, shocked to find her talking to a police sergeant.

"Question of a car," she said. "Frederick!"

"You his father, sir?" the sergeant said, and looked at a note-book. "The car found at this address is reported missing. It's in the name of Frederick Onslow Trothe. Not insured, not—"

"Missing from where?"

"The garage it was supposed to be picked up at by the agency. Car's here. I came to get a statement—"

"I know nothing of any car. "I've got to get back to London. Goodnight!"

Out we went, and Consuelo couldn't hide surprise. It was easier to go through London rather than make a wide turn west. The night was more smoky than foggy. I couldn't find a word to

149

say. I could see that little boy—curious, I couldn't see him as a man—being sent down from his university for a civil conviction. I *could* see Mr. Ebbleton's twinkling grey eye.

Ruin.

Consuelo sat away from me, little fingernail between her teeth. I didn't want her to feel sorry for me, or condemn Frederick.

"I expect we've been followed," I said. "They're pretty certain to report my movements. Routine check, that's all!"

"For myself, I don't care."

"I'm glad you're with me!"

But there was more than that, and she knew it, and smiled and looked away.

"I'm glad too," she said, to the lights swinging past. "I'll do anything for you. Anything. You believe that, don't you?"

I looked at her.

It's difficult in these days, when it's too often apparent that the fabric of at least part of our society is rotten with spies, agents and liars of one type or another, to trust any human being for any reason.

But I knew as I looked at her that I'd found a woman, and a beautiful woman, direct in principle, incapable of deceit, contemptuous of lying.

"Yes," I said.

I couldn't have said a word more if I'd been paid. I sat back, pretended to doze.

But the mind was very much at work. That I could think coldly about Frederick was a surprise. I hadn't ranted. I hadn't cursed Ebbleton. Even while the icy thought occurred that Frederick might have supplied the drug, I'd known what to do. But it wasn't what I'd have done a few days before. Perhaps Mel's death had, in fact, made a difference.

Beyond what I'd been—and I thought I'd been a fair father, at any rate—what was a *real* father? Somebody to come to and confess? Somebody to laugh with? Share a joke? They'd both been able to do that with me until I'd gone to Geneva. Even so, they'd flown out to stay with me, and when I went home we were always together.

Excuses.

That's what I had to tell Consuelo.

"Poor little things," she said, from an altitude, very much so, and surprisingly. "I don't even remember my father. I went from school to school. I can't remember worrying much about anybody. I was rather new-girl at times, of course. A little lonely. I got over it. My mother married somebody else. He didn't want us at home. He died about ten years ago. My mother wanted me to stay with her. That's where I am now. No, Edmund. I don't believe this about no-mother-no-father-chop-his-poor-bloody-head-off. Some of us need help of a particular kind. Others don't. Some want somebody to run to. Others don't. Some are easily tempted. Some are not. All some of us *really* need is to take somebody's hand we can trust. To know it doesn't belong to anybody else, even for a moment. Ever. After that, a house and a garden, and a couple of dogs or so. Is there anything lovelier to think about?"

Her voice trembled, I caught the flash from the corner of my eye, but she looked away.

"Simple," I said, as though it were *fait-accompli*. "What isn't simple is what's to be done in the next couple of weeks!"

"There's nothing we can't do if we put our minds to it," she said, in the tone of Miss Furnival at the office, succinct, confident, more or less in pretty good copy of myself at certain times. "If your son's anything like you, he can be pulled round. But he's a bit of a weak member. A little yeh-yeh, a little long-haired, torpidly fashionable, terribly anxious to make money and not quite sure how. No voice, no style, no rhythm, so singing's out. Even folk-singing. And what's left? Something quite awful called 'work.' Which singers don't do. They only sing. That's what he told me in Geneva, last time. It's such terrifying nonsense!"

"I'm a little tired of minors doing anything they think fit. I'd never have dared!"

Consuelo laughed, settled into the collar of her coat.

"I've had the most flat-footed afternoon," she said. "Really, one doesn't know anything at all about the other half. How *do* they manage? The raw stuff's quite defeating!"

"They mind their own business," I said. "It's what they've always done. They've come through very well, I think!"

She frowned, sitting away.

"If you'd seen what I saw this afternoon, you'd be outraged. They oughtn't to be allowed to live like that. I'm doing my instalment-buying report. It's frightening, how little people have to live on!"

"They don't look at it like that. So far as people are concerned, statistics mean very little."

She looked at me in surprise.

"But what about that study you made? Income, rent, instalments, all that. It's exactly what I've tried to copy. You said it would cause an absolute furor, remember?"

"And it didn't, remember? Figures don't alter the facts that made them. Compare the people you've been nosey-parkering to their parents or grandparents. They're a thousand times better off. It wasn't reports. Simply process of time, that's all. When they're tired of enjoying poverty, they'll work their way out of it. With their heads. That's where 'poverty' is. Joining the Market won't lessen poverty anywhere. It'll simply increase the aggregate. Which was never my idea."

"Does that mean you won't be going back to the department? Even if it's re-formed?"

I was led into that one. I couldn't even give myself a straight yes or no. A small circle of confusion.

"We'll have to see," I said, and opened the glass divide to show the cabman along the Strand to Berry Court. "Wait on this corner, please."

The watchman let us in and said he hadn't seen the young ge'mun for a coupla days.

"Lots of messages for him, sir," he said, and nodded at the rack. "I've heard the telephone up there since I come on, too."

"I'll take them," I said, and reached. "If he has any callers, put them on to this number."

Three of the messages were from his grandmother, the first, three days before, the last that morning.

We walked the two flights and I used the key.

Patti, by any comparison, was impeccable mother of order. How he could live in such a disgusting manner was beyond me. He'd been brought up to put things away. Mel allowed no nonsense. Was this a result of the badgering of earlier years? Didn't people want to remember the way they were trained? Was resentment satisfied in throwing things everywhere, putting nothing away, flinging paper on the floor, leaving piles of used cardboard plates and cups on chairs, and a dozen glasses over the mantelpiece among heaped ashtrays, invitation cards, letters, books? Poor books. Not one of them seemed in a state to be picked up, much less read. This was, indeed, a true court of vice.

"Look through those papers, will you?" I said to Consuelo. "See if he had any appointments to keep. Classes, lectures. I'll go through this."

I knew what I was looking for, and sure enough, in the brief-case I'd given him, with an automatic lock, there were three heavy packages with the pink band, a carton of something else I'd no intention of looking at, two boxes of phials, and a long serrated envelope. In one pocket was a thick wad of pound notes, in the other a thinner pile of five-pound notes, a number of dollars, and a small book in his handwriting. I put them all in my pockets, and went to the door to call the watchman.

"I can't find anything," Consuelo said. "His books are all here."

"Collect any letters, notes, numbers, names, addresses, I'll take the notebooks."

I gave the key to the watchman.

"Tell the administrator Mr. Trothe won't be coming back. Ask him to call that number and I'll talk to him. Wasn't the place ever cleaned?"

"Woman comes early, sir. He wasn't out of it, she couldn't. Youngsters, they lusherates in the gravy, they do. All the same, that age. Wasn't for the women, we'd all be in a slop!"

He strung the books downstairs, and I gave him a present for his trouble, and asked the cabman to drive to my club.

"Shan't be a moment," I told Consuelo. "If there's an enquiry, they'll have very little to go on!"

"What about the car?"

"That's up to Gilman. I'm not wet-nursing any more!"

The club was fairly quiet. I went to the cloakroom, locked myself in a stall, put the powder and pellets down the pedestal and flushed. That was that, but the phials were another problem. The stokehold was just beyond the firing range, but I wasn't sure if the stuff would explode or not. I went back to the cab and told him to drive to St. James's Park. Opposite Marlborough House I stopped him.

"I'm going to walk across," I told Consuelo. "Meet me on the other side!"

She asked no questions, and I thanked Heaven for mist and a cold night. Even so, two couples—God bless them!—hugged each other on the bridge. I remembered Mel, thinking of Frederick, wondering what convolutions of the mind would have been necessary to foresee, all these years later, that I'd be trying to save him from prison almost on the spot where his bride-mother and I had stood. I felt a close sense of Mel while I opened the box and shook the phials out of the layers. They fell in small glitter into dark water, not even a splash. The couples didn't move. I tore the notebook and boxes into bits and sprinkled some in one wastebasket, some in the other.

154

I didn't take a filling breath till I was back in the cab.

"That's half the job done," I said. "Wish to God I could meet the brute who supplied him!"

"I've got a vac of coffee here," Consuelo said. "Why don't you let me take you back in my car? I've got some whiskey in the pouch!"

20

On the way down, we doctored the coffee Consuelo had brought, still hot, and ate her sandwiches, I think one of the most satisfying meals I ever had, and when we got to the house I thought we were stopping for another traffic light.

There were two cars in the drive. One, I knew, was Yorick's.

"I'll make myself scarce," Consuelo whispered. "In the kitchen. Forget me till they've gone!"

She hurried round the side.

Mrs. Cloney opened the door.

"'s two gentlemen here, sir—!" she began.

"All right," Yorick said, behind her. "Sorry to disturb you, Edmund. Bernard and I came along for that drink you promised us. Two minutes, that's all."

"I hope you made yourselves at home."

"Oh, rather!"

He shut the door. Bernard stood up. He was pale.

"My father was out shooting this afternoon," Yorick said, as though he had a sore throat. "His gun exploded. He was killed instantly."

I could only look at him.

He took two cartridges out of an envelope, and held them up.

"You know these, Edmund?"

"I use them myself."

"Look at them."

I gave both a thorough examination. One was whole, and the other had been fired, and cut across at the copper disc.

"That one had an explosive charge in the neck," Yorick said. "When the hammer hit, it burst in the cartridge chamber. A chap we employed as handyman can't be found. We're after him, but I don't think we've got much chance."

"I'm at a loss. Deeply sorry. Anything I can do?"

"We came to ask whether you'd consider going to work earlier. Immediately. Now, in fact!"

"I told Lord Blercgrove I'd be ready at the end of the month. Have you any material on these organisations? How many, who they are?"

Bernard took a file out of a briefcase.

"This is what we've got so far," he said.

The telephone rang, and I picked it up, still reading.

"Mr. Trothe? This is Angela Masters. I'm speaking for Mrs. Paul Chamby—"

The line seemed to go dead.

"Hullo!" I shouted. "Hullo!"

Ridiculous word, I've always thought. But I knew then, beyond doubt, the house line was tapped.

"Mr. Trothe? I thought we were cut off. A terrible thing's happened. Mr. Chamby's had an accident with a car on the ramp of his garage. Mrs. Chamby's absolutely, well, like a lunatic. She's calling for you. Could you possibly come over here, sir? It's quite clear!"

"I'll be there as soon as I can."

They'd both heard it over the relay, and they stood, so far as I could see, chewing a rather large cud.

"If it wasn't an accident, I suppose he'd be about number twenty-something on the roster," Yorick said, looking here, there, up and down behind his glasses, making his eyes look like dwarf polyps of clearest pale blue jelly. "Your turn seen, possibly? The score's two in one day. What's the answer?"

"I'm going over to Paul's," I said. "Mrs. Cloney'll give you some dinner. I'll meet you at the office at eight tomorrow. Arrange a tattooist, shots, the lot. Right?"

"Yes, sir!" Yorick said, for the first time in my experience showing the smallest sign of respect.

I picked up my hat and overcoat and went down to the kitchen. Mrs. Cloney was having a quiet chat with Consuelo.

"Come on," I said. "We can dine later. The two gentlemen would like their dinner now!"

"Oh, Mr. Trothe!" Mrs. Cloney started, bless her. "You're never going to *dare* leave this—"

"Dare because I must," I said, and followed Consuelo out. "Goodnight, and please give me a call at six!"

We went out to the car, and waited for the engine to warm.

"You can't come here any more," I said. "I shan't be here. Thing is, I don't want to lose you!"

She clasped her hands on the wheel, and smiled in the light of the dashboard.

"You couldn't," she said. "Just tell me what you want done."

Fortunately—sensible girl!—she started to talk about her morning class in economics, and we were in something wildly absorbing about the structure of continental banks when we turned into Paul's lit gateway.

A policeman asked for my license, looked at the name, and handed it back.

"You're expected, sir," he said. "Keep right. There's a big hole in the drive!"

Police cars were parked along the shrubs. The garage had no roof, and the doors were in splinters, stacked against the wall.

Consuelo didn't look at me.

Angela Masters, tall, silvery-blond, slim in black, met us and took Consuelo away. I went in to meet Moira. She was pale, brownish under the eyes, sitting in the corner of the divan. She looked at me as if she'd never seen me before.

"It was a bomb in the car," she said. "Williams was backing it out of the garage. Paul was using the Ford. I was going to do some shopping. I went back for the list, and I heard this tremendous crash. I thought the house had come down. Paul was inside the garage, thank God. Would you believe it? Filling his lighter. That's what saved him. Only a broken leg. Scratches. And poor Williams. Know anybody with a grudge against Paul, do you?"

Different tone, another woman, hard, with a glitter I'd never seen before.

"Any suspects here?"

"Everybody's been with us years. The gardener was on the front lawn all the morning. Never saw anybody. You can't see him. He's asleep, poor boy. I'm in a heap. And I'm so frightened it'll happen again!"

I put a hand on her shoulder.

"He'll be out of the country in a short time," I said.

"We'll have to give up this house. I don't want to. Question is, where'll he be safe?"

She folded her arms and looked at the flowers.

"You don't think it was our own people trying to put him away, do you, Eddy?" she asked in a small voice. "I mean, he knows enough to make a lot of trouble. If he opened his mouth!"

I must have stood there with my mouth wide open.

"But, Moira!" I managed to say. "How could you possibly think of such a thing!"

"Think, hnh!" she said tiredly. "I know a little bit. I was in it, too, y'know. I'd put nothing past that dirty lot!"

"Take it right out of your mind," I said, quietly, distinctly. "You're on the wrong tack entirely, and one of these days you'll be sorry you ever allowed yourself to think it. Now, be a good girl, take a pill, and go to bed!"

"Eddy, do me a big favor," she said, and rolled off the cushions, and stood. "Tell that bitch Masters to leave, will you? First time I've had the chance of getting her out of the house. Nobody's going to get Paul while I'm alive!"

To say I was shocked is abuse of language.

"I'll ask Miss Masters to go to London and take charge of the office," I said, groping. "Of course, I'll take her back with me!"

"Take her where you like," she said, punching the cushions. "I see the bitch here again, I won't be responsible!"

"You're sure there's nothing more I can do? The police are all round the—"

"Not worried about the police or anything else," she said, bringing a long plait over her shoulder to tie the ends. "I just want that bitch out of this house. Everything happens for the best. Now I get *my* way!"

I said goodnight and went out to find Consuelo and Angela in the small study.

"Mrs. Chamby thinks it might be a good idea if you left with us and took charge of the London office from tomorrow morning," I began, in my crispest this-is-the-way-to-do-it. "There's a lot of stuff coming in and nobody to handle it—"

"I thought exactly the same," Angela said, calmly. "In any case, I can't *bear* her!"

I looked at Consuelo, and got the sort of look that says You're Absolutely Correct Don't Say A Word, and stood aside for them to go out.

"Angela's going to stay with me tonight," Consuelo said. "So we'll run you home, first!"

"Never in my life have I been driven home by *two* women," I said. "I can pick up a car at Hurcell's Yard. *No* argument!"

"But that's most ungallant, and utterly disappointing!"

"Then I'll accept a drink. Perhaps two—"

Consuelo smiled. It was a nice smile. It made her even more— I couldn't quite think of the word—dangerous occurred, but I put it aside.

"Ah," she said. "Nah y'r talkin'!"

"Worst attempt at Cockney I ever heard. You sound like a sixth-former at St. Excrucia's 'doing' Liza Doolittle!"

Her eyes opened in a mazy—quite lovely—stare.

"My favorite part!" she whispered. "How could you possibly—!"

"I'm ready," Angela said, coming in, pulling on black gloves, holding a small black crocodile make-up case. "Never want to see this dis-*gust*-ing place again!"

"You've got to think of the Company, surely?" I said, more to keep the conversation on a certain level. "Can't leave like that!"

She swept round, and the long black coat emphasised height, slimness and silvery-blond, fine-boned beauty.

"Of course not!" she said. "I *love* Paul. I'd *never* leave him!"

All very well, but I realised that any notion of getting in touch with Tanis through the Company was solidly and absolutely not on. Two "romances"—especially at top level—would simply not do. I had to find another way.

21

Bluish-yellow arms semaphored out of darkness, and a light shone red, black, red, black and morse buzzed dah-di-dah-dit, dah-di-dah dit—the letter C for Calling—and I dragged my other self out of a void to pick up the telephone. The clock said 3:16.

"Hullo, Trothe?"

The Blur's voice.

"Speaking!"

"Hawtrey's been found dead on the night express from Lincoln. I'm going to London now. Meet me there, five o'clock?"

Invitation, command, anything you like.

"No trouble!"

The 4:30 express wouldn't do. I put on the clothes I'd worn the day before, had a nip of whiskey, and backed the car into biting sleet. The heater helped, and I drove past our holly tree in ripple of scarlet berries, wondering if the curious luck of this year came of its absence in the house last Christmas—for the first time, I suppose, since the place had been built—and the missing bunches of mistletoe at any door, especially over front and back, to bring love on all coming in or going out, and joy for the year, and the Eden kiss of Adam and Eve for those standing under. But Mel had said she was taking the children to her mother's place in Torremolinas, and I stayed in Geneva. Her mother and the children had gone, but Mel hadn't. She'd stayed behind, feeling unwell, I'd found later. I could guess where in fact she'd been "unwell." Mrs. Cloney had told

me she was "proper 'eartbroke" that the house had been un-
decorated, and unblessed. When I thought of it, so was I.

I ignored speed signs until I was almost at Hyde Park, and I
passed Big Ben at 4:58, which wasn't bad for the weather. The
night porter took me up, and I had time for a cup of thick tea
in the cubby down the corridor before the Blur came in, seeming
to bring a shiver of Kentish hoarbreath with him. He wore shooting jacket and corduroys over pajamas.

"We've got to start, Trothe," he said, pulling off his gloves.
"I don't care what the result of the autopsy is. Somebody's got
to be in Regsmund to see if there's a party. Our man's too ex-
posed. We wouldn't get his report until well after it happened.
When could you go?"

"The only brake's my son. He's not well."

"You don't need to stay there. All you have to do is to
verify."

"And make an example?"

"Exactly. Or two. Which papers?"

"Eck. Simeon Rotbart Eck. Everything's in order. Just left
Aden. Working for Shell. Before that, the Congo. Union
Minière. Eleven years merchant navy, Liberian, Panamanian.
General electrician. Five years prisoner of war in Russia. Transfer my savings from Lagos to Barclay's Bank, Hamburg. Let's
say, six thousand-odd dollars. I'll send a couple of thousand
to Regsmund. Rent a place. Paint out. Print cards. Who's our
man?"

"A waiter in the Café de l'Europe. It's on two floors. Ground
floor, bar and coffee house, downstairs beer and pigs knuckles.
His name's Ants. Latvian. Mother was English. Parents died in
Sachsenhausen. He's been extremely useful in little ways. But
he's limited. As you'll find out. Very well. What time?"

I waited till he finished writing.

"Ambulance at the east door at nine. Notice in the midday
papers. I'm in St. George's Hospital. Overwork, appendicitis,

anything. Transfer to a nursing home. Incommunicado. Messages to odd friends—"

"Then?"

"Hamburg via Paris this afternoon. Regsmund tomorrow. And what about Frederick?"

"Cuthbert Bainbridge will visit him and put everything in order, never fear!"

Sir Cuthbert, whom I knew of old, was Harley Street's most famous physician. I wondered how he'd get along with Dr. Norris.

"Excellent. Very well. I'd like to see the tools, first. Then the music!"

Music was code for explosives and chemicals, and Sidney Taylor waited to take me across to Room 405. The items were laid out on tables, some of the most innocent rubbish I've ever seen, and the deadliest. Sidney had been in charge of that room for more years than I could remember. He was known as the Banger, because pretty nearly anything he touched went *bang!*

He showed me a series of small discs which stuck to everything, and exploded in anything from one minute to about half an hour.

"Can't guarantee it exactly, but it *will* go off in that time," he said. "These stickers are excellent workmen. They're about half an hour as well. Now, these plungers—they're called that because you've got to trigger them—like this—before you set them, they're the most destructive. A dozen'd pretty well wreck this wing!"

"They all stick? To anything, wood, metal—"

He waved a hand.

"Their only drawback," he said. "Once you've stuck them on, triggered, you can't get them off, and you can't stop them going. Those little discs for example, they'll smash up any car or truck. The stickers'll take out a part of a wall. Easily make a nasty mess in this room. Wouldn't be anybody alive, I can guarantee that. The plungers'll make more of a mess than any grenade. Explode on impact. Push the timer, you've got at least half an hour, and they'll level a room twice this size, roof and floor, too!"

I was given a choice of sprays to clean off fingerprints, destroy paper and textiles, and draw tears. I picked out some of the best tools I'd ever seen. My toolbox had been given an almost Château-vintage crust to tell of age in service.

At 9 o'clock I was taken by ambulance to St. George's Hospital. I'd swallowed a pill just before, and I blanked while we made a Caesar's progress through traffic obeying the siren.

I woke clear-headed at a few minutes to eleven. Sidney took an ice-bag off my head and gave me a towel I didn't need. My clothes had been changed to well-worn trousers and a jacket of foreign cut. I wore brown boots and I could feel a big toe through the right sock. In an inside breast pocket I had a purse with thirty pounds and about the same in francs, a seaman's discharge papers, a packet of references Scotch-taped at the folds, a couple of letters from friends in Lagos and Tetuan, a bankbook, odd bits of paper with telephone numbers, receipts, a laundry bill from a seaman's lodging in Gibraltar, and a Thomas Cook's ticket cover, to show I'd gone through Madrid to Paris two days before.

Miss Roule helped me in a final check of detail. She did, certainly, have a brain. She picked up the little things I might have missed, including a stub of paint for my hands and feet to take off the clerkly pallor and give the nails a workman's dun. At the end she gave me a small well-burned briar, a flat, round tin of cut tobacco, and a razor-sharp flick knife.

"No germs," she said. "It's new. There's a slop-chest shorty on the chair next door, and I thought a cap might be the thing. Blackened badge. It's the old Blue Anchor line. You were on board the *Aramis*, weren't you?"

"Fined for getting drunk in Durban. Only black mark against me. Sixth anniversary of freedom. Correct?"

"When, that year, did you arrive in Berlin?"

"You mean Cologne, surely? I didn't get to Berlin for another seven years. That's because I came in at Hamburg on the *Tong-king*, went up there and met what was left of my family. There are two less now. Ebert died a couple of years ago, and Paula wasn't long behind."

She shut the file and put it behind her back.

"Ebert had a ten-year-old son—"

"He's almost seventeen and went to sea as apprentice electrical engineer on my letter of recommendation. Due at Simonstown next week, Cape Town week after."

She gave me an old Onoto pen with a squat nib.

"You might practise your signature a few times," she said. "It should at least have the *shape* of the one on your papers!"

"Let's see. Tongue-tip left side of mouth, and chew. So? Undt zo, nein?"

"The flourish underneath means lack of confidence, does it?"

"On the contrary. I'm an individualist. There are days when I sign backhand. Depends on how I feel. Remember, I firmly believe that evil came into its own with the invention of the printing press. That wash of print made possible books and newspapers. Bad thoughts, twisted news, lies. Take print and paper out of your life. What would you be, and where?"

"Something demure making with petit-point, and helping with tea every Wednesday? Squire's at-home?"

"You see? The old lad's got a case. You'd be surprised how many go for it!"

"You have three minutes, sir, and they're flashing you!"

I picked up the telephone.

"Trothe here."

"I'm calling from Grasstree. To wish you the very best, and a quick return. Hawtrey undoubtedly was murdered. I shall have a report later today."

"Thank you, m'lord. I should be back here in ten days or so."

"Don't let them off too lightly, will you!"

Miss Roule held out my slop-chest shorty, a blue, double-

166

breasted affair in thick nondescript, and I put on the cap, picked up toolbox and bag, and clicked my heels in goodbye.

She curtseyed in opening the door, and I went out to the right, down the back stairs to the waiting cab.

So far, well enough.

But I had one fixed idea of my own.

I intended to meet Tanis, though certainly not as I then was.

22

Miss Roule had sent my own suitcase to Jamie Worsley at the airport. I took off the cap and coat, and when we got to the departure building, I paid off the cab, gave the toolbox and bag to a porter, checked them to Paris, brought a plastic holdall for the short coat and engineer's cap, and went upstairs to Jamie's office. My suitcase was where he always kept it, in the small lavatory at the side. I took very few minutes to change from the skin out. Mr. Eck's clothes went in the holdall, into my suitcase, a handy carry-on size, and I walked down in time to take the next flight to Paris.

I went to Claudine's hotel at the back of the Gare du Nord. We'd known each other for years, though downstairs she made no sign, and neither did I, but we had our usual glass of champagne up in my room a few minutes later. I'd known her since the German occupation. She must have been in her seventies, though on her day she looked little more than a fastish, and quite lively forty.

It took half a dozen words to explain Tanis, and she was enchanted to go off and put the call through to Geneva without mentioning a name, and leaving a number—not the hotel's—to telegraph the flight and arrival time.

"That one's in love," Claudine said, when she came back, nodding the shut-eyed weight of an expert. "Can't hide it any more than a May morning. But you don't want to stay here!"

I looked at a wallpaper of crippled lilac, a bare electric over

168

a hand basin, a kidney-dish bidet, and a bedstead that seemed to groan as I watched, and shook my head.

"I confess this was only to make the connection," I said. "This is a very private liaison—"

"I understand perfectly. You must go to my sister's. It's forty minutes. My son'll take you. I'll meet the girl and send her on. Better. No little tales, eh?"

"Will you also arrange the menu?"

"Is there any need? She has a kitchen. I speak with respect. Or, let us say, with reverence. She has a duckling. Ah! In cognac, with dates. And a lamb's tripes in cream. But tell me, what palate do you suppose this glorious monster will leave you? She will devour you!"

"The table, at least, has to be of that standard!"

"I send my especial friends from this noise and grime only to take advantage. She has logs in the fireplace. Pine, with apple and walnut shavings. In bed, it adds, no?"

"And of course, the same champagne as this?"

"Naturally. You haven't seen Georges lately?"

"It's been years. I'm not active any more. Why?"

She shrugged.

"I wondered, nothing more. You are going out?"

"No, I'll sleep here tonight, if I may? Seven o'clock call. Chocolate and croissants!"

I was enjoying a plate of cold turkey and a bottle of Montrachet, when Claudine came up to say my car would be downstairs next morning at nine to get me out there about thirty minutes before Tanis.

I had a hot bath and went to bed with most of the newspapers, looked at a couple of front pages, and fell asleep.

It was two minutes past one when the telephone woke me, a specimen of those old ringle-dringle brass and vulcanite tricks, where you disengage a cornucopia and have to claw for the earpiece.

169

"Two men have enquired for you," Claudine said softly. "A car will be here in a few minutes. You will be ready?"

It doesn't take me long to dress, and the porter took the bags down a steep sidestair, pausing to warn me at the turns, and himself fell down the last three or four and cursed magnificently in breathless silence.

"They were not of the police," Claudine whispered. "Both young, thirties, perhaps, German, I should think, I'm not sure. They didn't talk enough. One said he had a message for you. I said I didn't know you. The other said they'd be back. They won't find you where you're going. Enjoy everything. Time's too short!"

We made good speed out of the city, northwest I judged, and I went back over my journey of the day, trying to find a gap where I might have been careless.

I couldn't think of a time or place. Might the call to Tanis have been picked up? Between the time of the call, and the arrival of the two men, whoever they were, there was ample time to fly from Geneva. But that put Tanis in a circle of white light. I couldn't believe she had anything to do with the underground on any level. But I thought of Ghislaine. And of my friends, Bernard and Joel. They were sure they could convict.

I realised, of course, that what I was doing, in supposedly full possession of my senses, burst into highest pitch of midsummer madness. In all probability, M.I. had informed Paris that I was passing through. I'd made no fuss about going to Claudine's place. A tail would have placed me. Claudine would be known as one of the most extraordinary women on the list. Then, why send two agents she wouldn't recognise? I trusted her absolutely, since having got her husband and two sons over the border into Spain in 1941, we had worked—the word might be amicably— together over many a year.

I sat back, a little sleepy, unworried, and watched the dark roadside wink by beyond the moan of the car.

Tanis was near.

23

We ran over the cobbles of a drive and stopped at a huge gate. It wasn't a door. A postern opened, and light shone on the silver hair and sideburns of a porter in an orange waistcoat with scarlet sleeves. Whoever was driving the car didn't wait for me to thank him. He'd gone. I went through the little door into a vestibule so spacious, that one lamp over a long desk glinted on a couple of suits of armour, a few hanging standards, and a red and white tiled floor. The rest was black.

A woman in grey, wearing a white lace cap dipped a knee, smiled welcome, and took a bunch of keys from her belt, bending her head to the left. She had a small torch that lit the tiles to a platform without a gate. She pressed a button and we went up a couple of floors, stopping at the exact level, and I went after a black shadow and a moving white ball, along deep carpet—I couldn't see anything—to a door.

Her key opened it and I went in to a lit room so exactly what I would dream of, that I stopped, and stood there, and she went out and left the door open. I looked at the chairs, tables, silver, a yard-long candle burning beside a prie-dieu, and the porter came in with my suitcase. Behind him, a waiter with one of the same bottles I'd shared with Claudine, and a salver of sandwiches. They both went as sprites, and if I very much wanted a glass of champagne, I wanted far more to sleep, and I undressed without a thought, with no prayer, and put a knee into the best bed I ever slept in, and perhaps I slept before I was all in.

171

I woke to the aroma of coffee, in many ways I think the most civilised way of taking hold of the senses.

A maid, who might have been the porter's wife, in starched cap and apron, slid a newspaper under the sheet—so that it wouldn't fall—and said the day was fine, the sun was warm, but snow would come later.

I drank a cup of par-excellent coffee, bathed in a tub of fat porcelain sides, shaved in a flowered bowl, towelled in fleece, and generally had a most wonderful half-hour in an entirely different century, when people knew how to live, and made sure they did. Or, at least, their women did.

Dear me, to find such a woman today.

I walked through an empty foyer, and roamed—that's all I did—a wintry countryside for almost two hours, squatting on a gate, looking at geese, appraising fat cattle, happy to watch a three-month porker rooting in yards of turf, attended by a slidden-eyed gang of hens, waiting for a rich peck.

Curiously, in that time, feeling for Tanis seemed to cool, or wither, I'm not sure. I could think of her simply as someone I had to meet, not, as before, a goddess whose body I must worship, go mad for. That wasn't what I felt. I asked myself what the devil I *did* feel, and I couldn't answer. Consuelo presented herself. I turned away.

I was there because I'd said I'd be there. For a reason. But the reason didn't seem so important as it had.

But the sheer surprise of meeting Tanis, in a white caped-coat, pillbox cap and white topboots, coming through the main door as I went in from the garden put anything else out of mind. She was even more beautiful than I remembered, trembling, so that I had to take the pen from her and sign her in, and when I got up to the room she was in the bath.

I suppose the hours that followed have become a sort of milestone in my life. We didn't talk much. We never had. I told her I was there on a chance visit, and that I might have to go back at any moment, depending on governmental whim.

She said she'd taken a couple of days off from her paper in lieu of a vacation she hadn't had. I waited for her to say something about going to London to cover the Birmingham Fair, but she didn't. I thought that a little strange, but I passed it over. There's nothing like pillow-fighting—without pillows—for passing things over. We got up late and strolled along the river before dinner—a partridge with new potatoes and peas grown under glass, and a tart of small strawberries—and went to bed. Rain was heavy on Sunday morning. Bed, with drawn curtains, shaded lights, and the newspapers was the only answer, and we got up for luncheon —(is there any feeling more exquisite than being weak from love's wonder, cold-bathed, in fresh linen, taking a small hand that grips, looking into eyes still pinkly moist from the throes of that last love-cry, and dawdling a way into a shadowy bar for a superb champagne cocktail?)—and I lunched on the duckling—a masterpiece—though Tanis chose a steak because of poundage. We went through the garden afterwards, and rather sadly I remembered my own, in the rose pergolas, well cut back, a reach of water lilies, and the massed tints of early blossom in the greenhouses.

A sudden scream of warning retched out of two white flowers in a silver vase on the foyer desk. Two white-anythings had always been sign of emergency, clear out, go.

I don't think my voice changed, and I'm almost sure my manner didn't, and on the way to the lift, I went on telling her about an old rambler that sprouted little yellowish rags until I'd grafted a Hugh Dixon, and ever since had covered the south wall of the coachhouse with blood-red blossom that scented into the library and both bedrooms above.

"I would so like to see your house," Tanis said. "I saw pictures in a review. My mother also has a very old house. But so different. We have grapes. Every kind. Perhaps next summer you will visit us?"

"Of course. Love to. Here, in France?"

"In Hungary. Near Budapest. She prefers to live in Switzerland. We have Swiss passports. I was at school there."

She was speaking rather more than tensely, I thought, but I said nothing, and didn't ask questions, because the waiter was at the door of the suite with coffee. Between the cups a telegram doubled the warning.

"I knew it couldn't last!" Tanis said, shaking her hair free of the silk scarf. "I had a little grasshopper rik-rik in my ear since I woke up!"

"Well, now, let's see what it is, first," I said, holding the envelope, no hurry, pouring her a cup of coffee. "Now you pour me one, and I'll read it for both of us!"

I tore open the flap.

"Return immediately," I read aloud. "Request files G10 and 8 Ops."

G18 had been Claudine's old number.

"We aren't lucky," I said, distantly calm over a jumpy inner sense. "Why don't you stay here tonight? I can't see you to the airport. I have to go to the Air Force field. And visitors, however exquisite, aren't permitted!"

"I'd like to stay, but not without you. Anywhere is a desert without you, my one darling!"

The telephone buzzed.

"Sir, the messenger would like a signature of ink for the telegram, you please forgive me this disturbance?"

"I'll be down immediately."

We kissed as though our lips had been welded and might tear if they came apart. She held her cheeks, looking at me with such an utter longing that I went back and crushed her perfumed tenderness, wondering whether there was any real need to go so soon, or if I could run things fine, and stay on, at least that night.

"In any case we'll have a lot more time in London," I said. "Let me know when you arrive, that's all."

"My newspaper is taking a place for me. I think a hotel—"

"Too public. At any rate, for us. We want to be by ourselves!"

"Ah, my one darling!" she whispered, tightening her arms. "Of course. And I shall be in bed when you come back. Don't be long. I suffocate!"

I've always thought it curious how the mind works, or at any rate, my mind. Even while I was half-drunk with thought of her, I still had a flashing memory of Consuelo, and a half-dream became certainty that she would be much more the woman, even if I wasn't sure how that could be possible. I half-laughed at nonsense, the mind's absurd froth, that runs over when least expected. But the better part of my senses were at work on Claudine's warning. Two white flowers—two white-anythings—were sign of absolute danger. Claudine was not the type to stampede. Where did the danger lie?

Claudine herself held open a door to a small office behind the desk. The flowers were gone.

"The car is waiting," she said—for her—sharply. "You have no time to go upstairs again. You will go to Arras by road. Wait at the hotel across from the station until your bags arrive. Continue your journey by rail!"

"How does all th—?"

"You have friends. Georges is careful, no? It's enough? Don't complain, eh?"

I put my arms round her in a hug, and she hugged me.

"You leave to me what to tell *her*," she said, pointing upstairs. "Your bag is in the car. Give me your airline baggage tickets. I will send them this evening. Go with God!"

I had no need to be told that my friend Georges Pontvianne knew where I was and perhaps—from the evidence—where I was going. It was discouraging comfort of a kind. If the French Service was helping me, who'd informed? It might have been useful to know, but I had to think of the next few moves. I could catch a train from Arras to the frontier, but was I to be stopped? If I were, how could I, Edmund Onslow Trothe, explain clothing and tools, and Simeon Rotbart Eck's papers? If I were detained and had to call the British Consul, what reason could I give for being in France when I should have been in Germany? The more I thought of it, the more extraordinary seemed my conduct. Fatuous was hardly the word. Disgraceful, certainly. I know what I'd have said about anybody else.

We swayed on Citröen springing over miles of roads in stone setts, floated on asphalt between vineyards and orchards, and Arras came out of the poplars, shuttered for Sunday, few people in the streets, and we stopped at the hotel opposite the station.

A porter came out and took the bag and briefcase and I went in with him to get a room. One had been reserved in Claudine's name, which the chauffeur had given the porter. I went out to present him with a tip he'd remember, but he'd gone. The street was clear.

Upstairs, an electric fire warmed arctic air, and the maid had folded the bed cover. It seemed a good idea, and I took off overcoat, jacket and shoes, and lay down to look at the ceiling.

I woke to knocks, darkness, and three red bars of the electric fire. The porter came in with the toolbox and bag.

"The express stops at eleven-ten, sir," he said. "The restaurant's open. Would you like me to bring you a drink?"

"I'll go down," I said, and sat up. "If you take the bags across and get me a place, you won't regret it."

"First class, sir?"

I nodded, and he went.

I seemed to be moving in a small dream. Sunday night in a French provincial town, newspapers on wooden holders, a smell of black tobacco, and a haunting sense that I oughtn't to be there, all tended to spoil a sole in white wine, but they didn't. I walked across to the station, agreeably surprised at new steel carriages, and a corner seat. My bags were in the rack, and I'm sure the porter's smile could have lit the station.

I expected to be touched on the shoulder at any moment. I went into the buffet car, and had a coffee and cognac, and

176

dallied 'with a magazine. The more I thought of the past thirty-six hours, the more I wondered. Untrustworthy, lax, imprudent, I heard them all, but none seemed to match the contempt I felt for myself. Adolescent, perhaps, but there were overtones of inexperience which I couldn't claim, and anyway, mine hadn't been a schoolboy passion.

I woke in a jolt to find a uniform asking for my passport. I was alone. The bar was shut. I got up and went back to my compartment, and the train stopped as if a stretched rubber band had been released by degrees to normal. I've often wondered why porters on the Continent always have red faces. I think it's the weather. We got out into a kniving wind and a drift of snow like pellets. A passport officer looked at me, stamped my passport, and I followed the porter to the Customs bench. With a show of keys, I opened all three bags, and waited. The Customs officer looked at my passport and at me, chalked a pink scrawl on each bag, and the porter strapped them, and we walked across the tracks to the smaller, local, Regsmund train. I was a little surprised.

At least, I was in Germany.

24

I took the Eck bag to the lavatory, changed, put my own
overcoat and homburg in with the rest, washed the umbrella
handle clear of prints and left it on the hook behind the door.
But I had a nasty little surprise on opening my own suitcase.
The short blue coat and cap should have been in the plastic
holdall. The cap was not. But I'd tied the holdall in Heathrow.
Why would anyone take a cap? Nothing else was missing. I took
the homburg out of the other bag, tore the hat band a little,
ripped out the lining and generally dusted it down until it
"went" with the coat. I'd just finished when the collector came in.
I gave him my Cook's ticket cover, offered the difference, but
he said there was plenty of room in the second-class carriage,
and carried the toolbox for me. I offered him a drink, but he
told me to go five carriages to the rear in about an hour, and
he'd give *me* one. I suppose it depends on how you look and
what you say.

I slept again and woke to a creamy dawn with blowing snow.
I walked down five carriages, but my friend had gone. His
relief was freshly-washed, shaved, and fed, and nodded next
door to the buffet car. I had an excellent breakfast, read the
papers in German, and went back to the compartment and
slept till we were actually in Regsmund station. I handed the
bags through the window, and got out in biting winter. The
knocked-in hat, seaman's coat and the drip at my nosetip perhaps roused a brotherly sympathy in the cabdriver. I told him
I was just home and wanted a cheap, clean hotel. He nodded

without wasting a moment, and drove me around the station, passing a built-over two-story town that seemed quite new, and stopped in a sidestreet at a doorway in a neon-scroll *BOEHM'S.*

"Friends of mine," he said. "They won't rob you. Eat with the family, my advice!"

I went up a flight of waxed stairs to a spotless room with six chairs about the walls, a round table in the middle, and a cuckoo clock. A big woman came from an ironing board in the next room, fair curls close to her head in pins, white apron chin to ankles, and a smell of the laundry. I wrote in the book, showed my passport, saw her hands crinkled with water, and blue eyes in a chubby smile. She climbed the stairs with two bags and I followed with the lightest. I didn't feel exhausted so much as somnolent. She showed me the bell, and shut the door. The room was small, freshly whitewashed, a Sacred Heart was framed over the bed, and gross invitation lay in a real German counterpane. I had a hot shower in a box where careless soaping could mean shattered elbows, took a pill, and got into a feather bed that sank down. And down.

I woke a little before six next morning. Even so, the street was alive and so was the house. I could hear a carpet sweeper. I didn't shave. I washed, combed, dressed in a blue turtleneck, worn blue canvas trousers, the short overcoat, and the hat, sleeve-brushed, but knocked-in. A little girl gave me a cup of coffee, and I said I'd be back for the noon dinner.

Out in the street I saw a number of men wearing a leather cap with earflaps that looked just right. I ambled along, turning off here and there as fancy took me. I've never bought a map anywhere. I just like to walk and look, at shops, houses, people, they're all one to me, and I don't think I'm ever happier than when I'm "lost," because then it's time to find a good café, and sit down, order what I feel like, and find out where I am. That's what I did, and the waiter was very helpful. He drew a rough

179

plan on an old menu, though had I been stupid enough to follow, it could have landed me in Istanbul.

Instead, I went down the smaller streets, and just after eleven o'clock *eureka!* I found what I'd been looking for.

Between a women's clothes shop and a grocer's, a shoemaker sat near the door with the last between his knees. A boy sanded a sole at one of the machines. A sign in the window offered a half-space cheap. It was just the right size.

I stood in front of him, hand to crown of hat, other hand in pocket, heels together, jerky bend of shoulders, everyman's decent greeting to a fellow. His name, from the sign, was Jabotinski, and so I addressed him, asking the rental of the half.

He rested the butt of the hammer on the sole.

"What trade?" he asked, and I imagined I was dealing with a cast-iron Lutheran.

"Electrician. Just off a ship. Repair what you like. Radio, washing machines. House wires, strip lights, it's the same."

"Round here, you got a trade. Month in advance!"

"I put a division down the middle. Paint my side. Clean the window?"

He nodded, and took a tack out of his mouth.

"A month in advance, you could dance a mazurka!" he said, and hammered in the tack.

I walked to the corner, noted the name of the street, and started for Boehm's pension, surprised how near it was. I kicked the snow off my boots and climbed the long stair to my room, and packed my suitcase.

A lunch of several kinds of sausage and boiled beef, with dumplings and cabbage, made suitcase and toolbox a heavy load, but I took a cab to the station, checked the suitcase, and found Jabotinski's shop only two streets away.

He raised the hammer as I entered. I thought his eyes held some of the feckle of iron filings. Two men lounged in the doorway.

"This is Huldtmann, a carpenter," he said, and pointed at the other. "Metzler, a painter. If you're going to spoil the place, spoil it good. First, a month in advance!"

I gave him the envelope with the rent in clean notes, and while he wrote a receipt, I told the two what I wanted. Both I'd describe as old-time workmen, serious and painstaking. Huldtmann drew a plan, and Metzler took note of the colors and size of the area, and both went off to start that afternoon. I went along the main street to a radio components house and bought the items I needed, and on the way back, ordered a sign painted. A few doors down, I got five hundred handbills set for the next day, and my first job, fixing a switchbox that must have dated from Bismarck. It didn't take long, and I warned the printer he'd better get the place rewired before he went up in smoke. It didn't please him, but my handbills were free. Back at the shop, the carpenter had begun putting up a heavy bench he'd had in his yard for years. It was just what I wanted, and when he'd chiselled and planed it looked new. Next he put up the tool racks, and then began the division down the middle of the shop, about eight foot long by six high, with a half door and counter-top to interview my clientele. He was about finished when the painter came with a boy, pulling a truck with ladders and planks. I went for a walk along the main street to be out of the way, and to see if I could spot the Café de l'Europe. I didn't, but I got a street directory at a tobacconist's, and noted the address. It wasn't far, and the stroll wore off some of the sausage and dumplings. I knew I'd have to watch the table. That sort of feeding becomes a habit. It tastes so good, it's a penalty to stop eating.

The café was on a busy crossroad in the usual tangle of power cables and telephone wires. A news kiosk held the corner, with a shuttered flower stall. The windows were steamy from heat inside, and it seemed fairly busy for four o'clock, but then I remembered coffee-and-cake time, and went in. At the tables on the Family side, women talked in groups seen through the flapping entry door. At the bar, men were drinking by themselves, in pairs or at the small tables. Nobody seemed in a rush, and the barman didn't bother about me while he listened to a small radio by the till.

At my right, an ornamented doorway led down a stair with a CLOSED notice on the lower level. That, I supposed, was the cellar. A prickle that brought a shiver ran spine to nape, and burned. Downstairs was killing-ground. As I stood there, a scheme developed, grew, annealed.

The barman listened to a yell of *goal!*, opened his arms to the customer's cheers and handclaps as if he'd been responsible, and tied his apron tighter coming to me and another man just in.

"Sorry to keep you," he said, as if he weren't. "All right now. We're two up. Three minutes to go. Yours'll be?"

"Beer 'n chaser," I said.

He moved only his eyes to the other man, got a nod, and walked off. I wondered if he were Ants, the contact. Limited, the Blur had said. But I was suddenly remembering the missing cap. Who could have taken it? Claudine? Hardly. Tanis? Why? But the coat might also have been reported. Cheap it certainly was, but nevertheless uncommon. And very warm. But I had to get rid of it.

The drinks came and I looked at the barman's acne, black hair in lengths reaching over his ears, bald spots between, brown teeth, tear-y eyes, a fine specimen of the world-conquering Nordic male earning an honest living in healthy airs of tobacco and alcohol. Another barman came in and looked up at the clock, but he couldn't have been more than twenty or so. I spilled the chaser under the counter, drank half the beer, got my change, and left to look for a men's shop. I found a big corner place lit by strips that made everybody inside a pale blue, and bought a squeaky, thick leather coat, and a cap to match, gloves, and a pair of storm boots. My hat and shorty were bagged, and the shoes came with me in a wrap.

Outside snow was falling, and I was glad of the new leather. I felt distinctly warmer. At the top of my street, a man in a buttoned jacket walked a barrow, possibly of vegetables, and I held the parcel in front of his down-bent face.

"Listen, cheerfull" I said. "You want this, you're welcome!"

He gave me the perfect never-catch-'em sideglance, but he saw the name on the bag, and tore it open. The hat fell out, and he trapped it as a ball. He held the shorty up, sniffed it, opened it, and in a big grin, hustled it on, took the cap off, crammed the hat on, and held out his hands in thanks. He was too frozen to talk.

25

I got down to my place, surprised to see the carpentry finished, with a duckboard I hadn't ordered under the bench, and the painter starting on the second coat of quick-dry. It looked very good. I couldn't rack the tools because the varnish hadn't set, but I put out the instruments, pigeonholed the components I'd bought, and hung the spools of wire.

Jabotinski la-la'd a cracked tenor, using a machine beyond the division.

"I see you don't like to work messy," he called. "Me, I think so. But a man gets careless. He earns a living, he don't mind a cobweb. You do me a bad turn, here. I spend money. That's stupid!"

"You'll feel better," I said. "Other men have to work, painters, carpenters. Mouths to fill. How else, without?"

"On my money? That's charity. Ease the conscience, not the problem. So? Politicians don't have to think. It's a new race. They crept up. We don't know we got 'em. But they got us!"

I couldn't "place" his accent, and I didn't want an argument. I coughed what might have been agreement, and asked the painter if he knew where I could get a few bricks to put the stove on.

"Go through here," Jabotinski called. "Take what you like!"

I went round the division to the little door and down a passage hung with rolls of leather on pegs—that's where the smell came from—and out to a long backyard, with the house stretching three-quarters of the way, and the end closed by a green trellis. My torch lit a small stack of new bricks beyond an open doorway. I was amazed to catch a glimpse of black leather armchairs, rows of bound books, a reading lamp, and undoubtedly a Brancusi flying up on a white marble base. In the house of a shoemaker? Brancusi?

I piled a dozen or so bricks under my chin, and took them back to the shop, packed them in a square and went out for more. This time I took a slower pace and got a fair glimpse of a well-lit room which didn't fit in that district, not that it was any business of mine. I went back again and squared the bricks to hold the electric warmer, wired it up, and switched on.

"Careful man," Jabotinski said, through a crack in the boards. "No more work with the door open, eh? So the boy goes to sleep?"

"I like to work with my coat off," I said. "You wear sheepskin. The boy doesn't. Place is an icebox. Was. Tomorrow, it's where people work!"

"Listen to the industrialist, hah? Make the place warm. Give them music. It's comfortable? Pay less!"

The painter winked down at me from the ladder.

"He's the one who knows," he said. "Such an industry he's got. Him, one boy, two machines. Your boots die of old age in here. Three weeks you go in socks!"

"Cures your corns. Mr. Eck, not to be rude. Where's my tenant from, if people ask?"

"People in uniform? I'm from the other side of the wall. Dresden. Six years enjoying the hospitality of the working class. The first democracy. The worker's paradise. Which would be better, be sick now, or wait till we get outside?"

"I know," Jabotinski shouted over the hum of the wheel. "I was also a guest. Who wants to rattle bones?"

"I heard enough and buried enough. I got a good bed and I'm looking for hard work. That's money. Then I settle down here."

"Not married?"

"Was. Five good years. Then they took her. She went first-class. Standing."

"Mine, too."

"Ovens?"

"Overeating!"

Metzler shifted the ladder, looking at me with a step-leg cuddled against his cheek, a strange eye, hard, solid blue.

"Careful!" he whispered, and let go, tapping his ear. "It's everywhere again. Don't do to talk too much. Keep it down!"

"Same lot?"

He blew out his cheeks *phooh!* looking at the ceiling.

"Stronger. More money. More to shout about. If I knew enough to join them, I wouldn't be working here!"

"What d'you have to know to join?"

He folded his arms and looked at me, eyes down, smiling.

"Enough to want it all back again? No, friend. That's what I said. Never. Next time, I'll fight *them*. Here. In the street!"

Jabotinski came in yawning, taking off his apron. He wore a lambskin suit, handmade boots, and a blue silk muffler, all dirty, and he couldn't have washed for weeks.

"How long you going to be?" he asked, glancing about. "Mnnn! Smart place we're going to have. Same color for me, Metzler!"

"Be about an hour more. Paint outside tomorrow?"

"It's better. More money? Once they get a hook in, when they let y'loose?"

"I have a sign for the window tomorrow," I said. "Radio. TV. Appliances."

"I'll have one. '*Jabotinski. At your feet.*' That's all. What time you start in the morning?"

"Seven."

He threw me the keys.

"Lock up. I'm here at nine. Mornings, I like to read. Good-night!"

He went out through the back, and Metzler winked, touching his head.

186

"A little bit," he said. "He's Yugoslav. In and out of the cage. He'll tell you one day. More ideas 'n a monkey. Half of 'em's crazy. The rest, I'm not sure."

He went back to painting, and I began to wire two small radios. To the onlooker there wouldn't have been much difference between the two, and one was, in fact, a radio I meant to work in the shop. The other wasn't. It was a pretty little job with a duty all its own, and while I worked on it, that burn spread in the nape.

At a little after seven-thirty, Metzler put his ladders and planks against the wall, lined up pots and tins, dipped brushes, and went over the few spots with a rag. It was a different place from the morning. The boy tapped on the door to take out the gear, and Metzler put his account, in neat figures, on the bench, leaning to watch me use a soldering iron smaller than a pencil.

"Delicate stuff," he said. "I wish I had a trade, so. How long's it take?"

"To learn? Assembly, all types, months, if you've got the hands. And memory. Know what you're doing, design your own, that's years."

"Like painting. Looks easy. It's a lifetime. Listen, I mean what I said. Careful about speaking. This town's full!"

I shook my head, counting notes.

"That's it, and thanks for a fine job," I said. "The other? I don't care what they do. What they say. Moment I hear anything's moving, I'm back to sea. I don't argue. I cut the cable, I go!"

"Lucky. Well, I enjoyed it. See you again!"

There was an odd sadness in him, but I had enough to think about, and just after nine, I knew I could finish both sets next morning. I squeaked into my coat, pulled the cap on, locked up, and walked through falling snow to the Café de l'Europe.

The bar was crowded and so was the family side, but I went downstairs to the cellar, a room about sixty foot square, lined with wooden panels, high-backed settles both sides with a table between, one long table down the middle, and smaller tables on both sides, mostly filled. At the far end, two doors were In and Out to the kitchen, and a halfmoon bar took the other side. To my left, a passage led to a men's and women's, and a door up three steps marked PRIVATE/ADMINISTRATION.

A head waiter nodded to the cloakroom on the right, and I checked my cap and coat. He walked down to a place at the long table, and gave me a card. I ordered a schnitzel and a glass of beer, and went down to the men's room, a big place, shining white, with a little grey entellus to hand one soap and a towel. Steam pipes ran along the far wall, and, I judged, power cables cased in wood. I wanted very much to look into the room marked PRIVATE but there was no light under the door, and people were coming along the passage. Before the schnitzel came, I saw a green baize board to the left of the bar. A couple of men were reading the notes and talking to each other.

I told the waiter I was going for a drink, and walked down to order a bottle of lager. I don't know what I expected but I almost cheered to see that an important event was advertised for two nights later. The cellar would be closed after lunch, to re-open for lunch on Saturday. The other notices were about billiard matches, tennis, and a coach to a Sunday football tie. No mention of the 43rd Veterans whatever-it-was. A little disappointed, I went back to the table, and the waiter followed with my drink and the schnitzel.

After I'd had a couple of bites, he bent over me to ask if everything was good, and I said very.

"I was wondering how about a table for some friends. It's a birthday. Friday night?"

His head lolled back in a gesture of despair.

"Ah, sir!" he breathed, almost ecstatic with apology. "But you see, Friday night, we're shut. It's the night of the comrades-in-arms. Friday, they remember their sufferings. I didn't suffer. I never got to the front. I was shunting trains, coupling trucks. I only lost a leg in the bombing. That's why I'm here. So to see

188

them all suffering, all over again? Ah, sir, a sentimental heart like mine?"

His face was a blank of innocence. I guessed him to be a Berliner, because they and the Cockneys share the same comic sense, wickedly satirical, deeply human.

"Lads of the old brigade, eh?" I said, helping myself to mashed potato. "I'd have thought they were tired of it!"

"Who, them? Now they've got the youngsters on it. The cadets. Daddys' joys, every one of 'em. And they're the worst!"

He had to go off, and though I'd have liked a few more words with him, I'd heard enough to be perfectly happy.

Odd, I was thinking of that counterpane. And for some reason, Consuelo.

26

I wrenched out of sleep at a little after five. The blackened badge on the missing cap went mistily away in the dream. For a few moments I lay there in cold amazement at myself. Whether a couple of days in a different milieu had done something to recharge a sedentary mind, or if the Xth—the warning—sense had sparked during sleep, but I was forced to examine the torpid dolt I seemed to have become, and ask myself when, at what stage, I'd considered it necessary to stop using my brain.

My suitcase looked ordinary enough but wasn't. Whoever opened it used a special key. Had the thief also looked at the Eck papers in the lid? He—or she—would have to know where to find the latch. If somebody at M.I. had asked Georges Pontvianne's lads to help me if required, why take the cap? Might such open warning have been given by Claudine? If Georges had told her, then obviously she'd ask questions about Tanis. What would she find? My conduct must have assured her that so far as I was concerned Tanis meant bed, and nothing more. If there'd been a tape working in that room she wouldn't have a doubt. It told me a great deal about myself that I hadn't once thought of it.

I had less time than I'd imagined. Georges perhaps would warn his West German colleagues, or, certainly, his own sources here.

How far would I be allowed to go? It wouldn't take them an age to get "on" to me, and after that, how long would they wait, and what could I say? If I'd come here direct, Pontvianne, perhaps would not have been warned because Claudine would have had nothing to report. But if I was merely passing through France, why would M.I. tip Georges to look after me? Hadn't I made an original error in going to Claudine's place? Why had I gone there? Because it was a hideaway and I knew I could trust Claudine. But anathema lay in any thought of making love to Tanis in a wallpaper of crippled lilac and a plaintive bedstead. Wasn't my going there a childish misuse of privilege to please myself?

I was in a most serious situation of my own making. I deserved anything I got, an unacceptable thought, but I had to put up with it. While I showered and dressed, I thought of Mel, the children, the house, Gilman, but they seemed far away, never any real part of me. My name was no longer Trothe. I felt like an actor whose part in a play had become his own identity, not for a couple of hours, but for the rest of his life. It was a curious feeling but it didn't worry me, and the whiskers didn't, the clothes didn't, the room didn't. I was surprised I got along so well with Mr. Eck. We must have had a lot in common, though for the moment I wasn't sure what it might be. Unless, of course, it was a mutual desire to create a healthy shambles among a sordid pack.

The street looked like a woodcut pulled on dirty paper. I shut the door without a sound and felt thankful for the calf-length boots. Slushy snow was over the ankle and snow met me on the corner. By the time I got to the shop I had a pad on both shoulders. I put the warmer to work and started on the radio set, first. Once it was working, I put it up in a corner and went back to the other. I'd almost finished by the eight o'clock news, when Huldtmann came in with timber and tools, and Metzler followed with the truck and ladders.

I went out to get some breakfast, even happy about the snow. It was good cover, and I was glad to see the Café de l'Europe open and the paving cleared in front. Only the Family part was open for breakfast, of coffee, a plate of sliced sausage, cheese and ham, a fresh-baked loaf, a lump of butter and an apple jelly. As a good German I had to eat the lot and forget the figure, though I mourned and exulted at the same time. A curious feeling, but there's nothing like food with a taste.

I had to find Ants. Three men in the bar were washing down and two behind the counter dusted bottles. Two more came in with trays of glasses. None of them looked like an Ants. But then, nobody in the business ever looks like anything. The barman I remembered wasn't there.

I took out a cigaret, feeling in my pockets for a match, pushing back the chair, walking as far as the flap and putting my head in.

"Could I buy some matches here?" I said, at large.

A youth handling glasses nodded next door.

"Want a light?" the short waiter asked, and took a box out of his rolled shirtsleeve. "Take the lot!"

"I'll pay for them—"

"Lot of things I want paying for," the waiter said, wiping the legs of an upturned chair. "Matches'll never be one of 'em. Never take money for a match. Not like a knife. You give a coin. But matches? It's bad luck!"

"Free matches, good luck?"

"Something for nothing's always good luck. Least, I think so!"

I lit the cigaret and offered him one, but he shook his head, putting the dusted chair on the table top, picking up another, and I went back to my table.

Matches, used three times in a sentence with knife and luck, and a final sentence—"Least, I think so!"—couldn't be hit on accidentally.

While I poured another cup of coffee, he came in, looking about to find me, and brought a booklet of matches on a saucer.

"Sorry, sir," he said breezily. "Mind if I have that box back? Got an address in it!"

It hadn't, but I gave it to him, took the booklet, and made a sign for the check. He looked over at the waiter and thumbed at my table.

I'd found Ants.

In the gloom outside, sleet blew icy splinters on lips and eyelids, and I huddled, stamping flat in freezing slush to keep from slipping. Well down the street I took out the booklet in a doorway, tore off the match comb and put it in my pocket, and looked at the cover. The front advertised a brand of beer, inside, a copywriter's dithyramb about the pleasures of drinking it, and on the back, a list of addresses for dry throats. One had a dot against it, and a pencilled 4:30.

I tore the cover in shreds, and let them go a few at a time. I couldn't see more than twenty feet so I was fairly certain I wasn't being followed. I got back to the shop and found my handbills. Huldtmann's boy stood watching the other working the machine.

"If you want to make some pocket money, you could drop these for me," I told him. "Along the main street. Leave one where it's wanted. Don't waste any!"

"My boy'll help," Jabotinski said. "He's sweethearting. He can use the money!"

"Pay him more," Huldtmann said, from the top of the ladder. "You'd skin a toad for the croak!"

"Who gives me money?" Jabotinski asked, hammering. "The help don't like the pay? Go somewhere else!"

"You charge enough, God knows!" Huldtmann said, winking at me.

"I work the best," Jabotinski said, in a stifled voice, as if he spoke against his will. "Ten, eleven hours. No overtime. I'm wrong?"

"When you work for yourself, who stops you?" Metzler asked.

"Visitors, that's who," Jabotinski said. "I told them, I don't want them in here. I got my license to open. I pay my taxes. Leave—"

"A moment," I interrupted, without turning. "I need a license to work?"

"Well, Mr. Eck, you need it, naturally—"

"Who do I see?"

"The Town Hall. I thought you had one!"

"You didn't ask for it!"

"A month in advance covers a lot of ground," Metzler said, painting up on the ladder. "See the trade grow first. Then the license. You don't profit, you save money!"

"The latter-day honesty," Jabotinski said, peening leather on a cobble. "First, take out the license. Then you get the visitors. You are ex-combatant? Sailor?"

"That's an accident," I said. "Army."

"So they'll drop in. You join, or you don't. You join, you get the trade. You don't, you get what you can. It's not enough, and I don't keep lodgers!"

I pointed down at my boots.

"I've got two, and I stand on them," I said. "I told you. The moment I see anything, even smell anything I don't like, I'm back to sea. The investment here? It's nothing. I was land-hungry, that's all. Now I'm getting seahappy again. It's this snow. I don't like it. Africa, India, that's what I like. A man can live in a shirt and a pair of shorts. That's where I ought to set up!"

"I've got a boy you could teach," Metzler said. "Six months, he'll work for nothing!"

"If I stay, I'll take him and pay him. No taste in nothing!"

"I endorse the doctrine," Jabotinski said, flipping tacks in his mouth as if they were breadcrumbs. "Working for nothing, charity, voluntary this, that, and the other, it's a curse!"

"There he goes!" Huldtmann said, puttying a nailhead in the lintel. "When do we start on nationalised insurance?"

Jabotinski looked round at me in a grimace of pity.

"Talk to them, try to teach them, I tell you, Mr. Eck, the provender's too rich. That's Europe's disease. What you don't under-

194

stand, laugh at. Laugh. The bray of the mule. What's a mule? Look at the parents. A horse and an ass. You feel hungry, Mr. Eck?"

"I know it's well past midday—"

"Good. Then I invite you, my friends, to a midday table. Here!"

He untied the apron and threw it to the boy, and we followed down the passage to the yard, into the first door, to a pantry lined with cupboards, and beyond, to a dining room panelled in pale cypress, with silver and china massed in open dressers, a fine collection of pewter along the mantel, and a long table laid at one end for four, and at the other for two.

"Boys sit by themselves," Jabotinski said. "But they also have to learn how to eat. Outside to wash!"

While the others waited to use the "social" toilet, Jabotinski poured a schnapps, and waved to me to help myself. I found the atmosphere a little like the club. I filled a glass of beer and lifted a toast to the roof. Jabotinski raised a finger in thanks, and dropped in a chair by the gasfire, and the air cushion *faffed!*

"It's a rotten existence," he said, in a different tone, more authoritative and far less the shoemaker. Curiously, the lambskin suit, boots, blue muffler, dirty enough under light, at that distance gave him a certain elegance. "I don't see what's to become of us. I'm sick of the juice of nails. They don't need shoemakers at sea. Here I serve a need. But as myself, brain, what else? The politicians are going to destroy us. They must. There's no recourse!"

Huldtmann circled a forefinger at his right eye, winked, and walked to the bar.

"You've got a feeling for politicians," I said.

"No feeling whatever, and I'm hungry," Jabotinski said, and lifted his glass to Metzler's toast. "In the spring I'm going back to my country. South of Dubrovnik. It's beautiful. At least, that's

195

memory. I have a feeling I shan't come back. You know the poetry of Rilke?"

"I don't like poetry. It's a pastime for the idle."

"Hm!"

He pulled out a chair at the head of the table, and a woman came out with a long dish of beef, carrots, lettuce hearts, turnip and Swede slivers, button onions and parsley, reminding me of Mrs. Cloney's Brown Bess Pot. We helped ourselves and passed the dish to the boys. Nobody said a word. Jabotinski used a fork and a crust of crackly loaf. Huldtmann and Metzler had forearms on the table, tucking in. The boys gulped and champed, all of gusto, of manners none.

I saw Jabotinski looking at me.

As an electrician, many years at sea, how should I eat?

A simple question.

I used the fork as a spoon, helped by a heel of the loaf and tried not to be self-conscious. But I should have practised, and I hadn't.

The others finished, reached for a toothpick, explored as speleologists, brrfrrmmped, made gestures whether of apology or admiration wasn't clear, and when the woman came in with the coffee and a plate of cakes, we followed Jabotinski to the fireplace.

"I'm a lonely man, Mr. Eck," he said, as small fact, back to us. "I am, therefore I live. I never believed that drivel about I think, therefore I am. Only a lopsided economy permits such untruths. If the fool couldn't think, what's he doing? Listen, while this gastank fills such balloons, thousands of millions of humans die without a mark. The *real* truths, which could give them a better life, they never heard. They were condemned. As this generation is also condemned. The majority never grow past fourteen years of age, mentally. Not all of them achieve so much. Cinema, television, newspapers, books, who're they for?"

"All right, who?" Huldtmann asked, pointing the toothpick.

"I don't read newspapers *or* books. Don't get the time. Haven't been to the cinema for years. Television? The wife likes it. So?"

"You answered all the questions," Jabotinski said tiredly, and put his glass on the mantel. "Good work, sleep, eat, talk nothings, die. That's it. I vote, therefore I am. Democracy!"

"Well, I'm lucky," Metzler said, bracing for attack in a wide, pale eye. "When I think what I came back to, and what I've got now, well, it's not the same world. Listen—"

Jabotinski almost danced.

"But, damn it, naturally!" he shouted. "Rebuild the nest. But the animal stays exactly as it was. The only thing you didn't rebuild was yourself!"

"Look," Metzler said, as if he'd been bottling something. "I like coming here. I like everything here. I know you're not where you ought to be. I like *you*. Sometimes. But sometimes you talk like a Commie. I don't like them. Tito's or any other sort. And I won't listen to it. God damn them all. They don't let a man live in peace with himself or anybody else!"

Jabotinski raised his hands in calmest surprise.

"Have I ever said anything different?" he asked mildly. "Haven't I been through as much, lost as much—or more—than anybody here? For the same pack of fourteen-year-olds? The brains older than that, the rocket heroes, the bureau-aristos, they've got everything, town place, country place, cars, the gilded pheasant. Except the freedom to come, go express themselves freely as humans. How do they grow? Inwards?"

"Doesn't bother me," Huldtmann said, filling a pipe. "They can stay there and rot. If they come over, I'll be back in the line again, I'll tell you that!"

"You and your line!" Jabotinski said. "If they start, they'll come over in a hundred years. When the ash stopped being radioactive. The people you ought to be worried about are here. Outside there!"

"We know all about it," Huldtmann said, and put the pipe away. "Perhaps we ought to tell Mr. Eck what to expect?"

The shop bell rang faintly, rang again, rang and kept on ringing. Huldtmann and Metzler put their glasses down. They both had the air of being caught. They stood, hands at sides, watching Jabotinski. He drank, put the glass down gently, and looked at me.

"No need to tell you anything," he said. "These are the visitors. Sooner than I expected. But you're registered at Boehm's and you've had handbills done. It's known who you are—"

"I haven't said a word—!"

He waved his hands, and nodded at a boy to open the street door.

"You've got all your papers?" he asked me. "Paper, more important than skin!"

"All I came with," I said, touching my breast pocket. "Why do I have to worry about visitors?"

"Once upon a time, they were marching these streets in brown shirts. Since then, they learned a lesson. I tell you, be careful what you say. Let's go in the shop!"

The boy had opened the door for two men stamping snow off their boots, shaking their hats.

"Don't make yourselves comfortable!" Jabotinski shouted.

"We came to see Mr. Eck," one of them said. "That you?"

They looked a couple of typical small townsmen, mufflered, about forty-five, below my height, both with a smile about the eyes I'd often seen in police officers. The radio played "Entrance of the Little Fauns," which I thought apt.

"We got your particulars at the Boehm Pension," the taller said. "We represent the Ordgarten branch of the Reunion Movement. You were with the 225th Engineers—"

"The 227th, later the 51st, after Sebastopol. I was wounded—"

He lit a cigaret, blew smoke at the match *hauf!*

"We have your particulars. My mistake. I don't need to tell you what a welcome you'd have. Deep-sea man, too. You'd find plenty of ex-Navy men to talk to. We're trying to tie this town up!"

"Tie it up?"

"We're making sure who's with us, who's not," the second man said, and lit a cigaret off the other's. "There's a lot of business coming your way. That's if you know what y'doing. Your papers are all in order, that's why we—"

"What d'you mean, order?"

The smiles were open. The shorter licked his moustache.

"We vet everybody," he said. "No use trying to cover anything. You'll meet a relation of yours, Seidesmanner. Why don't you come along and meet everybody? Don't worry about money!"

"I'd be happy to," I said. "Seidesmanner, he was a cousin of my mother's. He must be getting on. Last time I heard, he was in Bremen—"

"Moved here two years ago. Selling tractor spares. I can see you're going to have a real business. This place won't hold you long!"

The other turned from looking at the warmer.

"This fire one of your jobs?"

"Made it this morning."

"If the price's right, I'd like one!"

"Ready tonight!"

"Uh, any politics? I mean, any party?"

"Been at sea too long. I think the government's all right. Time being. And I'm a Roman Catholic, if that's anything?"

"Does you no harm. Enemy's in the East, not upstairs!"

They were buttoning their coats, and the taller squatted to look at the warmer.

"Trust a sailor," he said. "You'll make a fortune. Any of you others want to join us?"

He was looking up at the group in the doorway, more threat than question.

Metzler moved, looking from Jabotinski's boots to Huldtmann's, twisting his head as if his neck hurt.

"If Eck's going, I will," he said. "Might as well. See what it's all about!"

"That's the spirit," the man in the doorway told the snowy street. "Jabotinski, how about you?"

"Get out of my place, you skulking rogue!" Jabotinski said, without raising his voice. "Take your filthy friend with you!"

The man going out looked at Huldtmann.

"We didn't hear from you, Sergeant-Major," he said quietly, ignoring Jabotinski. "I think it's time you came, too. Your son's got an examination soon, hasn't he? I'm told he's a smart boy, that right?"

Huldtmann rasped the whiskers across his face, glanced at Jabotinski, and shifted his feet.

"I wanted to keep out of it," he said. "Don't see any need for it!"

"Won't take them Russkis long to shove that wall down, will it? When they do, it won't take them long to get here, will it? If they do, it won't be too comfortable for the girls—got three, haven't you?—will it? Eh?"

That Will It? cut like the tip of a whipcord. I suddenly realised that both these unremarkable little men were thoroughly well-trained, practised, without a vestige of any feeling, and most dangerous when most friendly.

"Make up your mind, Huldtmann. Time's short. The children are growing. What'll they say?"

"All right!" Huldtmann shouted, and flapped his hand. "What the hell!"

"Seven o'clock. Tomorrow night. No need to dress up!"

The boy shut the door behind them. I went over to the bench. Huldtmann took a saw from the bag and chose a length of timber. Metzler leaned on the counter flap.

"I'm a dirty coward," he said. "But if I don't like what I hear, I'll tell them all to their faces!"

"Get to work!" Huldtmann said irritably. "Why don't you come with us, Jabotinski? Make us feel better!"

"Why? Let this Catholic salt season the dish for you. It needs only one to bend. The rest wilt!"

200

"What, exactly, is your objection?" I asked him, one eye on the clock. "If these men are getting together to protect themselves if the Russians attack—"

"Fairy tales! They make bogeys of anybody to suit themselves. Power's in the Bundestag. They get there by vote. As they did last time. I'm stubborn, Mr. Eck. Couple of years ago I had the biggest shoe factory in this part of the country. I wouldn't give them money. I wouldn't let their people in to hold meetings. Now I'm here. Half a shop. Go next door. Her husband, the same. Big business. He killed himself. They say. Go anywhere you like, any street, any farm. I tell you, Mr. Eck, they got this country in a fist!"

"You're staying with Boehm?" Huldtmann asked. "Ask him!"

The mention of "accidents" was interesting, but I wanted to be at the rendezvous at least thirty minutes before to look at the place.

I put the tools back and got into my squeaker, sorry to be leaving them at such a time. A boy came in, trod snow and shut the door.

"Mr. Eck? Mr. Lambert, the printer up there? He'd like to see you about that wiring job. Soon as you like!"

"First fruits!" Jabotinski whispered from the other side of the boards, and hammered.

"I'll come with you," I said, and turned off my light.

We walked into a white float. I didn't hear traffic until we got to the main road, and we almost walked into a waiting cab. I thanked the boy and said I'd be in later on. I opened the door and gave the address.

"I didn't want to go anywhere in this," the cabman said, half-seen. "I can get up there. You'll have to walk across the Square, though."

I wasn't worried about being followed. When I paid, the cabman pointed to a white blank and said it was About There. I had to feel a way over the tramlines, get into the small park, find the path, and cross the other street. I might have been alone in the world. A tobacconist's shop was lit and warm, and the girl told me I was six shops off to the left, look for the green and red sign, and turn downstairs. Sure enough, there it was. I went downstairs, put a wet coat in the cloakroom, walked into a comfortable bar in candlelight, waiters busy, white-coated barmen, barrels in a row behind the counter, and the tables almost full.

I sat on a stool and ordered beer. Ants wasn't there. I walked over to the newsstand for a paper, and got a most unpleasant surprise.

Druxi sat in the middle of a booth against the wall.

27

I'd known her since the Paris of 1940, perhaps not then twenty, studying at the Sorbonne, tall, elegant always, with an entirely American air of the well-bred. She looked now like a seedy busker. Bony fingers held a cigaret, which she drew till the ash glowed, and blew the smoke out of the side of her mouth in an appalling scowl. She was made up theatre-fashion in reds and blues, a feather drooped, a wide brim hid her eyes, and a sealskin draped her shoulders. I recognised her more spiritually than physically. I'd always admired her as one of the dedicated. Now she couldn't have been anything except what she looked, a good sort, rather common, hard times, no hope, and making the drinks last.

I was sure she wouldn't recognise me. My hair was uncombed, my beard had grown, I wore bifocals, and I walked in a stoop and shuffle.

But I knew, then, that C.I.A. was "in," and they took the business seriously, or she wouldn't be there.

While I sat and read the paper, two or three men went over. She waved a hand that seemed a foot long, as if she were waiting for her escort, and they bowed and went away. But she didn't refuse the drinks they sent over.

Ants came up behind me. I didn't see him till he gestured at an unlit cigaret. I gave him a box, and went back to the paper.

The barmen knew him, and two of them came down to get books of tickets for something to do with football.

"You're new here, sir?" Ants asked me, putting a napkin under my drink. "I know most of the regulars. I used to work here. You wouldn't like to take a book of sweep tickets, would you? It's for the hospitals. Your book has a winner, you're on the ten per. *Plus!*"

The *plus* decided me. I took the book, paid, and he gave me a pen, pointing to the blank name and address.

"Willi!" he shouted at the nearest barman. "God's sake get their addresses clear. Win a hundred thousand, no address, where d'you look?"

The barman nodded, pouring at the barrel, and two men came between us, asking about tickets. I gave Ants the pen, tore out the receipt, finished the drink, nodded between their heads, and walked out. Druxi was talking to a young man. Light shone on waves in his hair, firing an opal in a ring on his left-hand little finger. Opals, my grandmother maintained, were an unlucky stone. I wondered how I was to get in touch, or whether I ought, and decided not. I could be a nuisance, or worse, she could be.

Snow still fell and I walked back to the shop as if I'd never done anything else. I was surprised. I'd dropped into Eck's boots as though I were he. I could have laughed, kicking through slush, thinking of myself as a pseudo-member of the Common Market. How did I feel about it? My beer wasn't cheaper than in Britain. The food I ate certainly wasn't. My radio parts were too expensive, I'd thought, and by comparison with the same space at home, my half-rental with Jabotinski was exorbitantly high, and so were the accounts of Huldtmann and Metzler. For that matter, I'd never noticed prices any lower in France. If anything, remembering past times, every-thing—and newspapers—was far more expensive. Higher wages, transport costs, taxes, explained a lot. But where was the ad-vantage?

To the officers of any workman's union, to a cartelist or banker, the benefits were patent. But what about me, Simeon Rotbart Eck, workman, trudging through the streets of a small

German town, or Gerhart Huldtmann, carpenter, or Johannes Metzler, painter? When all the signatory paunches had moved from one dining table to another, all the pates scratched bare of ideas, all the papers signed, and all the fanfarronading trumpets drained of spittle, and that big Charlie had blown his nose, what about us?

Thinking back to conferences, charts, studies, reports, I was a little aghast. I'd accepted the idea. I hadn't thought of the reality, of an Eck, having to live on the money he could earn. I wasn't an "average" electrician. I was fairly certain that most Ecks wouldn't have two thousand dollars in a savings account. I'd spent far more than an Eck might in the same circumstances. I'd done it to give an idea that I meant to drop anchor. But as a Common Marketeer, what did I feel? I hadn't thought about it and I couldn't answer, but I was fairly certain that anywhere in Britain, in the same job, given the same chance, myself as Mr. Eck would have had a better life.

I was passing Lambert's Futurtyp, and went in to a hum and jog of machinery, the proud smells of ink and raw paper. Lambert came from a desk in mass of guillotined paper strips, paste pots and wire spikes drooping handbills.

"Ah!" he shouted, and sounded like a distant child, "When could you start? Tonight there's time. I'll close down these two presses at 10:30."

"I'll be here," I said, and he raised his fists, elated. "Send your boy down to the electrical store. This is what I want."

I wrote quantities on one of the paper strips, wire, sockets, and the other stuff. It wasn't much of a job. With half a brain he could have done it himself, but in any notion of power, most people are still in the miracle-half of the last century.

"Hear you'll be with us tomorrow?" he screeched, over the clattering start of another press. "You'll get a copy of the newssheet in the morning. Boehm's place? Best food there is!"

Who'd told him where I lived? News travels fast in small towns, but here it seemed to spin. I went back to Boehm's in a solid field of snow—it might have been the North Pole—and found the little girl doing homework at the table in the middle of that bare, shining room. I'm not particularly fond of other people's children, but I could have picked her up, chair and all, and bussed her soundly, if only to salute a sprouting mind determined to rob a book of learning. She smiled one little dimple at me in that refrigerated light, and I went on upstairs, suddenly cut to the heart, remembering my Patti. I didn't dare to think about her. That run of syllables rippled across my head like the rattle of a stick on palings. I shogged it off.

It was no longer part of my life. At least, I wanted to think it wasn't, but it was certainly unfinished business, and while I took off my coat I could hear that run of syllables again, and for the first time I was sure I'd heard the name or seen it, and probably, because of pressure or carelessness, missed it in some way. The thought annoyed, tantalized, but there was nothing I could do, at any rate, for the moment.

If I hadn't been looking for it with a loup I'd never have seen the message marked in Ants' book of sweep tickets. The pages had been dipped in water, dried, and the run of print had cleverly been used to touch—with a little help—certain letters which made up a six-letter code that I was able to read without using pencil and paper. I understood what the Blur had meant by limited.

Master Ants, that little man, was attempting blackmail.

I want five thousand pounds in my bank cabled advice Ants Uncle Dasti died Baat ex Beirut Lebanon account 4-11-230-P Bank of Tunis sent Hoilke Café de l'Europe here names and dates ready or nothing be careful.

Be careful meant he had another source of payment, possibly. Druxi came up, smiling painted blue eyes and scarlet lips. He might get more from C.I.A. She wouldn't hesitate. I knew Druxi. I never met a warmer-hearted cold-blood. I could, of course, drop the entire thing there and then, catch the next train out, infinitely confident that she'd take care of everything. I knew perfectly well she would. But I was thinking of Mel, and Frederick, and Mr. Von Hollefendorm and his ilk. I could save Druxi a little trouble and C.I.A. some money, and possibly relieve myself of a good deal of chagrin in some future hour, thinking back and wishing to God Almighty I'd put aside all the indolent let-somebody-else-do-it, instead of making quite sure the job was done, thoroughly well done, by myself, all on my little own, or as an old Cockney friend of mine used to say, on me own bloody Jack.

That was my original intention, remained so, and I gave myself twenty-four hours to carry it out satisfactorily, and then go for the Dutch frontier.

At a few minutes to the hour I got the "other" radio in working order, plugged into the light switch, and at three minutes past, tapped out a message to our monitor, telling London to expect me on Saturday or Sunday, and to cross Ants off the list. Then I read the paper until the half-hour, and at thirty-three minutes past, I listened for my call sign, and got a clear K, and A-R.

I switched out, dismantled the set and put it in my over-coat pocket. I was thinking of going out for supper, and I was held rigid by two timid taps at the door.

I took one pace and flung it open.

The little girl smiled her dimple, holding a plate with a steaming glass. I could smell rum.

"My papa said if you'd like to enjoy the fire, you could drink this downstairs," she whispered. "If you'd rather not, I brought it up!"

"I'm coming down," I said, and got my jacket. "What's that I saw you studying? Dolly's history?"

"No," she said, leading the way. "Algebra!"

That lidded me very nicely, and we walked through the shining, bare room, through the scrubbed and polished kitchen, to a room dominated by a fat-bellied porcelain stove taking one entire corner, that cast a pall like a hot blanket.

Mrs. Boehm, as I'd expected, was the big woman, now without the apron, wearing a flowered dress. Her hand was soft and damp but the grip told of character. Mr. Boehm came in through the door to the bedroom. I could see another counterpane thicker than mine.

"Ah, Mr. Eck, such a pleasure!" he said. "I've been longing to talk to you. I was second mate, steam and sail. Got malaria in the Philippines. So I came home and married. That was worse!"

He was tall, grey-eyed, stubbly grey-haired, thinnish—which surprised me, thinking of the kitchen—and, at face, the best type of merchant-seaman, evidently easygoing, but I judged he'd be strict on the bridge.

"I like that entire area," I said. "I used to like China. One place, Macao. Now, there was a dream!"

That started him, and while I sipped rum and lemon, he gave us an outline of twenty-five years or more, port to port, mostly in sail, and I could see my suppertime slipping away.

"How do you find things here?" I asked, when I could. "Better than they were?"

"Excellent!" he said, but he didn't look at Mrs. Boehm, and she didn't move or smile. "We're going to Canada!"

"Great country. Do very well there. With the kitchen you have here, you can't miss. So the young lady'll grow up a good Canadian!"

"I hope," he said, and looked at her. "I don't want her going through the same hurricane as her mother. I want to go as far inland as possible. In the middle. Where I can have a sailboat on a lake, and no speeches or processions!"

"Getting bad?"

"Some people, they're never happy, Mr. Eck. They've got to be stirring the soup. Old stuff. Stale. So I sold the place, and we're waiting for our papers. It's lucky I've got a trade apart from seaman. I have a master's certificate, of course. But I'm also a good plumber. I'll lay the best pipes in Canada!"

"And I'm trying to settle down here?"

"Might suit you. If you can stand politics, all right. When you get them coming in, examining your books, asking questions, well, you have to start wondering!"

"Just like the last time!" Mrs. Boehm said, suddenly, and the little girl got up and sat beside her. "No, Mr. Eck, we had enough!"

"They asked all about you," Boehm said, putting his feet on the stool. "They went through your room. Didn't touch anything, of course. Just looked at a few things. I stood in the door. They say anything to you?"

"I'm going to be at the meeting tomorrow night, that's all."

"That's sense. I ought to be there, but I'm taking my wife to her brother's. You're working with Jabotinski?"

I nodded.

"Fighting for nothing. Arguing for nothing. He won't last in his own country, he can't last here, and he won't go anywhere else. So?"

"But why *should* he?" Mrs. Boehm asked, sitting forward, suddenly, beating her knee. "Who *are* these people? Why should *we* have to leave?"

"Get some peace," Boehm said, dismissing it. "Mr. Eck, somebody gave Paula a message for you. No need to take it if you don't want to. My daughter's not a messenger for anybody!"

"Who was it?" I asked the child.

"It was a man. It was snowing. I couldn't see him very well. He said it was for you. By the time I had the door all the way open, he'd gone. I couldn't see anything!"

At my nod, Mr. Boehm gave me a crushed envelope, without name or address.

I tore it open, and took out a sheet folded in four, and opened it. Exactly in the center of the fold, I saw what I'd expected.

209

"What's that, a joke?" Boehm said, frowning. "Somebody playing stupid tricks?"

"It's a sample of paper from Lambert's, that's all," I said.

"Not what I want. Look at it. Rubbish!"

I turned the sheet back to front, held it up to the light, and tore it in bits. The little girl threw them in the fire-door.

They hadn't seen the capital M, overtyped by a capital O, which makes a fair symbol of the perched owl. We all knew it very well.

Obviously, Druxi had found out where I was. The owl was her clear invitation to get out while I was in one piece. I wondered if she knew who I was. Georges Pontvianne might have told her. Ants, I supposed, must have tipped her that one of H.M.'s lads was busy. It was a million to one he'd sold her the information, and was going to take another five thousand from us as a little gift. Limited, the Blur had said. I intended that Master Ants should be extremely so.

"Will you be with us long, Mr. Eck?" Mrs. Boehm asked me. "I can let that room—"

"I'll pay you three months in advance," I said. "I know when I'm well off. That's a wonderful bed!"

"Make it a month, and tonight you get a hot water bottle!" she said, and pushed the child. "Boil the water!"

I took out that broken wallet and counted out the notes.

"Lucky I went to the bank," I said. "I have to be at Lambert's to do a job. Shan't be home till three, perhaps. Be all right?"

"You have the key," Boehm said. "I'm looking forward to more talks. Listen, anything you want, say the word. You know?"

I looked him in the eye.

"Thanks, shipmate!" I said.

Sentiment carries its own weight in men of goodwill.

He put his fist on my shoulder, and shook hands, turning away. Mrs. Boehm looked up at him, and smiled at me, and I went clattering down the stairs.

28

By the time the master printer came in at a few minutes before two o'clock, the wiring in that part of the shop was done, and I got my coat on while he answered the telephone on Lambert's desk.

"Yes, he's still here," he said, and looked at me, listening. "Mr. Lambert wants you to go round to the Café de l'Europe for a drink. It's business."

"I could do with a sandwich," I said. "Tell him, yes!"

Snow still fell lightly but it seemed warmer. The walk took some of the kinks out of my back. I'd been hunched under the roofboards for a couple of hours, stripping rotted wire, putting in new, and worrying about Druxi. Once she had her teeth in, she'd never be pried loose. I had to find out where she lived. I didn't want her near the café when things happened.

I was surprised to see the place still full when I got there. An orchestra was playing in the Family part, the bar was crammed, people drank on the stairway, and downstairs was crowded. I put my coat in a bulging cloakroom, and did a sideways crawl to the bar, and luckily, or he was watching for me, Ants came behind the counter, and pointed across the room.

"Mr. Lambert's got a table over there, sir!" he called. "He's expecting you!"

I pushed through to follow him over to a corner booth.

Druxi sat between Lambert and Heinig, and the young man with the waves talked to a flashy blonde, perhaps of the theatre, possibly of the street.

"Ah, Mr. Eck, allow me!" Lambert said, half up and nodding at Druxi. "This is Miss Lisalotte Wesse, you know, the famous *diseuse*. She's taking the hall. We want a sign in electrics. It has to be ready tomorrow. I'm doing the bills. Look, sit down!"

At my heelclick Druxi merely stretched her lips, and went on looking at her drink. The others didn't bother. Ants brought some more drinks, put mine down, and stood at Druxi's right shoulder, looking about the room.

Lambert took out a pencil and drew a sign. In the noise, I understood he had the iron frame and sockets, and wanted Miss Wesse's name in yellow, the place in red, and the title of the show in blue. I saw no problems and said so, and Druxi gave me another of those broken-glass smiles. I still wasn't sure if she recognised me, but from the way Ants fussed about my ashtray, I was fairly sure he was pointing the finger.

The young man and the girl went without my seeing them. When Ants put another refill in front of us, I raised mine and drank it down without a breath, wiped my mouth and stood.

"Early call in the morning," I said. "Thanks for the invitation. Been a pleasure, Miss Wesse. Been admirer 'yours 'long time. Best o' luck!"

Again that stretch of the lips. She might have been drunk. I knew she wasn't, because she'd poured most of her drinks on the floor. I could feel the soles of my shoes were wet. Of old, I knew that nobody could apologise more prettily to a waiter—or tip more generously—for spilled drinks.

Ants wouldn't take any money, in a wave of a fat palm patronisingly refused a tip, and went into the crush at the bar. I got my coat and pushed a way out to the street, feeling the arctic edge of a rising wind turning slush to ice underfoot.

That, I suppose, is what saved me.

I'd just turned the corner of the street. Boehm's neon scroll was out. A lamp here and there made dirty amber splashes on plowed-up mounds of snow. In between spaces were blacker, and snow began to fall in large flakes.

I saw the shadows before I heard the splash of feet. How many there were I don't know. I hit the first in the mouth, thanking my stars I'd bought ribbed gloves. The second caught a short right to the jaw. The third kicked me in the upper thigh. I managed to pivot and jab the flat of my heavy boot against his taut knee, and it cracked like a stick. His scream frightened the others. I caught one turning and hit him in the back of the neck. The other was unluckier. He caught the full weight of both boots in a jump at the base of his spine. The others were running. A couple on the ground were sitting up. I booted both in the face, in the plexus, in the groin. Another saw it and tried a running start. He got the same, and so did the others, three each. If any one of them was on his feet within the month, he was a better man than I, and I wished him luck. I turned a couple of them over. They seemed an ordinary type, probably paid a few marks for the job. By whom? I couldn't believe Druxi would. Ants might.

I was cut on the cheek, an ear sang tenor, the thigh and a shinbone ached, and my right hand was badly swollen. But I was lucky. That type of mob makes a sad mistake in attacking a single man. They never rehearse. If that lot had taken the trouble, I'd never have had an earthly. They were all youngsters. I went through the pockets of all of them, but beyond a little money, nothing. I left their clothing open to give them rather more than their fair share of night air, and—I hoped—a healthy pneumonia, and went on down to Boehm's, waited a moment, and went in.

I was careful in going up the stairs, more than careful in opening my door, but all seemed serene. I examined my bag, looked at the bed, opened the wardrobe, but nothing had been touched. I had my own way of leaving things, so I was sure. I looked at the corner of the linoleum I'd edged up to loosen a floorboard where I kept my sticker-friends. Nothing had been disturbed. I took off my clothes and got into bed, absolutely certain I was about to enjoy my final night chez Boehm, and for the first time in many a long year, relishing the thought of my own enormous Elizabethan fourposter.

But reaching for the switch I had to turn, looking at a small table in shadow of the wardrobe, and sat bolt upright.

The engineer's cap, badge to the fore, grinned its peak at me. Druxi? It was the sort of joke she liked. A further warning? Georges Pontvianne?

In any event I knew time was short.

I didn't sleep as soon as I'd imagined, or as well as I'd wished.

29

My coffee came up with the *Veteran's Newssheet* under the toast. Miss Lotte Wesse had a page to herself, with critical acclaim in floral inserts, having the privilege to present herself in readings from Shakespeare, Goethe, Schiller, and as I'd thought, Ibsen and Shaw. It was right up her street. I wish I could have stayed. But there *I* was, on page three, with a résumé of my career accurate enough to make me feel uncomfortable. Where did that detail come from? And so soon? At three minutes past the half hour, I switched in to our monitor, gave him thirty seconds to come on, but he didn't, and I closed out, packed the set and started walking to the shop.

It was a dull day. I looked for marks of the night before's brawl, but the pavement had been swept.

I called in at Lambert's on the way, found the lights going strong, and the master printer said they didn't know themselves and hoped I'd do the same for the back of the shop.

"Mr. Lambert's at Miss Wesse's hotel," he said. "He took the posters over. See the piece about you in the sheet? I envy you. Never been out of this town. Too young during the war. Got in the Youth Corps for a couple of months at the end. Didn't even get a uniform. Then it was all over. Didn't do a damned thing 'cep' clear the streets and pile bricks, four-five years. Then I came here, and that's it. Been here ever since. Can't get a day job. Wife doesn't want to move. Can't grumble. It's a good living. Wish I could see Miss Wesse. Like the rest of them. I only set the posters and lick my chops. But if Lambert's there, I got to be here. That's *it!*"

"How can I see him?" I asked. "I want some cash. I have to do the lights for the hall."

"Station hotel," he said, pointing over his shoulder. "Two minutes' walk. Listen, take these cards. Joh Pensen. Her pianist. Just back from the States. Make a piano talk. Wish I could hear him. No luck!"

The cards made a good excuse to get away from that mumble. The fellow was an excellent workman, merely an nth of a human being, nothing more than the thinking part of the press that employed him. While I walked, feeling flakes melt on my face, I laughed inwardly, thinking of Simeon Rotbart Eck's hatred of all print. I'd never before been at all curious about him. His was an identity among others I'd picked up quite by accident, and I'd studied what was known of him until I'd been able to meet members of his family as one of themselves. Now I began to wonder about that little hero, frozen into the ice at Stalingrad, resurrected by an alien, and used successfully three times, almost four, in areas of duty he could never have known anything about.

The porter at the Station Hotel sent me up one flight to Number Three, and went on reading the paper. That was the sort of hotel it was, and the door was open. Lambert sat in a three-cornered chair smoking a small cigar with the stench of disaster, Joh—I recognised the wave and the opal—Pensen practised, making no sound except the muffled rat-tat of his fingers, on a dummy keyboard stretched between two tables, a waiter cleared dishes, and Miss Wesse could be heard talking to somebody in the next room, though a radio covered what she said.

Lambert signed he wouldn't be a moment, Pensen went on dabbing, the waiter didn't give a damn anyway, and I stood there, listening to Miss Wesse's voice getting louder till she came through the door, long fair hair in Ophelia swirl, a worn blight of a pink peignoir, raggedy lace slippers with bows bowed down with grime, a fattish script in one hand, and a glass of water in the other. At least, I thought it was water, until she teetered on seeing me, smiled with one side of her face, hiccuped with the other, and stood unsteadily in front of me.

"Listena this!" she commanded. "'Come, sir! I would you make use of your good wisdom, whereof I know you are fraught, and put away these dispositions, which of late transport you from what you rightly are!'"

"May not an ass know when the cart draws the horse?" I followed, reaching back to school, and a term of King Lear. "'Whoop, Jug! I love thee!'"

She gave me the glass.

"'This admiration, sir, is much o' the savor of other your new pranks,'" she intoned, looking over my shoulder. "'I do beseech you to understand my purposes aright. You are old and reverend, you should be wise!'"

"I've come about that sign for the hall," I quavered. "I want some money!"

She made a regal gesture, and almost fell down.

"Pay this—scroyle—his fardels!" she bawled, and blundered splendid progress to the bedroom, hiccuped, and slammed the door.

I knew she'd recognised me. We'd been through that act, or something like it, before.

"Couldn't you have waited at the shop?" Lambert said, annoyed. "Got to come here and cause a lot of unnecessary trouble?"

"Mr. Pensen's cards," I said, and gave him the package. "I haven't got the time to wait about. You want a sign, I want the stuff. I don't have the capital to take chances—"

"What d'you mean, chances?" Lambert said, angrily, and took out a wallet. "Trying to make an exhibition out of me? How much d'you want?"

217

I gave him the sketch and a list of stuff.

"All you have to do is sign that, and I'll take it to the shop and collect. Pay me for the work and time, that's all!"

He signed it, Pensen tore the wrapper and looked at the top card, propped it against the wall, and went on thumping fingers on printed notes. I went out behind the waiter, and he shut the door.

"Don't know how she stands up," he marvelled. "Bottle of gin for breakfast? Three bottles a day. Whiskey at night. How 'she do it?"

I could have told him she poured it down the bath, but I didn't. I'd seen the flesh of her breast when the peignoir fell open. Alcoholics don't have that skin.

I wondered why the drunk act would be necessary, and judged she would know her own business best. I sent Jabotinski's lad to get the items, and went to work on a radio that had come in. A little solder put it right, and a woman sent a boy with a message about a refrigerator that wouldn't work. She lived round the corner, in a little dark house, one of a row that suffered from Allied bombers those years ago. The marks were still there. The kitchen smelled of soap and old sacks, and one wall was only of mortared brick without plaster, and the floor sloped. I'd seen some scantling coming in, and I went out to get a few pieces, cut them to size, and put them under the near edge of the refrigerator, so that it sat square, and firm. For the rest there was nothing wrong, and I refused to charge. I hadn't said much up to then, and she hadn't spoken a word.

"Thank you," she said. "I thought it was just part of the curse on us!"

"These things don't go wrong on their own," I said. "Man who put that in ought to be kicked!"

"They nearly didn't bring it in," she said, a little thin, trembly voice. "They know about the houses here. I was surprised you came. I never thought you would!"

"I'm new here," I said, getting into my coat. "You've got years of good service in that."

"It's wonderful company," she said, running a hand over the enamel door. "Got it cheap from the neighbour. Her husband died. I know what that is. My husband's in there with the children."

She nodded at the mortared wall. I thought she meant they were next door. She went over and put the flat of her hand against it. For the first time I saw her eyes. They stared as a dead dog's.

"That's why I wouldn't move or let them finish here," she said, touching the mortar with her little finger. "I think of the Resurrection. They'd come out, wouldn't they? That's all I'm waiting for. I almost forgot how they look."

I got down the dark passage without being able to think of anything to say. But then I had an idea.

"If you'd like a small radio, I can send you one," I called back to her. "Cost you nothing!"

"Oh, my God, no!" she shrieked. "We heard them coming on the radio. That's when it happened. They got me out. Not them. I just listen to *them*. That's enough!"

It was, indeed, and I let myself out, grateful for the nip of an icy wind. I saw that most of the houses were rebuilt. In many of the walls, niches had been cut for small vases of paper or plastic flowers. Those buried when the bombers passed over were not forgotten.

The boy grinned when I shut the door, holding frozen finger-tips to the warmer.

"You didn't know she was *mashugenar?*" he asked, in the sloppy grin of the half-grown that dried as I looked at him. "Mr. Heinig was here. Wants to see you soon's you can. Mr. Jabotinski's sick in bed. Mrs. Lauter's gone for the doctor."

"Look after things till I get back. If the printer sends the sign, put it on the bench. Don't go out!"

It was snowing hard. I passed Lambert's boy going down with

the skeleton sign, and took a bus to the corner. The café was busy, and I went downstairs, kicking lumps of ice out of my boot-soles, swinging my coat over the cloakroom counter, to Heinig's office.

"Ah, right!" he said, from behind the smaller desk, and waved at a chair. "Just want you to sign membership papers. This one asks you to keep the rules. This one promises you'll vote with the committee. Right?"

I nodded, and signed in my best backhand.

"That'll be five marks," Heinig said, using a blotter.

"You're going to pay that, plus my drink bill tonight," I said, putting the pen back. "That's for the warmer. Cheap, too!"

He stuck a pencil behind his ear and grinned.

"Bargain," he said. "When are you leaving that rathole? We're going to close him out of this town. He won't land anywhere else, either. Look, go along here, about a dozen doors. Dorft's got a fine place empty. Six months' rent free, main street, and more than five thousand clients ready. Taken?"

"You bet," I said. "Like somebody told me the other day. The luck's turning!"

He pointed his finger.

"Stick with us!" he said. "You're doing a sign for Miss Wesse? Good. She's giving us a show tonight. Look, do us a big favor. We've only had a house electrician. Have a look at the stage out there. See if you could do a better job of lighting. Anything you want, ask for it!"

Luck was certainly turning, though I didn't need half as much. I looked at the stage. The "lighting" was strings of colored lamps. I made a sketch of spots, and smaller points in cluster, and a ring in a trough on the floor to shine up at the swastika. I made a list and took it to the office. Heinig picked up the telephone and dialled.

"All be here after two o'clock," he said. "Still at Boehm's? Best place. When you leaving that rathole?"

"Get my tools out tomorrow."

"You'll do!"

He didn't know how much I wanted to tip that desk on top of him. I got my coat, and walked back to the shop in a boil. I was sorry for Jabotinski, for everybody.

I saw exactly how Mr. Schickelgrüber had got things done.

30

By the time the Wesse sign was ready, I felt like lunch. I went out to see Mrs. Lauter. She made a sign to wait, and came back to call me into the dining room, through to the big room, rather less grand by light of day, still showing the bent of the book-man and art lover. It *was* a Brancusi, and he had a Chagall, a Labisse, and a Nash among other good things on the walls. She went up a short stair, and held open a door.

Jabotinski lay against pillows. He looked ill. The room was small, with only the bed, and a chair piled with his clothes.

"Mr. Eck, I think I'm going to the hospital," he said, in a throaty voice. "Could I ask you to pay the boy and the woman? Just keep an eye on things. Won't be long. Perhaps ten days—"

"Don't count on me," I said. "I don't think I'm going to last. Like I told you, Mr. Jabotinski. Moment I hear what I don't like, I'm out. It's happening!"

He nodded at the ceiling.

"Any books you want, take them with you. My pleasure!"

"I'm not a great reader. Anything else I can do?"

"Nothing, Mr. Eck. Clock's making a full turn. I'd have said it wouldn't happen. Once, I was professor of Sociology. I don't mention the University. My wife was a teacher of language. Wrong race. One day I came home, she'd gone. I couldn't find her. Never did. That was 1941. The mayor of the town we lived in was a friend. They wanted to take me away. I was 'con-taminated.' Also, a Slav. But the Mayor hid me. I was in the shoe warehouse he owned. Night watchman. He had hundreds of forms there. All sizes. Leather got scarce. I learned to make a good boot from worn-out tires and canvas. End of the war, I was a shoemaker. Still couldn't get leather. Or shoes. I went into business with the Mayor. We bought more old tires than anybody in the world. We made the best working boot. And we made money. He died, and I left, and came here. I opened a factory. It's still there. You know what happened. That's how it is. The fourteen-year-olds are in charge. The tragedy, Mr. Eck? They don't know they never grew past the age of puberty. That's the disease people don't know they've got. That's the one that kills!"

It was said almost dispassionately. He closed his eyes and turned his head. I muttered something and went down the stair into the sitting room. I could have put that Brancusi under my arm so easily. Mrs. Lauter wanted to serve a meal, but I went out to the shop, and sent the boy instead. I carried the sign on my shoulder up to Lambert's, left it against the desk, and went on to Boehm's. I still had a lot of pettifogging little things to do. A lunch of roast pork and apple sauce, and a red plum tart put me in a much better mood. The dining room was full. I didn't know anybody.

I went along to the station and took out the suitcase, caught the fast train down to the Junction, checked the suitcase, and caught a bus back. It took almost an hour longer, but I saw a little more of the country. In summer, it must have been something like the farmland round Trothe Close. I couldn't help smiling. Mr. Eck didn't have the entire area to himself. In any event, I intended to be Mr. Trothe within twenty-four hours, and devil take the hindmost.

I went to the hall, a two-story concrete Bauhaus affair, double door in the middle, canopy over, circular window each side, torn posters in the spaces overstuck with those of Miss Wesse. I climbed out on the canopy to fix the sign, and wired it back to the board, no trouble except frozen fingers and feet. I stamped in a snowstorm to the café, and took about an hour to set the lights. I was switching off when Ants came down with a hot whiskey.

"Compliments of Mr. Heinig, sir," he said, and put the tray down. "Haven't had the cable yet!"

"Everything takes time."

"You'll be here tonight, sir?"

"Hope so. Weren't you going to give me the names of some of the people here?"

In absolute silence my voice couldn't have been heard very far, but with the orchestra going, and a radio strident in the bar, I was sure no mike could pick me up.

"Point them out when they come in tonight, sir. Notice they don't print anything?"

He might have said more, but I turned back to the lights. He hesitated, took the glass off the tray, and went upstairs. I wasn't playing his game for a moment. I used the spray to give everything a thorough blow-down, and got off the stage to look at the dark room. At the long table, a silver plate and tankard were laid at the head, and at the left and right hand. All the rest down to the end were china, with a lidded glass pot. Left and right, smaller tables were laid for twelve, and at the end, behind the bar, where I was to sit, there were eight glasses. I couldn't see a menu or a list of names, and the green baize board at the bar had gone.

It was a little after seven o'clock, just time to go back to Boehm's for a bath and change, pick up my sticker-friends, and get set for a quick start.

When I was dressed, I looked at every article I had in the room. I sprayed anything I might have touched, even in the unlikeliest places, bedhead, chairhead, under the washbowl, round the shaving glass, over the wardrobe and chest-of-drawers. Every article of clothing not on my back I put in a sheet of newspaper in the washbowl. One puff of the other spray reduced it all to a fine ash, paper as well. I took the ash in handfuls and filled another sheet, though in the handling it came down to a small greenish pile. I swilled the bowl, first, and opened the window a crack to let the ash go, little by little, in the wind, a faint whistle. With the cleanser spray I took out marks on the floor, walls, bathroom, doors and window. I was standing on newspaper. I went over everything, sprayed where there was doubt, opened the door with my cap, sprayed the handle on both sides, and the panels inside and out. The newspaper sheet went in my pocket and I went downstairs.

The little girl was not in the room, the table shone plastic red, and the place glittered in the bluish glare of striplight.

31

I'd forgotten I'd given the boy the key, and he'd gone. The shop was dark. I rang, kept on ringing. Nothing. I went back to Lambert's and laid out tools and items. The printers shut down two presses and I started work. After about an hour, when I saw I'd have to tear out roofboards, I slapped my hands and got off the ladder.

"Back about ten or so," I called. "Better cover your machines. Going to be a lot of dust!"

They waved, went on folding paper. Snow was thick. I couldn't hear my footsteps, or see anything except a feathery pelt. Shops were closed. I saw shadows go by, but I couldn't see the other side of the street. I passed our shop and had to go back. I rang and kept my thumb on the bellpush. I could hear the bell faintly through the glass. The street lightened. Head-lights bleared against a black fall.

"Eck, is that you?" somebody shouted. "Here, I've got the key!"

Metzler came running, and held up a key ring in the light.

"Jabotinski had some kind of stroke," he said, opening the door. "We just took him down to the hospital. The housekeeper's there with him. You still want to go to this meeting tonight?"

"That's why I'm here. I have to finish this job at Lambert's. Doctor say what's wrong with him?"

Metzler shrugged. He was wrapped in a thick shawl. Ice crystals on eyebrows and moustache made him a Methuselah.

"I had to wait downstairs," he said. "Huldtmann stayed with him. Anyway, he's got friends!"

"I'm one. How can I help?"

"Nobody can. He lets them hunt him out. He won't last. He was disappointed you joined. Us going didn't!"

"I like the quiet life," I said, inclined to spit away a taste. "What have they got against him?"

"Anything they say, he's got an argument. Ties 'em up in knots. Very funny, up to a couple of years ago. Then his workmen didn't go in, then he had to sell his factory, then he came here. He wasn't always a shoem—"

"Any idea where I could buy some flowers?" I said, spraying the bench. "Fine time to ask!"

"Flowers?" he said, and sniffed. "What's that stuff?"

"Prevents freezing. Electronics don't like the cold."

While the crystals dripped from his shawl he was thinking, and I'd filled the place with a mist that sank down, below waist level. I knew I'd left no prints.

He locked the door behind us and kept the key to give to Mrs. Lauter. We got into an old DKW, and he held the road by bumping the off-fore tire against the kerb. We crossed the main avenue, and turned right, and stopped.

"See what I can get," he mumbled, pulling the shawl over his mouth. "'bout a dozen?"

While he was away I went over the plan by detail, and couldn't find a weak joint. I was depending, as always, on nobody except myself.

Metzler came back laughing.

"Flowers, this weather, he thought it was very funny!" he wheezed. "They aren't fresh. Everlastin's, they are. All right?"

"Splendid!" I said. "Where are we going?"

"In here. Hold tight!"

We turned down an alley to a car park behind the Café de l'Europe, with a watchman's lit hut, a bright spotlight full on the gate, and four men round a red-hot brazier. Two of them leaned in, breathing white clouds against the light.

"Metzler. To meet the committee!"

"All right!" one of them shouted. "Open up!"

He saluted as we went in, and the gate slammed behind.

Metzler parked, and I followed him into a porter's area with a time clock and colored cards. We passed a glass wall of the kitchen with a dozen or so cooks behind stoves and pots, and through a fire-door to the passage, almost opposite the men's. The office was open. Heinig saw us and beckoned.

"The *lights!*" he said. "You've got real stuff. But, look. When the bugles go, the chairman'll ask you and the other guests to leave, see? You'll be full members at the *next* meeting. 'jections?"

We shook our heads.

I looked at a pair of palish eyes gone curiously bright. I knew them too well. They belonged to any minus-ego, conscious of power and ready to apply weight. I wished I could have refused in suitable terms if only to see what would happen. But that wasn't my game. It wasn't Metzler's, that was obvious, and suddenly I was admiring Jabotinski for intransigence.

"Right," he said cheerfully. "Metzler, go upstairs and wait till Mr. Prell comes in. He's got some news for you!"

He slapped Metzler on the back to knock off a few more glittering drops, and we went down the passage. A partition had been put up that fitted tight against both walls. We had to pull it aside, and the noise of about two hundred men came as a roar from the cage. I never saw so many bald heads in one place. Ants, in a red jacket, saw me without surprise, and pointed, over many heads, down to the left of the room.

"Take a whiskey with you, sir!" he shouted, almost unheard. "Sign for it down there. Be with you in a minute, sir!"

Reaching the other end was real work. I pushed through a crowd wearing old tunics, or sporting field caps, mess jackets, and all sizes of bemedalled others in plain clothes. There were many greyheads, but most were late-forties, fifties, with a few youngsters, perhaps their sons. They all seemed prosperous tradesmen, out for the night, from the shouts of laughter, relaying the jokes they'd heard since the last time, and making sure of plenty under the belt for added good humor. When I got to my corner, the group near me weren't simply drinking. They toasted something I couldn't hear, drank head-back, ordered another— while I stood there with my whiskey untasted—drank that, and ordered a third. I didn't want to be pulled into it. I got in the shadow and stayed there till Ants came back. He was a real waiter, quick, good-humored. I wondered which one of us had been in touch with him before, or how we'd made contact. Beirut and Tunis seemed to provide evidence.

He came over with another whiskey and put a bar chit and pencil down, cleared a place at the guest's table, and pulled out a chair.

"Man at the head of the table's the guest of honor," he said, beside me as I signed. "General Prell. *Mr.* Prell. He gives the orders. He's from the central headquarters. On his left, there's Joh Pensen. He does a lot more than play the piano. On the right, somebody called Svertlov. He's not here yet. Heinig went out to the airport to meet him. Bad weather."

"Ever hear the name Hollefendorm?"

He shook his head, slowly, thinking.

"Can't remember it."

"What are those wreaths on the flag for?"

"One's for somebody called Josef Platz. He died a week or so ago. The others I don't know. Didn't get the names. I'll hear them tonight when they call the roll. Tell you tomorrow!"

He went back to the bar, and I sat there wondering if Mr. Platz could have been the man I'd speared, or if the others might have been Tanis and Ebbleton. I was almost sorry I couldn't stay overnight to learn.

A roar of *HOCH!* dinned, and the crowd on the stairway swayed back, an aisle was being pushed open, and the rear ranks gave way to let Druxi through, on the arm of a tall man in a blue uniform with the ribbon of the Iron Cross. Druxi, at her regal best, wore a white costume with sequins glinting on the shoulders, a small hat with an osprey plume, and waved a foot-long cigaret-holder which kept her admirers at reasonable distance. She was surrounded, and jeroboams of champagne were passed overhead. Men reached in glasses, brought them out full, made way for others, and Druxi appeared, plume first, lifted on to a table, and the General climbed beside her. All glasses went up in a shout, and the General raised a white shoe to drink a toast, drowned in a roar. Everybody drank, and many smashed the glass. Feet crunched splinters, voices called for brooms, the General was speaking, not a word heard, and Druxi put her arms round his neck and the room howled laughter.

I looked at my watch. I had a few more minutes. But I had to take care of Druxi.

I went round the long table into the crush, veering for her place at the first side table. I passed about a dozen other women all buxomly mid-thirtyish, being cuddled by groups of admirers. I was bumped, rebumped, smiled at, apologised to, shoved, almost thrown bodily, helped up, bowed to as an old comrade, carried along by a shouting scrum, freeing myself in ways known to footballers, and at last, managed to suspend myself over Druxi's shoulder, trying to keep off by a hand on the table.

I'd been careful to place the little finger under the rest and extend the thumb laterally, a warning signal in the past. She got it immediately, put her hands together, and tried to push back her chair. I helped, and when she was standing, held her arm to support her in the crush and let myself be pushed closer.

"Blow!" I whispered, using the old catchword, and pulled away, almost laughing to see her eyes, like a startled cat's, brilliantly aware.

I watched her go, followed by the General, and saw him make a gesture of accord, turning to wave to the other women.

The head waiter took the microphone from the stand, tapped twice, and said that Miss Wesse was going to change for the entertainment, and all honored and estimable guests, naturally, the ladies, should retire, and gentlemen, please finish your drinks.

I wasted no more time.

I went to the men's room and took a towel from the entellus, and to get him out, asked him to buy me six cigars and keep the change. While I washed a couple came in and went out. In the pause I put stickers over the steam pipe joints I could reach. Others came in, and I combed my hair and beard, polished my boots in the machine. When the room was mine I stuck discs over the boards covering the power cables, and for makeweight, stuck a few over the pump and pipeline, which, I judged, ought to lead to the kitchen.

Bugles sounded nearby, almost smothered in a roar of cheering. I went out to the passage and joined the crowd making boozy way to find places. I was carried along to the head of the middle table, and reached out to stick a disc under the edge, stuck another under the place at right, but I couldn't get round to the left. The "radio" set I'd put under the light-trough shining up at the swastika flag would explode in about twenty minutes or so. I allowed myself to be pushed along the length of the table, setting a disc here and there, and got down to the end, joining a small crowd at the kitchen door. I stayed just long enough to fasten a couple of plungers to the big boilers in the corner, a few to the festoon of refrigerator pipes, and three in almost a perfect triangle—for better effect—on the gas main.

Time was short but I wanted to find Metzler and get him away. I went back in the main room, thick with smoke, bawling groups packed tight, rumples of red faces, and edged nearer the staircase, dropping stickers on the way, planting more under the ledge of the bar. I looked down at the little radio. Its own light, a cheery red, one of a cluster, was on. Heinig came down from upstairs, and passed without seeing me, talking to a man

231

I thought I knew, fair, high cheekbones, and a blue glance brightly sidelong, deceitful.

Ants came behind me, head up, a question.

"Friend of mine here, somewhere," I said, and slipped a disc in his inside pocket, easy enough in that crush. "You might tell the barman upstairs to open a bottle of champagne. New boys, long life, eh? Have a glass for luck!"

"I will, that!" he said, all roly-poly smiles. "I'll phone. Be up there the minute they sit down!"

I went through a thinning crowd to take the flowers from the cloakroom, and had a last look at the room. All the tables were filling in a scraping of chairs, laughter, splintering glass and shouts of "Pay Up!"

Metzler was coming down from the bar, lightly for his size, happier than I'd ever seen him.

"Do me a big favor," I said. "I left my tools in the DKW. I've got to finish the Lambert job. Could you come round in case they won't let me in?"

"Certainlyl!" he said. "Let's get my stuff."

I put the flowers under the flag, thinking of Jabotinski, and his wife who'd died of overeating, and all her sisters, and Andrew Furnival and Tom Law and all the others, and Paul.

But most of all I thought of Melisande, and her note.

I stuck a few plungers to the stairway supports, and went out in thick snow, waiting with my back to the power pole, sticking plungers in a double row of three. It was concrete, carrying a lot of weight. It could only fall on the café.

Metzler came out and we went, head down, round the corner along the lane to the car park. Only the watchman sat in the hut. Metzler shouted and the gate opened on remote control. I walked down to the DKW parked in darkness. The crowd inside were singing "Lily Marlene." I couldn't think of any song we'd sung in English that hit so hard in memory, or that brought so many of the Salt of the Earth to live a young day again.

"Get in," Metzler said, wrapping his shawl. "I'll whistle you

232

down there. Glad we couldn't stay. Got to see about painting the Public Hall tomorrow. Biggest job I've ever had. See how it goes?"

"Drop me at the end of Boehm's street, will you? It's right on your way. Wish I'd brought my coat!"

"I'm three minutes from my supper and a lovely warm fire," he said, pulling off the shawl. "Take this. Take it, else I'll throw it in the road!"

I had to take it, and we stopped on the near corner. I got out, he took his foot off the brake, and went off in a wave of a red-woollen glove.

I turned down my street, and jumped into a doorway. There were two, perhaps, three cars outside Boehm's and light shone on a uniform half on the step. I turned about and walked fast as ice would let me. A telephone booth was alight on the corner, and I went in, grateful for the warmth. I dialled, asked for Miss Wesse, and somebody said very good, hold, please.

"'lo?" Druxi said. "Who's this?"

"A rude fellow. The air bites shrewdly!"

"Wish I could think of the follow-on!"

"From this time, daughter, be somewhat scanter of your maiden presence. Look to't, I charge you. Come your ways!"

"I'm leaving tomorrow. Had a wonderful tour. Went to Tunis, Beirut—"

"Useless. So's the guide. It's snowing hard. I wouldn't go out if I were you—"

"Ah, but the show *has* to go on!"

"It doesn't, y'know. Bed's the best place!"

I saw a taxi coming and put the phone down. Luckily it was kerb-crawling, snowblind. I hit the window as it passed, and it stopped.

"I want to go up to the bus stop," I said, and got in.

"You're on my way else I wouldn't start," the cabman said, trying to get his wipers to work. "Don't think you'll get many cabs tonight. Look at it!"

"My old mother's been waiting there for the past hour. Nothing running from Brauberg!"

The words weren't out, and the back of the cab seemed to lift. The windows rattled. The "radio" set must have blown. But the café was behind, and two streets over.

"Getting a rough wind, too," the cabman grumbled. "Everything happens the same time!"

We came out in a clear stretch of road, and he picked up speed down to the bus stop, a long cement shelter. Half a dozen people waited, all of them looking down at the way we'd come. I paid, and tried to give him a fair tip, but he refused with a grin, slammed the door, gunned, and got away.

I wrapped the shawl and stood in shadow. Nobody spoke. They were all watching the road.

"*Looks* like a fire," an old man said, squinting over his coat collar.

The sound shook.

"There you are!" a woman said. "I *told* you it was an explosion!"

"Well, we're safe enough here," a man said, calmly, in the darkness. "I don't know what the fuss is all about. If it isn't Ivan, and the Mongols, whatever else it is, we're all right!"

Headlights flashed down at the corner and a long shape turned. The people with me went forward almost with new life. The bus pulled in, a door opened, and we lined up.

"This is express to the Junction!" the driver shouted, taking money. "Any of you're getting off in between, wait for my mate behind. There's something going on down there at the café corner. I had to turn off. He won't be so lucky. Police got everything blocked!"

"What is it, a fire?" a woman asked.

"Everything was red down there," the driver said. "Sounded like the gas going up!"

He drove on, and I thanked Metzler for the shawl, pulling it round my shoulders, making a hood for my head, grateful for the bus's heating, that came on slowly, warmly, like the half-felt hand of a mother.

We skidded in snow that flurried against the windscreen, defying the wipers. The driver must have known the road inch by inch, and when we stopped, I knew it wasn't the weather. He opened the door.

Police came on. One, in black leather, stood by the driver.

"Shan't keep you long!" he called. "Just show whatever documents you've got. Letters, anything. Want to know who you are, that's all!"

I picked Metzler's license out of my pocket, thanking the gods I'd had the chance of taking it when he went to get his shawl. Fortunately I had all the accounts I'd paid, a handful of dogeared paper. When the policeman came to me, I—sleepily—pulled page from page, straightening them out till I came to the Metzler account, and his card. I handed them up, he looked at them, and gave them back.

"Where are you going, up the road?" he asked me.

"Collecting some stuff early and getting back. I've got a big job—"

He raised a finger and went on. I huddled down. Moments went by. There was an argument in front. A woman shouted that just because a man didn't happen to have a piece of paper on him, that didn't make him less than her husband. There was some laughter, and then the door closed, and we went on. I must have slept because I woke to see the station wheeling toward us.

I got off and walked, one of four, through the main lobby, over to the other side. I thanked God and Metzler for the shawl. While I got my suitcase from the baggage room, the express's headlight flashed down the line. Suddenly I didn't feel cold.

The train rumbled in, and I got into the second-class carriage, wonderfully warm, and all to myself. We were in the station about three minutes. When we moved I couldn't believe it. Well outside the Junction I went down to the lavatory with the suitcase. I took off the heavy boots, cut the uppers to ribbons, and put the soles through the top of the window, one now, one then. They'd been good friends. I took Eck's trousers and coat off, sliced them, and let them go through the window. I couldn't for the moment part with the pullover. I wore the Trothe shirt over it, tied the tie, pulled on the Trothe trousers, put on the shoes, got into the jacket, and looked at myself in the glass. The thick beard made me clench my teeth, but it had to be done. There was just enough icy water in the tap. A lot of cream, and a new blade made a surprisingly easy shave. My face was thinner. I combed my hair in the old style, shook out my overcoat and put it on, stamped my feet, tore up every scrap of paper and let it blow through the window, put my passport in my breast pocket, and walked out, myself once again, except for a hat. I didn't want to destroy the shawl. I left it on a pile of luggage in the corridor.

A first-class compartment was vacant and I shut the door, took off my overcoat in adequate heat, and sat in the corner. I hadn't long to wait.

A ticket collector slid the door, followed by a passport officer. I handed over ticket and passport, explained that I was going back via the Hook instead of flying, and the collector said he didn't blame me, and the buffet was still open, three carriages up.

I went along the corridor, walked into an even warmer bar, fairly well crowded, ordered a double whiskey straight, lit a cigaret, and lay back, ready for anything, not sure what it might be, and absolutely careless.

32

I'd always had a soft spot for Holland. The entire country's pin-clean, and even in winter the gardens are a joy. I had plenty of time to catch the Hook packet, and went out to The Hague for lunch at the Hotel des Indes, a *rijstafel*, of dozens of dishes that brought back early days in Java, memories of a gentle people, a glorious country, and sorrow, that the worst type of politics grew monsters and chaos, though how, is one of the smaller human mysteries. I bought a Hilhouse homburg after lunch, and with one of those fat little cigars with the long twist that makes them almost a foot of pure leaf, burning a heavenly aroma, I caught the train to the Hook, went aboard to an excellent cabin, slept for a couple of hours, and sent for coffee and the papers. Tucked away at the top corner I saw there'd been an explosion of some sort at the Café de l'Europe in Regsmund, and firemen were still digging bodies out of the debris.

I could find no smallest response within myself, certainly not a grace-note of regret. If I could have been sure I'd exterminated the lot, I'd have been perfectly happy.

In that mood I got to London and went to the club. It was early, but I called Green Tree 14, and took certain pleasure in getting the Blur out of bed.

"We've had a fairly full report," he said, almost jovially for the hour. "You've done marvellously well, Trothe. I knew you would, of course. Stay at your club till I get in touch. You'll be 'leaving' the nursing home tomorrow morning, happily 'cured.' That means you'll be free to come to the office at 11. Your son, by the way, is under the care of the doctor in your village. He's staying with the parson, there. He's one of the principals in the United Churches Council against drugs, or something of the sort. The charges were quashed. The parson and the doctor made themselves responsible to the Court. They'll tell you more than I can. Your daughter is in Morocco, apparently quite well. Your house is exactly as it was. Gillian has all that well in hand. A most satisfactory state of things, I think you'll agree?"

"I'm quite happy."

"Good. Then at eleven tomorrow?"

I called Paul, and had a few minutes chatter about my "illness" and listened to details about plastered legs, and so forth.

"When're you joining me, Edmund? Time's getting short!"

"I'm thinking about the end of the month. Just want to get some details straight."

"You won't be able to do too much tomorrow. What about the day after?"

"I'll let you know. Is Miss Masters at the office?"

"She is, yes. And your office is ready for you. Go and see it!"

I suppose it was the greatest temptation I'd known, and yet any thought of leaving the Service was repugnant, or, more than that, shameful. I didn't bother to analyse the feeling. Enough that it was there. Any thought of breaking with the life I'd known since youthhood caused indescribable discomfort, especially since I hadn't reached the top, or, at any rate, the goal I'd always set myself. Suddenly I felt tired. I'd had little more than a week of another sort of life, different work, mental strain, but it was quite enough.

I was thankful for being myself, and I turned to the quiet comfort of the club with a feeling of absolute relief, ready to sleep for a week. There was no report in any of the papers I read, and I asked for those of the day before, but they too, were blank. I slept like a log and woke to a grey morning, of rooftops and

238

chimneys in London's own breath, and never in my life felt better.

Dr. Norris told me little more than the Blur, except that Frederick was well and responding to treatment, and that I couldn't see him for at least a week or so.

"I don't like that!"

"I'm sorry, but it's part of the regime Sir Cuthbert Bainbridge and I decided on. He's being brought out of a peculiar emotional state. We're exceptionally fortunate that Tomsett's been willing to accept the responsibility. He has two nurses. That's about all there is, except that he's far better."

"How long will this take?"

"It entirely depends on him. He's a ward of the Court for six months. He'll continue his studies during that time, but he'll be under restraint to avoid any chance of his taking drugs. That's the crux of the problem!"

"I wish I'd realised it was as serious as that!"

"It's been going on for a very long time. You're not in the least to blame. He knows why you can't see him. He'll be far more amenable when you do. Come and see me when you arrive."

I was almost glad Mel had gone. I don't know what she'd have done. I didn't quite know what to do myself, and thinking made the whole affair preposterous. I decided to ignore it for the moment.

For some reason, as I passed the railings along the Mall, I thought again of that run of syllables, the name of some mythical African. I got to the office and a most kind welcome from Miss Roule, with a pile of correspondence, some household bills, and a report from Cloney that forced tulips were out and he'd taken them to the church. It reminded me that while modest Mr. Eck had been thinking of destruction, others, humbler, had been creating.

I asked for the African files and when they came over, went through them with a needle-point. As though I hadn't seen it before, a name began to take shape, at times spelled in one way

239

and at others differently, sometimes with one name and then two, three and four. I took out of my middle drawer the piece of paper I'd filled with syllables in a run. I hadn't been far off. Just far enough to be wrong. I could have kicked myself. I called Sir Ryder Chapman, reminded him of Jerome Cavendish's introduction, and spelled out the name and its counterparts.

"Doesn't ring anything for the moment," he said. "Sure you're spelling it correctly?"

"Very far from it. That's the devil of it!"

"Can be most annoying, I agree. I'll make enquiries here. A barrister? Ought to be simple!"

"I've combed the lists. We've done all we can—unofficially—but nothing's come up. The Registry Office name's quite different. Doesn't appear anywhere else!"

"That's usual. If he's ever been through our agencies, I'll have him for you by three o'clock. It takes one of his own people to sort this out, you know!"

At a few minutes to eleven I walked into Miss Tulliver's office to a pleasant greeting, and as Big Ben struck the hour, she opened the door and I walked in to meet the Blur.

He put a pen in a marble tray and came round the desk to meet me.

"Ah, Trothe, what a remarkable effort!" he said, warmer than I'd ever known him. "I'll show you the report later. Look here, several things have happened. That young woman, Desarbier's arrived in London. She's at the Savonia—"

"Here?"

"You didn't expect her?"

"Absolutely not!"

"Must have come in by tacit agreement between the Police and one or two other departments, I shall know which shortly. She'll be arrested later. With the worst imaginable consequences. I don't think I need enlarge. I don't want to give evidence. I don't wish to be questioned about certain periods. I'm sure you don't. But anyone she gets to defend her'd be a perfect fool if he didn't go in feet first. The case couldn't be heard entirely *in camera*. There'd be publicity of a peculiarly obnoxious kind. I don't want it. Others don't. It'll orbit some of the most controversial matters of the past few years. Won't do. We've got to get that woman out of the country. Tonight!"

I was confused, run-up. Why had she been allowed in? Bernard had said he'd known she was coming. Why hadn't the Blur stopped her? Hadn't he been told? Almost impossible to consider. Who else would want her in? Somebody could be giving him a little of his own treatment? Politics? Somebody in the Cabinet? Who?

He'd said "we've" so he counted me as one with himself. But that might be dangerous. If she were found with me, where was the proof that I was acting for anyone except myself? I'd be caught red-handed with the goods. And Tanis could also tell a tale.

Then, where was I?

"I'll make everything quite clear," he went on, without waiting for me to speak. "I say without fear of denial that your present position in the Service is due to my constant regard of your welfare. You may not realise it, but I shall never forget what you did for me. I felt—I still feel—I owe you a great deal. You have the necessary intellectual attainments, of course, which made things so much easier. I have no hesitation in saying that if this matter's pulled off, as I think you can, then you may look forward to a most—ah—satisfying future!"

The Lord God—the Power behind Power—talking to a very small archangel. I was being fed the swill of patronage. Swill. But he held the bucket that filled the trough, and he nominated the snouts to be fed. I had to keep both ears cocked. I could be broken with a word, and he was the type who'd crush.

"I wish my mind were clearer," I said.

"I quite understand. But this has peremptory importance. Now I'll tell you what must be done. Down at Famlingham

Sound, there's a converted E-boat. It's crewed by men who'll keep their mouths shut. I suggest you meet this young woman, invite her down for the weekend, go aboard, and you'll be taken within an hour or so to the sister yacht club on the other side of the Channel. You could catch the train to Paris. If you wished, of course. What?"

His meaning was plain. I chose to ignore it.

"Why me?" I asked. "Why not anyone else?"

"Her testimony can ruin you. You know it. Doesn't matter what you deny. It can also damage me. And a number of others we both know. They're all heavily implicated. I'll warrant there'll be many a long sigh of relief when it's known she's gone!"

"Perhaps irrelevantly, but what did she expect to get from me? I can't think of a moment when I distrusted her!"

"Oh, but of course not! And when *you* were at work, did you ever give anyone the slightest reason to distrust you?"

"It went on for a long time. Day after day. For months. Not the smallest shadow. What, exactly, was she supposed to get from me?"

The Blur pulled down his cuffs as if a sermon were in order.

"That disarming little trull was beautiful, accomplished and hard-working when I knew her," he said, quietly. "She never made herself in any degree cheap, or vulgar or forward. I made the running. We met socially. Wherever I went, she seemed to be. She had a sense of humor. Presently we began to play a game of exchanging new stories. The sort of glossy bedroom joke. The one who told a chestnut first, paid for lunch. We never discussed anything to do with what we were doing. I never at any time gave her so much as a zephyr about anything I did. She never said a word to me. I respected her for it. I thought I had the genuine article, a quite lovely girl who rather liked my company. She often came to my office. At the end of the day when I signed letters. The gloaming. Awfully romantic. But it never entered my head that she might misuse an introduction to some of the people we met, or plant a 'bug' in my office, and in my flat. They slip down in the furniture. Difficult to detect. But every word one says thereafter is broadcast. With you, rather different. But you don't think you were the only feather in her cap? Any more than I was. You were extremely useful as a pointer. You introduced her, quite innocently, of course, to people she required to know. And used!"

"But I don't understand why she's so dangerous here. Why wasn't she dangerous in Geneva?"

"But, Trothe! Obviously, because our people can hold her for questioning. You'd have to give evidence. I would. And a number of others. Would you want that? I wouldn't. I'm being entirely selfish. Understand me. It's got to be your way, or mine. Yours, let us say, will be nicer? Is that the word?"

"I fail to see any reason for hurry."

He sat back in the chair, swivelled to look through the window, and put the tips of his fingers together under his nose.

"At eight o'clock tomorrow morning, you'll be put in arrest as a suspected person," he said, as if he were reading it. "The evidence is available. You know it. You'll be incarcerated—if you go there, you'll understand why I use the word—in Wormwood Scrubs, one of the most horrible prisons in the country. Its hundred-year-old stink of urine, excrement, unbathed flesh and stale sweat gets in one's clothes. I went there once on a visit. I had to destroy everything I'd worn. I'd be glad to save you a disgusting experience. But if that were to happen, then innocent or not, you'd be finished. You see that, don't you?"

There was nothing for it. Any thought of weeks or months in that charnelhouse of the near-dead unnerved me. I knew it could be done. I was in Presence of the Management.

"Very well," I said, and got up. "I shall first settle a few matters here. What if she doesn't want to go?"

"Then we shall have to take Draconian measures!"

"I don't accept that. For a moment. I'll do what I can."

"My car's waiting for you. The chauffeur's name is Gaylor.

243

Tell him where you wish to go. Taxis report. We don't want too much of that. She has until about seven o'clock. They'll give her till then to know where she goes, whom she talks to."

"And if we're followed?"

"Not in *my* car!" he said, looking out of the window.

I called the Savonia and was told the lady was out till four o'clock. I left a message without a name that the call would be repeated at 4:30, and went down to meet Gaylor, a tall, broad anonymity in grey whipcord. He opened the car door on seeing me, touched his cap, and stood, looking over my head. I didn't ask how he knew me. I got in and told him to go to my club.

During the ride, I thought about myself, what I'd done, about Mel, the children. I had a call in to Patti's hotel in Morocco in fifteen minutes. I hadn't the remotest notion what I was going to say. The prospect of meeting Tanis didn't in the least excite me. I was probably too tired. Thinking about myself, I was inclined to wonder where I was going, to what end. I seemed to be sacrificial ox. I hated the idea, though hate as I might, I couldn't see any way round it.

Gaylor parked and I went in the club to take my call. While I waited, I called Dr. Tomsett. Out. I left a message. Dr. Norris was still on his rounds. Constable Parnes was down in the village. Mrs. Cloney was shopping, and Mr. Cloney had gone to the Coop. The hall porter cut in to say there was a lady on the line for me. Immediately I thought of Consuelo.

"Lady's name's Scoones, sir. Mrs. Marjorie Scoones. Called several times. Put her on?"

"Please."

"Edmund?"

"Yes. What a surprise!"

"Oh, Edmund. I so want to speak to you, if I may?"

"Of course. Where's best for you?"

"I'm at the Hyde Park—"

"Then how about Harrod's restaurant in twenty minutes?"

The call to Patti was being held and the porter came to signal a frantic *"on!"* and I nodded.

"Patti? This is—"

"I know, and I'm answering only to tell you I don't want anything to do with you, do you understand?" Patti's voice came clearly as if she were next to me, speaking naturally, calmly, herself. "I spoke to Mummy, you know. I don't care what Gilman or anybody else has to say. You told her if she came to London for my wedding you'd have her arrested. I don't want to see you or talk to you again. Are you—"

"I think you might listen to what—"

"I think we all listened for long enough. To a liar. You took our money and spent it on women. I had nothing for my trousseau. Your lickspittle Gilman gave me a tale—"

"Come back here and let me show—"

"Never! As long as I live. You murdered Mummy. But I won't let you touch Freddie's money. My husband's got that in hand. Keep out of my life, you nasty creature!"

I put the telephone down, carefully, wondered if I could contain myself, considered the possibility of flying to Morocco, damned it for a wrong move, barely made slow way out of the car. I saw a pink bundle that I loved to carry, that smelled of soap and talc and the sweet of Mel's milk, and fat feet, and dimples in knuckles, and the voice of a strangled seraph calling *da!* which at that time I'd thought one of the minor, more lovely miracles of my time. I thought of holiday months at the sea, and school visits, and suddenly a dryad running slender legs where a dumpling had toddled before.

We were at Harrod's before I was ready. I hadn't long to wait.

Mrs. Scoones came in rather hesitantly. I was amazed to see a distinct resemblance to Mel. She was thinner, quite smart in a dark ermine coat, but she looked oddly sere, and a little bent at the neck.

"Edmund, it's so good of you, such a busy—!"

"Do let's sit down and tell me all about it. How's Pamela?"

245

"She's in Canada. She called me last night. Apparently there's quite a large sum of money there, and Mr. Gilman's got a lawyer in Montreal looking into it for her. She thinks the world of you for the introduction!"

"Good. Now, what's worrying you?"

She pulled her gloves off, took the menu, ordered pate and mushrooms, with a half bottle of claret, and I said Nothing, thank you.

"A package was left for T—do you know, I *can't* say that person's name!—at Pam's about a couple of weeks or so before all this dreadful—well, anyway, he wrote to her, and said it was for Freddie. Well, with one thing and the other, she forgot all about it. A few days ago, a man called while she was out, and asked for Freddie. Mrs. Tewkes said he didn't live there. Well, he frightened the poor soul with what he said, and when he came back, Pamela saw him. She didn't take any nonsense. She said she'd call the police. The man laughed at her and said she'd be getting Freddie a few years for pushing. She didn't know what 'pushing' meant, and the man said it was selling drugs. She burned the package. You can imagine her state!"

"Indeed. And?"

"Well, it was getting quite awful, and the last time the man called, Pamela telephoned me and asked if she could come over. Of course I said yes. Do you know, she hadn't been in the house five minutes when there was a ring, and there the man was!"

"I see. Then what?"

"I couldn't see him very well, and there was somebody else with him. He threatened he'd carve his initials on both of us if he didn't get his money, and he'd see Freddie was sent to prison!"

"Did you give him any?"

"We hadn't ten pounds between us, and he wouldn't take a cheque. He wanted seven hundred pounds!"

"So you went to the bank—"

"I didn't. I ordered him off the step—"

"Excellent!"

"—and I said if he dared come again, I'd call the police. They went away. At ten o'clock the telephone rang, and it was the man. He said 'I'll cut the pair of you up!' and I put the phone down. He called every hour on the dot. The same every day till yesterday. He rings and rings till we answer. My nerves simply won't hold out. We were afraid to call the police because of Freddie, but we couldn't find him, and we couldn't get hold of you. Pamela went off to Canada. I was left alone. Last night he rang all night again. I had to disconnect the phone. I can't stand it any longer. This morning he said he knew all about Ebbleton, and he was going to let the police know if I didn't 'hand over' by two o'clock. He's coming to the house!"

"Did you tell him Pam'd destroyed the package?"

"Oh, yes! But he didn't believe it!"

"Right. Now, give me the key to the front door. You stay here and eat your lunch in absolute peace!"

"Oh, Edmund!"—the tears shone—"I knew I could depend on you! Mel always said—"

"That's right. I'll leave the keys with Daimler Hire. The chauffeur will be outside the house at six o'clock. You go to a cinema and forget all about everything. You won't be worried any more!"

For the second or third time in my life I kissed her cheek. I'd quite taken to her.

I knew exactly what to do, and where, and I took my time, sending Gaylor for lunch, to meet me at the Savonia at six.

It was ten to two when I reached the house, and I went into the drawing room. My new mini-friend shone black steel in the palm of my hand. I put it back in the holster, and walked about admiring some beautiful jade, wishing the oils were mine. At the desk I scrawled a note, and as I put the pen down, I saw the man come up the steps.

He rang, and I opened the door.

He seemed an ordinary sort of street corner yob, in an over-coat of "swinging" cut and a surprisingly small-brimmed hat that looked—as my dear mother used to say—"like a pimple on a hay-stack" and I almost laughed, hearing her voice.

Another man crossed the road, a similar type, using perhaps the same tailor and hatter, a little older. Both were brawny, both walked toes-turned-out with a deliberate placing of the feet, rather like old butlers.

"Want to see Mrs. Scoones," the man in front of me said, obviously a Londoner, but not my idea of a Cockney.

"I was asked to deputise," I said, in my old schooldays part of Teazle, with a soupçon of Macbeth to cheer things up. "Mrs. Scoones, poor twigish, has been taken to a broging fast. I'm afraid she's been overdoing it. My wife was called to the rokpron about—oh, I suppose an hour or so ago—and she sent this gloot to me at the fab. Are you the furniture people Mrs. Scoones has to pay?"

"Eur—oh, um, yes, that's right, furniture!" he said, and black eyes reached under that ridiculous brim. "You paying out, are you?"

"Mrs. Scoones asked me to, and I'm only too happy to oblige. I was a great friend of her husband's. Oh, such a regal being! They're not making crowns for his like any more. Now, how much was it?"

I looked a yard away at the scrawl. He must have seen the £700. I'd meant him to.

"Se'n 'undred, it was. Cash!"

"That is correct, to the penny. Very well. Just let me get my hosh and guft, and we'll be off—"

"Off, where to?"—sharp, hard, of the dark street—and he was suddenly huge in the doorway. I could quite imagine what the two women had felt.

"Oho, well!" I wheezed. "To my bank, of course. Who carries that sum about in these glaubrous days?"

"Where's the bank?"—eyes still hard, a dog about to fang— "'s it far?"

"Near Chancery Lane. I haven't my pergwis today. I'm off to clatch wof tonight. We'll have to get a cab. Why doesn't your friend whistle one up? Don't be alarmed. I'll pay!"

I tottered in to get my coat, buttoned it awry, put the homburg on slightly askew, shook out the umbrella, and the performance to the door, the oppity-bump-oppity-bump down the steps, with a little luck might have put me among the Barrymores.

We got in the cab and I tremoloed Chancery Lane, and sat back. One squatted on the extra seat, elbows on knees. Both hands were heavily ringed. They could cut. I felt the strain, that seemed to dry the air.

I hugged the umbrella.

"I'd monted going vergling through the burnish glom," I said. "I always go to Soho. Best foit, best moshutal. Been vergling there all cassotin glup. They all know me. They like me because I speak sroch. French or Belgian, it's just tuish. Did you not know? I was bedroozzled, almost intrincally fodder in, the first time!"

"Foit's lovely," Mr. Smallbrim said. "I've had it!"

Neither dare look at t'other. When they did, it was corner-of-the-eye-and-away.

I drooled double-talk. I simply looked out of the window and let it bubble. The man next to me started to shake, the other snorted, coughed, and both lay back and giggled, but quite helplessly. It was curious to watch them, neither with a healthy guffaw, both of them giggling and shaking, coughing, and then, as suddenly, sitting up, straight-faced, feeling pockets for cigarets which seemed to be loose, neither offering one to the other, neither offering a light.

We got to Chancery Lane by High Holborn, and I tapped the cabbie to stop.

"We can walk from here," I said. "There's no need for you

to come in the bank. Just go round the corner to my office. The secretary won't be there yet. I gave her till 3:30. I still have to do my vergling, and quamtats won't wait. But as men of the podlif, you know that!"

I paid the cabbie, and went into my gone-at-the-hocks totter, down Chancery Lane. It was after the lunch hour and there weren't many people about. Tyndal's Court was my property. We were waiting to rebuild. It was reached by a narrow lane with three doors on one side, two on the other, all dummy, barred windows, and just around the corner of the L bend, a flight of steps led to an overgrown garden darkened by a warehouse wall at the end.

"If you'll be kind enough to wait for me, it won't take a moment. I've ordered it ready, and you might be good enough to sign a receipt—"

"Sign nothink!" Mr. Smallbrim said, sucking down smoke.

"You can't expect me to hand over seven hundred pounds without a frovish!" I said, all saintly indignation. "How'll I get my money back? This is *my* money, you know!"

"Go and get it!" Mr. Smallbrim said. "Always talk about a fro-whatever-it-was. Don't be all night!"

As I'd thought, they didn't go down Tyndal's Court, but stood on the corner, watching me till I turned into the imposing office of a printer that looked like a private bank. I waited a few moments, looking through the window. They were giggling, doubled up, standing to breathe, giggling again. They didn't walk down. I knew why. They were giving themselves leeway for a fast start just in case I wasn't all I pretended to be.

I came out, stuffing nothing into my inside jacket pocket, and when they saw me, they turned and walked down. I followed, and when they looked round at the end, I pointed my umbrella to the right. When I turned the corner they were strolling a few yards ahead.

"Just up the stairs to the right," I said, in a fine flutter. "I believe I've a touch of tchocachich coming on!"

The lane was quiet.

"Come on, cut the 'ckin' lark!" Mr. Smallbrim mouthed, and came toward me, hand out. "Give us it 'ere. I'll count it!"

I gave him possibly the most brilliant smile he could ever have known.

"With quite unutterable pleasure!" I said, in my own voice, and drew my stand-in friend. "With the compliments of my son, and so many others like him!"

They halted in mid-pace, Smallbrim a little in front, mouth O'd in surprise, eyes squeezed in a new thought. I shot twice, no sound, no flash, no smell of powder. Both twisted, Smallbrim first, falling against each other, dropping backwards in a knock of worn-down heels.

Blood flashed in a runnel.

I footed them both over, went through their pockets, took a dirty notebook out of Smallbrim's breast pocket, and two folded sheets of paper. He had a gun in the right-hand trouser pocket. A wad of notes bulged in a bag tied about his neck under the shirt. The other had notes in all his pockets, and a gun in the left-hand overcoat pocket. I'd noticed he was left-handed. I was lucky with the two pieces of paper, worn with use, listing names and addresses. Freddie was there, and so was Ebbleton, home and business, and the address in Kensington. Mrs. Scoones' was handwritten with her telephone number. The notebook was filled with addresses most with nicknames. I took everything, walked out to Chancery Lane, turned right into Holborn. I caught a bus to Farringdon Street, and took a cab to Daimler Hire. I wrote a card to Mrs. Scoones, telling her where Freddie was, that he'd appreciate a visit, and to try to forget the nightmare of recent days. I addressed the note to the house, handed over the key, and took a cab to the office.

The briefcase I'd given Frederick was in my private drawer. I took it out, added the notes to the pile I'd taken from the two yobs, and put it all in a long envelope. Sergeant Quatrell was on duty and I asked Miss Roule to send him in.

"I want somebody to go along to the Great Ormond Street Hospital for Children," I said, and gave him the envelope. "That contains money. It's been collected rather painfully. It has to be anonymous. I want somebody I can trust to take it to the Almoner at the hospital. Deliver it personally. I want a notice in *The Times* that it was received. No names, no packdrill!"

"I'll do that on me way 'ome, sir!" he said, in a grin. "My pleasure, sir!"

Yorick came through while I was clearing the desk.

"Edmund? Oh. Um. How about lunch tomorrow?"

"If I'm in London, yes."

"It's oyster-and-turtle-steak day round the corner. The pub, upstairs. My table. I bought it. Recognise it by the family glass and the pot of orchids. Nothing like feeling at home!"

"Indeed."

"Just finished a band rehearsal. In the village. We bought a sousaphone. Gigantic thing. Entire population's *seeth*ing. All twenty-eight of them!"

"D'you play it?"

"With *my* lungs? Couldn't get a squeak out of a tin whistle. I'm going into a decline. Rather grandly, on the whole. Comforting thought. I shall never be entirely at peace till I'm carefully wrapped in silk and put into my sarcophagus. A maddening job in carved agate. Tear phials for the mourners, of course. I'm practising *rigor mortis* as I stand here—"

"For God's sake, go home!"

"But that's where I am. Love to see you here at any time. I was hoping to exchange a gasp or so with Gillian—"

"Why didn't you say so? Why drool on?"

"Often asked myself that. But near-corpses are always a little shy, what?"

I pressed the button to connect, and heard the receiver lift. "Mr. Trothe's office!"

"Darling! I adore your 'office' voice. Which perfume d'you

gargle with? I can smell it from here. It's the most erotic flux I've ev—I"

I must say I was a little surprised.

When I went out, she stood, cuddling the receiver. I said Goodnight, and got what I thought was a very *tiny* smile.

33

Gaylor waited outside the Savonia, touched his cap when he saw me, and I went in to ask the receptionist to send my name up. A thought, almost a dream, a ballet, of Consuelo, and music I hadn't thought I knew, seemed to invade, possess my mind while I was put on to Tanis' room.

"Oh, my heart's darling. I have been waiting for you! Where have you *been?* Don't you know I suffocate with love for you? Please come. I will call for the scotch and soda?"

We met as two waves merging. I felt the softness of passion's breasts, and the firm jelly of marvellous hips, the unutterable wonder of love's own pantheon within the living mouth.

"Darling, get your little bag. We're going to the sea!"

She pulled away, almost with fright in her eyes.

"Ah, no!" she whispered, frowning. "Tomorrow I have—"

"Get your bag!"

"Darling, I have the appointments made—"

"You have only one appointment. With me. Are you coming or not?"

She looked at me straight as I've ever been looked at.

"Yes, I will go with you," she said, perhaps in surprise. "But I must be back at least tomorrow night. Excuse me, please?"

She was still tender, but I sensed a something, not quite distrust, that was new, perhaps of the moment. She was sharply intelligent. There might have been a tone in my voice, or my eyes warned her. I had to be careful. If she refused to go, then something really untoward could result.

I heard her speaking Hungarian, a language I recognised but don't know, and she seemed to be arguing, pausing to listen, arguing again, and then she was angry and clapped the phone down.

"What stupidity!" she said, in a rare temper, coming in. "I don't start till Wednesday and they insist I go to Birmingham tonight. I told them Wednesday. Enough!"

But she was considerably more upset than that little matter appeared to be worth. I wasn't in the least troubled. I knew the phone must be tapped, and I was fairly certain there were microphones recording every word we spoke. All I had to do was play the eager lover inviting his mistress to the sea.

But I wasn't eager. I felt less lover than prison escort.

While I tried to get used to a notion which was absolutely foreign to anything I'd imagined I felt, I was suddenly appalled to find that any feeling I'd ever had, mental, physical, sexual, whatever it was, had quite gone. While she moved about in the other room, I tried to examine myself. I'd never thought I was flibbertigibbert. Love affairs were all strictly loyal, of the time, until one of us went away and there was no longer opportunity. Tanis was quite different. I'd fallen in love with her. Or I'd thought I had. And if I hadn't, and was certain I had, then it was my miserable duty to find out what was the matter with my method of thinking, feeling, doing. Clearly, in terms of commonsense, I was a great deal less than I'd imagined.

Patti's contempt still scored in the raw, unjust or not. I didn't want to think about it. Memory of Mel brought that abiding sense of shame.

Yet, the cause, the true reason, wasn't in Mel, wasn't in Patti, wasn't in anything except the new, never-thought-of-before, and repulsive idea of Tanis and the Blur. To think of her with him was disgust in itself. One's own passion always seems correct, of exquisite pleasure, a marvel of the senses. In others, a vulgar joke, prime of all dirty stories. Whatever the reason, and I was in no mood for a post-mortem, that tenderest flower, which I'd been pleased to call my love, was dead, door nail dead, and the words weren't any deader than the senses. I might have been a robot.

Tanis stood in the doorway in a raincoat and brogues, carrying a small dressing case.

"I'm ready," she said. "Do you think we shall have any sun?"

"It's going to be fine. I ordered it especially for you."

"Aren't you going to kiss me?"

"You know what happens when we kiss. Let's be off!"

"You have something strange," she said, and opened the door, out, to the lift.

I had, indeed. So strange, that I couldn't explain it to myself. But she was no longer Tanis, my love, my single wondrous passion.

She was merely the Blur's ex-piece, and I was getting rid of her.

The nicer way.

34

We were both more than a little distant on the way down, though I managed to keep small talk going by pointing out places of interest. I suppose she learned more history in that short time than in all her school years, most of it fictitious, but that's beside the point. We stopped for petrol when it was getting dark and I asked if she'd like a drink. We went in the pub, a "modern" place of oak panels and apricot lights, smelling of beer and something they'd put in the lavatories, and we sat on a very hard bench. I asked her to try Black Velvet. They had the champagne, and I took charge of the tankards and mixed in the Guinness, if I say so, with considerable style under the fixed regard of three waiters and the few clients who'd got up to see what was going on. I poured what I thought was a fair ration for us both, and offered the rest to the barman. One of the clients thought he'd like the same in a fairly loud voice, but when he asked the cost, he, in a word, desisted.

Tanis loved Black Velvet.

She drank again, put down the tankard, looked sideways at me, that liquid Come-To-Bed look, and put a hand on my knee, or rather, rubbed the patella.

"Darling one," she whispered. "Something is wrong. What?"

"I'm on home ground. This isn't the Continent. I've got to be careful. You don't need to be told that!"

She nodded, appeared more at ease.

"I found a beautiful small apartment," she said. "I thought you would find one for us?"

"You must have been lucky. I'd like to pay the rent and etceteras?"

"If you insist, that will be so wonderful of you. I shall have more for my pretties. Do you love me?"

"Of course."

"But so English!"

"With a dozen looking at us?"

"Kiss me!"

A command I resented for some idiotic reason. But I leaned forward. Impossible not to feel "something" when those lips were on mine, not in a kiss, exactly, but a sexual envelopment that blacked out everything whether in time or place. We came to, and I found the entire room in a stare.

Blah.

"Rooms are upstairs," some chap called from the shadows, and people tittered. Tanis got up, without hurry, and left me with a smile, and her going brought silence. For the moment. The barman, a decent fellow, divided his time between giving me change and admonishing the would-be cicerone, though had I been alone I'd have shut the ruffian up a bit sharp. Words and voices heated with the moments, but I took no notice, gave the barman a little extra for his trouble and walked out to the car.

"Only about twenty minutes, sir," Gaylor said, touching his cap. "I just called the harbor. Everything's ready!"

"Was that wise? Calls are recorded."

"Private line, sir!"

"Good. In the event of trouble, use your head!"

"Been told what to do, sir!"

It was hard-lipped and stone-eyed. Gaylor was only a chauffeur's cap and buttoned tunic, two grey, curiously depersonalized eyes and a mouth of zinc-y teeth. Anonymous, yes, but I owe him a great deal. So does the Blur.

Tanis got in. Gaylor shut the door and away we went. She leaned against me, we held hands, but never mind what we did, I couldn't feel anything for her. I don't think I've ever been more truly astonished in my life. Thank God, she must have felt the Black Velvet and dozed on my shoulder, and I was never more thankful than when the tires rumbled over the boards of the pier. She woke sleepily and Gaylor opened the door. The sea breathed at us. A lighthouse flashed white and left everything blacker.

"What is this?" she asked drowsily. "A quiet place."

"Remember I promised you this? A couple of days drifting from harbor to harbor? Weather's fine, a moon tonight. Come on. This way to Arcadia!"

She came happily enough and a seaman saluted at the gangplank of a fair-sized motor launch.

"'evening, Mr. Trothe, sir," he said, and tried to take her dressing case. "Welcome aboard, sir!"

"Wait!" Tanis whispered, and looked about, stepping back. "What is this? Where is the hotel? I don't want to go on this boat. I will not!"

"Tanis," I said. "Come on, now. We're going for the little voyage you said you'd enjoy—"

"No, I want the hotel. Please let us go back—"

Gaylor, a broad shadow behind her, bent, picked her up like a babe in arms and carried her down the gangplank. She started to scream but it was choked. I followed, the seaman waved a white sleeve, pulled at the gangplank and Gaylor jumped for the shore.

"She's right, sir!" he called. "No trouble there. She knows!"

He was shadow, and gone.

The seaman opened the door of a small bar, probably the best-stocked I've ever seen, all in dark polished wood and scarlet leather cushions. The sort of heaven one would like to die in.

"Just help yourself, sir," he said, with all the generosity of the mariner, owning nothing and unabashedly presenting everything, if not with love, then certainly with a warmth unapproached elsewhere. "Be some lamb chops and salad in ten minutes. Don't like chops, there's steak. No steak, chicken. Got some tinned turkey. Christmas puddin', anybody interested. Dock the other side about n'hour'n five minutes. No wind, sea's glass, and lights are bright, sir!"

I nodded. I didn't exactly know where I was, and I wasn't in any mood to appreciate lower-deck badinage. At any rate, for the moment.

I took off my overcoat and hat, had a wash, poured a very good drink, tasted it, felt a brute in thinking of Tanis who'd really feel like one, took the bottle and a soda, and went across to the cabin. I knocked but she didn't answer.

I went in.

She lay on the bunk, coat off, shoes off, staring at the ceiling.

"Why did you do this?" she asked in a small voice, without looking at me. "Do you destroy my love for you?"

"You didn't come to London because of that. In any event, it's all over!"

She sat up. She might have been smiling, but I wasn't looking directly at her. I poured the whiskey. Anything I saw was out of the corner of my eye.

"What are you going to do?" she asked, in an ordinary tone. "Don't you know my newspaper will ask for me?"

"You'll be in Paris tomorrow morning. If you'd stayed in London, they'd have found you in a prison!"

"Ah, but, Edmund! I have all my permits. I insist I am taken to London!"

"Drink this and think again. I was to have been arrested as your accomplice."

"But what nonsense!"

"Of course it is. The same 'nonsense' as your 'love' for me."

Cold alarm was in her stare, and she sat straight, putting the tumbler on the table.

"Edmund," she said, in the vibrant husk I knew, and had loved. "Please, you cannot treat me in this way. You know I love you. Why do you think I came to London?"

"To finish off the damage you'd already done. I don't know what you expected to do. I don't even know what you've done. But why did you take the trouble?"

She stood and turned her back. Without heels she was a small girl.

"I told you I love you. Love has no reasons. It *is* reason. What has happened in these hours? How do you change so much? Why have you done this? What shall I say to my newspaper?"

"Tell them that friends saved you. Perhaps from ten years in prison. Take my advice. Tell your German or Russian people we know what you're doing. You can also tell them I've resigned. I'm going into private business. As to love, tell that to Lord Blercgrove. You're expert at making fools out of fools. Is that part of your pleasure?"

"But, Edmund," she barely said, and held out her hands. "How can you change like this? Darling, what have I to do with Germans or Russians? I have only my small place!"

"Why didn't you tell me you knew Lord Blercgrove?"

She raised her head in startled surprise.

"But my darling, of course I know Lord Blercgrove!" she whispered. "How many thousands do I know from every country on earth? For two years I was cultural attaché. It was my business to meet them. Entertain them. Lord Blercgrove was very kind. Always very courteous. Why? You think there is something? How? Look at me, Edmund!"

"The usual bait. What else?"

"You imagine? What has happened to you? You know there is no other man!"

But I was remembering Room 1021. If they had enough evidence to arrest—and no magistrate would sign a warrant unless he was convinced—then she was playing a game. Why? Hoping I'd order the launch turned about? Why? What did she hope to do? What *could* she do? If she knew she was in danger of arrest, why would she argue? Why not accept in good grace, get off and go free? Was she relying on the power of the "patrons" who'd brought her in? Unless, of course, she really did love me and wanted to be with me.

"Darling," she whispered and came toward me with that walk that was all hips and flaunted breasts. "Let us take off our clothes. At least be comfortable. Yes? When have we been alone and in clothes so long? Come. My darling. Off!"

She unzipped, and the skirt fell. The blouse came off and flew over her shoulder. I undid my tie, unbuttoned my shirt, took off the jacket. By that time, she'd gone in the bathroom, throwing her bra over the chair, perfectly beautiful legs, and one exquisite breast catching a small diamond in light on the nipple.

I emptied my pockets and looked for a place to hide my stand-in friend and the holster. There wasn't one. Every drawer and cupboard was locked and so was the little desk. While it balanced by the strap, she slid the partition, and I pushed it in my overcoat pocket, ripping at my tie.

"Ready, darling!" she whispered. "Let us be ourselves only for these moments. But how I have dreamed of you!"

Naturally, at such a time, there had to be knocks on the door.

"B' y' parn', sir. Cap'n's compliments. Like a word on the bridge, sir!"

"Tell him to send me a note!"

"On the bridge, sir. Wait' take y' up, sir!"

A blowfly could take lessons in persistence from a matelot with an order from the Bridge. I hadn't a chance of sending him away. I looked at her, and she put the towel round her beauty as a toga, and blew me a kiss. I took my jacket. I didn't think the visit called for a tie.

"Shan't be long—"

"You have time, my one darling. I shall think of you. Come to me quickly. Quickly!"

I'm not sure if the lower deck heard, but he seemed to be frowning into wavy black distance when I went out. I followed him up a short ladder and he turned toward the charthouse. A shadow moved there, and I went toward it.

An electrifying supershock is what I had.

Yorick.

"Hullo, Edmund," he said, as if we'd just met in the canteen. "Straight from Davy Jones' locker, what? One of the few things I do rather well. We'll dock in about forty minutes. Give you time d'you think?"

He smiled a little tiredly at my surprise, and tapped a small loudspeaker over the desk.

"It all comes over here," he said, as if in apology. "The patter's not exactly Proustian. But you seem to be well on top, what?"

"Much rather be anywhere else. Can't we just sail along? *Must* we go in there?"

"Dock rules. Either we go in when we're told, or we stay out. And I can't afford to. I've got to be back to protect an alibi. Nuisance, but we bear our cross!"

I began to see that the Lord Imbrett was a great deal less than the idiot I'd presumed him to be.

"How many of you are there aboard?" I asked him.

"Myself, Polworth, and Jones the engineer. Why?"

"I can't think why we let a couple of ordinary chaps—not to mention Gaylor—become involved. If we were stopped now, what could we say?"

"I agree. You people of the older generation, you know, I think you're all mad. Quite mad!"

He said it, keeping the wheel steady, watching a lit point on the compass.

"What permits you to say that?"

He drew a deep breath of impatience or pity, I'm not sure. "Edmund. Consider. La Goulasch was mixed up with the Blur. Then she's mixed up with you. If that's what you prefer to call it. Before that she was one of those angel children. She got mixed up with my father. Why? Because the Big Hand employing her likes to keep in touch with those in responsible

263

positions. I've seen the list. It's really impressive. The Blur's talked to you about it, hasn't he?"

"Well? I don't see what you're getting at."

Yorick pushed the spectacles a little farther up his nose, and turned the wheel a fraction.

"Well, let's pretend we're in school again," he said calmly. "If the men who were leaders a short time ago, and now are in advisory positions, if they can be smirched in any way—the easiest is morally since we're all such disgusting hypocrites— then the social fabric's destroyed to that extent. When morals can be shown to be rotten, then there's no claim to honor. Without morals and honor, there can be no true authority. People begin to question themselves. Doubt their governments, put no faith in their ministers. Politics become suspect. So do the men, those elected, and more than them, those behind the scenes. The 'great' names, let's say. The Commie lads knew they've lost the economic battle. We've won hands down. But they can still make excellent friends on the moral and social front. Now, then, Edmund. Consider. A plus B plus C equals ABC. Therefore, if Lord Imbrett lends a launch—all they need do is find out who occupied dockspace on the other side—and aboard was Mr. Trothe who's directly connected with the Blur—"

"But I'm not!"

"Forgive me if I insist. All they have to do is look at the Service roster. Which they have. Or La Goulasch couldn't have gone unerringly to you. Then, as witness, you have La Goulasch, herself. She's being shanghaied—any other word for it?—out of Great Britain against her will. She's going to be left in France against her will. Why? Because Lord Imbrett, Lord Blercgrove, and Mr. Trothe—among others—don't want her to tell what she knows. In other words, A, B and C have something to fear? What?"

"I don't understand what you mean by 'she came unerringly' to me. Why me? Nothing was ever more accidental. What

264

could she get from me? Let's say your reasoning's correct. What real harm could she possibly do me?"

"You'll soon be in a most important position. A hint of immorality, and where are you? Pictures in the papers. Headlines. Gossip. And the damage in people's minds? And internationally? Who's to be trusted?"

I could only look at the glow of the French skyline.

The sudden change in Yorick put me off-balance. I realised that he'd cultivated—and his father must have helped—a droll fool's outer skin. He was, in fact, distinctly a brain, obviously with M.I. but I wondered why he'd take command of the launch.

"If this adventure's so stupid, why are you here?" I asked him.

"In case of accidents. I'm trying to protect my late father's name. And please let me give you a word of advice. Don't go with her to Paris. Don't leave the ship. Gaylor's waiting for us. Go back with us. That's an alibi."

"I can't do that. How could I simply discard her?"

"Preferably on the prongs of a hayfork. I've told you. She's a snake!"

"I think I know something about human beings. A little about women. I can't believe it!"

"Up to you, Edmund. You know her name's not Desarbier, don't you?"

"Nobody's yet been good enough to tell me. If it's of any importance?"

He gave the wheel a fractional turn, watching the compass, appearing to make up his mind.

"I feel it's necessary," he said suddenly. "If only to force a decision. Her name's Bernice von Hollefendorm. Daughter of a man you may remember?"

It didn't even surprise me.

Watching dark, almost-smooth water flowing past, feeling the slightest tremor of engine power underfoot, a small movement of the deck side to side, aware of stars in bright cluster beyond the glass of the wheelhouse, I wondered what might come next and really didn't care.

"Her youngest brother's probably in London. Sigmund. A real Nazi firebucket. Carrying on the family tradition, and so forth. Wasn't she telephoned tonight while you were at the hotel?"

"How do you know?"

"I got the report before I left. He was recently in Regsmund."

"That really does disappoint me!"

"I'm sure it must. Especially if you consider that Ebbleton was his older brother, alias Rolf von Hollefendorm!"

"I should have brought an overcoat," I said, starting to feel a sharp breeze.

"I just got over incipient phthisis. Lovely word. My teeth get in the way. I thought I was pleasantly ready for the tomb, but the nurse kept sticking needles in me. Awfully pretty, too. Gives one something to live for. And that's a pity, really. Well, there it is, Edmund. That little reptile was part of this Nazi business. She supplied copious information about you, your wife and family. There's no burke to the issue. They'll go on till they're satisfied they've dealt with all of us. I prefer joking about it, but it's not a joke. My father was on the list. So are you. So, I suspect, am I. You singed a little of the carpet. It's not enough. Regsmund's a small place. There are others, larger. We've got to obliterate!"

I began to agree with him on the way down the companion. I thought I'd do the best in present circumstances. While I opened the door, I determined to put her ashore, and leave her.

Tanis lay on the bunk with a sheet over that hid nothing. She looked at me with that fiery, tenderly tearful glaze I knew and loved. Or had. I poured two fingers and offered it to her. She shook her head.

"We dock in ten minutes, Fräulein von Hollefendorm," I said. "Then you go alone to Paris!"

Without looking at me she slipped her legs over the side of

the bunk and stood, turning her back, pulling the sheet about her shoulders, greyish in an aura of bright hair.

"It's now you must tell me this?" she said. "You have known all this time? You didn't know I hated you from the time I was a child?"

"How could you hate me? Why?"

She turned halfway, staring, almost, I thought, smiling at the bulkhead.

"Why?" she whispered. "Don't you know what I was told?"

"Who told you? Who knew?"

"My mother. She saw you. I was being born. Do you know the meaning of Bernice? Victory-bringer. My father thought I would be born on the day of victory. I was born on the day of his death. I thought I must hate you. But I began to love you. Edmund, you know I love you, don't you? Don't you, my one darling?"

Torn. It's the only word, torn. If I ever see my soul, I'm sure it'll show the scar of that moment.

"Tanis, listen to me. On the other side, when we land, you're free. Tell your people you're of no further use. I'm seeing you safely to France. After that, finish. That's all!"

The coldest-blooded thing I ever had to say.

She turned to me. Her face was lined deep in sorrow and I could have sworn she wasn't acting. I wanted so much to put my arms round her.

"I was almost not ready to do this," she said. "Edmund, I'm going to kill you."

The muzzle of my mini-friend looked at me.

I knew that fist had tightened. But she didn't know much about a firearm's quirks. The trigger pulled easily. So far. But then a release came into play to operate the silencer. She didn't find it.

I dived, grabbed, threw her in the corner cross-buttock, and scooped up the gun.

The walls of the cabin slid thunderously in screech of wheels

267

overhead, and we were out in the night, with the French coast dark on the sealine.

Polworth, a shadow, jumped in, picked her up, and before I could move, lifted her over the rail, and let go.

"Hang on, sir!" he shouted, and grabbed me while the deck tipped. We seemed to fly up in sudden roar of engine power, and keeled, kept on the turn, cut again and again through our wake, white, thrashing torn wings of phosphorescence.

Nobody, nothing could have lived in that spume.

The roar moaned away to a pulse, and the deck steadied.

"That's that, sir!" Polworth said, and slapped his hands, reaching up for a switch. "Good riddance to bad rubbish, eh?"

The walls rattled down, clicked in place, and the door slammed shut.

I sat against the bunk.

The pillows and bedlinen were still warm.

35

Gaylor left me at the house when the sun was well up. We'd dropped Yorick at Mellonhamp on the way. Four solid hours we'd spent cleaning the launch. Anything that might have been touched was given hot soda water and a pumice rub, and a sluice with the power nozzle. When ex-Chief Petty Officer Polworth was satisfied, we washed our hands, had a drink, and fell in the car, for myself, exhausted, though Yorick wasn't much better. He slept all the way.

I didn't.

I was never so excoriated by horror, shame, bitter regret, absolute self-contempt.

"Let's get it right, now," I'd said, on the steps at Mellonhamp. "I took her to the station. She was going to Birmingham on the 8:10. Then I went home. You know nothing. They can't rock Gaylor. My side's airtight!"

"Hope it sticks, Edmund. I passed several friends of mine at quay-side and out in the bay. However, *a bientôt!*"

He was certainly a different man. No longer an office boy. But I was too crumpled to wonder much about anything. I'd been guilty of cold-blooded murder many times before. Some of them had affected me in quieter moments. But passing time perhaps had softened. Thinking of Tanis picked up and thrown overboard made me feel physically sick. When Gaylor left me I stood for a moment listening to the morning. I was trembling.

The house gave warm, peaceful welcome. I felt I didn't deserve it. A tremendous storm came over. Thunder shook the windows, and that's all I remember till Mrs. Cloney woke me, on the study couch, still in my overcoat, just after nine.

I couldn't stay in the house. There was a fast train at 11:30 and I went up to dress. Mrs. Cloney made me tea and boiled eggs. She wept a little about Mel, and I gave her some money for shopping, and walked out in an edged snow-wind for the station.

Thankfully, nobody was about. The train came in on time and the newspapers took me to London. Nothing seemed to have happened in the rest of the world. All I could think of was a girl pulled down in that vortex.

Accomplice After the Fact. No hope of mercy from any Judge.

Father, and now, daughter.

I hadn't any idea what to do with myself. I couldn't bear another walk across the park. I went instead through Little France and out to Parliament Square. Small rain sometimes wet my face, froze my nose. I thought I might go in the Abbey, but the place had always reminded me of the belly of a dried whale. Hollowing echoes, the clump of tourist feet, memories of the nobility, most in hired robes, with their lunch sandwiches carried in their coronets, and the wonder of a thousand years of prayer. Humans on their knees pleading for what? How many generations of anguish and disappointment? How many moments of happiness? How many marriages? What of love?

Ah, Mel!

Tanis!

You lift in that murderous froth and your hair, that I loved to run through my lips covers your beautiful mouth. I could have run from the thought. But I was in Whitehall, huddled in my coat. I had little to do, and Miss Roule was off that day. But it was somewhere to sit, perhaps to think. I went into the building and the messenger saluted.

The room was tidy, cold, loud with silence. A note lay on the pad.

The handwriting gave me quite a jump. Consuelo's. I hadn't seen it for a long time.

Dear Edmund, this is to welcome you home. Rouley told me. If you feel well enough—!—you could telephone Gover's Grange 23 and I can be in London in an hour or so. This, of course, is only on the offchance you get this in time.

Consuelo

I telephoned, and she must have been sitting beside it. "I'm so happy you're here! If I'd known where, I'd have met you. Are you absolutely well? May I see you?"

"Completely. Isn't it rather a long way for you to come?"

"Just to see you for a moment and make quite sure you're in proper condition, that's all. I shan't sleep a wink if I don't!"

"I'll meet you at Claridge's at four, or thereabouts. That gives you time—"

"Watch me go!"

The door opened as if driven by a hurricane.

Miss Roule came in and stood tiptoe, hand to mouth, a perfect expression of astonishment. She wore a mink coat and cap, and calf-length boots of soft leather. I'd understood she was wealthy. Her appearance underlined it.

"Oh, Mr. Trothe!" she whisper-screeched. "I'm most frightfully sorry. I didn't think you'd be in!"

"But not at all," I soothed. "Anything serious?"

"I've got a confidential letter here. It was among Mrs. Trothe's things she left in Paris. It came in last night with the compliments of M'sieur Georges Pontviannel!"

She gave me a long sealed envelope from the steel cabinet.

There were receipts for clothes, perfume and accounts from the hotel. But the folded paper had been written in red pencil with a point that had crumbled.

From Mel.

Darling Edmund, my sweetheart, I must tell you while I can think. I don't know what's happened. It's as if I've been standing beside myself, watching somebody else do the most frightful things without being able to stop them, or say anything. I sold the house. I spent the children's savings. I sold everything I could. I gave it all to Terry. I knew it was wrong. I couldn't do anything. I hated you. I wanted to hurt you. I don't know why. Edmund, my darling, please believe I love you. I love you more than you've ever known. More than I can tell you. I never had any words. I was always a little bit frightened of showing too much. I was a fool. A prig. I gave it to Terry. I don't know why. He isn't the man you are. He's a swine with a conscience. That makes him pitiable. I pitied a swine. I became a swine myself. The more swine, the more I wanted to hurt you. And poor Pamela. What can I say to her? What? And why? Why? That's what I've been thinking about. Why?

I could almost hear her saying it.

I didn't want Miss Roule to see me make an utter fool of myself. I folded the paper and put it in my private drawer.

"Off to my club," I said. "See you tomorrow. And thank you!"

"Oh, Mr. Trothel" she mourned. "I'm so sorry I disturbed you!"

I walked along to Trafalgar Square, frozen in a whistling wind. I turned down Pall Mall. I was thinking about everything and nothing. The moment I thought about anything worthwhile I turned away. The club was quiet, lights were dimmer than usual, and unwrinkled newspapers overlapped in the racks. I took a handful and started to read, and it was then that a little pink memory-tab seemed to tickle the back of my mind, bringing into focus Paul's report, based on an exhaustive summary I'd made, which had caused the Blur's displeasure. To test the climate, I telephoned Miss Tulliver's office, and her relief said she'd find a copy and send it over. She did, and after I'd read it, I had no need to take notes in order to compile a precis—including personal experience—that must certainly cause any careful reader to think twice about our entering the Common Market until a healthier economic condition had been attained at home, and far better terms offered. As senior industrial power, with more potential than any other two of the countries already in, that was our right. What we'd needed was a Churchill at brilliant height of his gifts as negotiator-statesman. What we'd had were merest bargaining politicians, and Cholly simply brushed them aside. He could afford to.

One augustan broadside from a Churchill would have sunk him.

But I had to wonder what had been wrong with me that I hadn't been aware of the obvious. I'd been using my brain. My faculties were unimpaired. The figures were correct. My calculations were exact, borne out by other authority. Cholly and his advisers knew. Others must have had serious doubts. Why hadn't I realised what was happening long before? And had I seen it, would I have thought of making a counter-report, possibly against Paul's wishes, clearly to the detriment of our department, and irredeemably inimical to my career?

I was cold that daydreams of Tanis and others could have blunted or destroyed an exceptional talent—some said—for being able to locate and destroy mare's nests at tap of a pencil. I'd been partly responsible for creating this one.

Out of a void, I remembered an Arab sage I'd seen, squatting in the sand beyond Aden, a bundle of blue linen crisped in an ovenlike sun, and somebody's saying he was there to examine himself and his world. Had Mel's death put me out in the dry sands of self-examination? Was I being stripped willy-nilly of that air of godism? Was I awake in the wilderness of what-was-left, beginning to doubt, even to deny, what I'd believed before? Had running after the girls anything to do with that unforgivable blindness? Daydreams were the worst drug of all, and I'd certainly daydreamed. It was the most—apparently—innocent sort of pleasure, but it could become a habit. Had I become

273

addict? The facts were in front of me day by day. They were part of a duty I had determined must be a success, ending in the signing of the Treaty of Rome.

That, as I saw now, as Paul had seen, would have meant certain economic disaster for us, and many a penal year to recuperate.

In my small way I would have been responsible.

In those frigid moments I had to wonder where else I might be wrong. Was I so hopelessly muddled, purblind, behind the times?

Were the children correct? I couldn't for the life of me see where I'd gone wrong, or pinpoint the moment I'd started going stale. Unless, of course, it lay in hanging on to the lessons of childhood, which, unthought, became the pillars of what I'd always considered to be a decent life. But did a "decent" life have room for a Tanis or any of the others? A Mel left alone when she needed me? Was that type of brutal insensitivity inherited? Could the children have got it from me? I'd always been privately contemptuous of people who gave way to their feelings, whatever the cause. Feelings, sentiments, were privileged matters. Their realm was bounded by the four walls of one's own room. But my grandfather, a Victorian down to frock-coat and muttonchop whiskers, had thought it perfectly natural to weep in public. As a child I'd been quite shaken. Nobody else seemed to think it strange, certainly not my father. Then why had I been able to think differently?

Who'd taught me?

36

The walk to Claridge's did me good. The atmosphere in the foyer and lounge, created by more than one generation of civilised people, was something of a tonic. Consuelo got up from an armchair looking simply beautiful, pinkish from the drive, sparkling in a healthy way that I don't think I'd often seen, that might be described as dangerous, though I'm not sure why.

We had an excellent cocktail, and I suddenly decided to drive home with her. The drink might have loosened a taut rope somewhere, but anyway I felt a great deal better, and I wanted to see my house again. We went out in almost-darkness and we talked—I've never been able to talk to most people—I can't think what about, and by the time we got to Trothe Close, I was quite sure we'd known each other for the past three thousand years. Unfortunately, just as we were turning down at the Hollow, Dr. Norris came into the headlights walking his dog.

We slowed, I called, and he came over, breathing clouds of breath and pipesmoke.

"Look," Consuelo said hurriedly. "I've got to be at class early in the morning. May I go now? I'll be in by seven, all dew-y. May I call you tomorrow?"

"Or I'll call you. Thank you for a wonderful drive!"

"My own strictly private enjoyment, I assure you!"

She went off in a rrmpf! and I turned to meet Dr. Norris. He seemed a little off-hand, until I realised he wasn't quite sure how to open the ball. He knew I hadn't been in any nursing home. I led him on, talked about this, that, and nothing. Frederick was doing very well. I didn't press for details. It was too late to call on Dr. and Mrs. Tomsett. I had to make a special visit to thank them for real kindness in helping to save a young idiot from the life-long scar of preventive detention.

Dr. Norris became his usual calm self, when I asked him what the outlook might be, not only for Frederick, but for the others? Thousands? Millions?

"Fear of God used to have some effect," he said, tapping out the pipe. "But it's losing ground with youngsters. Every time those chaps in space climb out of a capsule, the idea of God recedes a little further. That picture of the earth seen from the moon absolutely petrified me. To think of all of us crawling about that little ball held in space—by what?—and worrying about aborting a thirteen-year-old, or some young rascal swallowing a dose of rubbish, really one's dwarfed. Imprisoned in littleness. I'm really terribly sorry for this generation. We were certainly adventurous physically. The world was ours to roam in, foot, sail, steam, what you will. But they're roaming the psychic world. Exploration of the senses. Sex? They've gone past it. Doesn't mean much any more. Cure? Possibly. But I'm not sanguine. Frederick's better material than most. That's in his favor, of course."

"I always thought you were an optimist."

"I am indeed. I'm only looking at the facts, and as those clever Russians say, drawing the proper conclusions!"

Parnes met me in the eye of his white torchlight as I turned down the Lane, a monument of good health and sanity. He gave me a hearty welcome, told me the place wasn't the same 'thout 'ee, and there had been visitors after dark on two nights, but by the time he got down to the gates, they'd drove off, ah.

"That's a little strange. When was this?"

"Let's see now, zur. Two nights ago, the last. So I'm kippin' one eye open, and Cloney's lain with a shotgun close 't hand, ah!"

He came with me to the front door. Everything appeared in order, but curiously, while I felt for the key, I lived again my killing days and found no comfort in their memory. What I had once accepted as brilliant adventure now seemed nothing more than the most sordid type of barbarism.

I looked about almost hungrily, I suppose, at pictures, china, carpets I'd known since boyhood, that had never changed place since they were put there perhaps half-a-dozen generations before, some of them long before that.

Everything shone, I was glad to see. Mel had always insisted on soap and water, and after that, wax. The aspect of coldness I seemed to pick up came, perhaps, from the absence of her touch. The vases were empty. I felt glad I hadn't brought her letter. A doll of Patti's stared at me, still in the glass-cupboard. There was hurt in thinking of her. I wondered what I might have said to Mel. "Darling, this is our new son-in-law, whose name I don't know. Patti's going to have babies by him. This is what we sweated in love for!" It sounded absurd but it wasn't. I don't know what Mel might have said.

The telephone rang. I had to look for it. Somebody had sensibly moved it out to the hall in the light.

"Hullo?"

"Edmund! What tremendous luck!"

"Yorick! Where are you?"

"Not far. They said you might be there. Had any reports of 'visitors' recently?"

"Tonight. I just got here—"

"May I come over? Two moments, not more!"

"Wait for you!"

The library fire was laid, and while I lit it, I was beginning to wake up to the fact that I might have to deal with somebody, perhaps not an ordinary burglar, trying to break in. Mulling it over while the fire took hold, I felt sorry I'd left my super-mini in my locker at the club. My automatic, my talisman, I hadn't seen since before the funeral. It ought to be handy at any time, not on the hip, but in the little shoulder holster, that fitted just under the arm, quite the prettiest I ever saw, which I'd taken off one of Himmler's people who'd got in the way. I had a good blaze going, and went out to the kitchen to put the kettle on. While it dribbled a tune as it filled, I tried to remember the last time I'd put my friend in the desk.

I couldn't.

Blue-green flame under that kettle wasn't hotter than the flame that suddenly burst inside me. I shut the thought out of my mind, took down the teapot and teacaddy, ready, and went to the desk in the study. The holster was exactly where I knew it had to be, coiled about by its polished strap. But my friend wasn't in the holster. I went upstairs and into my room. I searched methodically. I looked through the suits. Nothing. Every drawer and cupboard, the chest of drawers, both wardrobes, nothing. I pulled out shirts and socks, handkerchiefs, bathrobes, pajamas, every unlikely place. I went from room to room. Inch by inch. I was frozen stiff and sweating for the tropics.

Nothing.

But I'd also been wearing overcoats.

I hurdled the stairs to open the closet. I fumbled through raincoats, dusters, peajackets, towncoats and then to the heavy fawn where careful Mrs. Cloney had hung it in its proper place as Mel had taught her. The right-hand pocket held a weight. I felt the patch. It was the shape of the automatic.

I could have gone on my knees to pray thanks, but the kettle was screaming. The water was overboiled and I refilled, breathing easy again, thanking God, however incoherently, and wet through with the sweats of absolute anguish.

How I could be such an utter fool really did distress me. This type of idiocy—forgetting where I'd put things or forgetting them altogether—was simply not like me. I was generally cold-brained, methodical, a planner to extreme limits. My career was based on exactly that. My reputation flourished on it. But twice in a row I'd forgotten what must have been my most priceless possession.

I went back to the closet, and took it out of the overcoat pocket and pushed it roughly, as a friend, into its proper place, my hip pocket.

While I poured a cup of tea, the bell rang and startled me into slopping it on the floor. My nerves were not what they were. I felt the rage almost rip tissue inside me, somewhere. While I stared at the cup, I realised I must have been turning the house upside down for the past half-hour. But if I'd stopped to think, I must have gone immediately to my overcoat.

Why?

Why should I carry it in my overcoat? I never had. It had its own place in the desk, or on my hip. It had never been anywhere else.

I opened that damned door as though I'd never done anything else all my life.

Yorick came in on rubber soles, a ghost in a black coat with astrakhan cuffs and collar.

"It was Father's," he said, slipping out of it and leaving it piled on the floor. "May I speak freely? La Goulasch has been found. On a beach south of Ostend. This afternoon."

I'll never know why, but I felt the tears burn. Perhaps there's so little beauty in our time, in women or anything else. When it's gone, there's grief for those of us who've known it, and God forgive me, I had.

"I shall always regret my part in it."

"I concur. There was a search of all craft in Famlingham tonight. My launch was one of those given a thorough overhaul. Thank God, we'd repainted!"

He took the whiskey and rested it on his knee, sitting forward, staring at the Rowlandson over his right shoulder.

"I was called less than a couple of hours ago. I'm warned

279

that an article of women's clothing was found aboard the launch. They didn't say what it was!"

He wasn't staring, so much as ogling, over the rim of the tumbler. He drank, licked his lips and put the tumbler down.

"Edmund, you have an automatic, so I'm told, and a Scotland Yard permit, issued in late 1939?"

I swallowed a mouthful of weak whiskey and water, and came up for air.

"Yes. It's official."

"Where d'you keep it?"

I put my hand behind, and gratefully, with deep thanks to my guardian angel, gave it to him, butt first.

"Thank you," he said, and took an envelope out of his inner pocket. "This isn't loaded, is it?"

"It always is."

"Dear me. I hadn't realised you were quite so bloody-minded. All for the best, possibly?"

He lifted his glasses to read the number on the barrel, and looked at the envelope. He raised his head, pushed his glasses farther up his nose, and stuck his tongue in a back tooth.

"What's the number of your little friend?" he asked gently.

"237395. A 21."

"That's the number of the automatic found on the launch. This one isn't yours!"

I looked at it. Same size, same maker, but not mine, and not loaded.

"I'll get rid of it," he said. "Of course you'll report your loss to the police? We've got some pretty questions to face, haven't we? Let's decide on a few answers. Might cheat the hangman, d'you suppose?"

For the first time I had a fair idea of the type of people we were up against. I could see the staff work and split-second timing involved, the daring little plan to bounce the baby in our laps, that could make us hoist of our own petard.

But even while I admired, my mouth was quite dry.

37

Trees polled for the spring stuck gnarled black fists out of a foot of snow across the Common. I trudged the only footprints in all that white space. Neither milkman nor baker had been round. The trains were late. I should have heard the 7:11 whistle at Truscott's Battle. Fog rolled down in the dip. Not a bird flew, and I couldn't see smoke from any chimney. I turned into the constabulary house. Late ramblers brooded brown under a ceil of crystal snow. Good sign. Thaw coming.

I rang the bell.

Parnes opened the door, florid from a wash. I could smell soap. And beer.

"I've been trying to get you," I began.

"Oh, moi dear good God, zur!" he said, in half a voice. "The missus and me, we had a ploy down Gridgen's Round. All us families, it was, ah. Come from ev'ywhur. So we had a few. I just got home. The wife ain't here yet. Was it 'portant, sir? Please to come in!"

I followed him in, to a couple of hundred years of smoke from wood fires, hams up the chimney, laundry strung on three lines in the minimal kitchen, a white-scrubbed table with official forms piled square at two-inch intervals, an inkpot, and one pen in a holder dug from a piece of driftwood. I'd made dozens as a boy.

I knew he was still a little drunk.

"I came here twice to report the loss of a firearm," I said, not

281

severely, not cheerfully. "It's a nuisance. Those people must have broken in!"

I might have struck him.

He shut his eyes, ran his hands up and down his shirt front, and pushed his mouth up to squeeze the parting in a blond moustache.

"I'm not too far in the Sub's books. Sub-Inspector, sir. He'd dig me in, he would. Hope y'll let me say this mornin', sir? I could still say last night, though. I got the excuse the lines was all down, see? Snow's right thick. Nothing couldn't go through!"

"Do whatever you think fit. But for heaven's sake stick to your story. There's the number, make, and when and how and where I think it was stolen. It certainly was not lost. Be certain. It was stolen!"

"I'll fill out the form, sir. Get it over the wire this very mornin', ah. You done me a favor. I takes that very kindly, sir!"

"Thank you, Parnes. I'd like another of Mrs. Parnes' seven-pound pots of marmalade. Best I ever tasted. And a flitch. If there's any more sausage, up to ten pounds. Mrs. Cloney'll pay."

"Thank y', sir. Be delivered on the dot. Any trouble, y'know I'll do me level best, sir!"

"Don't doubt it for a moment, Parnes. Good morning!"

I went down to catch the 7:40, knowing I had a strong friend and almost a cast-iron alibi.

During the time of the lying-in-state, and in the days after the funeral, at least a couple of hundred people must have been in the house to sign the book or leave flowers, messages, condole, or just stand and stare. I wasn't present. Everybody there was witness that I stayed in my room, for most of the time out cold with seconal, and I felt all the better for it, even if I hated to waken. A surprising number came from Iron Curtain countries, where, so it was told, I wasn't liked, and dozens had dribbled in up to quite late even on that Saturday evening.

Thinking things over, I felt secure on all fronts.

The club was still in the hands of charwomen and porters. It took a few minutes to pick up my letters and take my stand-in friend from my locker.

I crossed St. James's Park—how many generations have thrown how many tons of buns to how many flights of ducks?—Mel! Such a broken-bottle wound when I think of you—why?—because you're among the dead? Do we pity the dead for having gone, or ourselves for staying?

And Ghislaine, those poor, broken fingernails that once I felt in delicate touch upon myself, I think of them, of you, and I yearn, I hunger to help you, if only I knew where to go, whom to see. God knows what else they did to you, those loyal and dutiful guardians of western miscivilisation, what other horror you endured before you broke, brave sweet. If to Christ I knew who those "guardians" were, don't you think I'd kill them as I'd kill flies, as I've killed before? Don't you think I would? But Ghislaine, I assure you! That killing, of how many no matter, would be my most consummate delight. Kidnappers and torturers, those who take pleasure in the screams and faints of their victims, are their lives more sacred than those of flies? By comparison with such offal any housefly, God knows, is limpid heart of cleanliness.

I hadn't got my hat and coat off before Miss Roule held up the telephone.

"Firearms Section, Scotland Yard, sir," she said. "They've been calling for the past half-hour!"

The constable at the other end took me step by step through all the detail, and as I gave him the answers I knew he was filling up a form.

"You've got no theories how it was taken out of the house, sir? You can speak your mind. It's all strictly confidential!"

"All I can think of is that after the funeral—for two or three days after—there were about a couple of hundred visitors to sign the book. The library, where my desk is, was open to everybody. The firearm was in that desk. I'm not sure if it was locked or not.

I wasn't in any condition to verify. Beyond that, the house has been broken into—"

"Ah. I'll get on to that report, sir!"

"I suppose it'll be some time before I can have it back?"

"Have to be decided if there was any carelessness involved. Meantime, your permit's in abeyance. Understand that, sir, don't you?"

"Yes. Could you tell me how and where it was found?"

"A 'nonymous phone call to the local police, sir. They found this woman's dress and your automatic wrapped up in it. 'Course, a firearm, that's very serious!"

"Anybody know who the dress belonged to?"

"Dressmaker identified the label, sir. A Miss Consuelo Furnival."

I thought I'd gone quite mad. I had to grab at sanity.

"That's rather surprising. I haven't been approached about it?"

"I don't doubt you will be, sir. Anyway, if there's anything else, I'll call you!"

My automatic and my ex-secretary's dress found on the launch of the late ex-head of my one-time Service? It looked as if, in all truth, I'd have to answer some very pretty questions. But I had a few to ask myself. Who'd planted that firearm in my overcoat? Who'd substituted it for mine? Could it have been Yorick, himself? But why should he?

I didn't know what to think.

Miss Roule brought in a note.

"Delivered by special messenger, sir. Scrymgour, Tyle's, the Canal Banking Syndicate."

The note was handwritten, asking me to call a number, and signed with two initials.

Miss Roule put me through to Sir Ryder Chapman's office.

"Ah, yes. Mr. Trothe. I—uh—felt it might be more practical to confine this to a telephonic conversation. The man whose name you require *is* a client of many years. I can only tell you that

284

he's very well found, both here and in the United States, in South America generally, and anywhere in Africa he's absolutely number one behind the scenes. Have you a pencil? The name is Obowepetawe Ngogajike Goiwokeke Njagowikijo, and there are others, let's call them extraneous, which he uses on occasion. A syllable from each name makes another, or a syllable here and there. It's not confusing to the African, of course. However, what's important here is that I find he's your son-in-law!"

"Does he act as banker for African students, do you know?"

"He has accounts in various banks here. He's United Kingdom representative for many of the African governments. He also recruits mercenaries, buys arms, planes, anything that's wanted—"

"Does he ever act for the Russians and Chinese?"

"He's done a great deal of business with them over past years. He's a likeable sort, but a *very* fast dancer. One has to be a small-print expert. Remember, he's a barrister!"

That was when I sat back to take stock of my position. Clearly it had been known that Tanis and I were rather more than friends, that I had been "friendly" with others, including Ghislaine, that my brother-in-law was Terence Ebbleton—how long had it been known that Rolf Ferenc von Hollefendorm was Tanis' brother?—that my wife was his mistress, that he was friendly with my son and daughter, and that she had married an African entrepreneur, banker, whatever-he-was, involved in subversive activities among African students, that my son had been concerned in drug-trafficking.

And Mr. Edmund Trothe, with his experience, in his position, a merest lily-i'-the-field, witless, where he was not, indeed wot-less, in short, a very vagabond of innocence?

If I were in the Blur's place, what would I think after reading those reports? And if I were in a soft spot politically, or fearful of some type of scandal, would I need a better scarecrow?

Once arrested, I'd have a devil of a job proving that I had never suspected, that nothing I had done was in any degree disloyal, that I had been guilty of little more than leaving my family to fend for themselves.

Was that why I had been given this—interim—desk? To hammer another nail in the coffin? If the name of my son-in-law had eluded me, could I have made a reasonable defense? Could I have said, truthfully, that I didn't recognise Mr. Obowepetawe, didn't know he was my son-in-law, had met him only once, coming out of a bathroom?

I had no hesitation in sending the name over to M.I., and I really didn't care what the consequences might be, for anybody, Patti least.

Curious to find oneself suddenly disliking one's own child.

"The Lord Imbrett and Mr. Joel Cawle, sir!" Miss Roule said, on the intercom.

"Ask them in, and see if you can find us some coffee!"

"Sorry about this, Edmund," Yorick murmured, with more than usual weariness. "Stand by for a dirty 'un over the poop!"

"I've sent for some coffee. Hullo, Joel. Fog's coming up again. What's wrong?"

"The night you went down to Famlingham, you remember the details?" Yorick asked.

"I think I do."

"You stopped for a quick one?"

"Did we?"

"Didn't you? At a petrol point with a pub next door?"

We pulled up three chairs near the window.

"Yes, we did. As I remember, we were both rather thirsty. Anything wrong with that?"

Yorick shut his eyes, blew out his breath, and took off his spectacles. Joel crossed his feet and sat back, looking down at the traffic.

"Why?"

"Probably the most expensive thirst you'll ever fail to enjoy. The attendant at the pump's a collector of ancient automobiles. The Rolls-Royce happens to be a special pet of his. Gaylor, I suppose, all disarmed by boyish enthusiasm, went out of his way to give the most impressive details. Including the engine registration number. Deadly and damning. Because after you'd left, the barman had an altercation with somebody, and had to call the police. The barman wanted to call you as witness. He didn't know who you were, but the lad outside gave him the car's number. Gaylor had taken the trouble to change the plates to two belonging to the Service. What he couldn't change was the engine registration, which Rolls-Royce instantly identified as the Blur's property, and his father's before him. Question, whom were you with that night?"

A flight of armoured bats seemed to lager in my stomach.

But the mind functioned.

"I was with a friend of mine, a woman, whose name I refuse to disclose," I said, and sat up to pour coffee. "We were having a drive in the country before she caught a train at Euston. What else?"

"Changed car plates, the Blur's car, a woman who disappears, is later found drowned, your automatic, your secretary's name —no connection, it's been proved—in the matter of a dress— Edmund, if you were a flatfoot, don't you think your nostrils might twitch? Just a little?"

"Prove that Miss Desarbier was with me!"

He took a folded paper from his pocket and held out a facsimile of a receipt from the Griffon & Grelles Arms, Four Went Waye, for a telephone call to a London number.

"If Tanis Desarbier wasn't with you, it seems rather more than a coincidence that whoever-else-it-was would know that number," Yorick said. "He left that hotel within minutes of her call. Obviously she warned him. Did she know where she was going?"

"I think she might. I gave her more or less an itinerary of where we expected to go."

"That's it, then. That's how he knew. Very well. Was there

enough time, after leaving the pub, to catch the 8:10? We've tried it. It took forty minutes."

"If we left the pub at about a quarter to seven, there was ample time. Provided everybody keeps his head, I don't think they'll get very far!"

Yorick pushed himself out of the chair, stood, buttoned his jacket.

"I think you forget the Blur," he said, and looked at Joel. "You've got the most unpleasant part of the egg. Say your little piece, and we'll *imshi!*"

"In stopping for a drink, you broke two rules," Joel began. "Not to be identified, and not to drink in public."

"Neither of those rules apply to me!"

"Under the circumstances, of course they did. The death of a woman known to us as Tanis Desarbier is being investigated by Scotland Yard at the request of the French and Hungarian governments. Chief Superintendent Hockley of the C.I.D. is in charge, and he's responsible to the Home Secretary, who reports to the Prime Minister. We were called at four o'clock this morning. If it appears necessary, the Blur's prepared to make a statement."

Yorick pushed his spectacles farther up on the bridge of his nose.

"If he does, it'll be at the expense of everybody else," he said. "Especially you, Edmund. But that's not all—"

"Look here," I interrupted. "I've got quite a number of friends in Fleet Street. This is the sort of thing they eat. Please remember that!"

Yorick set his tie, looking down at the lamp.

"All that's been thought of," he said, almost sadly. "Doesn't do to say it out loud and too often. The charge could conceivably come under the Official Secrets Act. Then it might be a very long time before you had the chance of talking to anyone but the prison chaplain!"

"But you're in rather a bright spot, too," I said.

"I know. Go on, Joel!"

"In the light of what's happened, and what might happen, it's considered that your usefulness is irremediably impaired. You will therefore consider yourself free of any promise, of any kind. Before seeing Superintendent Hockley at 11:00 this morning, you will please see the Lord Blercgrove at 10:45!"

"I'll think about it. I refuse to be chivvied for any reason!"

"Chivvying is as chivvying does," Yorick said quietly. "There'll be a police escort ready. That'd lead to several very serious steps. They'd have a warrant, of course, which'd mean they could hold you in custody and apply for remands as they thought fit. Wouldn't do you any good at all. Since I'm up to my cruppers in this, I'm a little apprehensive!"

"You don't imagine I'd mention you?"

He turned to me, head on one side, the prime-comedian look.

"Edmund," he said, in mildest reproach. "Do you think it even entered my head? No. We're here to warn, that's all. If you'd gone all strawberry-woo to that office this morning, you'd have run slap into something that might—but I doubt it—have tipped your onion-cart. But the best was first, and the worst is last. Where, exactly, do I stand in this? In the mud, of course, as usual. But what's my story? What are you going to say?"

"Exactly what I know, up until the moment we turned back for London. The bypass is just beyond Four Went Waye. I could have got her to Euston in time. I never heard Famlingham mentioned. What's Gaylor going to say?"

"We're going to beard the bloody old fool now. He talked to this lad, and took you on to the bypass, and back to Euston. No frills?"

"None. Perfectly ordinary journey. Two old friends, private conversation, and where more private than in a car? The same car had been used by Mr. Colethorne to take the body of a dead man to Service headquarters. The plates remained. What more?"

Yorick folded his arms, looked at me almost under the lenses, and smiled—the word must be beatifically—at me.

289

"Edmund, the more I see and hear of you, the more I'm sure I'm in the presence of irrepressible genius. I believe you've resolved the quantum. I'm off home to celebrate. As ever, my thanks. And please don't worry!"

I saw them to the door.

I had too much to think of to worry about anything.

38

I had to think back to my time with Tanis.

I surprised myself, because apart from the adventure of bed, I couldn't remember very much. I wasn't sure what she believed, or what she'd said, if she had any opinions about anything, or if, as most of them seemed to do, she took her opinions readymade from the Party, and didn't care about anything else beyond the odd jump. I was reminded of Jabotinski's theory about fourteen-year-olds. It seemed to be very much at work wherever one looked.

But a Scotland Yard enquiry was different. The correct course, it seemed to me, was to answer each question without shilly-shally. No police officer would ask to see me without first having made exhaustive enquiries. Consuelo hadn't called me. If she'd been told about the dress, she'd have asked me first, I was sure of that. Why hadn't she been told or warned? Why hadn't the police been to see me about the automatic instead of telephoning? Nothing fitted right. I felt the nudge of M.I. I was grateful I'd been shown that long-distance telephone receipt, because I hadn't remembered the name of the place. I might have denied having been there at all. That would have been fatal.

The Blur's office called to say his lordship would like to see me immediately.

I had a few mutinous moments.

I could resign and walk out. But there was threat of arrest. Imprisonment. I couldn't believe it. Then why not defy the Blur,

Room 1021, and all the rest? It would be the first conscious—or, for that matter, unconscious—act of outright disobedience since I'd entered the Service. It would be, in the circumstance, not merely irresponsible, but caitiff.

For some reason, I thought of Frederick.

He hadn't considered me, hadn't thought about himself as a member of the family, still less of his position in society, even so with a small s. He'd ignored his name, his position, education, responsibility, all that had made him what he was.

But any attempt, on my part, to ignore an official request, or to refuse an order, would be an infinitely worse crime. Death was the only excuse.

We all had to die, and the day was coming. That was perhaps the royalest thought in life. A moment was marked in time, a day in the calendar, unknown, but the clock would bring them by, mine, Frederick's, everybody's.

Then why worry? Why bother one's head about the Blur, or some Inspector Chiff-Chaff from Scotland Yard? Well, for the same reason that Frederick had to be taught to bother his head about me, about his duty to his family, and his place in society.

We were given life—poor Patti!—true, without choice, we existed, and whether we liked it or not, we had a duty because our salt was earned in conformity with the rest of human life, and we had to obey, because obedience was an essential part of the bargain of living.

Death was merely the end of obedience, which, like a relay-runner's staff had to be handed on to those coming behind, if, that is, they had any sort of race to run, the wit to see, the will to give their best, and the grit to try.

I no sooner had the thought digested than over the road I went, just in time for a magnificent cup of rare Soochow somebody had brought Miss Tulliver. The silver tea service seemed to take some of the burthen out of the air.

"I'm hoping we shall box a bird or so today," the Blur said, easily, pursing non-existent lips to sip. "The police are getting quite close. Errol's taken over what's left of this Nazi business, as you know. I thought he'd earned it. He's got a score to pay off. Now, as to yourself. Joel gave you the outline? You're rather too closely involved. Might be some—ah—publicity. Official enquiries are always touchy. Pity these aren't the old days. A gunboat solved most problems!"

"Scented notes and velvet slippers?"

"Getting that way. Nothing to look forward to, except join the Common Market, what?"

"That's no longer my opinion!"

He glanced—no more—at where I sat, and turned the chair.

"Atlantic Alliance of some sort? With help of the Commonwealth and the European Free Trade Association? Informed opinion seems to be hardening in that direction. But I always thought you were the great champion of the European engagement?"

"Time, and a bystander's point of view make a difference. It isn't covering needs in the way we thought. There's nothing of the exigency of the future in its method of thinking or working. You must have seen Chamby's report?"

"I was disappointed. The more so, since I understand he used your figures. Of course, we all know they can be made to mean anything!"

"On the contrary. Those figures have only one meaning. If we deliberately planned to ruin ourselves, we couldn't choose a better way!"

The Blur sat up. His profile, in itself, was a threat.

"I don't think I quite understand you," he said, at his weariest. "One moment you're all enthusiasm and columns of figures. And the next, a complete *volte face*, and the same figures mean something else!"

"We'd been studying everybody but ourselves. When we took a later assessment of our position, in relation to the others, then quite clearly we were faced with disaster!"

"Oh, now, Trothel Theatrics apart—"

"I insist. The figures tell the story!"

"Then what's the answer? We can't blow hot and cold. And you can't throw away a career for the sake of a guess!"

I suddenly thought of the porter at Heathrow, and Sergeant Quatrell, Mr. and Mrs. Cloney, Dr. and Mrs. Tomsett, Parnes, and all the other unknown—but no less real—innocents.

I had to see myself exactly as I was, the training I'd had, the life I'd lived, the man I'd become. Here I was, a creature of the moment, with that experience behind me which conferred a right to something called an opinion, that thrown in one scale or the other could affect a decision which might in greater or lesser degree touch the lives of millions.

"I've been guilty of impulse, but I don't think I ever guessed in my life," I said carefully. "I believe our entry into the Common Market at this time would mean a worse cat-fight than ever. Everybody scrambling for a larger slice of the same joint. The little ones going under. Monopolies taking over. Unions more powerful, and the socialists easily outnumbering all the others."

"Hasn't happened yet!"

"Wait till we join!"

"I asked, what's the answer? Join the United States?"

"The time's coming when the United States'll join us. The answer's in one currency, and a cooperative system. In banking first, then agriculture, industry, research, and everything else. Otherwise we sentence the European working population to a type of slavery for the same wage, lifelong. There's no way out because there's no room for manoeuvre. You sell for so much, there's so much profit, and so much for wages. That's the Common Market way. By cooperation, everybody shares. Whatever anyone buys gives a profit. That profit, on everything, is shared by everybody, nationally—"

The Blur stood, slapped his hands, almost as a washbowl Pilate.

"Sorry, Trothe. I simply don't begin to understand you. I don't think I'd bruit much of that abroad, if I were you!"

294

"The figures support it!"

"Chamby's essay's based on them, I understand? But he's resigned. You've just come from a nursing home. Who'll bother to read arcana? I don't think we—"

Miss Tulliver came in.

"Chief Superintendent Hockley, m'lord!"

The Blur got up to go to the door in person.

"Ah, come in, Superintendent!" he trumpeted, in his Special Occasions voice. "Make yourself comfortable. This is Mr. Edmund Trothe, a colleague of many years. You got the material I sent over?"

Chief Superintendent Hockley wasn't the sort you'd think of as a policeman. Medium height, bald, thin face, small moustache, stoop, he might have been a librarian somewhere. Except that when he spoke, one heard the crust of authority. He rarely looked directly, but always slightly to the side as though wondering what sort of specimen he was dealing with.

"I did, m'lord," he said, taking off a woolly overcoat. "I suppose you know Constable Parnes, do you, Mr. Trothe?"

"I've known him for years!"

"You're quite a hero of his. I'm glad of that. Very glad. He's a witness in the theft of that firearm. Curious business, I thought. I mean, whoever stole the firearm, bought that dress, gave that name, wrapped the firearm in it, left it where it'd do most good, well, that's about what I'd call malice aforethought!"

"That's the whole idea," the Blur said. "Make all the trouble possible for everybody everywhere. Scandal kills far more painfully than a bullet!"

"This young woman had quite a record," the Superintendent said, flipping the pages of a thick file. "She must have been warned that night. But if she was, why would she catch that train? Why not hop it from the hotel? And if we were trying to trap her, why wasn't somebody keeping an eye on where she went?"

"I think I can explain that," the Blur said, in his best Power-

Behind-Power style. "She had a French passport. Forged, of course. She entered the country as a tourist, but the C.I.D. man on duty was sharp enough to take note. His warning went to his own department, they got on to us—a delay of an hour or so—before the necessary steps could be taken. She didn't go to the hotel she was supposed to, and—as I imagine you know—looking for one tourist in a day's intake isn't the easiest job. She could have gone anywhere. Fortunately somebody—her brother, possibly—booked a seat for her on that train to Birmingham. That information was also sent in. When it was reported she was at the Savonia, we managed to tap the line and got a couple of very useful telephone calls. Obviously she was supposed to meet her brother in Birmingham. He may have warned her. By using another passport, she could have caught the Cross-Channel ferry that night or the following morning. What happened between then, and when she was found drowned'll always be a mystery to some of us. After all, others were out for her blood, as well!"

"Mr. Trothe," the Superintendent said, and if he couldn't have been more genial, I didn't like his eye, because I've never liked policemen's eyes, especially those long enough in the Force to achieve highest rank. "You were a friend of hers for some time. Did she ever talk of suicide?"

"I never met anyone further from the thought."

"You think it was murder, accidental death, or what?"

"Absolutely no opinion. She was a very fine swimmer, in fact."

"You didn't think of going up to Birmingham with her?"

"Why? She was reporting for her newspaper. Reporters are generally fêted at that sort of thing. I didn't feel it was any sort of place for me."

The Superintendent crossed his knees, shut the file, and looked at where the Blur's shadow might have been.

"Y' see, everything seems to fit, including the gaps. People's time sense is nearly always off. Everybody at Four Went Waye deposed it was *after* seven-thirty you went out. Which case, you couldn't have got to the station for the 8:10. The chauffeur says you went away at well *before* seven. Four Went Waye's directly on the route to Famlingham. There's no other way to get there. Five dependable witnesses swear they saw a Rolls-Royce go over Famlingham pier just before nine. Two of them thought it was a hearse. Four of them saw the launch put out. A fisher-boat skipper and three crew swear they passed her out beyond the Mert Rock buoy. The Hon'ble Errol Hinter—beg his pardon—Lord Imbrett—swears the launch wasn't out. The crew swears it wasn't. The launch was repainted next day. But she only had a repaint a couple of months ago. Lord Imbrett says that was only a red-lead-and-mastic job his father had done to underlay the new. But this is the very launch picked out by some anonymous caller, who said Tanis Desarbier was on board. That's where Mr. Trothe's automatic was found wrapped in the supposed-dress of Miss Consuelo Furnival, which it wasn't. I mean, what a lovely skein o' shoddy!"

"Somebody took the trouble to make it so," the Blur said, in charm of urbanity. "We're very far from dealing with clods, you know, Superintendent. These things are all planned to the last detail. They go wrong because of carelessness. It's the only reason we ever get anywhere!"

"That's exactly my experience, my lord," the Superintendent said, with—what I thought—might be described as a "silky" little laugh. "Mr. Trothe, what time did you get home the night this Desarbier woman caught the train?"

"I suppose at about 10:30 or a little after."

He nodded, ruffled the pages of the file, stopped at an entry.

"Very funny," he said, as if it wasn't. "How do you account for the fact that the dairyman down there, just been to the station to get the milk, not quite six o'clock, saw you in the Rolls-Royce of that selfsame number? So did the man riding with him, an odd-job gardener, working at your place. Both recognised you, and they both gave the car's number, about the easiest I ever saw to remember. Where had you been?"

"They're mistaken."

"Broad daylight? Two men who've known you man and boy? Mistaken?"

"Absolutely!"

The Superintendent closed the file, and with great deliberation put it back on the desk.

"Then, Mr. Trothe, you're at odds with your housekeeper, Mrs. Cloney. She says she found you on the couch in your overcoat. This is her sworn statement!"

"It was the day my wife died. I slept on the couch. Perfectly true. She's got days and dates wrong. Ask her again. You'll get a different answer!"

The Blur offered cigarets. Superintendent Hockley shook his head, clasped his hands and leaned back, half-smiling at the ceiling.

"We've all met that kind of witness," he said, gently. "But there's just another little point, here. If you were at the Langbridge Clinic for Nervous Disorders till Tuesday—and I've got the medical register—how could you see this woman off to Birmingham the night before?"

"There's such a thing as tipping a porter!"

"Quite. I quite see that. But the register gives you a large dose of sedative. Other medicines, here, too. You're saying the doctor and nurses who signed this were—let's say—mistaken?"

"You're looking at the day I went in. Not the day I came out!"

"Dear me!" the Blur said, at distance. "So even the Yard can make a bog, what?"

"I'll look into this," the Superintendent said, a little tiredly. "Well, I think that's the lot. For the moment. By the way, did this woman ever indicate she was a sister-in-law to you?"

"Never!"

"Beats me how some people live. A dead lie from the time they get up in the morning!"

I didn't move when he put on his overcoat. I felt like shouting. The Blur helped him on—a rare occasion, my God!—and walked to the door. The Chief Superintendent looked at me from the doorway.

"You've had enough experience of this sort of thing to know how unpleasant my job is at times, Mr. Trothe?" he said, almost cheerfully. "I've seen your record. If you'll allow me to say so, sir, I wish it was mine. Good day!"

The Blur went out with him. I found my hand distinctly shaky in lighting a cigaret. I knew perfectly well that the Superintendent had "scented," and he wasn't the sort to be blarneyed. Simply give him enough time.

Once again, in almost spotlit dazzle, I saw myself as sacrificial ox.

The Blur came back, all smiles, and shut the door.

"*Well!*" he said, rubbing his hands. "I must say I greatly admire your sang-froid. Didn't turn a hair. Very delicate situation, that. The business of my car stunned me. Fortunately, it's been too useful in other ways to give me much trouble. But we'll have to step rather warily for a day or so. If we can catch one or two of these fellows, the enquiry's a dead-letter. But you're the danger. You can be mired by some very awkward questions. Minutiae. We wouldn't like that, would we? How soon could you leave the country, and where'd you wish to go? I could arrange a flight to the West Indies this afternoon?"

I don't like policemen's eyes, and the Blur's I liked still less, especially at that moment. My Xth sense scalded in warning. I might be walking into a trap.

The Blur would merely have to raise a finger.

Supposing I went to the West Indies, a partner in the Commonwealth. I could be extradited on a charge of evading an enquiry. That I'd run away would point to guilt. Were I to implicate the Blur, he could easily suppress any statement.

But why would he try?

Perhaps my remarks about Fleet Street had been relayed.

Yorick had made a point of mentioning that it wouldn't be of much help. The fact remained that the West Indies was the one, absolutely certain place, where I could be held, and sent back, without a whisper anywhere.

I could have been absurdly mistaken, but that Xth—the warning—sense had always proved far too dependable a friend to be ignored. I also was aware that, from the moment, I had to watch for Mr. Colethorne, or a few of his friends.

"Sounds extremely tempting," I said. "I'm inclined to accept. But I shall have to see about a few things, first. Joel Cawle seemed in a strange mood this morning?"

The Blur almost waved his hands.

"Takes everything rather too seriously, Trothe. Accommodations, so forth? Taking anyone?"

"Possibly my son."

"Two, very well. Later today. You'll let me know, will you? Oh, while I remember. Lord Imbrett's memorial service. It's been postponed. All of us in one place, rather a pretty shoot, what!"

Outside, Miss Tulliver gave me a message from Miss Roule and I spoke over the intercom.

"Mr. Trothe? Miss Furnival. I'm in London!"

"Luncheon? The pub next door? Half an hour?"

"Wonderful!"

39

Consuelo came home with me after luncheon to get some files, and the typewriter. I had a crass desire to kiss her, and along those lanes was all opportunity. But I preferred not. Not for any reason, or lack of one. Simply not.

That surprised me, but I was perfectly happy about it, and that, too, surprised me. Somebody else seemed to be taking charge, and—it suddenly popped into mind—Barkis was willing.

She stretched her legs, and sat up.

"You know, Edmund, this is so completely different from anything I'd have imagined a few days ago," she said, "I feel I simply *must* tell you. I never meant to. We quite thought they'd closed in!"

"How do you mean, 'closed in'?"

"We were both sure," she said, beyond argument. "Rouley got some files for you a little time ago, didn't she? Well, there was one she didn't let you see. About an OAS agent. An absolute horror. You'd have found it very difficult to answer. She showed it to me. She couldn't destroy it, of course. I told her to leave it on her desk, and I'd 'lift' it. That's what I did, and it went in small pieces. In dear 'Father Thames, flow softly till I'—how does it go? Well, anyhow, that's how it went!"

"Destroying State papers? That's ten years!"

"I didn't care. I don't care about anything except you, and Rouley knows it!"

"I must say I always wanted to take a curry comb to that hair!"

Consuelo heaved in a laugh, and sat up.

"A wig, darling! She's got dozens. They all think she's blind as an earthworm. She isn't. Everybody thinks she's hideous. She's not. They all think she's pool—stuff with the rest of the girls. She's not. She's probably the best agent we've got. In her own way. She's in between jobs. And hopelessly in love with Yorick!"

"Can't be!"

"Noggins about him. Took me a little time to see why. I once thought him the original all-round *ache!* Now, of course, he's a multi-millionaire. Makes him rather more attractive. But she isn't exactly broke, either!"

"Often wonder why people like that work at all."

"She told me she was born too idle to do nothing!"

"Lucky for the rest of us!"

She put a hand on my arm, moved a little closer.

"May I lift a couple of strings of those button onions for Mummy, please? And a few of the tulip bulbs?"

"Help yourself. They're all marked."

It was still quite early. When I turned off the ignition I heard the slither of a bicycle behind, and Parnes jumped off.

"Ar'tnoon, sir! Been a bit of a free-thinker's ball here. I heard a car come down last night very quiet 'n I thought it might be you. So I nipped out. Wasn't you t'all. I never got a chance at seeing their plates. I called the radio car and they're doin' a patrol round here all night. No idea who it was, sir?"

"None. Any marks of entry?"

"Not that we could see, sir. They was down the side door. We had a look down there. All safe, sir. No, I come down, because the Inspector was on to me 'bout my report, sir. That firearm. 'course, I wasn't too steady at the time. I put it right, sir. Lucky. Lines was still down, any road. So it's all right, sir. Hope I didn't botch nothing up for you, sir?"

I looked at a pair of eyes honest as a terrier's, and felt an absolute tyke.

"Perfectly all right, Parnes, thank you. Come in and look round with me, will you?"

The front door hadn't been touched, but I was looking for signs of a time bomb. None of the side doors had been tampered with, and the terrace windows were all shuttered. Parnes took Consuelo out to the greenhouse while I got what I wanted, and I gave him a couple of bottles of scotch and the spare keys.

"Keep an eye on the place for me, and tell Mrs. Cloney to be more than careful. If I'm wanted, Dr. Norris knows where I am. If you should want me direct, that's the number of my club. I'll attend to the tradesmen tomorrow. And thank you for all you've done!"

Parnes gave me an old-time policeman's salute, that rare sign of civic respect, making me feel low enough to walk under the car.

"'pend on me to see all's right, sir. Anybody come messin' round here, they' get put in their proper slot, sir!"

I drove out for Truscott's Battle and passed the patrol car just outside the village. I slowed to wave, and a sergeant waved back, and on I went, knowing they'd got my number.

"Do you know, for the first time in my life I've got the colli-wobbles!" Consuelo said suddenly. "Rouley was right. You're not safe anywhere!"

"She said that?"

"Yorick told her. What are we going to do? I don't think I could go on if anything happened to you. I've lived with the thought of you too long!"

I put out a hand, felt the supple warmth of her thigh.

"Nothing's going to happen. Pity I wasn't there when they called!"

She rested her head on the seat, looking up at the roof.

"Edmund, would you mind terribly if I asked a—a question?"

"Do, of course!"

"Am I to understand you want to marry me? You haven't said anything, well, plainly, and I could be—"

"Absolutely my intention. Why?"

She held my hand tighter, turning away.

"I must tell you. I've got to. I know it'll hurt you. It might even spoil everything. But it's got to be said now. Then we both know where we are!"

"What?"

She sat up, smoothing the hair over her ears.

"I simply couldn't live in that house!" she said quickly, passionately. "Couldn't. *Couldn't!*"

I tried to smile at her.

Everything I'd thought, and hidden, for months, or years, perhaps, seemed to come in shadowy smother to confront me, once and for all.

"It may be the home of your family, and I'm dreadfully sorry if I've hurt you. Your memories, and—and—sentiments. But I felt the place muttering. Talking to me. It was *awful!* I could *never* stay there. Frederick'd always felt it, he told me. Even now, he can't sleep in the dark. He'd never live there. He said he always stayed with the people who work for you. He and his sister both agreed they'll pull the place down and rebuild!"

"When I've had my ration of daisies?"

"Oh, darling, don't say that, please! I'm going to take the greatest care of you!"

"I've been given a jolt, let's say, by the Revenue. I'd made the place over to my wife and children. By her death, the property reverts to me. I've revoked the deed which made the children part-owners. But death duties are enormous. If I died, they'd be impossible!"

She leaned to kiss my cheek, a marvellous, tender weight.

"You might regret whatever you do," she whispered. "Then you'd simply curse me!"

"I'd rather keep some of the furniture and pictures, and the other stuff that's really valuable, and sell the place. Build somewhere else. In the sun, perhaps?"

"But wouldn't you lose a lot of money?"

"I'd do that paying the tax, anyway. The piece at the back's been sold for a satellite town affair. Now they can buy the whole caboodle. More I think of it, the better I like it!"

I knew beyond argument I was right.

Why? Name? Social position? History? I—suddenly—felt relieved of a burden. That's what the house had always been, even in my parents' time. A millstone, a deadweight about our necks. Rates, taxes, upkeep were a constant worry. Death was not merely grief, but a financial penalty. Had the land at the back not been sold, I could then and there have been very near bankruptcy. Ebbleton—and poor Mel!—had in fact been of greatest service. It took me a little time to taste the joke, because, really, that's what it was.

I tried to sit apart from myself to examine my attitude.

Had anyone suggested selling the house even twenty-four hours before, I suppose I'd have bawled a quire or two of closely reasoned self-righteous nonsense about roots, tradition, and the rest, all of it demonstrably true and heartfelt.

I didn't believe it any longer.

Whether thought of having to go back there to live till the mutes once again put their threadbare tophats on the hall table —and roses draped yet another Trothe coffin!—had cured me of any desire to totter about the garden until I went meek into the same hole as my forefathers, I don't know.

I amazed myself. I didn't want the old order any more, didn't want mossy stones, split timbering, worn parquetry, creaking boards, loose tiles, rotten thatch. I wanted something new, of the new time, to share with a new woman.

Consuelo didn't require history, had no need to enter its shadow. She carried it without the aid of twenty-two rooms, staff hall, butler's pantry, armourer's cellar, saddlery hide, priest's hole, coach house, pigeon cote, lily pond, elms, yews, ivy, and all the rest of it—sentimental digression?—second thoughts during an affectionately proprietorial sweep of the known and dear?— last moment hesitation?—no.

Absolutely not.

Patti had known it—Patricia Melisande Onslow Trothe—had known it all from birth, she, at the moment, learning perhaps a little more about African tribal law in Marrakesh, would have voted for demolition.

God bless her.

Frederick had been part of it, and yet, behind my back, had said he'd pull it all down. I didn't doubt that he would.

I'd save them both the trouble.

40

I left Consuelo at her mother's place without even a kiss, because Mrs. Rolleston stood in the doorway. I was introduced, said a few words about the weather, refused a cup of tea I could have done with by looking at the clock, good-afternooned, and got off.

I haven't the faintest idea what I was thinking on the way to Paul's, but I stopped at Hurcell's Yard to telephone.

The maid put me on to Angela Masters.

"Cairo speaking. It might be a most inconvenient time to see Mr. Chamby, but I could be there in five minutes—"

"I'll make the appointment, sir. We have a patrol service at the gates. They'll have the name, Cairo. Is there anything else?"

"I need the package immediately. Including stamps. I don't require the label. All he need do is pencil the address. Is that clear?"

"Perfectly. Should the address be printed?"

"Please!"

What a blessing a brain is, and training.

Package was code for tickets, cash drafts, and anything else needed for a journey. Including stamps, meant for two people. I don't require the label meant don't expect me back, and pencil the address meant immediate and urgentest. Her enquiry about printing asked if she should book the flight.

I wove through lanes where an oncoming car could never have got by, but I came out almost at the gates of Paul's place, with a barrier painted red and white strong enough to stop a

307

tank. I said "Cairo!" through the window, and the bar lifted, and somebody waved me on.

Angela Masters, in black, stood at the half-open side door. A maid took my hat and coat, and Angela led up to the first floor by a way I'd never been.

"My ticket should be in the name of Perceval Onslow, company director."

"At your home address, sir? Very well!"

I had that momentary stab that it wouldn't be. But hurt passes.

Paul sat in a wheel chair, with a plastered leg up on a plank, directing two men pinning numbered flags on a map stretching across the far wall.

"Edmund-o!" he crowed. "Isn't she a beaut? We're plotting the pipeline route. Going great, so far. Come in here!"

He swung the chair wheels like a veteran, and we went into a boarded-off division. He nodded at the door, and I shut it.

"Just in case these lines are tapped, I had a woggiz put in. Anybody using the tap gets Moira or Angela reading off a shopping list. Or lovely music. Ever heard the old Aussie classic 'Cootamundra' have you? That's one we play 'em. What's on?"

"I believe I'm for the high jump!"

Paul wasn't surprised. He nodded.

"Yorick was over here last night," he said, and put a match under the alcohol burner. "The Blur's not too pleased about my report. He probably thinks you deliberately helped. He's responsible for information backing up policy. At the moment, he can't look too good!"

"He should have seen it before."

"You mean, we should!"

"I accept anything that's reasonable. It wasn't my business to cast doubt. The early figures were absolutely in accordance with, let's say, strategic theory. Later figures weren't. They were submitted, though. Nothing's been changed. It simply means that people up top can't, or won't, look at figures. The Blur obviously never did. You had to put it in so many words. With the usual painful clarity!"

Paul put a forefinger crossways between his teeth.

"What's staring you in the face oughtn't to be disregarded," he said, even sadly. "I must admit I didn't get the weight before. I was playing for the team. You see a lot more from the stands!"

"What's this got to do with us? Or with me?"

Paul poured boiling water on the tea.

"Policy's policy. It's got to be backed up. But we submit a negative, even a destructive report. And he's been backing us? He's got to give excuses for himself. The trend should have been seen a long time ago. But poor ol' Blur's not an analyst. He's a case-maker. Knock him off balance, he's a stink-beetle, ass-uppards!"

"But why would he go for me?"

Paul gave me a cup and I spooned honey.

"Sweet tooth's what I like," he said, pouring. "I'm sick of people dieting. Look, Edmund. You know the Blur by now. If he thought it'd do him any good, he'd fillet his mother. I told you Yorick was here last night? He was very worried. If they've got even half a case, you can be held. Till things blow over. Then it'll be all apologies. I told him you weren't that sort of bird. I didn't tell him about our business, though. Who else knows?"

"Nobody. The Blur invited me to fly to the West Indies this afternoon."

Paul stared infant surprise.

"Oh, my word, Edmund! And the story's what? Chamby? Ah, yes. He resigned rather than face the music. Trothe? Hm. Curious business. Very. Mixed up with some tart, or other. We're looking into it. Their combined report and summary? Not worth the paper. They've been removed. Policy? As before, but rather more caution. In other words, prudence. That's the Blur's key-word, Edmund. If everything goes right, it was his prudence. If it goes wrong, well, somebody—not the Blur!—wasn't prudent. And we take the can back? If I'd been asked for an interim report, there'd have been no difference. Except, we'd have been there to sing the high notes. As it is, I'm off before the end of the month. I insist *you* go this afternoon. No shennanigans!"

"I'm wondering whether to charter a taxiplane to France. I don't like the idea. It looks evasive."

"You've got a contract signed, you've got a ticket, and you've got instructions to meet your company's legal staff in Rome to-night. What more d'y'want? If the word's gone out to pinch you, what's the plan?"

"In the event of failure, and of your being asked what you know, then the less you know, the better!"

"Agreed. Angela's got everything downstairs. Moira's flown to Sydney. Our office in Rome'll fix the Egyptian visa. Yorick told me you were thinking of doing something utt'ly fat-headed, Edmund. In Germany. Were you?"

I was caught completely off-guard.

"I'd thought of it," I said, looking away, a little nettled.

He slapped the papers down, lifted them again and slammed them down.

"There's times I swear to Christ everybody's gone stone-bloody-*atcha!*" he shouted. "I mean, good God, how long'd you last?"

"Leading question?"

"Ah, my arse, Edmund! Listen, before I got this, I'd give any-body in the world a couple of rough minutes. Might go three. And after? Where'd I be? And I'm only a few years older than you are. You mean a man like you, brains, everything, you're going to live some assinine form of half-life? For how long? Trying to do what? You ought to be shoved inside, and sat on!"

I laughed because I had to.

"I'm beginning to believe it's not my cup of tea at all!"

Paul pointed his finger.

"Now you're talking! I'm glad of that, because I was going to

310

give you an ultimatum. Either you drop the idea flat, or never again come anywhere near me. See? There'd be nothing for you. Now, then. Angela Masters'll come out with me. If you've got a preference, you'll have to look sharp. There's vaccination and inoculation, and all that business. Anybody in mind?"

An extremely off-the-cuffish tone of voice while he turned pages, but I knew him far too well.

"Consuelo Furnival," I said. "If she'll go!"

He looked up, raising a forefinger in acknowledgement.

"Good luck," he said. "Can't go wrong, there. What're you doing about the house?"

"Selling it!"

He stopped the chair and half-turned to look up at me.

"Not making yourself an Ishmael, are you?" he asked, uncertainly, for him. "They're not going to be after you all your life, y'know?"

"I always thought a man was meant to have his own little place. To live, express himself. I don't believe it any longer. It's simply a threading of habit and indolence, with a touch of pride for color. Sunshine and the sea, please!"

"That 'place' is exactly what we want!" Paul said happily. Put up everybody coming in. Sort of a club. And head office. I was going to offer this, but it's just not the size."

"I'll put Gilman on to you."

We shook hands at the stairhead.

"I'll expect a cable tonight, Edmund," he said, and grinned the big teeth. "Just one tip. Don't go near your club!"

There were a number of places I had no intention of going anywhere near, and the club was one. Angela waited for me with three envelopes.

"I thought they'd slip into pockets a little easier," she said, and put a receipt form, and a pen, in front of me. "Fifty pounds in cash—all you're allowed!—air tickets, in the name of Onslow, letters of introduction, in your correct name, to Mr. Shoukary in

311

Rome, Mr. Chaddid in Cairo, Mr. Benson in Beirut, and Mr. Osterley in Teheran—"

"Oh, he's there, is he?"

"Went three days ago, sir. You may have to go to Bahrein from Cairo, but that will be settled there."

I went by the back road to Mellonhamp and enjoyed myself, thinking of nothing, looking at England, herself, in damp winter browns and ambers, that to me, at any rate, always held more of magic than any other land in gaudiest summer's bloom.

I couldn't see the house because of the trees, and I was at the steps before I realised I'd arrived. A footman took my name in, and Yorick walked out in slippers and shirtsleeves, carrying a beekeeper's gauze helmet.

"Oh, hullo, Edmund! What a pleasant surprise! Forgive the get-up. I've got some special queen bees I'm looking after. I'm trying to humble the African variety. They're a pest, but they could be made most useful. Let's go in here, shall we? Booth, we'd like some tea please!"

"Cer'nly, m'lord!"

We sat in a panelled study with a Sargent over the fireplace, a Gainsborough to my left, and a Picasso over the desk.

Almost without thinking, I told him about the Blur and what I imagined. When I'd said it, I thought it sounded painfully tenuous.

"You could be so right!" he said, sitting up from a sprawl. "He knows I'm safe enough. So are the others. You're not in the same push, are you? You're a sort of craggy citadel, out on your own, as it were. You could be most dangerous when you didn't mean to be. I mean, this fellow Hockley isn't the biggest chump on earth. He *knows* there's something. He knows if it goes as far as you, then it must go farther. How far? He'll keep digging at you. It can only lead to the Blur!"

"Let him dig. What can he find?"

"Supposing he's seen that M.I. film. But rather more than you saw. Again, the timing of the telephone receipt goes against

312

your story. It supports the barman and the others. You'd never shake those villagers of yours, would you? And supposing your fingerprints were found on the launch?"

"Couldn't have been!"

"How do you know? Now, pretend you're the Blur. If Mr. Trothe could be put away, conveniently, until things cool—all in good faith, of course!—then all's well. Remember, our friend Hockley's a terror. A *real* terror. He's a policeman. The only people in this are yourself and Gaylor. Talking to Gaylor's like addressing the English Channel. My crew are sailors. They never *did* know anything. Who else is there? Only you. Supposing you're found out in a misstatement? That's when your record'll go against you. They'll know you're telling a tale to cover yourself. And who else? Obviously somebody higher up. Whom? You see the Blur's on a very sticky pitch? That's why he'd love you to fly to the West Indies. You might stay there in perfect comfort. But—then again—you might be on the next plane back, and disappear on arrival. If I know the Blur, that's the form!"

"Why the West Indies? Why not here?"

"Too many things to go wrong. You're quite well known. Simpler to invite you to the coco-palms and do the job there. Wouldn't be a peep, never mind what sort of fight you put up!"

It was then, while I was absorbing the idea that arrest was rather more than a possibility—and blessing that Xth sense!—that I saw myself, if cloudily, bony hunkers folded in sun-crisped blue linen, staring up into the Face of living heat, really and truly examining myself and the world about me.

It was something I'd never done, never thought of doing, never had the time or felt the necessity, and really, there had never been any reason. Life went on day after day, and one took one's place in the machine that started with waking, bathing, shaving, reading the papers, and so on, until bedtime, and so, sleep. I'd never questioned it. The work I did always seemed reasonable, except during the war, and that, naturally, was exceptional. After the war and during the few months of rehabilitation, things were a little strange, but they soon picked up, and on we went again. I never remembered asking myself what I was doing, or why, or if there was something else I'd prefer to do. I'd never questioned that all I did was correct. I'd never worked in an atmosphere that permitted the incorrect in any sense, or that went against the good of the commonweal. I was part of a Service, that too often worked thanklessly, though never to its detriment, or other than in highest tradition of loyalty to the Sovereign and the body-politic. Sententious, perhaps, but then, facts often are.

But I was being made aware that a number of people had far more power than the Service intended, or the Law permitted, and not only misused, but abused, without a by y'leave or a word of protest anywhere.

That could only be because people like myself either turned a blind eye, or for the sake of a good opinion, fawned in complicity, or plainer still, licked boots. I should have let the Blur handle the Desarbier affair himself. I was baited by a fine mixture of threat and flattery, and I'd walked in, not so much as sacrificial ox, than as an old, broken-kneed milch cow.

In any event I had no right to be in that room talking to Yorick, no business to be confiding in a man younger than myself, much less to be seeking his advice. I realised I'd gone there in the same way that a rat goes up a drainpipe, in fear, the unthinking scurry, *sauve qui peut*.

I had no need.

"I hear you're i/c Nazis," I said.

He laughed, stretching a long arm to pick up the beekeeper's helmet.

"More or less, Edmund. I've bought a bar in Fräglechaben. We've got a man there. He knows who's been away. Who's been getting the welcome-home parties. Who's 'in' on the Jew bait. They'll be singled out for special attention. I've got the whitest jackets in the bottle biz. And quite the slowest poison.

314

It's absolutely death-dealing. Leaves no trace. And I wonder when there's been a blacker heart?"

"No conscience?"

"On that level?"

He picked up a heavy chair and turned it into the table, and I saw he was physically a great deal stronger than I'd thought. I wondered if the generally uncombed mop was a wig, or if he really needed spectacles. He and Miss Roule made a splendid pair. Some families acquire power as part of property, inherited and handed on. The Roules and Hinters—and how many more—had been trained to use it. Or so it appeared.

I had sudden, merest, gleam, of power-within-power. How had the late Lord Imbrett talked to his son? When? What should I have said to Frederick? When?

"I'm going to the airport," I said. "But *not* to the West Indies!"

He looked at the clock.

"Couldn't your Fleet Street friends help? A squib or two might do a lot of good. Still time to catch the late afternoon editions. Let's see—'Mr. Edmund Trothe, recently Common Market counsellor to H. M. Government—'"

"Leave that out!"

"—let them dress it up!—'takes the famous Blue Ribband flight to the West Indies this afternoon. Significantly, both the United States, and the Canadian Department of Commerce attachés are—"

"They'd chew the—!"

"My dear Edmund, let everybody know where you're supposed to be going, at least. You've got a handful of spades. When do you start playing them? Don't you know your friends expect it?"

That was when I felt I'd been literally booted off my hunkers.

"I'm very glad I came here," I said, and got up. "I wish you all success. In any event, I'm delighted to see you look after queen bees!"

"*Deus et Regina Gloriam in Aeternum?* There's really not much

315

else, is there? Never thought a lot of coco-palms, anyway. Had much more fun at Hampstead Heath!"

"*Sieh zu dass du sie los wirst!*"

He closed his heels in a clicking echo.

"*Dies wird mir ein vergneugen sien!*" he called, and put on the helmet in a dance of gauze. "Meet at the waxworks, possibly?"

I wondered, going away, how a humbler of rabid bees could turn a keel through seas which he knew must murder. But then, I remembered, he wasn't simply humbling, but trying to cure, a pest.

41

Watching briars reach thorny arcs from both sides of the lane to splash diamonds against the windscreen, I knew that surely, and not-too-slowly, I was becoming myself. Yorick's "your friends expect it of you!" hurt more the further I went.

I'd acted as a clerk and I'd been treated as one. I'd been passive. That, when I cared to think about it, was the worst crime in the book. I'd simply gone along with the Management out of pseudo-respect, and latterly, from fear of what might happen if I didn't. It was no help to wonder what Bernard and Joel must have thought, or for that matter, anyone else.

I caught a reflection of myself in the driving mirror. I was smiling, though not, I thought, healthily.

At Sloane Square, I garaged the car, and went in the callbox to dial Consuelo.

"I'm resigning from the Service, and joining Paul," I said matter-of-factish. "I'm leaving the country. Are you determined to waste time at that school? Is a cap and gown imperative? Or are there other things you might do?"

"If you're asking if I'd go to Teheran, of course I would!" she said, with what seemed to me that breath-held feeling before pressing the trigger. "Angela's been telling me. At least it'll be warm there, won't it?"

"Anteroom to hell at times. Thank heaven for ice. You'll have to look into passport, visa, inoculation, so forth. Financial details later!"

"Wonderful!" she murmured, in not quite a whisper. "I'll look

317

over the bagwash for a wardrobe. Is there a number I can call to let you know I'm ready?"

"I'll call you tonight," I said, and my voice was steady, thank God. "You'll be flying tomorrow. I shall meet you. We'll go on together!"

"Darling mine, I've *dreamed* of it!"

I took a cab to Oxford Circus, and went to an old friend of mine to get my hair cut shorter, clip a little off the eyebrows, and gum on a small moustache. Five doors down, I bought a pair of steel spectacles with blue lenses. I don't know why steel frames alter the appearance more than any other, but they do, and I almost didn't know myself. In Regent Street, I ordered three passport pictures from the quick-print chap in the arcade, and while they were being processed, went across the road and bought a cheap tent of an overcoat, a canvas bag, and, as an afterthought, a cap. Nothing so vulgarises the inner or outer man. When I'd bought a pair of clumpy crepe-soled shoes, I looked the part. I'll swear my own children wouldn't have known me. A cab took me to the Passport Office, and I went through the waiting crowd to Rodwell's sanctum, and asked his secretary if I might have a moment, showing a corner of my diplomatic Red. Rodwell came out, and held the door wider in welcome.

We'd known each other for almost thirty years, and he asked no questions when I told him I wanted an ordinary blue, in the name Perceval Onslow, with the profession of company director. He sent in a cup of tea while he was away, and in so many minutes I had my blue, with his best wishes, his secretary's smile, and the bite of a backstreet gust.

I was ready to sing my *chant du depart*.

One eye, at least, was always somewhere, looking for Mr. Colethorne. So far, I hadn't given him much opportunity, but I knew a little too much about him and his ilk to be careless.

I bought a couple of papers in the Tube. Nobody took any notice of me, but I watched everybody else, in between reading the *Standard* and the *Evening News*.

My name in both surprised me.

The *Standard* columnist was very flattering, and wrote that many of my friends would be at Heathrow to drink a stirrup cup. The *Evening News* gave a résumé of my career, adding, that significantly, The First Secretary of the United States Department of Commerce, and the Canadian, etc.

Yorick had done fairly well.

But if all the "birds" hadn't been boxed, then others, apart from the Press and my friends were going to be there. Those who run may also read.

My little stand-in friend made a reassuring lump under my arm. I was becoming fond of it. The job it did was incomparably better than my own. The two I'd left in Tyndal's Court took up about as much room in my conscience as a pair of trodden roaches.

But I'd promised to let the Blur know about the flight, and I got on to Miss Tulliver. She almost came down the phone.

"Oh, Mr. Trothe! We've been looking for you! Your tickets are here. It's the Blue Ribband flight. You've got fifty minutes!"

"Have them sent to the desk, will you? There's too much fog to venture into London!"

"His lordship's just gone, but he asked if you'd call him at Grass Tree. He won't be there, yet. I'll send the tickets off, sir. And do have a wonderful holiday!"

I still had plenty of time, and I took a cab to Heathrow, looking at a nineteenth-century London I'd almost forgotten, not a bit sorry to be leaving, if only once again to know the glory of sunshine.

I got out at the Customs Import section, changed clothes and shoes in the men's, and scuffed over to the International side, up a sidestair to the main hall, bustling as ever, in yellowish light that made everybody look bilious. Miss Tulliver would have warned the desk—and whoever was interested—that I was on the way.

Careful was the word.

I sat in the lounge near my airline ticket desk, and watched the people round about. Nobody was known to me, and there wasn't a policeman in sight. I went over and put down my ticket, passport, and health certificate.

"Baggage, Mr. Onslow?"

"This is it. May I have a holdall, please?"

I got a shoulder bag, with the airline insignia large upon it, and the ticket from my overcoat I hung from the lapel.

"First stop Rome, the rest open, sir?"

I nodded.

"The lounge is straight through. You'll be called in plenty of time!"

The desk was over on the other side of the hall from the Caribbean departures. Perhaps the weather had something to do with the queues, but there seemed to be hundreds of people lined up as if waiting for a bus. I had my cap well down, my collar up, the specs had steamed, and my lapel badge dangled.

I must have looked—as my grandfather used to say—a dissight.

A darkish corner invited me, and I crept over to lean against the wall, about a yard from the path where the porters were pushing trolleys piled with luggage from downstairs to the ticket desks.

I caught a glimpse of a man's face I knew, but couldn't for the moment remember, and when I looked again, I'd lost him. I didn't even know where to look. I scanned the queues, looked between heads, hats, and at faces with no likeness to suggest one nation, but only a varied humankind.

One by one, five uniformed policemen walked in as if they hadn't seen each other, and stood, as policemen do, unnoticed. I looked for plainclothesmen, but they know their jobs too well. I didn't spot one.

I don't know why, but it gave me a real jolt to see Bernard Lane and two men I didn't know walk through the Trinidad queue, and go behind the counter to the inner office.

"Mr. Edmund Trothe, passenger on the Blue Ribband flight

320

to Trinidad, please!" the loudspeaker boomed almost over my head. "Would Mr. Edmund Trothe please come to the information desk. Mr. Edmund Trothe, please!"

I stayed where I was. My glasses had steamed again. I had to look over the tops. Bernard came out of the office, and one of the men stayed at the counter. The other followed him between the queues to the end, where people were dotted rather than in line. Bernard made a signal well-known to me—by putting left-hand thumb and forefinger to the crown of his hat. It meant Nothing Doing. I had to bend a little forward to see who it was meant for. Well to my right, just behind the moving stairway, Joseph Colethorne, ever the newspaper-seller, stood in a group with three others, possibly policemen. There were men at each doorway, and at the top of the moving stairway, all, apparently, aimlessly unemployed.

I slouched out, deliberately passing within a yard of Colethorne a moment or so before Bernard met him, and went to the coffee bar. I bought a double ham sandwich, and with a paper cup topping a bottle of beer, went back to my coign. The sandwich wasn't so much comestible as decoration. Crumbs stuck to my woolly tent, and it made sure of a few in my moustache. But while I was biting into a mass of white pap and ham, I saw the face again.

I zero'd in over the top of my spectacles.

I couldn't quite see him. He was behind a woman with a couple of children. He appeared to be looking about. I hid my face in the sandwich, and when I'd bitten, raised the cup. He strolled off to the other queue, stood there while I chewed, and turned to his right.

I wasn't quite sure of the profile. He was fairly well-dressed, though not in the London style, or the Parisian. Not the Roman. He'd bought a Locke felt, which slightly changed everything. The loose blue coat might have been Mittel-European.

My mind clicked here and there. I was thinking of Bernard

321

and Colethorne and all their "friends." They were there to see I went on board that Trinidad flight, that was clear enough.

I was thinking of Consuelo, warmed in her grace.

The man turned, looking about. I knew I'd seen him before. He'd been coming down the stairs with Heinig, those nights before, at Regsmund. But I hadn't taken much notice. The name, Svertlov, came to me. Of course.

Even if he seemed older than I'd expected, there was no mistaking the full face, and the eyes that always seemed to be peering sidelong, cheekbones that caught light in sharp relief, a mouth pulled down more on one side than the other, palish gingery hair, and yet the more I studied—over the shining rim of the specs!—the less he looked like the pleading, crouching, hollow-eyed fellow I remembered, and the more he seemed the schoolboy of memory, older than myself, just beginning to wear the habit of a man.

No doubt of it, and I felt not surprise so much as a mighty elation I'd known—ah! but how long before!—a sudden lifting of the senses, rare at any time except before the kill.

Far at the back of my mind, I'd welcomed the notion that young Von Hollefendorm would try a crack at me. He wasn't of the blood or breed either to let go, or accept failure.

Not more than twenty yards separated us, but I couldn't aim at a sitting bird, and certainly I had no intention of challenging in garb that was lowest sort of disguise.

The lift doors to my left crashed open and the silhouettes of luggage trolleys rumbled nearer.

The noise took his attention, and he looked over in a general turning of heads, though most didn't look, or turned away.

I made a sudden step forward in a wide gesture of the right arm and flung off the cap. As I'd expected the movement caught his eye. I ripped at the moustache, one, two, and flicked them away. He turned to me, staring. He knew who he was looking for, and I let the tent slip off, flinging the spectacles behind.

He knew me, he must have done from the sudden widening

of pale blue eyes and the quick half-turn. His right hand plucked aside a rever of his overcoat. I waited until the hand was out and he almost leapt through the gap.

We were face to face, with about ten yards between us.

His gun was blue in the shadow of the overcoat.

The first luggage trolley was passing behind me. I fired while the porter was hidden by the pile of luggage. No more sound than a scraped shoe.

The trolleys were still passing. I pretended to put my hands in my jacket pockets, looking the other way. I knew there was no need for a second shot.

He was bending, slowly, glaring a freeze of amazement, holding his chest, with smoke wisping as if he held a cigaret.

His automatic clattered, and he fell on it, rolled, arms out.

The trolleys went on, the porters were shapes, there was no noise except the rumble of wheels and the murmur of the hall.

People turned, a man knelt, others made a group. A woman pushed through, shrieked Police! I kicked aside my sandwich remnant, raised my paper chalice, wished myself good health, drank, and followed the last porter along to the right, leaving a shouting bedlam. People were halloing for a doctor, first aid. I didn't see Bernard, Colethorne or anyone else.

I went across to my airline counter and asked for my bag. It was still there. Over on the right, policemen were running, which always makes them look longer-legged than anyone else.

"What on earth's happening?" the airlines girl asked, standing and craning.

"Summer is i-cumen in," I said. "Whoever wants this bag, it's theirs. And loud sing cuccu!"

I went into the cloakroom and had a wash, got, as it were, into myself again, and put on the homburg. While I looked in the glass, I was aware that I wasn't sure why I called it, or thought of it, as a homburg. But then—a sudden, breaking memory—that's what my father had always called that type of hat. I wondered if Frederick would ever have the same heart-clutching thought about me.

I seemed to look younger than I had, I felt infinitely better than for many a long day, and I simply did not have a care in the world.

Battle had yet to be joined.

I still had twelve minutes to walk about and be recognized. I intended to beard Room 1021 from Bernard down, and challenge the lot.

The hall seemed to have resumed its normal hum. A band was playing "A Life on the Ocean Wave" downstairs. I could hear the ferrule of my umbrella tap, tap, tap toward the Information Desk.

"Anything known of a Press party?" I asked the girl. "Some sort of hail and farewell?"

"Let me check, sir," she said, and went away.

I stood there, in the open, jumpy as grouse at the start of the season, pugnacious perhaps, but—I could think of only one word—ebullient, and that, Great God! I hadn't been for how long?

"Nothing marked, sir," the girl said. "There's something in a few minutes about a band at Gate Five. Nothing to do with it, I suppose, sir?"

"Hardly. Thank you!"

My flight was called as I turned away, walking toward the lounge, studying the floor, thinking of Patti, and wondering, and of Frederick, and worrying, if reassured by memory of Dr. and Mrs. Tomsett and Dr. Norris, and under all, revelling in a thought of Consuelo, so that I almost forgot where I was, or what I was doing.

I was brought to my senses by pairs of feet directly across my way.

Those in the middle belonged to Bernard.

The band was quite near, playing "Hold Your Hand Out, Naughty Boy."

To my left, Joel in a brown covert coat, moved in behind with two others. To the right, Colethorne stood with his squad.

Bernard tried to stop me by a cheerful greeting. I walked past and he turned to follow.

"Edmund!" he said, quietly urgent. "You're supposed to be on this West Ind—"

"I'm going somewhere quite different," I said, lengthening my pace for the ramp. "I suppose you know I settled accounts?"

"We were sure it was you. We were fairly certain he'd be here. Nicely done. But you really ought to be on the other side!"

"Allow me to judge. And by the way, a full report of every detail leading to this journey is with my Bank, addressed to Chief Superintendent Hockley at Scotland Yard. He'll get it if anything happens to me!"

I walked down the middle of the ramp with Bernard at my elbow, and the others closing in. There were three passengers in front, down at the barrier.

"Doesn't alter the route this afternoon!" Bernard said, at his grimmest, and came alongside. "I must insist you come with me!"

It was time to fight.

In a quick move I had my back to the wall, and showed the holster.

"How many do you want to lose?" I said. "I can take most of you!"

"Oh, now, please!" Bernard started. "I do wi—"

In sudden braze, a band blared, and echoes hung in the roof with a chorus of voices, tambourines and drums. The brass marched down from above us in a shouting crowd filling the ramp side to side, and light shone gold in trombones and trumpets, and a pelt of paper flowers and streamers almost hid us.

Bernard looked at me, and up at Joel, and shook his head. Nobody could have moved anywhere in that crush except down, and that's where I went.

Bernard, and his most un-merry men, stood in solid glower,

325

jostled by bandsmen and dancing members of the chorus, led by a tall man in a nylon coat, tartan tam o'shanter and enormous sunglasses, blowing fan-fa-ra's on a hunting horn.

The airlines officer took my boarding pass, and ticked my name on the list, lifting the rope to let me through. He turned to appeal to the crowd, waved his arms, opened his mouth, and undoubtedly he shouted, but I was next to him and I couldn't hear a word.

I gave Bernard and Joel a nod each which they didn't acknowledge as they turned to go, and the tam o'shanter took off the sunglasses.

Yorick.

"This is quits for the chair!" he bellowed. "Happy take-off!"

Beside him, a hoyden in a suit of the same tartan, and a high-crowned Dutch cap, with sunglasses of peony petals almost hiding her face, screeched a greeting I recognised but doubted, though the voice, exactly like an old gramophone record played too fast, cut the din like cheese wire.

The airlines officer thumbed me through the door and used all his strength to close it behind me.

I walked across puddled tarmac in blessed silence and a cold wind to the jet. Other passengers straggled from a door farther down. I stood behind them at the stairway, listening to fading noise upstairs.

A sense of hurry tingled hands, nape, scalp.

"Sort of so-long I like to see, sir!" the steward said cheerfully, taking my pass. "Package for you aboard. Bring it along after we're up, sir!"

A police car slithered toward us, made a wide turn, and went on.

I took a deep breath and walked the stair as though time were my property. A hostess took my hat, coat and umbrella, and I went in to a comfortable armchair. Another hostess bent over me with an armful of magazines. I took a sheaf and began to flip through, with an eye to the window. The door shut. The jets ripped and whined. We turned, taxied, bumped. There was still plenty of time to stop us and hoick me off, though I was fairly certain it wouldn't happen. Bernard must have taken my warning to heart. He knew as well as anyone that I meant what I'd said. Discussing the sin of killing, as a Christian, is one matter, but face to face with reality, all argument dissolves.

Belief, prayer, everything else apart, I had not intention of being taken off.

The jets screamed as if sound itself were unravelling, and then we were lifting, and I felt the bump of the undercarriage through an almost-unending sigh of relief. I hadn't known I was quite so keyed.

A large hamper tied in a bow of my school colors came down the aisle, and the steward put his head round.

"Compliments of Mr. Paul Chamby and the Lord Imbrett, sir!" he intoned, in a toastmaster's bellow. "'case you took a turn over the Channel, sir, there's a jeroboam of Krug on the ice, and be sure to give you"—he read from a slip—"Rouley and Furney's love, sir, and when in Rome, do the Romans 'fore they do you!"

"Thank you, steward. What's in the hamper?"

I pulled the bow and opened the lid, taking out a pad of damp tissue. In a plastic wrap, flowers grew, stocks, pinks, forget-me-nots, cornflowers, planted, apparently in a square of green matting. A card, stuck in a cleft stick, was typed WHEN I TOLD YOU I HAD PLANTED SEEDS OUTSIDE G106 I AM SURE YOU DISBELIEVED ME, BUT HERE IS THE PIECE I CUT OUT AND TOOK HOME. GILLIAN SAYS BEAUTY GROWS IN THE UGLIEST PLACES. BE GOOD. BE HAPPY, AND ENJOY WHAT'S ON WHILE IT'S THERE. THE JEROBOAM WAS DRUXI'S IDEA. HI! EVER, E AND P.

I put the card in my wallet, intending to frame it, and blessed Yorick and his Gillian for that idea of the band. Without it, I'd have been a loser.

"I'll take the Krug and the hamper off with me," I said. "You

327

might keep the flowers damp. And I'd like a glass of champagne when we're approaching the Channel, please!"

"Certainly, sir. That's about now!"

I was wondering if an R.A.F. fighter was going to come alongside and wag us down, but then I realised I wasn't quite so important as all that. Merely an ex-civil servant on his way to a new appointment, without a family, no property and therefore no address in the United Kingdom, of certain reputation and accomplishment, few worries, a regret here and there, and many memories, some to be cherished, most to be expunged and soonest.

The hard lump under my left arm was almost as comforting, in its way, as the dream of Consuelo. Next day seemed an age, and yet, at this time tomorrow, she'd be flying over the same stretch, perhaps thinking of me waiting in Rome, only a couple of hours away.

Far below, pulls of dirty cotton wool blew past, a bottle poured at my elbow, and the frosty, patchworked fields of France lazed by.

There was plenty of time to toast everybody else. But, selfish as ever, I raised that first glass to Consuelo and me.

Champagne has always been a great favorite of mine.

I don't think it ever tasted better.

ABOUT THE AUTHOR

Richard Llewellyn was born in Wales, where his first novel, the international bestseller *How Green Was My Valley*, was set. He died in 1984, having published some fifteen other novels.